Ample Make This Bed

Copyright © 2019 Terry Oliver

ISBN: 978-0-9813895-6-1

All rights reserved. No part of this publication may be reproduced, stored in a retrieval system, or transmitted in any form or by any means, electronic, mechanical, recording or otherwise, without the prior written permission of the author.

Printed in the USA and the UK.

Cover design by germancreative at Fiverr.com © 2019

The characters and events in this book are fictitious. Any similarities to real persons, living or dead, is coincidental and not intended by the author.

3rd Age World Publishing. Victoria, BC, Canada.

www.3rdageworld.com

2019

Ample Make This Bed

Terry Oliver

Ample make this bed
Make this bed with awe
In it wait till judgment break
Excellent and fair

Be its mattress straight
Be its pillow round
Let no sunrise yellow noise
Interrupt this ground

- Emily Dickinson *(1830 - 1886)*

In the secret hour of life's mid-day, the parabola is reversed, death is born. The second half of life does not signify ascent, increase, unfolding, exuberance, but death, since the end is its goal. The negation of life's fulfilment is synonymous with the refusal to accept its ending. Both mean not wanting to live, and not wanting to live is identical with not wanting to die. Waxing and waning make one curve.

The afternoon of human life must also have a significance of its own and cannot be merely a pitiful appendage to life's morning.

- C.G. Jung, The Stages of Life (1930-31)

Dedication

To my children, Ami, Sam and Joshua

CHAPTER ONE

'Spike? Over here! Spike!'

At first, Porter Drummond didn't recognise his nickname above the din of mourners talking at the top of their voices as they spilled over into the front hall, clutching drinks to their chests or holding them high above their heads. He was almost pushed back out the front door. He wedged himself against a door jamb to gain some forward leverage and side-slipped past a beefy man with his tie askew, holding a drink in each hand.

'Take it easy, mate. There's lots more where this came from.' The man jerked his perspiring head to one side. 'The bar's right in there – but it's a free-for-all.' He pressed his steaming face closer to shout in Porter's ear. 'Head for the kitchen, the stock's in there.'

Porter pushed past him and slid along the wall into the crush of the living room and glanced about for a familiar face.

'Spike – here, behind you!' came a woman's voice again.

He half turned and saw her. 'Ama?'

They struggled to get closer but the crowd took no notice and they swayed back and forth out of reach, smiling helplessly at each other.

'It's no use, I'm stuck!' she called, holding out one arm for him to grab. Their fingers touched but were pulled apart.

'Ama – stay there, I'm coming.' He dropped to his hands and knees, forcing himself through the forest of legs, which parted slightly at the unexpected pressure and he squeezed between them towards where she stood. He stopped at a pair of women's legs, made a decision and ran his hand up her calf. The leg twitched, the woman gave a startled scream and the crowd fell back enough for him to stand, face to face with her.

'Amarylis Waterstone,' he grinned. 'I'd recognise those legs anywhere.'

'Porter Drummond,' she smiled back at him. 'You haven't lost your touch.'

They hugged and stood swaying as the crowd closed in on them and the volume resumed its previous level.

'Dance?' he said into her ear.

She laughed, holding his hand, 'Why not?'

'Like old times. We haven't been this close for decades.'

'Not since London.'

'Not since The Old Vic,' he nodded. 'What was the production?'

'"Tis Pity She's A Whore'.'

'How could I forget? All those thrusting bosoms...'

'And all those bulging cod-pieces,' she grinned. 'Speaking of which...'

'Sorry – it's this heaving crowd,' he apologised.

'Not just the crowd, perhaps,' she said, into his ear.

'Perhaps not. What we need is a drink, Ama. To celebrate our reunion.'

'Hopeless - the bar's mobbed. It is a wake, remember?

'Some guy said the kitchen is where they store the booze...when was the last time you did a stage faint, Ama?'

'Faint? Right here?'
'Yeah, swoon – and I'll carry you out.'
'Ooohhh! Aaahhh!'
'That's it – louder... and slump!'
'Oohh God...I can't breathe!' She sagged against him and he grabbed her under the arms.
'Make room, make room!' Porter shouted. 'Somebody help her!'
'Okay – I'll take her feet!' said a tall man peering over the others at Ama slumped in Porter's arms, her head flung dramatically to one side. The two men carried her out through the crush of mourners, suddenly hushed and clearing a path for them, as Porter steered down the hall for the kitchen. As they arrived, he spoke to her.
'Okay, SnowWhite, you can wake up. Thanks, pal. She'll be alright now. What she needs is a good stiff drink.'
The tall young man lowered her feet and found a chair for her to sit on. He watched Ama's miraculous recovery, then glanced at Porter pouring out large drinks.
'Join us?' Porter offered him one of the drinks. 'Pretty convincing actress, isn't she?'
'Oh, I knew she was acting,' the man said, taking the drink.
'You did? I thought she had everyone fooled, except me, of course. How did you know?'
'Halfway down the hall, she winked at me,' he said, laughing and toasting Ama, who raised her glass to him and winked again. 'My name's Sy.'
Porter turned to stare at him. 'My god... you're not...
The young man nodded. 'Simon, junior. This is my father's wake. Cheers!' he added, holding up his glass again.
'I thought your dad was a tall man but I think you've got him beat. He was a good head taller than me.' Porter held out

his hand, 'I'm Porter Drummond, one of your dad's oldest friends. But I haven't seen him for a long time.'

'Are you related to Spike Drummond?' asked Sy. 'I haven't seen you since I was a kid.'

'Quite closely,' said Ama. 'Spike is Porter's nickname. And he and I haven't met since I was your age. My name's Amarylis Waterstone, better known as Ama, because nobody can pronounce it or spell it. Your mother invited me to come today although I only knew your dad for a short while. But I've known your mom through her work in the theatre – she's a brilliant scholar.'

'That's how she and Dad met – they both did medieval studies at Dartmouth College.'

'Where is she, Sy? I haven't seen anyone I know in this crowd,' said Porter.

'She's here somewhere. I'll go and look for her and tell her you're here.'

'How is she coping with all this?' Porter waved his arm around at the crowd of noisy mourners.

'Well, it wasn't unexpected. She and Dad planned this wake together when he knew he was dying.' Sy finished his drink with one long swallow. 'I think I know where she might be. There's another crowd downstairs in the TV room. You stay here and catch up with the rest of us – we're about ten drinks ahead of you. I'll see if I can find her and bring her back'. He loped off down the hall.

'So, Amarylis, where shall we begin? We've got off to a rather unusual start.'

'Well, perhaps we can start with our names. It feels odd calling you Porter after thinking of you all these years as Spike. And not many people even know my name is Amarylis. You never called me anything but Ama, so how about just Spike and Ama again?'

'Suits me. Porter Drummond was only my acting name when I trod the boards. My agent always insisted nobody would take me seriously with a name like Spike. But now as nobody takes me seriously anymore, Spike is fine with me – Ama.'

'I'll drink to that,' she said holding out her glass for him to top up. 'To Spike and Ama.'

'To Ama and Spike – cheers!'

'Well, now that we've got the star billing sorted, we can start the first act replay,' she said. "The last I heard of you, you were going on tour to Australia with that comedy where you jumped through a plate glass window.'

'The Front Page. Yeah, that was a great play. You and I had just split up so I decided to go with the touring company to Sidney and Melbourne for eight weeks.'

'Is that all? I thought you were away for years – you never wrote once,' she accused him.

'You left me, remember? For that northern actor – I forgot his name. Blanked it out of my mind.'

Ama smiled. 'Tim Hockney. That lasted for about three weeks. He was a notorious womaniser. Having a northern boyfriend was becoming quite fashionable back then. He taught me the Geordie accent – very useful, I got lots of TV and radio parts because of it. I wrote you, afterwards – twice, but you never replied. Sent them via The Old Vic stage door.'

'I never got them. The tour was so successful, they kept extending it – New Zealand, Hong Kong, South Africa. They must have got lost along the way. What did you say – come back? Beg my forgiveness?' He grinned, watching her reaction.

'I don't remember – more likely, the other way around. You were sleeping with that Scottish girl behind my back, as I recall.'

'Fiona. That was just a fling. We didn't do much sleeping. You were too busy with your first leading role in rep – in that Alan Ayckbourn play.'

'That's right, my new northern accent got me that part – Watford Rep, a tryout for a West End transfer. 'Absurd Person Singular.' The play transferred but I didn't – dropped for a bigger name and a worse accent.'

'Sour grapes?'

'Very. And I came limping home from Watford, seeking comfort – and find you in bed with the fiery redhead, Fiona.'

'It was just excess testosterone combined with opportunism – and she piqued my curiosity with her hairy orange legs. Made me wonder if... you know,' he trailed off.

'A boy's natural curiosity,' she nodded. 'And was she? No, I don't want to know.'

'Everywhere – armpits, too. Didn't believe in shaving – unnatural, she said.'

'Just a wild Highland lass. Must have been exciting, I'm sure, compared to me, your ordinary North London consort.'

'She was from Perth Rep. Not exactly the Highlands. Just down to the Big Smoke for a 'dirty weekend', as she called it.

Ama raised her hand to stop him, 'I think I've heard all I want of the fiery Fiona. Perhaps, more to the point – what is your current status, if I may be so bold? - single, married, divorced, co-habiting... all of these, none of these?'

'All of those, but none of those at the moment. You?'

'Similar, I guess – sort of mix and repeat a few times.'

'A few times? Which – all of those or...?'

'Married, divorced three times.'

'That's an impressive record, Ama.'

'Is it? A three-time loser. Depressing, I'd call it. However, I do have one daughter, as a consolation.'

'Does she live with you, or flown the nest?

'Off and on. She's away at present. I'm afraid she might break my record.'

'Sounds like my son, Patrick – a chip off the old block is the term, I think.' He picked up an open bottle of rye and poured them both another drink. 'A toast to our offspring – may they not repeat the error of our ways.'

She drank, then raised her glass again. 'To our renewed acquaintance.'

They drank, silently toasting each other, smiling and nodding beneath the steady buzz of the mourners. Spike looked around the swelling crowd that moved in and out of the kitchen.

'Do you suppose there's any food left or has this horde scoffed it all, Ama?'

'Try the fridge,' she suggested.

Spike opened it. 'Aha! The mother lode. Look at this, Ama.'

She peered over his shoulder and shook her head. 'It's all still wrapped in clingfilm, Spike. I don't think we should open it until Esther comes back – she may be saving it for later on.'

'Where is she, anyway? Sy must have found her by now.'

As if on cue, he saw Sy's head bobbing above the black clad guests, leading his mother by the elbow. She spotted Spike and waved her wineglass – spilling some of its contents over her guests like a blessing.

'Spike! - you made it.' She embraced him, pouring the rest of her wine down his back. She was more than a little tipsy. She turned to Ama. 'Sy told me how you were rescued by him from near suffocation, Ama.'

'My hero.' Ama smiled.

'Esther – sorry, sorry, sorry. Sorry I was too late for Simon and too late to be here for you at the end.' He hugged her again and held her close for a minute or so. She pulled free to gaze up into his face, tears welling into her reddened eyes and streaking her makeup.

'This wake is supposed to be a celebration and I can't stop crying. Every time I see another old friend here...' she stopped, dabbing at her eyes with a sodden handkerchief clutched in her hand. 'But you missed the reading of the will. Simon wanted you to be here for the surprise, didn't he Sy?'

Her son nodded, 'Shall I tell him or do you want to, Mom?'

'You tell him, Sy. I'll just start crying again,' said Esther.

'Dad left you the Mongoose,' he said, handing Spike the keys. 'It's still waiting for the dry dock, I'm afraid. Dad was too weak to begin painting her. But he was happy to think you would finish the restoration job you've both worked on for so long.'

'The Mongoose belongs to you and Esther, Sy. I only have a part share in her. You both know that,' said Spike, trying to hand the keys back to Simon.

'My only interest in the boat was to help Dad realise his dream, Spike. I'm like Mom, I don't like the sea or boats, except as scenery. Besides, I'm going to New York in a few days – be gone indefinitely.'

'Sy's right,' said Esther, 'I get seasick crossing the harbour on the Dartmouth ferry. We all agreed you were the one to finish the Mongoose. It's what Simon hoped for. Don't let us down, Spike.'

'It would be an honour and a pleasure to complete the project,' said Spike. 'It's true, the Mongoose was a shared dream – I just never expected it to end like this. I'll happily finish her, but I can only accept part ownership. Esther.'

Esther looked at her son and nodded agreement. 'Okay, Spike, we'll remain silent partners but you take responsibility for it.'

Sy shook Spike's hand and held out the boat keys. 'And if you ever decide to sell the Mongoose, we'll be there with our hands out for our share – agreed?'

'Congratulations, Captain,' said Ama. 'How about some champagne to break over your bow?'

'I'm afraid this bunch have demolished the champagne hours ago,' said Esther, 'but there's lots of wine – everybody brought some.'

'Not me,' said Ama. 'I brought some bubbly and hid it under the back-porch steps – for our surprise meeting, Spike. Do you think you can break through that crowd by the door, Sy, and find it?'

'Be right back,' he said and inserted his long bony frame into the solid wall of guests blocking the back door.

'Surprise meeting?' said Spike. 'You knew about it?'

'I told Ama I'd been in contact with all Simon's oldest friends and when I mentioned your name she almost fell over. Told me she had lost touch with you years ago and thought you were in Europe or Australia,' said Esther.

'So, when Esther said you lived in BC and were coming here for the wake, she invited me, too, at the last minute, to meet you again.'

'I was going to produce her as a surprise,' explained Esther, 'but we both got waylaid in the pandemonium. I forgot how popular Simon was and all his old graduates and colleagues and sailing pals just kept pouring in from all over. God knows where they'll all stay tonight. This is a big old house but there's only room for a few of them, unless they can sleep standing up.'

'I bet they'll stay right here as long as the booze lasts,' said Spike, staring at the revellers, 'probably still be here in the morning.'

Sy reappeared with two plastic shopping bags in his hands. He handed one bag to Spike and stuck the other one in a high cupboard over the fridge. 'For later,' he said to Ama.

Spike popped the champagne cork and filled all their glasses, keeping hold of the bottle.

'To Dad' said Sy, raising his glass.

'To Simon,' the others all said and drained their glasses.

'To the Mongoose,' said Spike, pouring out more bubbly.

'To Captain Drummond,' Ama toasted.

'To surprise reunions,' Esther proposed.

. She turned to Spike. 'When Simon got ill, I took over the department, to carry on Simon's modern English Shakespeare project.'

'That's a mammoth task from what Simon told me of it,' said Spike, 'and he was just nicely getting started, too.'

She nodded agreement. 'Yes, we'd only done a handful of the easier plays before he learned of his disease. He was going great guns until then, wasn't he, Sy?'

'Never saw him so happy,' he said. 'And then it all came to a halt, almost.'

'Why, what happened? He never really talked much about it to me,' said Spike. 'His illness, I mean.'

'That's Dad all over, I couldn't get him to tell me for the longest time. And he swore Mom to silence.'

'She never spoke of it to me until quite near the end,' said Ama, 'although I knew something was up.' She turned to Esther, 'You used to start crying for no apparent reason. I couldn't figure it out – thought it was marital problems but you wouldn't tell me.'

'Oh, I'm an expert crier now – been at it almost non-stop today. After Simon told me he was diagnosed with early Alzheimer's, he knew he would never finish the project. I tried to persuade him to continue but he refused. Said he would just mess it up and I should just go on with it myself. Made me promise not to tell anyone or we might lose our project funding.'

'But surely he knew they would find out if he stopped working on it,' said Spike.

'He'd figured it all out,' said Esther. 'Gave up all his classes and only kept his graduate seminars so he could focus more on the project – that's what he told the Dean. I drove him into his department office and he pretended to work on the plays.'

'Didn't his graduate students realise what was happening to him?' asked Ama.

'Not for awhile, but by the end of the term it was obvious to him he couldn't continue, so he asked for a sabbatical leave to do some research in London.'

'That's when Dad told me what was wrong with him and asked me to help. He said he wanted to end his life before it became obvious to everyone, and the Shakespeare project would be in jeopardy – that's all he cared about. So I agreed,' said Sy.

Esther took his arm. 'We can talk more later. Sy and I should be circulating – we haven't spoken to half the people here yet and they'll think it's strange.'

'Would you like me to help put out some of the food, Esther, while you see to your guests?' asked Ama.

'The buffet!... oh my god! It's gone straight out of my mind. No wonder everybody seems smashed – all this drinking on an empty stomach. Now, there's a ton of stuff in the pantry and plates and plates of aperitifs in the fridge here and more in the one downstairs...'

'Why don't you and Sy go down and deal with that, while Spike and I spread out the buffet in the kitchen.'

"Yes,' said Esther, 'I know it's a wake but it still wouldn't do for the hostess to end up flat on the floor. I'm already feeling giddy and there's hours to go yet with the buffet and the musicians arriving for the evening.' She handed her empty wineglass to Ama. 'I better start pacing myself, Sy. I can't drink like I used to. When your dad gave those parties for his grad students – I could keep up with the best of them.'

Ama opened the fridge door and began passing out the loaded plates to Spike to unwrap.

'I suppose it's alright for me to sample these now we've had the official signal to start,' he said, trying out items from each plate as it came out of the fridge.

For the next couple of hours Spike and Ama did the rounds of the friendly mourners and guests, while everyone talked at their loudest to be heard above the clamour. They managed to catch up on each other's past lives, in between meeting people, but they barely scratched the surface of almost forty years apart.

'I can't face anymore new people, Ama. Couldn't we find a corner to sit and talk to each other, instead of to total strangers?'

She looked dubious. 'That might not be too easy, Spike. We could try upstairs, I guess.'

They wormed their way past people perched all the way up the old oak staircase, eating from plates balanced on their knees and clutching at wine glasses as they passed.

'It's just as crowded up here as downstairs,' said Spike. 'Even the bathroom's full.'

'Let's try the bedrooms,' she said, opening one of the doors and then closing it quickly, but not before Spike glimpsed a couple spread-eagled on the bed, naked from the waist down. 'I hope that's a spare bedroom and not Esther's, Ama.'

'From what she's told me, she's used to wild parties when Simon was alive.'

They tried another bedroom with a locked door. 'That's probably Esther's room, Spike. Let's find Sy's – he won't mind, I don't suppose.'

At the end of the hall, a door stood ajar with several people sitting on the floor in a circle at one side of the bed, drinking and arguing. They looked up briefly at Spike and Ama, before returning to their heated conversation. Spike and Ama commandeered the floor on the opposite side of the bed and pulled a couple of pillows down to sit on while they leaned back against the wall. Spike had lifted a bottle of red wine from a side table in the hall which someone had abandoned. He filled their glasses and they drank silently.

'God, my throat's hoarse from shouting at people,' said Ama, 'and my feet are killing me.'

Spike reached down to pull off her sandals for her. 'That better?'

She wriggled her bare toes. 'Much. Now, what did you want to talk about?'

He slumped back against the wall and closed his eyes. 'Nothing. I'm talked out. For the moment, anyway – maybe in a while. Let's just sit and rest. I've forgotten how exhausting big parties can be.'

'Depends,' said Ama.

'On what?'

'Lots of things,' she said. 'I love them or hate them – depends on who you meet'.

'What about this one – love or hate?'

'I love it – except for my sore feet.'

'Would you like me to massage them for you? I used to be good at that, remember?'

'So you were, I hadn't forgotten.'

'I see – just hinting?' He lifted one foot on to his lap and rubbed the sole. 'How's that?'

'Bliss – don't stop.' She closed her eyes while Spike kneaded her foot from the heel up to her toes.

'You used to tell me folk tales – I remember that, too.'

'That's right, I did – to relax you. And massaged your feet till you fell asleep.'

'From Oscar Wilde...' she prompted.

'The Giant's Garden,' said Spike.

'I didn't always fall asleep.'

He slid his hand slowly up her calf. 'I remember that, too.'

She sat up and pulled him towards her so their faces almost touched. Before either of them quite realised what they were doing they were locked in an old embrace – a kissing match that covered their faces and necks in turn. It lasted for several minutes till they took a breather.

'God, I wanted to do that since the moment you came through the door,' said Ama. 'I've been fantasizing about it all morning, waiting for you to show up.' She kissed him again, more slowly this time, pausing to decide where to place the next one.

'Took you long enough to get around to it,' he said. 'I thought maybe I'd lost the old charm. Made me feel quite insecure.' He turned his cheek towards her. 'You missed a spot.'

'Did I? I'm out of practice – here?' She kissed the proffered cheek.

'Down a bit – no – over a bit,' he moved under her lips. 'Yes.' Their mouths met and they were off again, covering each other's face.

Ama pulled back. 'Stop. We're being silly.'

'I know.' He continued caressing her, his hands now starting to move down her body, his head following them, brushing his face against her clothing and then her bare knees.

'Spike,' she hissed, 'those people will hear us...'

He lifted his head from her bare leg to look at her. 'I won't say a word, I promise.'

'But they might see you – they're right there!'

'I'll hide.' He lifted her filmy summer skirt and put his head under it, kissing his way up her thigh.

She gave herself up to the sensation for a brief moment, then wriggled free, pulling her knees up and her skirt down and drawing his head back up to face her. 'Spike – not here.'

'Where, then?' He looked around. 'Under the bed?'

'You're being silly again.'

'I'm deadly serious, Ama. I want to kiss you all over.'

'Not under the bed, you're not.'

'On top of the bed -'

'In plain view?'

'Under the covers -'

'Spike – be serious, I want this as much as you – but not in front of an audience.'

'Ask them to leave,' he said.

'You ask them – besides they were here first.'

'You're making excuses – this is not the Amarylis Waterstone I knew of yore.'

'It certainly isn't – that was forty years ago. I'm an old respectable lady now.'

'Impossible.' He fondled the hem of her skirt. 'I remember these legs as if it were yesterday -'

'And they will remain a memory as long as we stay here,' she said. 'I'm leaving before I do something I will regret in the morning.'

'There's nowhere else to go, Ama, the house is crammed to the eaves with drunken mourners, all with the same idea as we have.'

'Not all, surely. This is a wake, not an orgy.'

'Give them time – wait till the music starts and they get their second wind.'

'Well in that case, we might as well go back downstairs and join the mourners,' said Ama, rising to her feet and slipping her sandals back on. She stood over him, waiting.

He ran his hands up the inside of her long legs.

She laughed and pulled him to his feet. 'What was that line from O'Casey you loved to quote? - about having your mind on higher things than a girl's garters.' She took his hand and they tiptoed out the door, unnoticed by the seated figures still deep in discussion.

Spike clutched the half empty bottle of red wine and he stopped on the landing to fill their glasses. Somewhere below them some fiddlers were scraping their bows as they tuned up, adding to the cacophony of noise from the revellers who were gathering around an upright piano. Ama leaned against him on the landing and they looked out over the heads below, sipping their wine and waiting for the musicians to begin.

'How long are you staying before you head home?'

'I have to be back for rehearsals starting in two days. I shouldn't have left at all but I promised Esther and she's done me so many favours. She and Simon knew everybody in the theatre throughout the Maritimes and they gave me tons of support with my project – God knows how I'll survive without them.'

'But you can't up and leave when I've only just found you after all this time, Ama – it's not fair!'

'Well come and join me down in Arcadia – you said yourself you were at a loose end.'

'That was before Simon left me the Mongoose. You heard me promise Esther I would finish it off.'

'Couldn't you sail it down to the south shore and meet me there, Spike? It could be your maiden voyage in it.'

'I haven't even seen it for ages, I've no idea what shape it's in. Sy tells me it's just been sitting on the mooring for over a year because Simon was too ill to work on it.'

'Perhaps we could go and have a look at it tomorrow – it might be fine. It's not that far to Arcadia and you could work on it down there – when you're not helping me, that is.'

'Okay,' said Spike Let's make this a night to remember.'

They surged down the stairwell, scattering mourners as they headed for the music coming from the living room. Three fiddlers sawed away around the piano, joined by two penny-whistle players and an old man in a battered fedora playing an ancient squeezebox. The tune was an unrecognizable jig but the revellers bobbed up and down, clutching at each other, barely able to move as even more mourners pushed and elbowed their way into the room to hear the musicians.

Ama hopped up and down trying to see. Spike bent down and boosted her up to look around, then lowered her back down.

He grinned at her, puffing slightly. 'You're not the sylph-like girl I remember, Ama.'

'That's what forty years will do to a girl,' she patted his belly. 'I don't recall this paunch, either.' She put her arm round his neck. 'Lift me up, once more, Spike. I want to see if Esther's around.'

Spike laced his fingers together to make a cup. 'Okay, put your foot in here.'

She eased off one sandal, holding it in her hand while she stepped up to look over his head. 'I'm facing the wrong way, Spike, turn around.'

He swivelled about, his face pressed into her stomach. 'Can you see her?'

'Yes, she's with the old accordion man... they're kissing.'

'Aww, how sweet,' he said, lowering her down. 'I'm envious.'

She pulled his ear. 'Of that old man?'

'I mean if they're not inhibited, why us?'

She gave him a peck on the cheek. 'With everybody watching?'

'Everybody, or nobody – this is a wake, remember? Anything goes.'

'Not for me, it doesn't, not in public.'

'For someone who used to act in bawdy restoration comedies, you've become strangely modest, Ama.'

She smiled at him, 'Yes – "I have by degrees dwindled into a wife." Only I'm not even a wife anymore.'

'Well, that's something to be grateful for, anyway. It just so happens, that I too, am unattached.'

'In that case, follow me.' She took his hand and led him back into the hall to the stairs going down to the rec room.

'Where are we going?'

'You'll see. Someplace I only just thought of.'

The guests in the basement rec room crowded around the temporary bar and a piano keyboard that a grad student thumped away at. Ama squeezed past a group blocking a panel door and pulled Spike after her, closing the door. He leaned against it, adjusting his eyes to the darkened room.

'Where are we?'

'The laundry room. It's not very big but at least it's private. See if you can find the light switch, Spike.'

He ran his hand over the wall by the door until he found it and flicked it up and down. Nothing happened. 'Probably the bulb's blown. Never mind, it's more romantic this way.' He pulled her to him. 'Now, my proud beauty...'

They leaned against the washing machine and clung to each other for a few moments in the gloom. She put her hand up to his face to trace his mouth before they kissed long and hard. They paused to touch each other's features in the dark. The only light came from a narrow gap at the bottom of the door, barely enough to discern their body outlines. He touched her lips with his fingers.

'You're smiling,' he said.

She brushed his mouth again with the back of her hand. 'So are you.'

They proceeded to explore each other in between bouts of embracing and kissing, their hands moving up and down their bodies, over and under their clothing, pressing themselves together in the dark.

'Talk to me, Spike – I need to hear your voice.'

'I'm right here,' he breathed in her ear. 'I'm not going anywhere.'

'I never realised how much I missed you all these years,' she said. 'Where have you been all my life?'

'Lost, waylaid, flotsam and jetsam, abandoned by you.' He lowered his head to her breast.

'Forty years,' she said, clasping his ears. 'Do you think that's significant, Spike?'

'Definitely symbolic – forty years wandering in the wilderness, searching.' He truffled his face about in her clothing.

'For what?'

He stopped, his face looming up in front of her. 'For you, obviously.'

'And now?' She resumed kissing him, feeling the dent in his stubbled chin with her index finger.

'A lot of catching up to do, Ama. Can't afford to waste anymore time.' He pressed himself against her and she felt him stiffen beneath his trousers.

'Spike?'

'Hmm?'

'Before we go any further, I think I ought to tell you something.'

'What?'

'The knobs on this washing machine are jabbing me in the back.'

He eased himself upright. 'There's always the floor, I suppose.'

'It's bare concrete, not even a bit of carpet,' she objected.

They stood swaying, arms about each other, considering.

'We only have one option,' he said. 'A knee-trembler. Are you game?'

'I've been waiting forty years for you to ask. But are you up to it? You have to do the heavy lifting – and you've already told me I'm too fat,' she said.

'I may need some encouragement to be up for it – the heavy lifting is not a problem.'

She lifted her light summer skirt with one hand and led his hand to her waist. 'Then help me out of my knickers,' she said, tugging down on his arm. He pulled them down and she stepped out of them. 'Now you,' she began unzipping his fly, searching for him, inside his pants. With her other hand she loosened his belt and his trousers dropped to the floor.

He stood stock still, relishing her touch on his bare skin. 'You've done this before, I see.'

'Not for a long time,' she said slipping down his boxer shorts and gripping him in her hand. 'Not like this.'

They fondled each other in the dark until she felt he was ready, then put her free arm round his neck while she steered him into her body. 'Now?' she whispered in his ear and he placed one hand on each cool buttock and lifted her onto him as she wrapped her legs about him. 'Gently, I'm not used to this, Spike.'

'I have only a folk memory of it myself,' he said, raising and lowering her with his hands while she clung about his neck and blew in his ear. They bobbed up and down for a few minutes and he attempted to lower his face to her breast. She loosened her grasp on his neck to undo her top, while he took one hand off her bottom, to raise her breast to his lips. Even as he did so, he felt himself going soft inside her with the exertion. She slipped off him, the two of them nearly falling to the floor.

'Oh Spike, I'm sorry – I am too heavy for you,' said Ama, panting.

Breathing heavily, he stood in front of her, feeling his knees turn to water. 'My fault – too ambitious.'

'It was nice while it lasted though,' said Ama, consoling, as she slipped her underwear back on. 'I guess I wasn't thinking too clearly when I suggested this place.' She extended her hand to take his, 'Are you feeling okay, Spike?'

He squeezed her hand. 'No damage, except to my wounded pride.'

They stood contemplating their next move, listening to the din from the revellers in the next room.

'I don't think we should leave together, Spike – it will look too obvious, especially as I probably look pretty rumpled,' said Ama, adjusting her skirt and patting her hair.

'You go first – they'll think you're the laundry maid,' said Spike. 'I'll follow you in five minutes. Meet you in the kitchen.'

'No, I'm heading for the nearest bathroom and hope nobody I know sees me before I get tidied up. Do you think my clothes are straight?'

'Turn around and let me feel your skirt,' he said, running his hands over her bottom and pulling down a bit of her skirt caught up in her underwear. 'There. Now the front...' he turned her round and checked her blouse buttons with his fingers, lingering on her breasts. 'This one doesn't feel quite right...let me see,' he attempted to slip his hand inside her bra before she pulled away.

'And perhaps I'd better check your fly is done up, too,' said Ama, stroking his pants. 'Hmm- can't tell without a closer feel...' She leaned up against him and slipped her hand down inside the front of his pants, cupping him in her palm. 'Everything seems in order.'

'Just shows how wrong you can be. We have all sorts of unfinished business,' said Spike.

She wriggled her fingers experimentally again. 'Yes, I see what you mean – but not here.' She withdrew her hand, smoothing the lump in his trousers. 'Perhaps you'd better wait here – till you calm down a little. I'll see you upstairs.' She kissed his cheek and cautiously opened the door. A wall of noise enveloped her as she slipped into the crowd.

Spike waited the obligatory five minutes then sidled out, with hardly a glance from anyone and worked his way up the stairs. There was no sign of Ama in the kitchen. He popped a chocolate ball into his mouth from a heap on a platter. 'Profiteroles – my specialty,' said Esther, coming out of the pantry with more loaded plates. 'There's someone you should meet. I think he's by the piano.'

They sidled through the dancing mourners until she pointed to the old squeeze-box player, standing with the other musicians. His battered fedora tipped to one side, reminded Spike of Leonard Cohen's last concert appearances. He had set off a minor craze for fedoras and now every folk rocker was wearing one. But this one seemed to pre-date Cohen's with its battered brim and crushed top.

She stopped to listen. "We'll wait till he finishes this song.'

'Who is he - a friend of Simon's?'

Esther only nodded, doing a little shuffle to the music and watching the old man play. 'Tried to get him to teach me the button accordion but he said he didn't know how to teach – only play by ear.'

The song finished and they launched into another, but Esther moved in to tap his shoulder and nodded towards Spike. The old man listened for a moment, then followed her as they moved out into the hall, away from the heaving bodies near the musicians. Spike joined them in the front hall.

'Spike, this is Fergus, an old friend of Simon's. He's a boat-builder.'

'And a mean squeeze-box player, too,' said Spike, shaking hands.

'Was a boat-builder,' corrected Fergus. 'Been retired a long time. Now I just mess about doin' the odd repair job. I like to keep me hand in. That's how me and Simon met.'

'Pay no attention, Spike. He's a master shipwright. He worked on the Bluenose and the Bounty in Lunenburg – very choosy about who he works for these days.'

Fergus acknowledged the compliment with a slight wave of his hand. 'Only the replica ships,' he said. 'I been playin' this thing about as long as I been messin' about with boats. Don't know which I likes best - probably the squeeze-box, but I'm better at boats'.

Spike laughed. 'You sound like Ratty in Wind in the Willows, doesn't he?'

'"There is nothing," said Esther, "half so enjoyable, as simply messing about in boats."'

Fergus nodded and grinned at them. 'That about sums me up, alright. I should have that carved over my workbench. To remind me why I keep goin'. I'll be 85 come the fall,' he added, almost to himself.

'Fergus, the reason I wanted to introduce you is so you could meet the new owner of Simon's boat. He left the Mongoose to Spike in his will.'

'I been wonderin' to myself what you was goin' to do with it now Simon's gone.' He shook Spike's hand again. 'Congratulations. That's a fine old boat – just needs a few more bits 'n pieces doin to it – an' a lick or two of paint...'

'She'll need more than a lick of paint, I'm afraid, Spike. But Fergus is right, the Mongoose is a classic old boat.'

The old man nodded. 'Built down the south shore in Mahone Bay, before the war. Simon told me she even did some time with the navy as a shore patrol boat. Still got the original engine in her, last time I looked,' Fergus said.

'I thought you might be able to share some of your expertise with Spike – help him get the Mongoose finished like Simon intended.'

Fergus eyed Spike for a minute. 'You know anythin' 'bout boats? You don't sound like you're from around here.'

Spike shook his head, 'I'm not in your league, Fergus – more like Ratty. I just enjoy messing about with boats. Small boats,' he added. 'I haven't seen the Mongoose for quite awhile but from what Simon's son has been telling me, I'm going to need your help. Are you free to have a look at her tomorrow?'

'Be glad to. Hate to see a fine old boat like her bein' neglected.' He cocked an ear to the music. 'Sounds like they need my steadyin' hand on the tiller in there – I better get back.'

'See you tomorrow at the dock,' said Spike as the old man headed back through the dancers to the piano.

'Good,' said Esther. 'I was pretty sure he'd say yes. He worked on it with Simon, but they stopped when Simon got too ill. He may be 85 but there isn't much he doesn't know about fixing up these old lobster boats.'

They worked their way back through the throng to the kitchen.

'Where have you been?' said Ama. 'I met an old friend of Simon's and got talking about Shakespeare.'

'You planning to do any Shakespeare in your new theatrical enterprise, Ama?' asked Spike. 'We've barely mentioned it, except that you're in rehearsal. What for?'

'An Edwardian Music Hall show to start off with, cabaret style, followed by Shakespeare's Twelfth Night.'

'You mean, like they do in England, for the summer tourists, end of the pier stuff?'

She made a face. 'You make it sound awful. I'm aiming for a tongue in cheek approach. More of a send-up, but mixed in with lots of nostalgia turns as well as some topical items.'

'So why Edwardian?'

'Simple. It's an old Edwardian era theatre with a break-arch proscenium, so we thought let's do it in Edwardian dress.'

'How about coming with me to see the Mongoose, Ama? I'm going down there now. I'll sleep there tonight.'

'I want to come with you. Wait a minute.' She picked up a plastic container with a few sandwiches left in it and quickly filled it with food from nearby plates. 'Okay, let's go.'

Spike reached up above the fridge to open the cupboard and remove a plastic bag. 'We might need this later.' He showed her the spare bottle of champagne they had hidden earlier in the day.

They edged their way to the back porch and went down the steps into the late summer evening. Spike looked at his watch. 'It's half past ten already and it's still light. Do you have a car, Ama, or shall we look for a taxi?'

'I left it in the neighbour's driveway.' She manoeuvred the little car through a patch of orange daisies, leaving two tracks across the lawn, onto the street. Spike climbed in beside her, grinning.

'Somebody's going to have some explaining to do tomorrow.'

'I'm blaming you – it was your idea,' she said. 'Where away, Captain?'

CHAPTER TWO

Spike steered her through the quiet streets of the university area, down to the docklands until he saw the old fishing boat masts and outriggers between the warehouses. 'Down here,' he directed, and Ama drove slowly down a narrow lane with only an occasional streetlight, to an old wooden wharf and parked her car facing the harbour.

'Sy told me it's down near the end of the dock. Watch your step and hang on to me – there could be missing planks on this old wharf.'

They made their cautious way along the dock. Spike stopped suddenly.

'What – what is it?' Ama asked him, looking nervously around.

'The Mongoose. There it is.' He played Ama's flashlight over the decks of the old fishing boat and stopped on the stencilled name flowing beneath the bow. He walked alongside, found the gap in the mahogany handrail and stepped aboard. The tide was in and the boat was almost level with the dock. He put down the parcels and held out his hand to her. 'Welcome aboard.' She stepped straight into his arms and they stood gently rocking with the boat while they held a long embrace.

'Is this a traditional sailor's greeting, Captain Drummond?'

'Start as you mean to go on,' said Spike. 'Nelson always said, "Hang strategy – just go straight for 'em".'

'I see – so this is how I can expect to be treated in future?'

'Damn right. Let's go below.'

'Aye, aye, sir.'

'There's a shoreline here for power,' he said, following the cable with his hand down the steps into the cabin area. 'Ah, here's the switch.' Dim yellow light lit the unpainted wooden interior and they sank down onto the shabby seat cushions covering the bunk type cabin seating.

Ama eyed the narrow benches. 'Is this where we sleep?'

'Never fear,' he said, rising and opening a narrow door leading forward. 'Have a look at this.'

She stuck her head under his arm to view the forward cabin with its vee-berth double bed, spread with two sleeping bags over a thick slab of foam, cut to fit the vee shape. 'This looks promising. A definite improvement over the laundry room, Spike.' She crawled up onto the berth. 'Is there any light in here?'

'Nope, only that extension cord in the main cabin. But we're used to the dark after the laundry room, aren't we?'

'Maybe there's some candles in the kitchen we could use,' she said. 'Much more romantic anyway than bare light bulbs.'

'There's no kitchen on a boat – it's called a galley.'

'Pardon me.'

'Honest mistake, don't let it happen again. Come out here and I'll show it to you.'

Ama backed out into the cabin and followed him towards a long counter at the rear of the open plan main cabin space, to one side of the steps they had come down. A temporary camp kitchen had been set up with a two-burner propane stove, kettle and a few basics of crockery, cutlery and pots.

'Voila... La cuisine!' He lifted a frying pan, encrusted with dried fat. 'Here is where I shall prepare sumptuous repasts for you.'

'But not in that, I hope.' She poked about the dusty collection of jars and cans, and unearthed some stumps of twisted wax candles. 'Now if we had some matches...'

Spike picked up a long-handled gas lighter beside the propane stove and clicked the spark a few times before it ignited. 'Pass me one of those candles.'

She handed him a drooping one, smiling. 'Remind you of anything?'

'I'm hoping you'll be able to fix that,' he said, lighting it and sticking it on a dirty saucer.

'I'm afraid the candle is too far gone, but as for you...' she carried the light towards the bed. 'If you'll follow me, I will attempt a resurrection.'

'All in good time,' he said. 'First let me show you a couple of things.' He led her around the other side of the stairs and opened what looked like a cupboard door and stepped aside to show her.

'Ah, the bathroom – I was wondering if we had to use a porta-potty, like camping.'

'The head', he corrected. 'Shall I demonstrate? No, best if you do it yourself while I explain.'

'Make it quick, then, because I've been holding back for ages – all that wine...'

'Right. First you drop your drawers – shall I lend a hand...?'

'No, that I can manage.'

'Now, are you seated comfortably? Then you can begin.' He stood with his arms folded, watching.

'I can't do anything with you staring – you'll have to leave the room.'

'I'm not in the room, it's too small for both of us. I'm in the doorway.'

'Well, close it then, till I'm finished.' She made shooing motions with her hands and he pulled the door shut and waited. After a couple of minutes, she called, 'Where's the teepee?'

'In the drawer, behind you.' He heard some scrabbling sounds. 'Find it?'

'Yes, what's next?'

'I re-enter, and continue the lesson,' he said, pushing the door open and leaning in through it. 'Please remain seated and pay strict attention. One false move and you may sink the ship.'

'Good god! Maybe you'd better take over...'

'Nonsense, you're a grown woman. If you're going to sail the seven seas with me, you'll need to learn how to operate a head. You can't expect me to wipe your bottom like a two-year old, if we're in the middle of a Force Nine gale.'

'Heaven forfend I should ever be in any such situation. Come on, then, get on with it. I feel like an idiot, sitting on the throne being lectured to.'

'On your left is a long wooden handle for flushing. Between your legs on the floor is a small lever. You lift the lever and it allows the sea water to enter. That's it. On your right is a red tap. You open that first to allow the bowl to be emptied. Right. Simple, but ingenious. Now you pump out the contents till the bowl is empty and you only see clean seawater in it. Go ahead, keep pumping. Now push the lever between your legs back down to stop the sea from entering. Good. And finally, you shut the red tap to prevent any backflow. Pull your drawers back up and you're done. You may now consider yourself an able seaman.'

'That was the most complicated pee I've had in my life. And believe me I've been in some strange places. Where's the tap for this sink? Don't tell me there's a whole rigamarole for that, too, Spike.'

'Nope, it's just a pedal by your foot there – pump it up and down, that's it, nice and steady.' He carried the candle back out to the counter. 'I'll leave this here by the stove and the gas lighter, in case you need it in the middle of the night.'

'If I do, I'm going upstairs and pee over the side,' said Ama, sitting down behind the table and attempting to push it away from her legs.

'It's bolted to the floor,' said Spike. 'So you'll have something to hang onto in those Force Nine gales I mentioned earlier. Well, what do you think of the Mongoose, so far?'

'Not exactly luxurious, is it – a bit rough and ready, I'd say. What do you think – is it how you remembered it?' She drew him down beside her on the bench seat and leaned her head on his shoulder.

'It's a bit musty from being closed up for so long but she's pretty comfortable compared to how it was before. Simon and Fergus have done a lot to her.' He looked around the cabin. 'Look at all that new panelling on the walls. That must be Fergus' handiwork.' He pointed at the steps. 'And the companionway was just a stepladder when I left. Solid mahogany staircase and handrail now. I'd say that's fairly luxurious, wouldn't you?'

She nodded in agreement. 'Is that slidey roof the companionway?'

'It's the sliding hatch cover – mahogany as well. The whole entrance and stairs is the companionway.'

'A lot of terms for an old lady like me to learn,' said Ama. 'A bit like being in the theatre with its whole set of terminology to get used to. Took me ages to remember 'prompt side' and 'O-P' were just terms for stage left and stage right.'

'Bit like port and starboard on boats for left and right,' said Spike.

'Probably all designed just to add to the mystique of the theatre and sailing so you can impress the public.'

'Like POSH.'

'And "deus ex machina."'

'By and large,' said Spike.

'Fly loft,' said Ama.

'Swinging the lead.'

'Break a leg.'

'Let the cat out of the bag,' said Spike.

'That's not a sailing expression,' objected Ama.

'Yes it is – google it.'

'I can't, there's no computer here – if you're going to cheat, I'm not playing anymore... besides I can't think of another stage term at the moment.'

'Let's change the subject,' Spike said.

'Okay. This may be thirsty work. Shall we open the champagne?' She passed him the plastic bag and he took out the bottle.

'It's not quite chilled to the right temperature,' he said, holding it out to her.

'It actually feels warm, Spike. I've never drunk warm champagne.'

'Another new experience for you to add to your seafaring lore,' he said, peeling off the foil and the wire cage. 'The champagne flutes are in the galley, no doubt. Will you get them while I ease the cork? I can't just pop it or the bouncing around in the car and the warmth will end with half of it on the floor.'

Ama pawed through the assortment of crockery on the counter and returned with two thick tumblers. 'We seem to be right out of champagne flutes.' She plunked the heavy glasses on the table.

'Tut, tut. These will have to do – unless perhaps we used your slipper...?' He pulled the cork slowly and it only made a soft thump.

'My open-toed sandals aren't up to it, I'm afraid,' she said, dangling one off her foot to show him.

Spike carefully half-filled the two thick glasses, letting the foam reach to the brim. 'To the Mongoose,' he toasted, clinking her glass.

'– and all who sail in her,' she said, tipping the warm frothy wine up high to get through the foam to the liquid. 'Mmmn...unusual,' she nodded, licking her white moustache.

Spike twirled his glass and drank it all off in one swallow, leaving a wide foam moustache on his upper lip, too. '"An unassuming little wine, but I think you'll be amused by its presumption."'

'Highly amusing,' she said leaning over to lick off his frothy lip.

He reciprocated and they amused each other, licking and kissing for a few minutes. Spike paused to refill their glasses and they had another round of foamy kissing. 'I think this warm champagne may catch on – in certain quarters.'

'Close quarters,' said Ama, licking his lip. 'Amongst the crew.'

'That sort of thing. Propinquity,' he said, undoing her blouse.

'Is that what they call it? Another sailing term, I suppose.' She undid the buttons on his shirt.

They stopped to pour out the last of the warm champagne.

'Any last toasts?' he asked.

'After you.'

'I propose we splice the main brace and then go to bed.'

'To propinquity,' said Ama, draining her glass.

'To the coming resurrection,' he said, emptying the last drops from the bottle.

'Let's just have the candle, Spike.' She brought the drooping candle over from the counter, then stopped and went back to search for a different one. She returned carrying a thick straight one. She lit it with the gas lighter and Spike switched off the bare bulb hanging over a beam. Holding the candle high for him to see, Ama perched on the end of the vee- berth.

'"How bright this little candle sheds its beam.

So shines a good deed in a naughty world."'

'Amen to that,' said Spike, taking the candle from her to put in a niche at one side of the bed. They helped each other out of their clothes, grateful for the forgiving light of the candle, and crawled into the vee-berth, unzipping the sleeping bags to make a top and bottom blanket.

True to her word, Ama performed the resurrection and Spike rose rigid above her.

'For what you are about to receive, may the lord make us truly thankful.'

'And amen to that,' she said, wrapping her legs around his back and pulling him into her.

For what seemed a long while, neither of them spoke, concentrating their attention on their goal. When at last, they achieved it to their mutual satisfaction, they lay wrapped only in the candle glow.

'Amarylis Waterstone,' he said at last.

'Porter Drummond,' she echoed his tone.

'I feel you ought to know,' he said, 'that you have succeeded in turning my carefully crafted plans tits up. I have been quietly ploughing my own furrow all these years and now here you are, wreaking havoc,' he said, turning her in his arms to face him. 'What have you to say for yourself?'

'I might say the same thing to you, only more so. At least you admitted that you have just been drifting, while I have been patiently sorting through the remnants of my former life, trying to make head or tail of what is left. Just when I began to feel it was starting to gel into shape, you reappear and I fall to pieces. Have you no shame?' She propped herself up on one elbow to study his face in the candlelight. 'No, I can see you haven't.'

'I am unrepentant. And you?'

'Ditto.'

'In that case, there is only one course of action,' said Spike. 'We must heed Churchill's advice – when you're going through hell, keep going.'

And they fell on each other again until they were finally sated. He rolled onto his back, conceding defeat. She sat astride him, panting and waiting to see if he was really finished lovemaking. But there was not a flicker of movement from him. She slid off him.

'Now what happens?' he asked.

'We talk, of course.'

'I thought that's what we had been doing.'

'No, mostly we've been avoiding talking. Playing games -

,

'This is the serious bit then – the rest was just foreplay?'

She nodded.

'Okay, you start,' he said.

'Alright. I'd like to know if you're trifling with my affections or if your intentions are honourable.'

'Which would you prefer, Ama?'

'Right now – I really don't know. I'd like some clarification.'

'And I already told you, I feel completely confused. How do we clarify things?'

'Well,' Ama said. 'Do you want to see me again or do I disappear back down to Arcadia like this never happened. That's one possibility.'

'No, it's not. No more disappearing acts – let's make that rule number one.'

'How do we make that work, Spike. I told you I have to go back. I should be in rehearsal. I'm only here to help Esther with the wake.'

'Can't somebody else stand in for you, Ama? Now that I have the Mongoose, we could live on it together – get to know each other again. See if there's a second chance for us.'

'I can't, Spike. I'm committed. Until this theatre project is up and running, my life will be Arcadia based. Why not bring the boat down to Arcadia? We could live on it there. I could help you – and you could help me. God knows I'm going to need it. That second chance for us might be waiting right there in that old theatre.'

'My acting days are over, Ama. I've put that behind me. I can't remember lines anymore.'

'Neither can I, most of the time. I just do bit parts. And direct instead. Not so big a thrill, but more satisfying.'

'I've tried it a few times – mostly with short fringe plays. Hard to start over again at my age and anyway, nobody wants to risk a full production on an unknown beginner.'

'If you came down to Arcadia, you could work for me, Spike. Direct a full-length play.'

'Work for you?' he said. 'You mean you call the shots down there?'

She pulled back from his shoulder to see his face in the light from the candle. 'Didn't I mention that I'm the artistic director? Probably why I was only a mediocre actress – too modest.'

'Amarylis Waterstone, A.D.,' said Spike. 'I must learn to treat you with more respect in future.'

'You can start right now by taking my offer seriously. And I could really use your help, too. Being the A.D. with a community theatre is more like being a general dogsbody than a big cheese. Maybe that's why I don't brag about it more – the title doesn't fool anybody in the world of local theatre. If anything, they probably think I'm a bit touched in the head to take on the job,' said Ama.

'You don't make it sound very appealing,' said Spike. 'I'm more interested in us getting back together, than me starting out again from square one, in the theatre. Not at my age.'

'Think of it as a way for us to get to know each other again,' she coaxed. 'You come down and help me launch my theatre – and I help you launch your boat. Does that sound more appealing?'

'Depends on which comes first – your theatre or my boat, I guess.'

'It doesn't have to be an either/or, Spike,' she urged. 'It could be a both/and.'

He considered for a moment or two, idly tracing the outline of her body in the candlelight. 'Do you know anything about boats, Ama?'

'Mostly what you've taught me – galley, head, companionway, port and starboard...'

'It's a start, I suppose.'

'And that's not all – I just remembered POSH, by and large, and letting the cat out of the bag – but I haven't checked that one out yet – still sounds more like a farming expression. You can see how fast I learn stuff,' she said, taking his hand and putting it on her upper arm. 'And I'm strong too,' she flexed her bicep. 'Feel my muscle.'

He moved his hand from her arm onto her breast. 'Very impressive – a powerful body.' He leaned over to kiss her nipple, then asked, 'I don't suppose you can cook, too?'

'My Achilles' heel,' she admitted. 'Does that mean I don't get the job?'

'Fortunately, I am a competent, if limited cook, if you don't mind vegetarian food,' said Spike. 'You can do something else instead while I'm preparing your dinner. You can't just lie about looking decorative, you know. You might get away with that on land but not aboard ship.'

'I could swab the decks,' she offered. 'Would that be useful? And you could show me how to tie knots.' She slipped her fingers down his body. 'I'm very good with my hands.'

He lay on his back for a few minutes, letting her demonstrate her manual dexterity before conceding, 'I can't deny you would be a useful asset to have aboard. I have to warn you, though, the wages are abysmal. Far worse than in the theatre. You'd be working for bed and board.'

'I accept,' said Ama. 'If this is what I can expect as an apprentice sailor on your boat.' She stopped fondling him for a moment and sat up. 'Now what about my offer? If I'm going to be your galley slave, I expect something in return.'

'How can I refuse – turn about's fair play,' said Spike. 'It will be turn and turn about, won't it? Not simply the occasional night aboard.'

'Nights aboard ship and days in the theatre,' she said, 'at least until we open, then it might be reversed. Is it a deal?' She stuck out her hand. He took it and pulled her back down beside him.

'You can be very persuasive, Ama. I hope you won't regret it. It's been a long time since I worked in the theatre.'

'They say it's like riding a bicycle, you never forget.'

'Except for the lines,' he reminded her.

'You won't have to worry about those anymore, not when you're directing.'

They lay quiet for awhile, each absorbing the implications of what they had just committed themselves to, waiting for the other one to speak first.

Spike broke the silence finally. 'I've arranged with Fergus, the old shipbuilder Esther introduced me to at the party, to come by tomorrow to give the Mongoose the once over – see what needs doing to make her seaworthy. I wouldn't want to take her anywhere until he gives me the all-clear.'

'I'll be going back to help Esther clear up after the wake,' said Ama. 'It's bound to be an all-day job. You could join us after you're done inspecting the boat.

Ama reached across him to blow out the candle. 'I must get some sleep or I'll be useless tomorrow.' She burrowed down beside him and he began kissing her again. After a few moments she held him off. 'It's no use Spike, I haven't the energy for anything more tonight. I'm way too old for our former marathon lovemaking sessions.'

'You go to sleep, I'll lie here and imagine how it's going to be for us,' he said, stroking her thigh under the cover. 'You don't mind if I keep holding you, Ama? I need reassurance.'

She took his hand and placed it on her breast. 'I do, too.'

They both slept so soundly he was only awakened much later by Ama sitting up and attempting to dress in bed.

'What time is it?'

She found her watch among the bedclothes and strapped it on her wrist. 'Nine-thirty. I better get up or Esther will be clearing up the mess on her own.'

He tried to pull her back down but she resisted. 'You said Fergus will be arriving and Esther is waiting. And besides I'm starving. All this energy we burned off, I need some breakfast.'

'There's nothing on the boat to eat except some canned beans and soup.'

'Yes there is, I brought all those leftovers, remember. Will you make some coffee on that stove? I don't know how to work it.'

'Only if you lie down here again for five minutes.'

She relented and lay back in his arms. 'Five minutes. I'm timing it.' She lay still, waiting. 'Well?'

'Be realistic, Ama. Five minutes. It will take me a few minutes to warm up.'

She consulted her watch. 'Four and a half minutes...'

'Ama. I can't do this on my own. I'm not a performing seal –'

'Four minutes – you're wasting time,' she said, not looking at him.

'Goddamit, Ama...' He threw off the covers and started undoing her blouse but she had put her bra back on and he couldn't undo it with her lying on her back. He abandoned this effort and began to slip her underwear down but she pressed her bottom into the mattress, foiling his attempt. He stopped and moved up beside her.

'Two minutes,' she said.

'A lot can happen in two minutes, Ama.'

'I'm waiting.'

'Okay.'

He swung his leg over and straddled her and began to tickle her around the waist, then moved his hands up to her armpits and tickled her hard. She bucked and tried to throw him off but he hung on.

'Stop, stop, ahh...ahh – that's not fair!'

'Do you give in?'

'Thirty seconds...'

He renewed his frenzied tickling and she squirmed, pulling at his hands, 'I'll scream, I'm warning you...'

'Do you give in? Give in and I'll stop.' He paused, waiting.

'Time's up. Get off.'

He fell back on his side and they lay apart, panting. After a few moments he said, 'What was that all about?'

'I don't know. Old stuff, maybe. Both of us wanting to have our own way.'

'I'm sorry,' said Spike. 'I was out of order. Going too far too fast – we barely know each other.'

'It was pretty childish of both of us, trying too hard for an old intimacy. I'm sorry, too.'

He took her hand and kissed the palm. 'Old days, old ways. I was suddenly back in London, when we shared that tiny bed-sitter behind Camden Town tube station, with no money to go anywhere. So we spent most of our time in bed.'

'Playing endless games, under the covers, like naughty children.' She stroked his stubbled chin.

'Or acting out scenes for rehearsals and auditions. Funny how I can still remember the lines for some of those parts, but give me something new and my mind goes blank.' He smiled at her, recalling their time together back then. 'Tickling was a kind of foreplay we resorted to, if one of us got cross.'

'I was much more ticklish than you and you took advantage,' she said.

He nodded, 'Just like now. But you had your underhand methods, too. Groping me suddenly and squeezing hard.'

'I remember – instant surrender.' She glanced at her watch. 'Let's get up, like proper grownups and make some coffee and then I really must go, Spike.' She leaned over and kissed him, then slid out of the vee-berth and opened the cabin door, re-buttoning her blouse and straightening her wrinkled summer skirt.

He pulled on his clothes and followed her out to the galley. They made coffee and carried the box of leftovers up to the deck. Spike slid open the hatch and was almost blinded by the morning sunlight pouring down the companionway. He led the way forward and they sat on the hatch cover over the vee-berth.

Ama looked around her. 'This is a big boat, Spike. Are you sure you can handle it?'

'Not on my own, maybe – but with a seasoned first mate.' He picked through the carton of food, eating the savoury items first.

'You can give me another lesson over breakfast,' said Ama, pointing. 'What's inside that big box?'

'The winch – for hauling up the anchor chain.'

'It looks kind of rusty. I hope it works.'

'Fergus will check it all over when he comes. God, this coffee is strong with no milk.'

'I'll bring some back for later. Can we stay here again tonight, Spike?'

'Sure, why not, if you don't mind the primitive conditions.'

'I love it – specially the candle-light.'

She munched a sandwich and sat contentedly beside him. 'I'm sorry I won't be able to meet Fergus and hear what his verdict is. I hope he thinks the Mongoose is seaworthy. So you can bring it down to Arcadia soon.'

'Yes, it's too bad. You'd learn a hell of a lot more from Fergus than I could ever teach you.'

'Why? Are boat-builders good sailors too?'

'Not necessarily, but lots of them are. I suspect Fergus is one of them.'

'I doubt I'd even understand what he was saying – probably all sailing terms like 'avast' and 'belaying pins' and 'keel haul.''

'And three sheets to the wind,' said Spike. 'Like us, last night. That's a useful sailing euphemism.'

'What for?'

'For being drunk.'

'Yes, I guess we were – although I don't feel hungover this morning, do you?'

'A bit,' Spike admitted. 'I'm not much of a drinker anymore. Can't drink, can't act, can't even make love very well. I'm not the man you knew forty odd years ago, Ama, as you're beginning to discover.'

'I'm not complaining. It's me that should be confessing, not you. I expect I'm a big disappointment to you from what you remember.'

'A little more... substantial, perhaps, but I always thought you were too skinny. Now, you're perfection.'

'I think that's a left-handed compliment, but I accept it anyway. And you're a changed man too, Spike. I don't ever remember you being so quick to apologise in the past. That's a very disarming side of you I've noticed.' She glanced at her wristwatch. 'I'm going now – no more sweet-talking me or I'll be here all day.' She stood and pulled him to his feet to kiss him goodbye. 'Save it for tonight.'

He helped her off the boat onto the wharf and watched her drive away, then walked up and down alongside the boat admiring his inheritance. From what both Esther and Sy had said at the wake, they were happy to have the Mongoose off their hands, so he had carte blanche to make whatever changes he liked. His first consideration was to make her seaworthy, all the rest could wait until he joined Ama down in Arcadia. If he was going to make it a live-aboard that she would seriously consider, he'd have to make it less utilitarian – more creature comforts to attract her.

He closed the hatch behind him and walked around on deck doing a survey. He saw sections of the hand rail that had been spliced in and only primed; some new planking on the deck near the stern and the whole of the aft cabin above deck, which had been added only roughly with no finish work done. The windows and cabin roof were sealed and waterproof but the door had only a padlock and hasp and no handle. He checked the wheelhouse locker for a key to the padlock and found several. It was while he was trying them out that Fergus appeared on the dock.
'Permission to come aboard, Captain,' he called down to Spike, who was several feet below him as the tide was now out.
'Hang on a sec, Fergus while I fetch a ladder for you.'

'It's right above you on the cabin roof,' Fergus pointed and waited for Spike to brace it against the dock for him. He lowered himself to the deck with practised ease and shook hands. 'I see you've started without me.' He looked at the bunch of keys in Spike's hand and pointed. 'That one.'

'You and Simon have done a lot of work since I saw the Mongoose last time. I was about to check out the deck cabin.' He unlocked the padlock and pulled open the door for them to enter. The room was empty except for some timber lying on the floor and a pair of sawhorses with a few hand tools on them.

Fergus looked around. 'Been near on a year since we done any work to her. We was only gettin' goin' on this cabin when Simon took sick.'

'What was he planning to use it for, Fergus? I know he mentioned it could be a saloon at one point.'

'That's what he wanted,' said Fergus. 'Somewhere comfortable on deck for Esther to use. She didn't like to go below when they was out of the harbour, he told me. She got sick as a parrot in any kind of weather.'

Spike looked around, peering out the windows on both sides. 'It will make a good day cabin alright. And could double as spare sleeping quarters, too. You've done a nice job on it so far, Fergus. I like the way you curved the roof-line to match the wheelhouse. I hate these square boxy things made out of plywood you see on so many Cape Islanders. They look like garden sheds. Spoils the look of these old boats.'

'I stopped work because I didn't want to do any interior finishin' without Simon's approval and he got too sick to even visit after a while. Didn't seem right to go ahead without him.' He took off his battered felt hat to scratch his bare dome. 'What was it you wanted me to do exactly, Spike?'

'I hoped you would give her the once-over and tell me if she's okay to use as is, or what needs to be done.'

'Well for starters, we need to charge the batteries and try to get the diesel runnin' so's we have some power.'

The old man connected the charger to the battery bank below deck and examined the engine oil. 'Look at this, clean as a whistle.' He showed Spike the dipstick and pointed to the clear golden oil on it. 'I reckon she should be fine once we get some juice to her. Simon had this old motor fully overhauled and has barely used it since. If we can get her runnin', we can take a tour round the harbour and get a feel for her.' He climbed out of the engine well and wiped his hands on a rag.

'Perhaps you can have a look at everything on deck before we go below, Fergus. Tell me what you think needs doing before I go anywhere.'

'Where you plan on goin', Spike – just local trips?'

'That was my intention, sort of get re-acquainted with her. But my plans have changed. I met a lady-friend at the wake who I haven't seen in years and she wants me to join her down in Arcadia. Says I could live aboard there while I'm finishing the work on it.'

'Women and boats. Like oil and water, some people say,' Fergus grinned at him. 'Course I don't put any stock in them old stories, but fishermen are powerful superstitious.'

'Oh, Ama has no intention of sailing down with me. She has to leave tomorrow and drive back for work.'

'Probably just as well, if she ain't used to bein' at sea. Could be seasick the whole way. Not much good to you if you met some weather. Things can blow up fast on this south coast. You'd be better to find someone with experience for your first trip.'

'It's for sure I don't want to take her on my own. But right now, with this hangover, I can't think of who to ask. That was some wake they organised.'

'I heard some talk last night that Simon took a drug overdose,' said Fergus. 'Wouldn't surprise me, he often told me he wouldn't hang around when the time came. Said he wasn't the type to sit about starin' at the wall in some old folks' home.'

'You and Simon discussed the possibility of him taking his own life, did you?' he said, choosing his words carefully. 'Have you thought what you would do, Fergus?'

'Think about it every day at some point. Course, I'm a lot older than Simon – at 85, I'm runnin' outta time.'

'What have you decided?'

'Well, I couldn't take a drug overdose like Simon – if that's what he did. Wouldn't know where to get any drugs for a start. Problem is, I still enjoy my life, or some of it, anyways. Long as I can keep doin' a bit of work, I guess I'll keep goin'. I'm sort of takin' it a day at a time.'

'No plans for doing anything drastic then, Fergus?'

'Kinda hopin' I'll just keel over, one of these days. Meantime...'

'- you'll go on 'simply messing about in boats',' said Spike. 'Speakin' of which, shall we have a look below?' asked Fergus. 'Check the stopcocks, see if there's any leaks anywhere.' He led the way, inspecting the sink outlet in the galley and then moving on to the toilet.

'The head works fine – tested it last night a few times,' said Spike.

Fergus nodded, looking for leaks around the rubber seals and then raising the hatches to expose the bilges in the main cabin floor. 'Bone dry,' he nodded with satisfaction. He got up from his knees with some difficulty and grinned at Spike.

'I'd say the Mongoose is in a lot better shape than I am – of course she's quite a bit younger'n me.'

The old man took his time, poking into lockers, checking ropes and tackle, digging into deck and wheelhouse woodwork with the tip of his Swiss army knife blade.

'Simon give me this last Christmas, said my old penknife was a disgrace to any shipwright.' He chuckled to himself, remembering. 'Told me if I ever got shipwrecked, I'd be glad of all the gadgets on it. I said the chances of me gettiin' shipwrecked anymore was almost zero – once was enough.'

They went in the wheelhouse and Spike handed the keys to him. Fergus gave the starter a quick two or three short bursts. The batteries were still weak but the engine caught on the third try. 'She'll soon charge up now the alternator's kicked in,' he said, pointing to the gauge. He let the motor run for a few minutes, then with the lines still secured he eased first into forward and then into reverse. The boat strained against the moorings in both directions.

'Guess we're ready to cast off, Spike. That's about all we can check, tied up to the dock.'

Spike climbed up on the wharf and let go the ropes, stowed the ladder back on the cabin roof and gave Fergus the all clear. The old man eased the Mongoose away from the dock and slowly steered her through the motley collection of empty fishing boats and other small craft tied along the wharf. Spike stood beside him in the wheelhouse, watching how Fergus guided his new acquisition into the open water of Dartmouth harbour.

'Steerin's good and tight, she handles real well. Can't test the autopilot until we get more open water.' He stepped back from the helm. 'Here, see what you think, Spike. Aim for the point – we'll go out past the lighthouse and you can open her up.'

Spike took the wheel and steered in the direction Fergus indicated. He looked at the old man smiling and nodding, and caught himself grinning with pleasure. Fergus winked and shoved the throttle forward, as they cleared the lighthouse point and entered the outer harbour. The Mongoose surged forward and the thrum of the engine increased, the tachometer showing 1100 rpms.

'She'll cruise nicely at 1300 revs,' said Fergus. 'See how she feels out here with a bit of a chop.' The brisk wind had stirred up the waves but there was no swell in the sheltered long outer harbour, as Spike edged the throttle forward till the tach read 1300rpms.

'Just puttin' her through her paces,' said Fergus, easing back on the throttle. 'I think we can take her back in, Spike. Turn her around, head for the lighthouse and we'll switch on the auto-pilot. See if she holds her course.'

The two of them watched the compass heading, Fergus nodding his satisfaction with the way the equipment responded to the steep chop of the outer harbour.

'Sometimes these auto-pilots gets confused in a followin' sea and start over-steerin' but she's keepin' her heading nice and steady.'

Fergus monitored the behaviour of the auto-pilot and Spike watched the wheel turning back and forth to the sawing noise of the automated equipment.

Back at the wharf, they moored the Mongoose and Fergus drove off in his battered old pickup. Spike locked up and went ashore to find a local bus to Esther's.

Ama was in the kitchen, still clearing up from the mayhem of the night before.

'Where's Esther?' he asked, looking into the living room. None of the furniture had been put back and the carpets were still rolled up behind the piano.

'She was up the entire night and she finally conked out an hour ago so I packed her off to bed.'

They spent the next few hours restoring the house to order while Esther slept.

'What was the verdict from Fergus this morning? Will the Mongoose sink if you take her out to sea?'

'Already have – well, the outer harbour anyway. Fergus and I roared up and down full speed for over an hour, playing with my new toy.'

'What did he say?'

'Oh, he had lots of advice. He said in his opinion, you were the best-looking woman at the wake.'

'Obviously a man of keen discernment. What else did he say – about the boat, I mean.'

'Well, he said women and boats were like oil and water.'

'Another old misogynist – I was wrong about him apparently – not so discerning, after all,' said Ama.

'To be fair, he said that was only an old fisherman's superstition, he didn't hold with it, himself.'

'Good old Fergus – anyway what did he say about the Mongoose?'

'After we eliminated you and Sy as possible crew for the trip down to Arcadia, he hinted he might come with me. He and Simon did a lot of sailing together over the years in his old sailboat.'

'Good idea. I think the Mongoose is too big for you to handle on your own. I don't want to lose you after I've only just found you again.'

'He left me a list of minor repairs to do and he's coming back in a couple of days to check on me.'

'I've put as much of this leftover food as I can into the freezer for Esther,' said Ama. 'She won't need to think about meals for a month.'

'I hope you saved something good for us for tonight on the Mongoose. I've collected half a dozen opened bottles of wine we can polish off onboard, too.'

They loaded their bags and the food and wine into Ama's old red Toyota and drove slowly down to the docks area. She parked on the wharf near the Mongoose to unload the parcels onto the fore deck. Spike stowed everything below and came back up with the two tumblers and one of the opened wine bottles. He searched in a couple of deck lockers till he found some faded canvas boat cushions. They sprawled on the vee-berth hatch cover to drink and watch the last of the sunset across the harbour.

'I think we done good,' said Spike, kissing her. 'We earned this drink.'

'We did,' she agreed, kissing him back. 'I'm glad Esther won't have to face that mess, at least.'

They went below to make some supper from the leftovers Ama had packed up. Spike lit the propane stove and she heated up a spicy black bean and rice casserole in a copper pan. He lit the collection of candle stubs and set them around the cabin interior. Ama switched off the hanging bare bulb and took the glass of red wine he handed her. They sat waiting for the casserole to heat through and nibbled on a few of the remaining aperitifs from the food box, sharing bites of ones they liked.

'I wish I didn't have to leave tomorrow,' she said, leaning into the crook of his arm. 'We could make a little nest here and hole up together. Illegal live-aboard.'

'Help Esther eat up all that food in her freezer.'

'Let's fill our plates and go up on deck for awhile longer and watch the boats go by,' said Ama, testing the casserole.

Spike nodded, refilled their glasses and they went back topside to sit on the boat cushions to eat their food. A tugboat crept by pulling a string of barges heaped high with gravel. It still hadn't disappeared by the time they'd finished eating.

'I hope the Mongoose can go faster than that, Spike or it will take forever for you to get to Arcadia. I want to get started learning how to live aboard.'

He poured out the last of the wine bottle into their glasses and held his tumbler up towards the sky, which had revealed clusters of stars to their eyes, as they became accustomed to the dark.

'"The moon shines bright"', he declaimed. '"On such a night as this,
When the sweet wind did gently kiss the trees
And they did make no noise, in such a night
Troilus methinks mounted the Troyan walls
And sighed his soul toward the Grecian tents
Where Cressid lay that night...."'

Ama paused for a moment to recall the lines –
'"In such a night
Did Thisbe fearfully o'ertrip the dew
And saw the lion's shadow ere himself
And ran dismay'd away."'

She continued, '"In such a night

Did young Lorenzo swear he loved her well,
Stealing her soul with many vows of faith
And ne'er a true one.'"

"'In such a night,'" said Spike,
"'Did pretty Jessica, like a little shrew,
Slander her love, and he forgave it her.'"

"'I would out-night you, did no body come;'" said Ama,
"'But, hark, I hear the footing of a man.'"

They laughed, pleased with themselves for remembering parts from that long-forgotten Merchant of Venice production. Animated now, Ama got up to pace about the deck. She turned to face him, 'You told me you stopped acting because you couldn't remember lines, Spike.'

'I can't. That was ancient history – no problem remembering that stuff, but anything recent disappears overnight. I can reel off Shakespeare by the yard, provided I learned it when I was young.'

'Well, when you come to direct for my theatre, I promise you won't have to learn a single line. Just teach them to act like that and I'll be happy.' She returned to sit on his lap and stroke his cheek in the darkness, which now enveloped them on the deck.

'On such a night as this, did the scheming Amarylis, flatter her love...and he did fall for it,' said Spike, standing up. He led her by the hand below to the cabin, still lit by the few remaining candle ends. He gave her one to put on the little bookshelf at the head of the vee-berth. They undressed in the semi-dark and stood feeling the press of their warm skin against each other. 'You want to try to raise the main or just heave-to?' he asked.

'I'm too tired to try raising anything tonight,' said Ama, crawling under the blanket. 'Let's just heave-to, it sounds nice and relaxing. Maybe in the morning...?' She curved her back to his body and pulled his arm over her like a cover.

In the morning, Spike was awakened by the sound of water running and the smell of coffee. He lay back and gazed at the square of blue from the skylight above the vee-berth. He swivelled round when he heard the shower stop and waited for Ama to emerge from the tiny washroom cubicle. She wore two towels, one on her head and another wrapped round her body, as she left a trail of damp footprints over to where he lay sprawled on the bed. She stood in front of him drying her hair and gave him an enquiring look.

'How is my amorous Lorenzo this morning? You want to push the boat out again?'

For answer, he tugged at the big towel and it fell away. She stood watching him looking at her for a moment, then lay down on top of him, pushing her still damp breasts against him and straddling him as she sat up in the confined space. They jockeyed for position, tussling to see who would end on top. For awhile they fossicked about, taking turns on the bottom, pleasuring each other. Finally, they lay still, panting and exhausted, content to lie together, touching but not moving, with her leg across his body.

'If we were at sea, we could let the waves provide all the motion. We'd simply hold on to each other,' said Spike, stroking her bottom as she lay on him.

'But who would steer the boat?'

'We'd put it on autopilot.'

'Can it see other boats coming? I wouldn't want to be run down by some big Chinese container ship,' said Ama. 'Maybe we should save our love-making for when we're in harbour.' She slipped her hand down between his legs. 'You want to go around again or shall we have some coffee?'

'What do you think – do I have what it takes?'

She waggled her fingers for a moment, then shook her head. 'Afraid not, you've given me your all. Never mind, let's have some coffee, instead.'

Spike joined her on the bunk bench by the table. They sat, naked, drinking their coffee and eating slices of carrot cake. She brushed some crumbs from his chest and he licked some off her breasts. Neither of them had commented on the ravages time had visited on their bodies, perhaps each waiting for the other to mention it first.

'Does it put you off me, seeing me stark naked in the daylight, Spike?'

'Did it seem like I was put off?' he said, kissing her shoulder and neck. 'How about you? I'm not the blonde Adonis of your youthful memories anymore.' He looked down and patted his paunch. 'At least women don't go bald and have pot-bellies.'

'It's rather nice to wander around our little den in the nude,' said Ama. 'I think I'm a secret exhibitionist. Are you sure you don't mind me like this - 'au naturel'?'

'I love it – I can't get enough of looking at you naked. When we're at sea you can go nude all day long, sunbathing on the deck,' said Spike. 'Of course, there is a downside. I won't be able to keep my hands off you.'

'You could always put the autopilot on. I wouldn't mind if we were on deck and I could see everything.' She moved about the galley, putting things away. 'This is fun. I feel like I'm playing house.'

'As long as you don't get carried away and go on deck in the noddy while we're at the dock.'

'I don't remember you as a jealous person, Spike. Have you changed?'

'No, I'm not jealous and yes, I have changed. Everyone has. Everything changes, according to the Buddha, nothing stays the same, remember?'

'God, I haven't done any meditation practice for years,' said Ama. 'Do you still meditate?'

'Nothing you could dignify with the word 'practice'. But I think about it off and on, and I've kept all my old Buddhist book collection. Occasionally I read bits and vow to start practising properly again.'

'Maybe we could practise together when we go sailing,' said Ama. 'Encourage each other.'

Spike put his arms round her bare body and pulled her closer to him. 'You don't have to encourage me,' he said. 'This is the only practice I want.'

She kissed him. 'Me, too. But perhaps in between times.' She glanced down at his lap. 'You know – while we're waiting.'

'You're not suggesting we could meditate in the nude, Ama? I doubt if even the Buddha tried that. My powers of concentration would be severely tested.'

She stood up and crossed to the bed to collect their clothes and bring them back to him. 'Too much over-stimulation is the problem. Time to get dressed and face the world.'

Reluctantly, they put on their clothes, with Spike insisting on kissing each breast before they disappeared from view. Ama buttoned his shirt and tucked it deep in his trousers. He opened the hatch cover and climbed up on deck into the heat of the August mid-morning sun and waited for her to join him. They drove across town slowly, aware of their imminent separation.
,

Ama parked her old red Toyota in front of Esther's garage and they knocked gently on the back-porch door before trying it. The door opened, so they assumed Esther was stirring and entered the kitchen.

'Hello – hello... Esther?' called Ama, going down the hall to the living room. There was no reply so she went upstairs to check the bedrooms, knocking on each door and calling Esther's name before she entered.

'Maybe she's gone out,' she said. 'Did you check downstairs, Spike?'

'I was waiting for you.' He rose from the stool and they descended the stairs to the basement. The rec room was empty but a light was on in Simon's cluttered study.

'Esther?' said Ama, pushing the door open till it bumped against an old leather armchair. Esther sat on the floor with her legs spread and a pile of old photo albums on her lap.

A soft bubbling snore came from the sleeping Esther and a glass slipped from her fingers onto the carpet. At one side of her a near-empty rye whisky bottle lay on the floor. Ama gave her arm a slight nudge and tried to wake her but Esther only breathed heavily in her sleep.

'She's drunk, Ama,' said Spike, picking up the whisky bottle and glass. 'Let her sleep it off.'

He urged her out of the study and pulled the door partly closed, turning off the lamp on the desk.

Outside again, they stood hugging each other before she finally opened her car door and got in. She kissed him several more times through the open window, then backed slowly down the drive. 'I'll talk to you tonight to see how she is,' she said. 'Keep checking on her, Spike – promise?'

He nodded and waved as her old red Toyota turned the corner, then wandered around the huge well-tended garden for awhile before going back into the house. He entered the den and saw Esther sitting in Simon's old swivel chair and went over to give her a hug. 'You finally surfaced. Ama had to leave but she'll call you later from Arcadia, she said.'

'I was just going to make some strong coffee,' said Esther. 'Shall we go upstairs?'

'I was hoping I could stay on here for a few days while I get the Mongoose ready, Esther. Ama has persuaded me to sail down to Arcadia and help her with her theatre project.'

'Please – stay as long as you like,' said Esther, 'the house is empty now – only me left.'

'Fergus was telling me how he and Simon did a lot of sailing together.'

'Mostly in Halifax harbour,' she said, 'nothing too adventurous. Although occasionally they went further afield – St Margaret's Bay or Mahone Bay.'

'Not Peggy's Cove?'

'Not very often – Simon said the approach is tricky if the wind's blowing hard.'

'Ama wants me to bring the Mongoose down to Arcadia so I can work on it there – and assist her with getting her theatre up and running. I told her I wasn't going anywhere until Fergus gave it his approval. He and Ama don't think it's a good idea for me to sail the Mongoose down to Arcadia alone. I've never handled a boat that size on my own before.'

'Well, it's not a sailboat, so you'd be under power the whole way. All the same, a strange boat in strange water – Fergus is right, someone who's familiar with the south coast to go with you is a good idea.'

'Are you still teaching medieval studies, Esther?'

'Only part-time nowadays. We do a lot of revivals of the old mystery plays and pageant wagon morality plays.'

'Is there any audience for that sort of thing today?'

'Only university audiences.'

'Ama told me she hopes to do modern dress classic revivals in her new theatre – maybe you can tour one of your productions down there.'

'It would only be a one-night stand, if we did,' she said. 'In a small town like Arcadia you'd be lucky to get more than a handful of people turn out to see it. Those old plays were more street theatre than formal theatre in the medieval period. Lots of slapstick and knockabout farce to keep the crowd's attention.'

'When Ama and I were in drama school they sometimes did a mystery play as part of the course work. I played the back end of a pantomime horse in a student production of Noyye's Flodde. Plenty of clowning and improvising stuff, the cruder the better, as I recall.' Spike grinned, remembering. 'Lots of toilet humour for old Noah to cope with. I think Ama played the dove in that show, flapping around the stage with a pair of old angel's wings from the Christmas panto.'

'Pantomimes and the Nativity play is all we have left from the old morality and mystery plays,' said Esther.

'What about the Canterbury Tales? That ran in the West End for years. It was my first job in professional theatre. I was a dresser for the chorus – helping the girls in and out of their medieval bodices in the quick-change area in the wings,' said Spike. 'Best job I ever had.'

'A wonderful musical, I loved it,' she said, 'but not strictly Chaucer. About as close as West Side Story is to Romeo and Juliet.'

'I still think it would be a great way for Ama to draw in the tourists for her new theatre. She says Arcadia is swamped with tourists looking for something to do in the long summer evenings. I'm going to suggest it to her. Maybe she can persuade you to bring a show down there.'

'It could be fun,' Esther conceded, 'and good experience for the students, to see how ordinary crowds respond, instead of elite university audiences.'

'If you came down to Arcadia, we could talk to her about it. And also discuss staging one of Simon's modern English Shakespeare plays.'

'Love to go, but not by boat. I prefer to drive.'

For the next few days, Spike alternated between working on the Mongoose with Fergus and helping Esther and some students sift through Simon's papers. Spike bought new mooring ropes with scuff protectors under instruction from Fergus and did the provision shopping for the trip. The old man advised Spike to empty the stale water tanks and refill them with fresh water, after he tasted the tea the first time.

Two days before they intended to depart for Arcadia, Spike received a brief email from Ama. *'Ocean disappeared, gone to look for her. Not sure when I'll be back. More later, love, Ama xxx.'*

After talking it over with Fergus, they decided to delay their sailing date until he heard more news from her and he returned to helping Esther and Fergus with the house and boat.

CHAPTER THREE

Ama had told Spike very little about her daughter, Ocean, except to hint that she was often in difficulty, financially, physically and emotionally. Sometimes to the point of nervous breakdown. Looking back now, Ama had to confess she had been over-protective of her only child, often to her detriment. Ocean had become too dependent on her mother and her attempts to break free and become independent often ended in disaster. She had an uncanny knack for choosing boyfriends with even more hang-ups than herself. This latest one was leading her into serious trouble. Ocean and her mother had argued so bitterly, that she left home and refused to say where she and Clay were going.

Ama had demanded that her daughter have nothing more to do with him, when she discovered Ocean and Clay had been dealing drugs with the local high school kids, until someone reported them. Clay had left Arcadia to disappear out of province. Ocean presumably followed him when she and Ama had had their latest altercation.

As she always did when she had problems of any kind, Ama drove to her friend, confidante and mentor, Kitty Langford. She parked her red Toyota outside the huge Georgian style wooden mansion and rang the bell. It was an ancient contraption of wires and tiny pulleys, that jangled a tinny bell on a spring in the kitchen at the rear of the house. Kitty's live-in housekeeper, Mrs. Spengler, a local fisherman's widow, eventually answered the door.

'Hello lovely,' she said, wiping her floury hands on her apron. 'I been bottlin' peaches and makin' peach pies. You're just in time to try one.' She gave Ama a hug and led the way through the dark old hall to the steamy kitchen. 'Trust me to pick one of the warmest days in August to do it. But Kitty come home with a carload of fresh peaches from the farmer's market, so I didn't have much choice.'

'Where is she, Sarah? I must talk to her, I'm in an awful mess.'

'I'm right here, dear, what is it?' Kitty sat at the far end of a long oak harvest table, looking more like a child in the heavy armchair than an eighty-four-year-old. She had a full-size long-sleeve smock covering her from the neck to her wrists, so that only her head of silvery blue hair and manicured hands with be-ringed fingers were visible.

'She insisted on helpin' me blanch these peaches,' said Mrs. Spengler apologetically, 'so I put her to work. I blanch and she peels and I bottle. We're a team effort but we could use some help slicing and stoning. Will I get you an apron so you don't splash on your clothes?'

Kitty smiled a near perfect set of pearl white teeth. 'If it's not urgent, dear, we could finish this batch and then take a break. I could use a nice cup of that gunpowder tea you brought me from Halifax.'

'It's not that urgent, Kitty. Bottling peaches takes priority.' She held out her arms for Mrs. Spengler to slip on a smock she was holding like a surgical gown, tying it behind her neck.

The three women focused on peaches for the next half hour, in the moist humid air of the old period kitchen.

'I tell Kitty this is too hot for her to be workin' here, Ama, but she don't pay me no mind,' said Mrs. Spengler. 'I said, what happens if you was her son, Gerald, at the door an' he finds her up to her elbows, doin' my work. He probably have me sacked an' then where would we be. Me out on the street an' her with no house-keeper, that's where. But she's a selfish old woman, don't care for anyone but herself, Ama. Isn't that right, Kitty? Am'nt I always telling you that?'

'You wouldn't be out of work long, Sarah. People in this town would be lining up to hire you,' said Ama.

'In the first place, Gerald doesn't pay her wages, I do. And in the second place, bottling peaches is one of the few things, I'm still good at – besides, they taste better when you've done them yourself,' Kitty said. 'Sarah complains if I help her, she can't ask for a pay rise. It's my sneaky way of being mean.'

'She lets other folk bleed her white, an' if I try to stop them, she accuses me of wantin' all her money, Ama. There's a constant stream of beggin' letters an' phone calls – or there was till I persuaded her to go unlisted.'

'I guess I'm one of those people, Sarah. Always knocking at her door.'

'No you're not, Ama. Kitty knows you're a real friend, just likes to have a good yarn with her.'

'Pay no attention to her, dear. If Sarah had her way, she'd have me wrapped in cotton wool so's no-one could get near me,' said Kitty. 'The plain truth is, she's right. I am selfish. I only like helping the people in my own community, it makes me feel useful.' She pushed herself up out of the big armchair. 'Help me out of this cocoon, Sarah and let's have some of Ama's tea. We'll sit out on the veranda, there might be a breeze off the harbour. It's stifling in here.'

Ama followed Kitty out to the shaded front veranda that wrapped around three sides of the house. Kitty sat on the old-fashioned wooden swing and patted the seat beside her. 'Sit down and tell me what's wrong, while Sarah's making the tea. If I ask her nicely, she may even bring us a slice of peach pie. We deserve it, don't you think, dear?' She sat back, gently pushing the swing with her foot, waiting for Ama to speak.

'God, Kitty, I don't know where to start. Ocean's chasing after that criminal she's been living with, who had to leave Yarmouth for god knows where, because they were reported for selling drugs to the high school kids. I'm way behind on the play rehearsals for the opening of the theatre; the theatre isn't ready for the fire department inspection and to top it all off, I've got involved with an old boyfriend from Victoria, who was at Simon's wake.'

'Is that good news or bad, Ama? I could never tell with old flames. Sometimes I got burned.'

'All I know is, we're besotted with each other, like a pair of teenagers. I can't keep my hands off him, Kitty.'

'But you're back here and he's gone back to Victoria. Is that the bad news?'

'What bad news?' demanded Mrs. Spengler, appearing with a tray of tea things to set down at the nearby table.

'That's what I'm trying to find out. Ama's found an old lover and now she doesn't know what to do with him, Sarah.'

'Only one thing to do with old lovers,' said Mrs. Spengler, 'you don't need an old lady to tell you that.'

'She's already done that,' said Kitty. 'Apparently the problem's not that simple.'

'It never is at your age, Ama, they always come with baggage.' Sarah set out two plates. 'Here, I brought you some peach pie for helpin' me. It's still warm. Kitty can pour out this gunpowder stuff. I'm havin' mine in the kitchen. I prefer proper fisherman's tea. You have any more problems with your old lover, you just bring him here to me. I never met one yet I couldn't satisfy. Ask Kitty,' she said grinning, as she retreated to the kitchen.

Ama and Kitty shifted to the porch table. The old lady poured out the green tea into the delicate bone china teacups she insisted Mrs. Spengler use for everyday, despite her protests.

'Sarah would have us using fishermen's mugs, if I let her,' she said, handing a cup to Ama. 'I told her I'm leaving all my good Spode to her when I die. She can put it in her china cupboard and never touch it, but while I'm alive I want to enjoy it. She says by the time she gets it, there won't be anything left. Now don't say anything more till I've finished this peach pie. I've been waiting all day for it.'

'What did Sarah mean, ask you?' said Ama, when she and Kitty had savoured the last crumb of the pie on their plates. 'She made it sound mysterious.'

'Oh, she was just being foolish. Nothing important.'

'You don't want to tell me? Or it's none of my business.'

'Sarah and I go back a long way, Ama. She's been with me since before Gerald was born. I was rather delicate during my pregnancy and needed some help with this big house. I sometimes feel Gerald thinks he has two mothers. We were two young widows together. She lost her husband when his fishing boat went down in a winter gale off Yarmouth, and left her childless. My husband Stephen never came back from the war. He's buried in Normandy in one of those endless war graves. Gerald was our only child. I still have all Stephen's letters. We planned to have a big family when he returned.'

'And neither of you remarried?' asked Ama, surprised at this revelation from Kitty.

'Oh, we both had our suitors over the years and sometimes...'

'Was that what Sarah meant, Kitty?'

'Not exactly, no.'

'You don't have to tell me if it's too personal. I understand – but I'm dying to hear.' Ama smiled at the old lady, waiting.

'I feel as if I were betraying confidences, in a way. Although Sarah mentioned it first, didn't she?'

'Let me guess,' said Ama. 'Two healthy women, living alone in this big house. You both took lovers?'

'From time to time,' admitted Kitty. 'Not for a long time now,' she added.

'Not so surprising,' said Ama. 'I did the same, three times. Only I made the mistake of marrying them.'

'Was this old flame at the wake one of them?'

Ama shook her head. 'I lost him – like you and Sarah. The other three were sort of replacements that never quite worked out. I should have followed your examples. Too bad I didn't know you back then, would have saved me a lot of heartache.'

'Following our example might not have been a good idea, Ama. That wasn't what Sarah was referring to earlier.'

'I guessed wrong? But you said you did take lovers...'

'We did but...sometimes we made the wrong choice, so –'

'– You changed beds.'

'In a manner of speaking, yes.' Kitty eyed her for a moment before continuing. 'It was a foolish prank the first time. We'd all been drinking too much alcohol, but after awhile it happened more frequently. Of course, we had to be very discreet. Choose very carefully. Some men would take advantage of such a situation. We were lucky. We learned that married men had a vested interest in keeping their mouths shut. This is a small town and we needed a pretext for our visitors. So, we both became involved in local charities. I gravitated to fund-raising and treasurers' positions, and Sarah preferred hosting kitchen parties here. She found musicians' outlooks on life more to her liking. But we both developed catholic tastes in lovers.' Kitty looked at her, smiling. 'I'm afraid I've shocked you.'

Ama laughed. 'You *have* shocked me. Surprised shock - not scandalised. I knew there was a reason we became friends.' She rose and hugged Kitty warmly.

'Birds of a feather...' said Kitty. 'Of course, you realise this is ancient history. Sarah and I are respectable old ladies now. Pillars of the community.'

'I should have put two and two together, with your background in New York Off-Broadway shows. Is that where you met your husband?'

'Stephen was a stage door Johnnie – wouldn't take no for an answer. So here I am,' said Kitty. 'More tea?'

'You are an old fraud, Kitty.' The two of them laughed and chinked teacups.

'Careful of my tea service, you two,' said Mrs. Spengler, coming back in to clear the table. 'Soon be nothin' left for me to inherit. What're you cacklin' about.'

'Old times, Sarah, old times,' said Kitty.

'You haven't been tellin' tales out of school, Kitty?'

'You put her up to it, Sarah, remember?' said Ama.

'Maybe I did,' said Mrs. Spengler. 'Thought maybe a little history lesson might be in order.'

'The thing I don't understand is, where was Gerald during all this?' said Ama.

'Stephen's family is a very old one in this town,' said Kitty. 'His great-grandfather was a ship chandler and his grandfather became a wealthy merchant, owned several sailing ships. My husband's father inherited the family business, married a local heiress at the outbreak of the First War, and went off with his Nova Scotia regiment as a young officer. He died in the senseless slaughter at Ypres, along with practically half his company. I found his gravestone when I went to visit Stephen's grave, after the war. Every young person should have to experience those silent acres of crosses. It would save a lot of future grief.'

'The men died young and left a whole generation of women with blighted lives, with no men to marry, no children to bear,' said Mrs. Spengler. 'It's them I feel sorry for, robbed of having kids.'

'You could say Stephen's mother was one of the lucky ones, although I know she didn't think so,' said Kitty. 'She was pregnant when he left for France.'

'And Gerald is a bachelor,' said Ama, 'so the family name ends with him?'

'Not for want of tryin',' said Sarah. 'God knows we filled his bed with eligible girls over the years, but none of them took, so to speak.'

'None that we know of anyway,' said Kitty.

'Kitty still dreams that someday a lost grandson will turn up on our doorstep to claim his inheritance.'

'I don't,' protested Kitty, 'not anymore. Anyway, I have only myself to blame, giving in to family pressure and sending him off to private school.'

Sarah looked grim but said nothing for a moment. 'I'm just as guilty, Ama. I could have backed Kitty up – but I secretly fancied him bein' in that posh academy, up in Antigonish. It had a great reputation for gettin' its graduates into university.'

'We were too ambitious for him and didn't realise we were losing him till too late,' said Kitty. 'If only I'd let him go to the local high school like he wanted to...'

'An' if we'd paid more attention to the men who passed through our beds,' said Sarah.

'Why? What did they say?' asked Ama.

'That boys lose interest in the opposite sex, in private schools,' Kitty said.

'I always said them places should be closed down,' said Sarah. 'Deprivin' old women of grandchildren. A big man like Gerald could have filled this house with kids, 'stead of leavin' two old women to rattle around in it.'

'That's a bit harsh on private schools – and yourselves, isn't it?' said Ama. 'I know lots of gay people in theatre, who never set foot in a private school.'

'So do I, Ama. When I lived in New York before I was married to Stephen, most of my friends in the theatre world then were gay. They always seemed to be the cleverest and the most talented ones. And loyal friends, too,' said Kitty. 'When you get your theatre off the ground, I'll invite some of my oldest ones to come to the opening.'

Mrs. Spengler cleared all the tea things and returned to the kitchen.

'Oh god, I hope I haven't offended Sarah,' said Ama. 'She sounded awfully bitter.'

'Don't mind Sarah, she can be rather blunt at times. But she has a right to be bitter, don't you think?' asked Kitty. 'She's seen too many blighted lives and it's made her a fierce feminist. She would have been a powerful suffragette in an earlier era. One of her favourite charities is the local women's refuge. She brings the new ones and their kids back here to feed and cosset them. Some days the kitchen is half full of children playing and making cookies. Sarah is a great believer in the healing powers of food.'

'So, one way or another you both have adopted grandchildren, Kitty,' said Ama. 'Do you ever stay in touch with any of them as they pass through the refuge?'

'Not as many as Sarah does,' said Kitty. 'She gets more cards at Christmas than Santa Claus. But I make sure any of them who want to go on to college or training can afford to. I had my lawyer setup a fund to provide bursaries for the hospice children.'

'God, you make me feel selfish, pestering you with all my problems,' said Ama. 'I'm sorry to take up so much of your time.'

'Nonsense, I'm not Mother Teresa. I enjoy your company and I'm flattered to be your confidante,' said Kitty. 'Now tell me the latest in your theatre saga – you know how interested I am in it. If I wasn't so old and decrepit, I'd be down there painting sets with you.'

'That's just it, we're a long way from painting sets yet, Kitty. We're still refurbishing the interior. Restoring that old Edwardian theatre is taking much longer than we reckoned. And now with Ocean disappearing again, I'm so distracted trying to track her down I can't concentrate on rehearsals or anything else. I'm hopelessly behind.'

Kitty patted her hand. 'Just tell me how I can help, dear. You'd be surprised at the resources I can call on – and not just in Arcadia either. You sound like you could use an assistant director, for a start.'

'That's the one bright light on the horizon. My old flame I told you about has agreed to come down and co-direct with me. He's reluctant to come out of retirement, but I persuaded him I would sink without trace unless he helped me.'

'From what you've told me, I imagine you could easily inveigle him to come to your rescue.'

'If you mean did I tell him he could have his evil way with me, you're right. Although who was seducing who is debatable. As I mentioned earlier, we fell on each other's necks.'

'You still haven't told me his name. Would I ever have heard of him?'

'Doubtful. He was never keen on mainstream theatre. Preferred political and avant-garde productions. His name's Spike.'

'Unusual name for an actor. Is it a stage name?' asked Kitty.

'No, it's a nickname. His stage name is Porter Drummond, which happens to also be his real name. His agent thinks like you. Told him no one would take him seriously with a name like Spike.'

'And did he want to be taken seriously?'

'God, yes. He was constantly after me to do plays with all his left-wing mates in the UK. They used to tour political cabarets up and down the country. Scotland, Wales, the north and the midlands.'

'I suppose the university student unions loved that kind of thing in those days,' said Kitty.

'Never went near them. They focused on the miner's clubs, working-men's clubs, union halls. We're talking about the whole Thatcher era. She epitomised everything the extreme left loathed. They demonised her. Spike really believed the revolution was going to happen. At least at first, he did. Later with all the factional in-fighting between the Communists, Maoists and Trotskyites and the Labour unions, he became disillusioned. Thatcher used the old divide and rule method to crush the miners and defeat the unions in

Britain. She had to use the riot police and army tanks to do it, but she won. Spike wasn't the only one to be disillusioned; the British left was in disarray for a generation.'

'I wish I had been a participant in those days, instead of a spectator down here in Arcadia,' said Kitty. 'I expect you must have been in the thick of it, Ama, with Spike for a boyfriend.'

'Yes and no. I went on a few marches and demonstrations and signed petitions but I was focused on my acting career. I was one of the ones Spike called armchair socialists at the time. We lived in two different worlds and eventually went our separate ways after I had a brief affair with another well-known actor. I tried to find Spike later but he had left the country, with a touring theatre company to the far east.'

'Sorry, dear, I'm not sure what I can help you with. Is it your daughter that's worrying you most? Ocean's run off with disreputable characters before – is this one any different.? Once she sees through him, won't she come home again like she usually does?'

'That's it, I don't know, Kitty. He's got some sort of hold over her, she won't leave him and now the police are after him. She could be charged as an accomplice.'

'She's not a child anymore, Ama. You can't shelter her from the world indefinitely. I think this diagnosis she had has made you even more over-protective. From what I've heard, ALS can take years to develop. Maybe she just wants to live her own life in her own way... sorry, I'm preaching again,' said Kitty.

'You're probably right. Maybe the problem's mine, not hers. Only I can't stop worrying about her, especially when I have no idea where she is.'

'Would it help if you did?'

'I don't know. I think so.'

'At the risk of meddling even more, can I make a suggestion, Ama?'

'If you think it will help me out of this mess.'

'Why not speak to her father? Let him shoulder some of the responsibility. Is he still living in Halifax?'

'Ronnie has his hands full with his new family and I imagine his young wife isn't keen on having Ocean disrupt their lives with her escapades.'

'Why, have you asked him for help with her in the past?'

'Not very often, but sometimes when I'm at the end of my tether I call him.'

'Sounds like this may be one of those times, Ama. Does he have any influence with Ocean?'

'He used to when he was on his own and she would go to stay with him. But since he remarried, they've drifted apart, I think. She never says much about him to me anymore.'

'Well, she is his daughter, that should still count for something,' said Kitty. 'My father could always be depended on to be on my side, when I was in any scrape in New York. Fathers and daughters are like mothers and sons, I've learned. It's a powerful bond, irrational but strong. I could never refuse Gerald anything.'

'It's worth a try, I suppose,' said Ama. 'Ronnie was always self-centred, like most good actors. Ocean was the only person he ever put before himself. Certainly not me.'

'What happened between you two, Ama?'

'Like I said, he was totally self-absorbed. His acting career always came first. He walked out on me once too often, and I wasn't there when he came back. I'd followed him out to Stratford, Ontario, from England and we both worked at the Shakespeare festival until I got pregnant. That put an end to my acting for a long time and when we split, I moved to Toronto and slowly began working again.'

'Didn't he follow you – try to get you and his daughter back?' asked Kitty.

'He was so wrapped up in his own life, he barely noticed I was gone. Occasionally he'd remember Ocean's birthday and send her a present. We'd see him on TV now and then in some drama series and I'd contact his agent to demand some support money. But he was never reliable as a source of income – too hit and miss.'

'All the same, it's worth a phone call, don't you think, dear?'

CHAPTER FOUR

Back at her house-sit, that Kitty had lined up for her through her network of contacts and friends, Ama chewed over what the old lady had said. Even when she didn't act on her advice, she always took some consolation from their talks together. Although there was a generation gap between them, she could say anything that was on her mind and Kitty was seldom fazed by it. More often the old lady surprised her with the breadth of her experience, as she had shocked her today, with the revelations of her and Mrs. Spengler's past lives.

She smiled to herself, moving about the big lavishly equipped kitchen of Kitty's absent friend, preparing some sandwiches to take to the theatre later. Spike would love this story of the two old ladies' intrigues, she thought, but could she dare risk breaking a confidence. One day maybe, when she felt more sure of him, but not yet. Meantime, she had more pressing concerns. She picked up the house phone, found Ronnie's agent's number and rang him, to leave an urgent message for her ex. Then she changed into her scruffiest old jeans and top, collected her bag of sandwiches and drove her old red Toyota to the theatre.

Unlike most theatres in small towns throughout the country, the Regency was not a former movie house, but an

Edwardian vaudeville purpose-built theatre. Erected by a wealthy merchant newly returned from London, and determined to provide a cultural palace for his affluent home town. Arcadia was in its heyday and no money was spared, to create a lavish theatre in the heavy Edwardian style. Etched glass, polished mahogany, heavy brass fixtures and an oversize glittering central chandelier were set off by deep red plush everywhere.

And herein lay Ama's problem. After a century's wear and neglect it was now, in these straitened times, shabby, faded and worn. Her initial enthusiasm for restoring the old theatre, by sprucing it up with a new coat of gleaming period maroon paint on the exterior, only made the interior appear even more depressingly dull and dreary. She knew there was no money to replace all the expensive original red plush carpets, swags and wall curtains. She mourned the huge bevel edge mirrors over the heavy mahogany bar, and in the restrooms and foyer, that had lost their reflective purpose as the silvered backings flaked and peeled off. It was hard for her to imagine the once polished and shining brass fittings, that had turned dull and black with age.

That was only the front of house and auditorium. As Ama knew, the whole of the backstage area was not only shabby and worn, it was dangerous. The open stair-steps to the fly-loft were riddled with woodworm and unsafe. The fly-loft itself, felt shaky underfoot and the heavy ropes for flying the scenery in and out, were rotten from disuse.

Ama sat in the middle of the auditorium in one of the worn lumpy red plush seats, trying to focus on her theatre renovation problems and forget about her wayward daughter. She was waiting for Claire Tremblay to show up. They had arranged to meet here to discuss how they could kill two birds with one stone – make the theatre ready for the opening performance and design a striking but simple set, which could be adapted for multiple plays. One thing she knew for sure, there would be no flown- in scenery. The fly-loft was out of bounds until further notice. She calculated that if she had the stairs boarded up, that would satisfy the fire officer and the insurance people. Flying scenery and props would have to wait for another day, when success might bring funds for repairs.

Ama heard a backstage door bang shut and two minutes later, a tall cadaverously slim woman in her sixties, in designer jeans and a knee length cotton smock, strode to centre stage and threw out both arms wide to declaim to the empty house:

'" ...Pardon, gentles all –
The flat unraisèd spirits that hath dar'd
On this unworthy scaffold to bring forth
So great an object: can this cockpit hold
The vasty fields of France? Or may we cram
Within this wooden O the very casques
That did affright the air at Agincourt?"'

Ama applauded. 'If we do Claire, it's going to be a miracle.'

Claire nodded agreement. 'It's gonna be a tough sell alright, but are we down-hearted?'

'At the moment, yes,' Ama said.

'Nil desperandum,' said Claire. 'I have a trick or two up my smock.'

'I was hoping you would. Everything I think of, is going to cost money we don't have.'

'Trust me, I have magical powers,' said Claire. 'With a bit of gauze and glitter and some lighting tricks, I'll conjure up any scene you like. I do it all the time in the most unpromising surroundings – warehouses, parks, church halls, disused factories – all smoke and mirrors, Ama, you'll see.'

'From where I'm sitting, I only see problems, Claire. A crumbling break-arch proscenium stage with curtains falling apart and a condemned fly-loft – all of which will cost a small fortune to restore. Where do we start?'

Claire disappeared into the wings and re-entered at the side of the auditorium. 'Come with me.' She pulled Ama from her seat and led her to the rear of the stalls. 'We start by getting rid of the first four rows of seats. Way too many seats in here to ever hope to fill anyway. Instead we add a thrust stage in the centre and two long ramps, not steps, one on either side of the new stage area. Ignore the proscenium arch and curtain, we don't need them. Replace them with lights and sound.'

'Smoke and mirrors,' Ama said.

'And best of all, cheap. Some recycled timber, a few sheets of plywood, a couple of rolls of used exhibition carpeting, and the services of a good stage carpenter, which you already possess....'

Ama nodded. 'Arthur. Another magician. You should see what he's done with the dressing rooms backstage. I love this idea, Claire.'

'I'm not finished, Ama, look up there.' She pointed up at the curving old balcony above their heads, dimly lit by the stage work lights. 'I want to show you something.'

She loped off on her long matchstick legs, through the shabby foyer and up the once-grand curving elm staircase to the balcony seating area. Ama followed her as Claire leaned over the balcony on stage left.

'Look at that old box seating. It's halfway between here and the stage. If we took out the two seats, you can have another acting area. And if we put in an open staircase from here to the box, and then to the side of the stage, we can link all three levels for entrances and acting spaces. And before you object, I have an old admirer who works with an exhibition joinery firm in Halifax. He has a warehouse full of used steps and stairs from old shows they've done. All we need is a local aspiring thespian with a pickup truck to collect them.' She took Ama's hands in hers. 'Look me in the eye and tell me that the prospect of a three-level thrust stage doesn't thrill an old director's jaded heart.'

'God,' said Ama. 'Do you really think we could do it?' She stared down at the stage, visualising how she might make use of Claire's design for half a dozen of Shakespeare's plays she wanted to do in modern dress.

'And with that new thrust stage section, we could easily put in a trap door, with access from the wings behind the proscenium arch. Another great dramatic entrance for you to use. If we can't fly them in from above, Ama, we'll bring them up from below.'

'More smoke and mirrors,' said Ama. 'I've never had a trapdoor to use before. Yes, please. Have you spoken to Arthur about it?'

Claire nodded, 'Piece of cake, he says. And speaking of smoke and mirrors, I've got an idea for the foyer area, too. Come on down and I'll show you.' She strode off again towards the entrance area.

They stood side by side in the middle of the old grand foyer and bar area, surveying the gloomy prospect before them. Ama felt the enthusiasm that had gripped her minutes before, begin to drain away.

'Reminds me of the Forum in Rome,' she said. 'All it needs is some ivy growing everywhere.'

'The glory that was Greece, the grandeur that was Rome,' Claire said, arms akimbo, glancing about. 'The ivy's not a bad idea, Ama, we can make some long garlands of it to hang around the bar. Now, what I had in mind was this. All these huge old bevel-edge mirrors are too expensive to restore – for the time being at least, so let's cover them up.'

'What with?' asked Ama, 'whitewash?'

'Period posters from the Edwardian era – reproductions, of course. Stick them up like playbills, overlapping each other. There's a terrific poster shop in Dartmouth I go in, every time I need inspiration. They don't need to be theatre posters, just period ones to add some flair. I happen to think poster designers are brilliant artists.'

'They would look great behind the bar,' admitted Ama.

'Not only the bar. In the restrooms, the foyer walls, anywhere there's an old mirror mounted,' said Claire. 'As for the bar, what we need is a giant tin of Brasso, get all the brass fixtures gleaming again. Perfect job for volunteers. This old mahogany bar will glow with a few coats of french polish. Do you know anybody who does furniture restoration, Ama? My contacts are all in Halifax at present.'

'I don't, but I'll bet Kitty does. She knows everybody in the county and she's keen to help out.'

'Good. The simplest way to transform the whole foyer is to suspend a cloth canopy from the ceiling down to the top of the bar and the front entrance area. Something filmy and light coloured so we can light it from above. Make it like a stage set as soon as they enter. Do you have a good wardrobe mistress, Ama?'

'Our wardrobe mistress is a man, as it happens. Frankie can adapt anything to anybody, from a codpiece to a vest of chain mail.'

'Perfect,' said Claire, 'let's get him working on our canopy. We can have half a dozen different ones to change from one show to the next. Cheesecloth is cheap and cheerful. So is burlap.'

'Old fish nets?' said Ama.

'Perfect – as long as they're free.'

'There are lots of redundant nets in Arcadia, along with fishermen.'

'The nets we can use – not so sure about the fishermen,' said Claire.

'Can we talk about the plays now? I've brought some sandwiches. Let's take them in the Green Room and make some coffee,' Ama said.

The two women made their way backstage through the scenery store to the Green Room which was covered in dingy red flock wallpaper.

'"Nightmare, darling – absolute nightmare",' said Claire, looking around. Grinning, she plunked herself down on an old sofa to stretch out her long thin torso, and kicked off her trendy ankle boots. 'Like my kinky boots, Ama? Ten bucks in my local Amnesty shop.' She glanced at Ama's sturdy old canvas runners, splashed with paint. 'What size are you? These are sixes.'

'Snap,' said Ama, 'can I try them?'

Claire tossed them over to her. 'Floor length mirror right there, if you can make them out,' she said nodding towards the flaking silvered mirror on one wall.

Ama tried them on and stood in front of the speckled mirror. "These old work jeans don't show them off to best advantage and my bum's too big to fit into those skinny pencil jeans, Claire.'

'My current squeeze loves women with bums like yours, Ama. God knows what he sees in me. Must be my fine mind.'

'Is he what brought you way down here from Halifax?'

'Partly,' Claire said.

'What's the other part?'

'The provincial museum department wants me to design a touring exhibition, based on the best of the holdings of all the maritime museums – wants it to tour across the country, and maybe a bit in the New England states nearby.'

'What – paintings?'

'Not only paintings – more a cultural mix of artifacts, to show off the 'richness of our maritime heritage', according to the blurb I was sent. Seems they got an obscenely huge grant from the federal government to promote tourism, to replace the collapsed fishing industry.'

'Oh god, does that mean I'm going to lose you, just when I was thinking you were going to be our salvation?' said Ama.

'Don't worry, it's not a nine to five desk job. I can set my own hours, decide when and where to work. I chose Arcadia as it's right in the heart of the south shore. Who knows, I might be able to exploit this as part of my cultural travelling circus,' Claire said. 'But for the moment let's discuss your project, not mine. Tell me more about your long-term plans, Ama.'

Ama poured them out coffee from a thermos urn and sat across from her new-found designer. She spread the sandwiches from her bag on the low table between them to share.

'I sort of fell into this role of artistic director by chance. At my age I wasn't looking for full-time acting anymore. Usual problems with type casting, in an over-crowded field of too many aging female actors. Plus, big parts meant too many lines for me to remember, as a 69-year-old, so I began directing as a way to stay in the game.'

Claire picked a small sandwich and broke it in half to nibble on from her supine position on the sofa. 'Not too many women directors working that I know, Ama. You must be one of the lucky ones.'

'Wrong. I barely had any work professionally when I stopped acting. I soon realised if I wanted to remain in the theatre, which is all I know, I'd have to look at community and fringe theatre jobs.'

'Can you survive doing that?' asked Claire. 'Judging by the size of the honorarium your board offered me, you'll soon be thinner than I am and I'm a professional anorexic.'

'So why did you agree to do it, Claire?'

'Same reason as you. I was looking for a challenge. Commercial stuff pays the bills but it starves the soul.'

'But this museum project sounds fascinating, I'd love to do something like that,' said Ama.

'It is, but theatre design is my first love. It's what gets my creative juices flowing. You mentioned on the phone that you wanted to do modern versions of the classic repertoire. How could I resist an offer like that? When you told me Peter Brook was your favourite director, I was sold. Love his productions. Leave all those fussy period costumes and sets for television, they do it much better than the theatre. The stage is for the imagination,' said Claire.

'I thought first of a modern dress Shakespeare, say Twelfth Night. But then I thought why not exploit the Edwardian theatre theme, with playwrights from then, Shaw, Ibsen, O'Casey, T.S. Eliot,' said Ama.

'How about a German expressionist play and a French farce?' asked Claire. 'On our new stage, we've got the chance to try anything - "therefore be bold!" Lulu – I'd kill to do Lulu! Do you know, I saw the new Paris opera house do Wedekind's Lulu last year. It was so breathtaking, I fainted with excitement. Better than anything the Met or Covent Garden ever did.'

'I'd like to do Brecht's Mother Courage on this new stage of ours – but it wouldn't fit for this season.'

'Maybe next, then,' Claire said. 'What do you want to open with, Ama? Something daring we can really get our teeth into. Rock them back on their heels.'

'I've already begun doing rehearsals of Twelfth Night. But you're making me rethink the whole season now. Save Shakespeare for later. Why don't we meet again in a few days and I can come up with a list that will work together on our new stage. Meantime, you and Arthur can decide how you can rebuild the theatre with just smoke and mirrors, Claire.'

'And I want to meet this wardrobe master as well, to get him started on our foyer makeover. Do you have a producer or co-director to share the load, Ama? I know how these community theatres work. I've seen too many people burnout after one season. Learn to delegate, that's my secret. Never do anything you can persuade someone else to do – under supervision, of course.'

'As a matter of fact, I do have a secret weapon,' said Ama. 'But he's still in Dartmouth, working on his boat to get it ready to sail down here to rescue me. His name is Spike and he's going to be my co-director.'

'Have you known him long, Ama? Does he know what he's letting himself in for, doing community theatre?'

'I haven't told him too much yet. I don't want to frighten him off. He's a professional actor I've known since drama school. He's new to directing but I think he'll be a natural. Providing I can persuade him to stay. We've only reconnected recently and I've had to use all my wiles, to lure him down here to Arcadia.'

'Sounds like you have some history between you,' said Claire. 'How long has it been since you saw him last?'

'That's the crazy thing, it's been over forty years and we bonded like we'd never been apart. I can barely wait for him to get here.'

'Well, well, this is all very intriguing. I hope he doesn't turn the tables and lure you off into the sunset on his yacht, Ama.'

She laughed, 'Spike's boat is no yacht. It's a converted old Cape Island lobster boat. Takes a bit of getting used to – but I quite like it. He wants us to live aboard.'

'Very romantic sounding. Although I expect the reality is rather different. I'm already curious to meet him. When's he coming?'

'Not for a couple of weeks. He's getting it ready for the trip here with an old friend of a dead friend.'

'Curiouser and curiouser,' said Claire. 'Better get to work on our play season ideas.' She sat up and wriggled her feet back into her ankle boots. 'I'm off to find Frankie and Arthur to get them started.'

Ama finished her sandwiches while browsing through the theatre's old play library, housed on dusty shelves around the Green Room. Nothing was in any semblance of order but she found actor's copies of several plays from past productions with their parts and cues underlined or highlighted with marker pens. A paperback edition of 'Oh What a Lovely War' caught her eye and she took it with her back up to the stage.

She had seen a production of Joan Littlewood's play, at the Roundhouse Theatre in Camden Town in London years ago, and it had had a powerful effect on her. She paced about the stage with the script in her hand, visualising how it might be performed in the revamped theatre of Claire Tremblay's design. The highly stylised production she had loved so much would adapt well to the three levels and runway entrances of Claire's imaginings.

'Oh, oh, oh what a lovely war,' she sang aloud, recalling the tune from the play's title song. The period was right although the play had been written much later than the First World War. It's combination of commedia del arte style, crossed with music hall-type numbers and a harsh Brecht/Weill approach to the setting and music, would utilise the full effects of the new thrust stage and multi-level acting areas. It made Ama wish Spike was here to share her excitement over all it's possibilities, as an opening show for the new theatre's season. Claire's offer of a trapdoor in the new thrust section made her think of a trench scene she could stage, with suitable pyrotechnics and sounds.

'Smoke and mirrors,' she said, gazing up at the balcony with fresh eyes to its possibilities, once Claire's linking staircase was added. Her cellphone rang, breaking into her reverie and she tried to ignore it but it continued ringing so she answered it at last.

CHAPTER FIVE

'Hello Ama, it's Ronnie. My agent said you left an urgent message – what is it, Ocean playing up again?'

'I need to talk to you, Ronnie. Ocean's in trouble.'

'You are talking to me. What's she done this time?'

'No, I mean we have to meet – face to face, and decide what to do. I can't handle this on my own this time. When can I see you – are you at home?'

'I'm working on a TV pilot in Montreal, Ama. I can't get away. On call all the time. Can't it wait until I finish here? We should be done shooting in ten days or so.'

'Absolutely not. She's in trouble with the police and disappeared on me. If they find her, she'll probably be arrested along with that thug she's living with. This is serious, Ronnie. I need your help.'

'You know I can't leave in the middle of a shoot, Ama. It could ruin my career if I walked off a film set – nobody would hire me again...'

'Jesus Christ, Ronnie! Can you for once think of someone else besides yourself. This is our only child and she could end up in jail, with a criminal record. What about her career?'

'Calm down, Ama. Let me think for a minute. For a start, I have other responsibilities, too. Ocean may be your only child but I have two more now, remember? And this is news to me that Ocean has a career. What as – a hypochondriac or a drug addict?'

'Ronnie, stop trying to weasel out of your duty as her father. When your child is in trouble you have to help her.'

For a minute there was silence. 'Okay, Ama. If you want to meet me to talk about Ocean's problems, you'll have to come here to Montreal. We can talk between takes I guess, but I can't leave the location. We're shooting on the docks – you'll see the green fluorescent signs posted when you get near. Phone me when you land and I'll guide you here,' he said. 'When do you want to come?'

'Right away – tomorrow. I'll call you from the metro station downtown.'

'Okay. Just remember you may have to hang around if I'm called on set, Ama.'

'Ronnie do you have any idea where our daughter is? Have you spoken to her recently?'

'Not for ages. Last time was when I met her on her birthday.'

'That was March! It's mid-August, Ronnie – what kind of a father are you, anyway?'

'The kind that works hard to support his children. Don't start lecturing me, Ama. I'm warning you. If you want my help....'

'Goodbye Ronnie. I'll see you in Montreal tomorrow – no excuses.' She snapped her cellphone shut and sank to the stage floor, staring vacantly around. Tears of frustration smarted her eyes and she rubbed them away. 'Goddamn you, Ronnie. You selfish bastard!'

She sat for awhile longer on the stage, attempting to recapture her mood before her ex-husband rang but it was no use. It all seemed irrelevant when she compared it to her only child's predicament. She was never able to put her theatre career before her daughter's welfare the way Ronnie did. How many times had she been forced to abandon a promising role when Ocean would disappear without a trace. Invariably Ama would drop whatever part she was doing to track down her wayward offspring.

At first, she had tried to enlist Ronnie's help, but he made such a scene and raised so many objections to interrupting his acting career, that she gave up asking him. If she hadn't felt so desperate this time and Kitty hadn't been so persuasive, she probably wouldn't have insisted on meeting him again. She knew he wouldn't be much help, but was determined he would at least share in the despair that was overwhelming her. It was a cumulative feeling that had built up inside her for several years, as she watched Ocean sink deeper and deeper into her miasma over her deteriorating health.

From being initially diagnosed as a psychological problem attributed to Ama's breakup and subsequent divorce, later re-assessments indicated Ocean had a physical illness, that no one wanted to put a name to, until more recently. When she began to exhibit symptoms that were variously similar to Parkinson's, then multiple sclerosis and possible Lou Gehrig's Disease, her behaviour became even more disturbing. At least to Ama, who bore the brunt of most of it. But this time, she was going to insist Ronnie play his part as Ocean's father, one of the few roles he ever turned down. She picked herself up off the stage floor, left the theatre and drove back to her house-sit.

Cooking was never one of Ama's passions but she had a stock of comfort food recipes, learned from her mother and grandmother in Devon, that she turned to whenever she felt depressed. After she split from Ronnie, she and Ocean had lived in a series of shabby rented apartments in different parts of Ontario, wherever her acting roles took her. When she was in one of these lows, blaming her daughter's behavioural problems on herself for not providing a stable home for her, she would concoct one of her comfort meals. These usually involved a lot of chopping, simmering, stirring and tasting, which she accompanied with plenty of red wine. Feeling the need for one of these meals, Ama had stocked up on supplies at the local farmers' market on her way home to her house-sit. With her arms full of vegetables, she had stopped at the stall of her favourite artisan bread baker.

'What is it this time, Ama?' said the woman behind the table. 'Not exactly comfort food weather.'

'Hello Gloria. I'll have one of those harvest loaves with the caraway seeds. Do I look that obvious?'

'All that shopping and your puffy red eyes are a bit of a giveaway,' said Gloria.

'I've got my heart set on a big potful of ratatouille for tonight. I usually make tons so I can eat it cold for the whole week. Come around and join me one night and we can talk about a play idea I have for our opening production.'

Gloria had played in several of the community group's shows and was an excellent character actor. She and Ama had developed a good rapport on the last show and often talked shop after the play ended. She was a keen supporter of the new theatre project and put in as many hours as her busy life permitted.

'I hear our new designer has some startling ideas for the theatre, Ama. Do you like them?'

'How did you know already? She only came by this morning.'

'I saw Arthur on my rounds earlier and he was full of it. Can't wait to get started, he says.' Gloria leaned over the table to tuck a large sticky Chelsea cinnamon roll in one of Ama's bags. 'I hope those red eyes are not what I think, Ama. It's not Ocean, is it?'

Ama nodded, tears spreading down her cheeks. 'She's gone again. I don't know where she is, Gloria.' She dumped her bags on the ground to fumble for her handkerchief. The big baker gave her a handful of paper napkins from her stall and came around to give her a hug.

'I thought so. There's rumours floating around the market this morning, about that lad she's been seeing.'

The two women stood silently holding each other as the busy market crowd flowed around them.

'Why don't I come by after the market closes, Ama? Give you a hand with that pot of ratatouille. We can talk properly then.' She gave Ama a last firm squeeze, loaded her up with her bags and returned behind her table to her queue of patient customers.

In the large old-fashioned kitchen of her house-sit, Ama piled her bags on the sink counter and set to work. The thought of Gloria's impending arrival made her look round at the shambles she had been living in these last few days. The long farmhouse table was strewn with papers, dirty crockery, library books and empty CD cases, newspaper flyers and unopened mail.

Before she began the ratatouille, she poured herself a large glass of red wine from the four-litre box of Shiraz, sitting beside the stove. A second box of white pinot grigio perched ready on the shelf inside the fridge.

Taking a large chef's knife and a wooden chopping board, she began slicing onions and fat cloves of garlic.

Ama wiped her eyes and stirred the onions and garlic round the big frying pan. She felt a sudden pang in her chest, thinking of Spike again. What will it be like with him back in her life? She added more chopped ingredients to simmer in the deep stew pan, as she felt her eyes fill again.

She didn't hear Gloria's knock at first, as she had Leonard Cohen's 'I'm Your Man' on full volume, through the powerful hi-fi speaker system in her temporary home. The owner had an impressive collection of classical vinyl records which Ama had been working her way through. But sometimes when she was really scraping along the bottom, the only thing that worked for her was Cohen's lyrics. She always carried at least three or four of his CDs in her luggage, wherever she lived.

Gloria stood in the middle of the kitchen, exaggeratedly gulping, goldfish style, until Ama turned the volume down at the end of the song. Ama gave her a hug and poured her a glass of red wine.

'Wow, you have got a powerful armoury of coping mechanisms,' said Gloria, 'I must remember to try them myself, next time Garth goes on a three-day binge and leaves me to bake all night on my own.'

'What's your favourite remedy, Gloria? I'm always on the lookout for new ways to get me through the night. I don't think baking will work for me. Too much risk of failure.'

'Sappho. "Beat your breasts, ye maidens, rend your tunics!" Perfect stuff for kneading bread dough and imagining it's Garth's head I'm pummelling down flat. Here's my contribution. Kaiser rolls. My own recipe. I'll just pop them in the oven to warm for a few minutes then we can have them with your ratatouille.'

They sat at the long oak table drinking red wine while they waited. Ama switched the record to some Chopin nocturnes and the two women communed silently for a few minutes, letting Chopin work his magic. The big baker waited for Ama to speak first.

Finally, Ama said, 'I'm flying to Montreal tomorrow, to press-gang my ex into shouldering some responsibility for our daughter, after all these years. It's probably a fool's errand but I'm going anyway.'

'I thought you told me you'd written him off years ago. Why the change of heart?'

'Kitty put me up to it. She said my approach was wrong. I need to get him onside and stop attacking him.'

'Have you spoken to him yet?'

'Yes, and got off on the wrong foot straight away. I can't talk to him on the phone because he's probably reading a script at the same time. I need to eyeball him in person. Make sure I'm getting through to him.'

'Kitty's a pretty shrewd old woman,' Gloria said, 'She say how you should go about getting him onside?'

'Ask his advice, appeal to him as a father. He's got two other kids as well now. Be humble, ask for help, don't demand it.

'Do you think it will work, Ama? The ex-wife as humble supplicant?'

Ama laughed, 'Not when you put it like that. Ronnie's self-centred, but he's not stupid. He'll probably see right through me.'

'Not if you're a good enough actor. Let him play the role of good dad this time, instead of going straight for the jugular.'

'You could pull it off, Gloria, you're a better actor than me. Maybe I should send you instead.' She rose and brought the heavy casserole dish to the table. 'Let's eat this comfort food and see if it works.' She served up two platefuls while

Gloria fetched the warm Kaisers from the oven and Chopin's nocturnes continued their healing work.

CHAPTER SIX

'Ronnie? I'm on the airport bus. I should be downtown in half an hour. Where shall I meet you?' asked Ama, trying to keep her usual tinge of annoyance out of her voice.

'Ama – Christ! All hell's broken loose here. You couldn't have come at a worse time,' he said.

'Why, what's happened?' Ama tried to keep the hint of suspicion suppressed but already feeling he was back-pedalling on his offer to talk yesterday.

'Seth, the director, has laryngitis, been shouting at everyone for the last week – speechless, can't say a word. The producer wants me to take over temporarily. I'm on the set right now, I can't talk to you, Ama.'

'Why can't the assistant director do it?'

'She's a trainee – producer doesn't trust her, that's why he asked me. I couldn't refuse him, Ama. Not when I've been angling for the chance to direct for ages. Can we make it tomorrow instead? Seth will be back by then.'

Ama swallowed hard and heard herself saying, 'I understand, Ronnie. I guess I can find a hotel and stay over. You're sure this guy will be back in the morning?'

It was Ronnie's turn to sound surprised. 'You don't mind staying over? I'm sorry about this, Ama. I promise I'll meet you first thing tomorrow.'

'Thanks, Ronnie. I'm really counting on your advice. I'm at my wit's end. You'd better get back to work, see you in the morning.' She rang off and stood for a moment replaying their conversation. Had she really asked for his advice? Ronnie seemed as surprised as she was.

She found a cheap *pension* on the French side of Main and propped herself up with pillows on the bed. She had picked up a copy of the Montreal Gazette, the English language daily and skimmed through the arts section to see if she could salvage anything from her wasted day. One of the little fringe theatre groups was doing a matinee performance of Ionesco's *The Bald Primadonna*, in French.

Ama had seen a production of this play in Paris some years ago before she came to Canada with Ronnie. All she remembered was the inane conversation about all the people being called Bobby Watson. And the postage-sized set, totally painted like a British Union Jack in red, white and blue. The wonderful absurdity of it had stuck in her mind, as a play she would like to put on someday. Maybe it could be part of another season of offbeat plays for her new theatre. God, she thought, I haven't even sorted out more than the opening play for our first season and already I'm planning for the next year.

The matinee didn't start until 3 pm and it was still only mid-morning. Who did she know in Montreal she could look up for lunch and maybe the Ionesco matinee as well? Most of her acting friends from her professional days were retired by now, too. She couldn't think of any theatre contacts she still had in Montreal. Skimming through her old address book that she kept with her mainly for nostalgia's sake, no names rang any bells, until... Jasper! Why hadn't she thought of him before? Was he still practising? Probably, as he was five years younger than her.

'Hello, Jasper Falkenham speaking.'

He answered on the first ring, obviously not over-busy with clients, Ama thought. Jasper was a trial lawyer she had had a brief fling with years ago. They had met when he acted as a free legal consultant on a production of the Merchant of Venice, helping her understand the points of law she faced playing Portia. He had insisted on discussing it further after rehearsals over drinks and dinner and eventually in her bed. He was comfortably married into an old Montreal family, had three children and no intention of altering this arrangement. It suited Ama at the time, intent upon her acting career.

'Hello Jasper, how is the Playboy of the Western World?'

'Pardon? Who is this?'

'Portia. Remember? 'The quality of mercy is not strain'd; It droppeth as the gentle dew upon the earth beneath...'

'Ama? Ama Waterstone? My God! Is that you?'

'None other. One of a long line of disillusioned actresses to pass between your sheets, Jasper.'

'Ama. Where are you?'

'Right here in town. Practically on your doorstep. I was hoping we could meet. I'm only here until tomorrow, then flying back to Halifax. Are you free for lunch? I'm paying. I want to consult that keen legal mind of yours.'

'Amarylis Waterstone. Jesus and Mary. This is my lucky day. I've been sitting here feeling sorry for myself with no client to distract me. Stay where you are, I'm on my way. Do I need my car or...?'

'No, I'm only a few minutes walk from your office, if I recall. I'll meet you at the *Prêt à Manger* on St Catherine's and Main, okay?'

'Ten minutes – Ama? Will we recognise each other? It's been so long. I'm old and fat and bald. How about you?'

'Me too – old and fat, anyway. Blue rinse hair.'

'You sound gorgeous.'

'So do you, Jasper. I'll be waiting. You won't stand me up again like last time, will you?'

'If I do, it will be against a wall, Ama.'

'Same old silver-tongued Jasper,' she said and rang off.

In the long hall mirror in her *pension,* Ama tried to see herself as Jasper might. Although she had been joking about her hair which still retained streaks of auburn amongst the gray, her face and neck betrayed her 69 years. She must remember to hold her chin up. She turned to look over her shoulder at her ample behind, which Spike swore turned his legs to water when she was naked. A pity she hadn't packed more carefully when she left. This skirt didn't do her any favours, she decided, holding in her tummy. It would have to do, as she hadn't planned on staying overnight. Or meeting an old beau. A quick brush of her still thick hair and a lick of lipstick, then she pulled on her favourite old tailored linen jacket and closed the door behind her.

The late August morning was warming up as the sun bounced off the plate glass store windows of St Catherine's street, making her squint behind her sunglasses. The *Prêt à Manger* coffee shop was only a block or two from her *pension.* She dawdled along, window shopping in the smart Montreal storefronts, preferring to be late than early to their meeting. Studying her reflection in the window of the store next to the coffee shop she became aware of someone standing behind her.

'Is this the face that launch'd a thousand ships, And burn'd the topless towers of Illium?' said Jasper, over her shoulder.

Without turning around, Ama spoke to her reflection. 'I think it's more like the Wreck of the Hesperus.' She felt his hand on her arm, turning her around and hugging her to his chest. She kissed his cheek then pushed him away, for them to have a good look at each other at arm's length. Fat and bald he was not, with a trim if thicker figure and only a slightly receding hair line. But older he most definitely was, with long creases in his face, pure white hair curling slightly over his collar and a slight stoop to his six-foot frame.

'I nearly missed you, Ama, I was so busy looking for a blue rinse elderly matron. Instead, what do I find?'

'Just an elderly matron,' she said. 'I lied about the blue rinse.'

He took her arm and steered her on past the doorway of the fast food chain. 'Let's go someplace quieter. This place is packed.'

'It's too early for lunch, Jasper. Couldn't we just have a coffee and sit outside in the sunshine?'

'Suits me. This is my stomping ground. I know an espresso café one street over, where I like to people watch.'

'And I'll bet it swarms with leggy French-Canadian girls who will show me up as a dowdy old lady. I'd rather find a park bench where I can have your undivided attention.'

'Have it your way,' he said, pointing across the street to a small city square with lollipop trees like children's drawings, in conical concrete tubs. 'I'll grab the coffees and you find a bench.' He ducked into the coffee shop and Ama crossed the pedestrianised street.

She sat on a molded lime-green plastic bench facing the small fountain in the centre of the square. Its sunflower shower heads sprayed a fine mist on three bronze sculptured children in frozen postures beneath. Ama tried to compose how she would ask Jasper for help finding her daughter. The realisation that Ronnie would never abandon his work for even a day, to look for Ocean had made her fasten on Jasper, the moment she thought of him. The fact that he seemed pleased to see her again gave her new hope. He was not only a lawyer, he was a resourceful man, good at his job despite his playboy reputation. She wondered how much that had changed. Jasper was still a striking figure she saw, as he approached her, his white hair curling over the collar of his pale blue seersucker jacket.

'No sugar, right?' he said, handing her the paper cup and sitting with one long leg folded across his knee. 'Where shall we start?'

'With you, of course. How is Delphine? And your beautiful children?'

'Delphine is Delphine. And the children have all flown the coop. We've been empty-nesters for many years.'

'But you still practise?'

'I still come into the office, most days. But I'm not the fire-eating ambulance chaser I used to be, Ama. The fire has gone out.'

'I don't believe that. You still look like a lady-killer to me.'

'Ah well, I was referring to work. And my reputation as a ladies' man is a shadow of its former self.'

'Delphine was a children's court lawyer – is she still?'

'Not anymore – she is a juvenile court judge nowadays.'

'I suppose your kids are all married with families of their own?' asked Ama, gazing at the bronze infants in the fountain.

'Charlotte has one, Elvire has two and Bo is still struggling with his gender direction. At the moment, he thinks he's gay but he may be bisexual, too. He's had lots of girlfriends.'

'Which makes you a grandfather three times over. Congratulations, Jasper.'

'Not too many playboy grandfathers out there', he said. 'Can't get used to the idea of a pipe and slippers.'

'Nonsense. I'll bet you've got a wallet full of pictures you're longing to show me.' She smiled at him, 'Go on then, let's see them.'

He grinned sheepishly before taking his billfold out of his jacket. 'You really want to see them or are you only being polite, to curry favour with me so I'll reduce my fee?'

'Both,' she said. 'And I'm envious, too. Only one daughter and no likelihood of any grandchildren...'

She studied the pictures for a moment or two. 'God, aren't they gorgeous at that age. Hard to believe they'll turn into surly teenage monsters.'

'You speaking from personal experience, Ama, or from insider knowledge about my three demons?'

'Bitter personal experience. According to my daughter, I am the world's worst mother.'

'Not possible. Delphine holds that title,' said Jasper. 'Apparently, having a juvenile court judge for a mother is about the worst fate that can befall any child. So I've been reliably informed.'

'God, I hope Delphine handles it better than I have, Jasper.'

'I've had to rescue her at times when they ganged up on her,' he said. 'But that was long ago, we're in calmer waters now that two of them are parents themselves. Delphine has been vindicated. The jury's still out about me, at least with my son, Bo.'

'My daughter, Ocean, is the reason I'm here in Montreal, Jasper. I came to talk to her father for help. He's here making a TV series in the old Expo site and giving me the usual run-around. Supposed to meet him this morning – now it's postponed till tomorrow.'

'Did I ever meet him, Ama? I have no recollection, but that means nothing these days.'

'I'm flattered you remembered who I was, Jasper. It was a long time ago. No, you never met him although you've probably seen him many times. He works non-stop. If he devoted a fraction of the time he spends on his acting career to his daughter, she might not be in this mess. His name's Ronnie.'

'Ronnie Waterstone – nope, no bells,' Jasper said.

'Waterstone's my maiden name. I never took his when we married. Jordan. Ronald Jordan.'

'Ronald Jordan! Is he your husband? My god – Delphine watches everything he's in. Thinks he's wonderful.'

'Ex- husband. We've been divorced for years, separated when Ocean was a toddler. A drag on his career. I'm afraid I can't share your wife's enthusiasm for him. Although I grant you, he's a good actor. Damn well should be, it's all he's good for.'

Jasper grinned at her, 'You sound all bitter and twisted, Ama.'

'Too right I am. I'd like to strangle him.'

'Now, now. You should learn to differentiate between the stage and real life. I'm sure Ronnie's a splendid fellow when he's not acting.'

'That's just it. He never stops. His whole life is a fascinating drama with him in the starring role. Please don't try to defend him, Jasper. I'm the one who needs your help.'

'Sorry, Ama. My legal training – learn to see both sides. I've met many bitter, angry wives in my long illustrious career. I have one at home.'

'Knowing you, I'm sure she has reason to be, Jasper. The difference between you and Ronnie is that you stuck with her and he's been trying to scrub us from his life for years.'

'Delphine and I have a working agreement. We live together but lead separate lives. The trick is always to put family first, anything or anyone else is secondary.' He stared into his empty coffee cup for a moment or two before crushing it in his tanned hand. 'It's not perfect, but it works. Most of the time.' He looked at her and smiled. 'We seem to be talking mostly about me, Ama. I haven't yet heard what the real reason is for calling me after all this time. Not just to hear about my love life. Which has never been quite the same since you left me.'

'Jasper, you forget how well I knew you. I'm fairly positive you never gave me a second thought until your phone rang this morning. And just for the record, although this may prejudice my chance of getting your help, I left you because I don't believe in breaking up a family. Even though you said Delphine would turn a blind eye.'

'Aha! Now we're getting somewhere. I knew you weren't after me for my famed sexual prowess.' He stood and put their empty paper cups in the recycling bin behind their bench. 'How about you tell me what I owe this pleasant little saunter down memory lane to, over lunch. You did say it was your treat.' He pulled her to her feet and put her arm through his. 'I hope you weren't thinking of making me eat my free lunch in the *Prêt à Manger* coffee shop. This is Montreal. We can do better than that.'

'Your choice,' she said. 'Not too pricey. Remember I'm an old lady on a fixed income. No expense account dinners in my current post. They gave me a title instead.'

He steered her down a side street to a tiny bistro with a *prix fixe* menu out front. 'This okay, Ama – not too steep?'

'Perfect. And there's a free table outside.' She edged past two women eating their way through the set menu and sat down opposite him at the empty table. She studied the menu briefly. 'You can order *à la carte,* Jasper, it seems fairly reasonable. I'll have the *prix fixe*, I think and a glass of *vin ordinaire.*'

'No need to be too spartan, Ama. Let me treat us to a bottle of something to celebrate our reunion.'

The waiter brought them a chilled Vouvray and took their order. While they waited, she told Jasper the background to her daughter's recent disappearance with the druggie boyfriend. Jasper sipped his wine, nodding from time to time but said nothing until she finished her account. The waiter brought their salads and topped up their glasses before leaving.

'From what you've said, it sounds as though the police want him, not her. If they get picked up, I'm sure I could make a case that Ocean was not really an accomplice, just along for the ride. With any luck, she might only get a reprimand and a brief suspended sentence. Unless, of course, she gets caught red-handed in the meantime, actually doing a deal,' said Jasper. 'The sooner we find her, the better.'

'We... does this mean you'll help me locate her, Jasper? I only intended to pick your brains, not involve you personally.'

'If we wait for the police to catch up with them, she could get into all sorts of mischief. This guy could be working with a dope ring, not just selling a few spliffs to some high school kids. What do you know about him, Ama?'

'Nothing good. That's why I'm so worried. Ocean has run off before on her own. Usually she went to one of her friends or a relative or even occasionally to her father. But not this time. Clay has his hooks into her and she does whatever he asks. God knows where he's taken her, Jasper.'

'If the police are after him, he's probably gone to ground somewhere safe he knows of. My guess is back to where he came from. Ocean told you his hometown is out of province. Where?'

'Stratford. In Ontario. She mentioned his father was a lighting technician at the Shakespeare festival theatre. That's how they met. His dad got him a summer job as a stagehand and Ocean went with a bunch of college friends to see a show there.'

'How old is she now, Ama?'

'Twenty-four in November.' She looked at him. 'I know what you're going to say. She's not a teenager anymore and I shouldn't interfere in her life. That's what Ronnie's been telling me to do since she turned eighteen.'

'Maybe he's right, Ama. They have to make their own mistakes. God knows it's hard to sit back and just watch them screw up. Specially the first one. Elvire is the same age and Delphine and I sat on her too hard – told her none of her friends were suitable, put unreasonable curfews on her, vetted all her dates... you wanna guess what happened?'

'She got married and produced two beautiful grandchildren for you,' said Ama.

'Not until after she put us through hell. Dropped out of university after one year. Went off to Europe on her own without a word. Didn't ask us for a nickel, got a job as an *au pair* in France, then as a crew member on a yacht; left that in Greece to follow some guy on a motorbike heading to Kathmandu. Ended up on an ashram in south India with hepatitis. That's where I finally found her. She was gone almost two years. Her sister got the odd postcard from a different country each time. I spent a fortune in plane fares chasing after her around the globe. Always dead ends. Delphine lost twenty pounds and became an insomniac, roaming the house all night long.' Jasper winced, recalling the pain of his loss. 'I know what you're going through, Ama, believe me. I want to help you find her.'

'Poor Delphine,' said Ama. 'Two years, with no word. My god, she must have been devastated. Do you ever recover from something like that?'

'Takes a long time. She and Elvire were estranged for months after I brought her back home.'

'And yet, she's married with a family now. And happy?' asked Ama.

'Contented. A devoted mother. Happy? I don't know,' said Jasper. '"Count no mortal happy till he pass the final limits of this life secure from pain." Isn't that what Oedipus says?'

'Show me her picture again, Jasper. I want to see her.'

He took out his wallet. 'Let me see a photo of Ocean, too. I know you have one. I carried Elvire's picture everywhere, just in case.'

They exchanged photos and sat silent, studying the faces of their offspring, searching for some clue to help them understand. Ama saw only a striking young woman with her father's smile, her arms protectively around her two small fair-haired children. Nothing to indicate the troubled girl she had been. Unless perhaps the furrow that crossed her forehead. She handed it back to Jasper with a smile.

'Happy ending for you all. I hope I shall be as fortunate,' she said.

'May I keep this, Ama?' asked Jasper. 'I'll need it if I'm going to help you find her.'

She nodded, 'If I wasn't already in love with someone else, I could fall in love with you all over again, Jasper.' She took his large hand and pressed it to her cheek. 'Thank you. I feel as if a great pressure has been removed from my chest.'

'And I'm starving,' he said. 'All this unburdening has left me feeling hollow. Let's eat.'

It wasn't until they had finished their meal and were polishing off the last of the Vouvray, that he asked her who she was in love with. Ama thought for a moment before she answered.

'You of all people know about old flames, Jasper. Spike and I go back to my drama school days in London. We only just rekindled, at the wake of a mutual friend in Dartmouth recently.'

'I guess that quenches this one then. I'll have to be satisfied with old friend status instead,' said Jasper. 'Still, I'm not proud, I'll settle for the crumbs from your table, Ama. Only one thing, you have to make me a promise if I'm going to help you.'

'I can't sleep with you, if that's what you're going to ask. I couldn't, not now.'

'I wasn't going to ask you to,' he said, 'but why not, just out of curiosity's sake. Am I so repellent? I could eat you for dessert right here, Ama.'

'I'm not immune to your charms, even now, Jasper. I have other reasons. Spike. Delphine. Elvire, to name just a few.'

He said, 'I want you to promise that whenever I have information about Ocean, that we meet in person. Over lunch, like this. That will inspire me to keep searching, knowing I'll get to see you again. Do you agree?'

'Gladly. I haven't felt this hopeful for ages. I know it sounds selfish, but your experience with Elvire has made me feel you really can find Ocean before it's too late. Where will you start?'

'Probably with the boyfriend. He's the one whose left some tracks. I've got lawyer friends and court contacts from here to Victoria and back. What did you say his name was - Clay something?'

'Clay Fordwich, from Stratford. Jasper? I can't pay you, except for your expenses. In fact, I can't really afford to fly to Montreal to meet you for lunch, either.'

'You pay for the lunches, I'll handle the rest. I can fly to Halifax to meet you, instead. We'll have a Lloyd's of London contract - no rescue, no fee. Then when we find her, you can owe me. It'll give me a hold over you, so we can keep having lunches together into our dotage. I understand there's some good seafood restaurants in Arcadia we can sample, too.'

Ama hugged him and she and Jasper parted outside the bistro.

For the rest of the evening she worked on ideas for the plays to make up her opening season and decided what she was going to say to Ronnie tomorrow. The TV news was focused on the debate over the Physician Assisted Suicide bill that was being forced on a reluctant government. They saw it as a hot potato that was handed back and forth between them, the courts and the medical profession. On a whim, she decided to phone Spike. She'd been thinking about him almost non-stop, she realised, since she left Jasper.

'Hello? Porter Drummond here.'

'Spike, it's me, Ama. I know it's late. I suddenly felt the need to hear your voice.'

'Ama? Is something wrong?'

'Not really. I'm in Montreal and I'm missing you, that's all.'

'Montreal? What're you doing there?'

'Supposed to be meeting my ex to talk about Ocean, but he's too busy with filming – maybe tomorrow, he says.'

'Does he know where she is, Ama?'

'No – hasn't seen or heard from her since her birthday six months ago.'

'I don't understand. Then why are you there?'

'Because he's her father and I want him to help find her. But I'm pretty sure it's a waste of time. If he stalls again tomorrow, I'm leaving.'

'What made you think he'd change after all this time, Ama?'

'An old friend told me I should give him the opportunity to get involved...Spike, I don't want to talk about Ronnie. Let's talk about us, can we? When am I going to see you? I can't think straight since I got back here. All I do is fantasize about us being together on the Mongoose. Then when I don't hear from you, I think you've gone off me. You haven't, have you, Spike?'

'Never, you won't get away from me this time, Ama. When are you coming back to Arcadia?'

'Tomorrow, as soon as I've met with Ronnie. When are you leaving? Is there much left to do on the boat?'

'Not much, she's nearly ready. Fergus isn't happy with the autopilot, keeps running off course when we take it out for trials so he's got it all apart at the moment.'

'God, how long is that going to take?'

'Maybe another couple of days, not more,' Spike said. 'Tell me about the theatre project. What have you been doing?'

'I've found this amazing designer who's full of brilliant ideas to change the interior, so we can play on three levels at the same time.'

'Three levels? I thought you said it was an old Edwardian proscenium arch theatre.'

'It is. And the best thing is it will hardly cost a penny.'

'He sounds amazing. I can't quite picture how he'll do it,' Spike said.

'It's all done with smoke and mirrors. And he's a she. Her name is Claire and you're going to love her. She's got me all fired up with new ideas for the first season. I've thought of a different play for the opening instead of doing *Twelfth Night*.'

'What's happened to your modern dress classic revivals idea – have you ditched that?'

'I want to use the theme of the Edwardian era in the revamped Edwardian theatre – plays about that period around the First World War,' she said.

'You're not going to do *War Horse*, are you? The rights would cost a fortune. Never mind the production costs.'

'Nope. Not going to tell you till you get down here. I'm only starting to work out the staging so I'll need your input.'

'Better have it all figured out by then, Ama, because when I get there, I'm not letting you off the boat for a week.'

'I can hardly wait, I've got so much to tell you, Spike.'

'Long as you can do it lying down, you can tell me anything you like,' said Spike. 'I'll tell you a few things I'd like as well. And they've got nothing to do with the theatre.'

'Sounds idyllic. I talk about plays and you talk about love. Are you sure we'll only need a week?'

'Better make that ten days – keep forgetting we're jerries, everything takes longer than you expected,' he said.

'Take as much time as you like, I'm available right now.'

'I wish you were, Ama. I miss you, baby-sitting Esther, instead of being with you.'

'How is she, Spike?'

'Distracted, mostly. She wanders from room to room, picking things up and putting them down in a different place. Sy and Ivy and I take turns staying with her. Supposed to be helping her clear out Simon's old stuff but really, she doesn't want to part with it. I get restless and fidgety not accomplishing anything. I'm starting to worry Fergus won't want to leave to come with me when we go,' he said.

'Oh god, I don't want to hear this, Spike. Please don't say you're putting off the trip.'

'I suppose I can try to go on my own. As long as I'm in harbour every night.'

'But Fergus promised you he'd come with you. Has he changed his mind?'

'He says he hasn't but I don't think he likes to leave home. He's 85 now.'

'It's crazy you sailing that great big boat by yourself, Spike. What if there was a storm or it broke down?'

'It's not that big, Ama.'

'What about Fergus? Why has he changed his mind?'

'Fergus says his sailing days are over. I don't like to press him. He's already done a lot for me, making sure the Mongoose is in good shape.'

'Let me talk to Ivy tomorrow and ask her if she can persuade her to talk to Fergus,' said Ama. 'I'll call you as soon as I hear from her, Spike.'

She was up early despite waking half a dozen times, dreaming incomprehensible pastiches with Ocean and Elvire running off together to an ashram and Spike and Esther being seasick in a storm on the Mongoose. She dressed hurriedly, grabbed a coffee and a croissant from the corner café before heading down to the old Expo site, to the huge geodesic dome that was now turned into a museum. Ronnie had told her she'd see all the film trucks, around the dome area where they were shooting beneath the monorail. It was after 9am when she arrived.

She saw Ronnie before he saw her. A cluster of technicians surrounded him and he was arguing fiercely with them. She stood by the catering truck waiting for her chance, and drinking another coffee the girl in the truck offered her. A long tracking shot was laid out parallel to the overhead monorail, and the camera crew were moving the dolly back and forth on the temporary rails. Three actors in 60s clothes stood waiting for direction, looking at Ronnie. He broke away from the tech crew and moved towards the actors, then saw Ama and stopped, hesitating before coming over to her.

'Bad news, Ama. The director's worse today – some kind of summer flu. They want me to continue the shoot without him, as it all went really well yesterday...' he paused, scanning her face to see how she was taking this.

'I don't care a damn about him, Ronnie. I came here to get your help with Ocean and I'm not leaving till I get some commitment from you,' she said. 'Where can we go and talk privately?'

'Ama, you're not listening. I'm in charge here and all these people are waiting for me to get started. This is a complicated scene and they need me to...'

'And I told you I need you to help find our daughter. Now stop stalling and take me somewhere we can discuss our plans.'

Ronnie looked back over his shoulder at the actors and crew watching them. He held up two fingers, then turned back to her. 'I'm sorry, Ama, it's impossible right now – you can see for yourself. I'll have the producer yelling at me in a minute if I don't get started. Maybe tonight, say after nine – no, shit, we're doing a night shoot while we're set up here. It will just have to wait for a few days more, I'm sorry.'

'You promised me if I flew here, we could talk about finding Ocean. I stayed overnight and now you tell me not for a few days more. Meantime we have no idea how much trouble our only child is in and you just say you're sorry. I told you the police are looking to arrest her, Ronnie. Don't you care?'

'At least she'll be safe if she's in custody. We can do something then. The cops will find her faster than we can, Ama.'

'And she ends up with a criminal record to follow her through life, is that what you want?'

'Ama. I've got to go – leave your hotel address with the PA and I'll try to call you later tonight, okay?'

He turned and hurried back to the camera crew before she could answer. A girl with a headset detached herself from them after a brief word with Ronnie and came over to Ama.

'Hello, I'm Stella, the PA. Ronnie asked me to take your details so he can be in touch later.' She held a pen and spiral notebook poised to write.

'Tell him the next time he hears from his daughter, will be from prison,' said Ama. She turned and stamped off to the bus stop without another look back.

Riding out to the airport, she stared out the bus window, not seeing anything but her reflection. She grimaced at herself, thinking of her conversation with her ex-husband. Why was she surprised at him when she had felt from the start it was wasted effort? But she hadn't helped her case by jumping down his neck in front of all his cast and crew. Poor Ronnie, she smiled ruefully, she had made him squirm publicly and he wouldn't soon forgive her. To hell with him, she had Jasper's pledge to cling to now. She rang his number at work as she had promised him she'd do after speaking to Ronnie.

'Jasper? It's me, Ama.'

'I was wondering when you'd call. Are we having lunch again today?'

'Afraid not. I'm on the airport bus to catch the noon flight to Halifax. I just wanted to tell you I've spoken to my ex this morning.'

'Was he as pleased to see you as I was?' asked Jasper.

'Just the opposite. Gave me the bum's rush,' she said. 'No time to waste on me or our daughter. Far too busy with his precious TV show.'

'What's it called, Ama? Delphine will want to know.'

'I never gave him a chance to tell me. Tore a strip off him in front of everybody on set.'

'That was a good move. I'll bet he can't wait to help us find Ocean now.'

Ama laughed, 'It certainly felt good, Jasper. I knew he had no intention of helping as soon as we met, so...'

'...You gave him both barrels. I guess it's my turn now to play good cop, as you've usurped the bad cop role.'

'Save your breath, Jasper. It was a mistake listening to my friend Kitty's advice,' she said.

'Can't believe she would have advised a broadside as an opening shot, Ama.'

'You're right. I did everything she told me not to do.' She gave Jasper a blow by blow account, venting her anger at Ronnie's selfish behaviour. When she finished, he waited a moment before replying.

'Okay, what's done's done. Now that you've got that off your chest, as your lawyer, I think it might be useful for me to invite Ronnie around to the house for dinner. Try to repair some of the damage from your full-frontal attack and get him onside. Delphine will be delighted to apply some massage to his bruised ego, I'm sure.'

'Can't imagine why you want to bother with him, Jasper.'

'I think I'll ask Elvire to come too. She can frighten him with some of her stories of her lost years in the wilderness. Maybe he'll decide he should help find his own child after all, 'said Jasper. 'Leave it with me.'

'Does Delphine know about me – us? She might not be so keen to get involved.'

'On a need to know basis, she will know enough not to inquire too closely, Ama. I told you we have an understanding. And she will be doubly sympathetic with your missing daughter and her favourite actor.'

'You know best, Jasper. I hope you're right on both counts. Ronnie and Delphine. Let me know as soon as you have any news. And Jasper? I'm doubly grateful too. For your help with finding Ocean, and for having you back as a friend.' She rang off as the bus was pulling into Montreal's Trudeau airport departures' drop-off. Her flight for Halifax was already loading.

CHAPTER SEVEN

After Fergus pronounced himself satisfied with the Mongoose, Spike tried to pay him but the old man refused, said he did it for Simon. He drove off in his battered old pickup and Spike paced round the docks on his own, thinking of the trip ahead.

Fergus had showed him the route on the chart he was proposing to follow. He had finally agreed to go with him, provided they went nice and slow. 'Simon and I liked gunk-holing, so we won't be standing off and running straight down the coast, Spike. We'll poke along in sight of shore while we explore all the bays and harbours between here and Bridewell.'

'Suits me,' said Spike. 'Give me some practice getting in and out of port and familiarise myself with this coastline – under supervision.'

Over dinner at Esther's that night, she talked of Simon's Shakespeare project and how much the graduate students loved continuing his research. They enjoyed finding modern English equivalents for the obsolete words and phrases, which baffled contemporary audiences so much. Esther mentioned how often Simon ran into resistance and often open hostility to his project from teachers, professors and other scholars.

'His standard response to these attacks was to quote Dryden's defence of updating Chaucer, because the sense of it is lost when it's barely intelligible to modern ears, unless they're scholars – like Simon. I plan to write a preface to the plays and use Dryden's argument, that he didn't update Chaucer for scholars and experts who didn't need it, but for ordinary people to be able to enjoy his work. He really demolished all the arguments against a modern English version – called his critics misers who wanted to hoard Chaucer for themselves and deprive ordinary people of him.'

'Sounds like the perfect argument for a modern English Shakespeare, alright,' said Spike. 'Too bad nobody reads Dryden anymore.'

'Except scholars, professors and critics,' said Esther. 'And my medieval studies grads – don't forget them. They know Dryden's defence by heart.'

The next morning Spike and Fergus followed the heavily indented coastline at a comfortable distance, occasionally changing headings but mainly running on autopilot. Around midday, Fergus idled the engine in the almost smooth water.

After lunch Spike took the wheel as they skirted round the famous lighthouse at Peggy's Cove. Masses of tourists crowded the smooth slippery rocks, taking endless photos of themselves, against the best-known backdrop in the Maritimes. Kids cavorted about near the water's edge despite prominent signs warning of the danger.

'Every year tourists get swept off those rocks and drown,' said Fergus, pointing to two young boys chasing each other on the black rocks, glistening with slimy algae. He shook his head. 'If those two were mine...'

'Be a shame if the authorities decided to make it out of bounds, though,' Spike said.

A while later, Fergus throttled back the Mongoose as he eased the boat into a tiny cove. 'You go forward and be ready to drop the hook when I give you the signal, Spike. Good sandy bottom here so we'll lay out lots of chain on it to get good holdin'.'

Spike dropped the anchor on a nod from him, watching first the chain and then the thick new rope he and Fergus had bought and fitted, with different coloured duct tape marking each fifty-foot length running through the cleat.

Spike unfolded some canvas chairs and they sat on the rear deck of the Mongoose in the late afternoon sun, drinking wine.

'Let's eat out here this evening,' said Spike.

Both the casserole and the wine vanished rapidly in the early evening air, which now had a hint of coolness as the sun dropped lower. Fergus fetched a bottle of Armagnac from his bag to go with Spike's coffee. They sat back watching a pair of great grey herons work lazily back and forth across the sheltered cove.

'To Simon,' said Spike, raising his brandy.

They drank a toast with the Armagnac, saying nothing for awhile as they watched the sun set in dramatic fashion over the water. Finally, Fergus broke the silence.

'Did you ever think of it yourself, Spike? Suicide.'

'A few times, but never seriously. At least not back then. Today, it's a different story,' Spike said.

'What's changed for you? Simon's death?'

'That's certainly made me think about my own end of life. It's more dying than death, I think. Death is a kind of blank wall. It defeats my imagination whenever I try to visualise it.

When we no longer enjoy the comforts of religion which our parents and grandparents relied on, it does present a bleak prospect.' He held up the Armagnac. 'I'm with Omar Khayyam - *Make the most of what we yet may spend*

Before we too into the Dust descend;
Dust into Dust, and under Dust, to lie,
Sans Wine, sans Song, sans Singer, and - sans End ... I used to be able to recite the whole of the Rubaiyat by heart – not anymore. I have to keep looking it up.'

'Will you and Ama each keep your own separate places, or both live aboard the Mongoose?' Fergus said, looking around at the unfinished state of the deck saloon.

'Ama's game to try living aboard but she's not used to the primitive conditions, so I think it will be more like camping out until the weather gets too cold. Not sure what will happen after that.'

'She told me that she has a big fancy house-sit, while the owner is abroad for a year,' said Fergus. 'Sounds like that would be a good spot to hole up for the winter. You sure as hell don't want to be livin' on an uninsulated boat when the snow flies.'

'Ama's dead keen to have me helping on her theatre project, so it makes sense to be living together ashore. I'll have to wait and see the set-up when I arrive. I might end up camping in the Green Room for the winter, if it's still a building site by then.'

Underway again the following morning, with Spike at the helm they followed the ragged coastline down the peninsula out of St Margaret's Bay. As a sailor, Fergus said he preferred keeping a good distance between them and the shore, so they ran down the bay using the autopilot. They sat on the forward hatch to keep an eye out for other boats while they sipped mugs of tea and studied the passing coastline.

'We seem to be running a bit closer to shore than before,' said Spike. 'Should I change the setting on the autopilot, Fergus?'

'You're right, we are too close. That's funny, I was sure I'd set a course well clear of that headland.' Fergus pointed up ahead. 'I'll come with you and take another look at the chart. Better turn on the sonar, too, Spike – this coast is covered with low-lying reefs.'

In the wheelhouse, he glanced at the compass heading, while Spike switched on the sonar. Fergus grabbed the wheel to turn it away from the shoreline. 'We're way off-course. What's happened?' Spike tried to turn the wheel again but the autopilot pulled it back out of his hands.

'You have to disengage it first before you can change course,' said Fergus. He reached across Spike to throw the lever but nothing happened, the autopilot continued its grinding and sawing noise.

'Jesus – look at that,' said Spike, pointing to the sonar screen. A long ridge of rocks lay dead in their path.

Fergus struggled with the wheel which yawed back and forth, pulling towards the land. 'Switch it off, Spike, switch it off –'

The grinding noise stopped and the wheel once again responded, as Fergus yanked it hard over and the bow swung slowly away from shore.

Neither one of them spoke, as they studied the rocks on the sonar screen edging closer. The ridge seemed to curve towards them. Fergus yanked the throttle lever back to idle and they began to wallow in the swell as they lost way.

'Go forward, Spike – see how much depth we have – I can't tell clearly from this screen.'

Spike ran to look over the bow, shielding his eyes from the sun to see the reef. He could vaguely make it out in the depths. 'Looks like it's pretty deep. Should we risk going over it?'

'Take the wheel, while I have a look.'

They changed places and Fergus studied the reef. 'What's the sonar say, now?'

'Nine feet. You said we draw four and a half,' said Spike.

'I think it's falling away. Ease her ahead slow, we should be clear,' said Fergus leaning as far out over the bow as he could.

Spike pushed the throttle forward just enough to give them some headway, watching the sonar screen and Fergus for a signal. They crept forward over the ridge of rocks with Fergus beckoning him on.

'Shit!' he shouted and made backing off motions. 'There's a huge one right in front of us.' He pointed as white water broke over the top of the submerged rock. 'Full astern, quick!'

Spike pulled the gear lever backwards into reverse at the same time as he felt a jarring bump. The Mongoose seemed to shift sideways with a scraping sound as they glanced off the rock. Fergus came stumbling back into the wheel house and grabbed the wheel from Spike, swinging it hard to port and shoving the gear lever and throttle forward. The Mongoose steadied as they came head on into the swell. He peered at the sonar screen and nodded to Spike. 'Fifteen feet...twenty feet.' He inched the throttle ahead to keep them moving forward.

The compass needle swung onto the new heading and held steady, as Fergus steered away from the reef and well off from the looming headland.

'What the hell was that all about? I thought you told me you'd fixed it,' Spike said.

'I did, we tested it several times in the outer harbour. The tide does odd things to the currents along this south coast,' said Fergus, 'that's why I like to have plenty of distance between me and the shore.'

'Maybe that's what was causing it to over-compensate, do you think?'

'Possible. But all the same I think we should stick to hand steerin', till we can have a look at it again. I don't trust it, Spike. That was a bit too scary for me.'

'Me too. Let's just take turns at the wheel from here to Bridewell.'

'You go first,' said Fergus. 'I'm goin' below to get us both a stiffener.'

He disappeared down the companionway and Spike clutched the spokes of the wheel. He tried to calm the nerve in his right leg which threatened to give way on him. He thought of what Ama had said to him several times. Maybe this boat was too big for him. What if it had been her instead of Fergus with him just now. The memory of how he had gone blank frightened him. Was it his age that made him freeze, instead of respond to the situation? His self-confidence evaporated whenever he became stressed, he realised.

'Here we are,' said Fergus, reappearing with two tumblers in his hands. 'Dutch courage. Drink up, this will steady our nerves.'

Spike took a large swallow and choked. 'Jeezus...'

'Ninety proof Jamaica rum. Never leave port without it,' said Fergus.

CHAPTER EIGHT

Fortunately there was a lull in the usual horde of summer visitors to the little port of Bridewell and they found a spot at the public dock. They squeezed the Mongoose in between two gleaming cocktail cruisers, whose owners watched nervously as Spike tied her up with her new mooring lines. Fergus shut the engine down and joined Spike on the wharf.

'Let's have a sun-downer before we eat, shall we?' said Spike. 'I'm still feeling shaky after our little escapade today.'

'Me too,' said Fergus. 'The Sail Loft pub has a patio deck on the waterfront.'

They finished their meal and sat drinking the last of the wine, content to observe the summer crowd of sailors and tourists while Spike tried to identify possible members of the local theatre company.

'Looks like we're out of luck, Fergus. I'd say this bunch is mostly summer sailors, judging from the bits of conversation I've been hearing. You go ahead and check out the other pubs if you like. I'm going back to the Mongoose. Had enough excitement for one day.' He returned to sit on the rear deck and promptly fell asleep. He awoke later at the sound of voices, with a foul taste in his mouth.

Two figures approached along the dock, deep in conversation. One of them looked up and called out.

'Spike – is that you?'

Spike turned to see an unsteady Fergus being helped up onto the deck by the other lanky man with him.

'Thought you were having an early night?' said Fergus. 'Spike, this is Justin, a fellow actor. Met him at the pub.'

'Pull up a cushion, Justin – it's too nice to go below,' said Spike. 'I'll fetch some more glasses.' He went back down the steps to the cabin.

'There's half a bottle of Armagnac on my bunk while you're there,' called Fergus. 'Had enough beer for tonight. What do you think of the Mongoose, Justin? Not quite the usual yacht that ties up here in Bridewell, is it?'

'To me they're strictly scenery,' said Justin. 'Look but don't touch. Never had the money to get in with this crowd. I am just a poor player. They occasionally invite us for a drink after the show for a peek at how the other half lives.'

'Are they keen supporters of the theatre?' asked Spike, pouring out the brandy he had brought up.

'They're mostly a transient bunch, looking for amusement,' he said. 'Reluctant supporters is a better description. Let's just say they don't come here because of the theatre, but if they're bored with eating and drinking and swapping yarns, they come along to see us.'

'Justin and his partner, Emily, runs the old Majestic theatre as well as playin' the lead roles in Taming of the Shrew. I thought he'd be interested in meetin' you, so I brought him back for a drink,' said Fergus.

'Fergus told me about your plans to help restore the old Regency Theatre,' said Justin. 'Perhaps we could do a joint co-production with Arcadia.'

'Maybe I should phone my partner, Ama, to drive over to meet you and Emily and see the show,' said Spike. 'I think I'd better call her now so she can sort out her plans for tomorrow.'

'Okay, I'll leave you to it,' said Justin. 'Come by the theatre in the morning and let me know and I'll save you some tickets.'

In the morning, Spike was woken up by Fergus walking about on the deck above his head. He crawled out of the vee-berth and surveyed the disarray in the cabin. Fergus appeared on the companionway steps and beckoned him up on deck.

'Come and have a look at this.' He crouched down near the bow and pointed under the waterline as Spike joined him. 'A little souvenir of our encounter yesterday.'

'God, that looks a bit ugly,' said Spike.

The two of them studied the long gash in the paintwork below the Plimsoll line, where the bare planking showed a deep gouge with rough splintered edges in the raw wood.

'Do you think I should do something about that before I leave, Fergus?'

'Not much you can do until you get to Arcadia, Spike and nose her up onto a dry-dock ramp for repair.'

'Will she start to leak, I wonder?'

Fergus shook his head. 'No, these old boats is double planked to handle abuse. It's only surface damage to the outer layer. I'd say it looks worse than it is.'

Fergus tidied up onboard while Spike went to find the marina laundry with his sheets and towels. He passed a tiny gelato ice cream shop and on impulse went in. The teenager dishing out huge scoops asked him what flavour he wanted.

He explained they were on a boat and he had no freezer, only a cooler.

'No worries, mate. We can deliver,' said the youth in a strong Ozzie accent. He pointed to an old-style delivery boy's bike outside. 'We get lots of you yachties ordering for dessert.'

'Are you just here for the summer?' asked Spike.

'Yeah, I been here for a couple of weeks, part-time. I crewed on a sailboat from Perth. Plan to go to Uni in Dartmouth in September,' he said. 'I'm Travis.'

'I'm Spike. I'm on the Mongoose, the old wooden fishing boat, amongst all the plastic yachts.'

Travis laughed. 'Spike – I like it.'

'I'm looking for a launderette, is there one in the marina or nearby?'

'Sure thing, mate. It's opposite the old theatre. I pass it every time I go to meet my girlfriend.'

'She works in the launderette?'

Travis laughed again. 'No way. She's got a summer job backstage at the Majestic. Wants to study acting when she finishes her uni degree.'

'I'm going to the theatre myself as soon as I drop off this laundry. Maybe I'll meet her there. What's her name?'

'Anna-Lise. She's French-Canadian, from Montreal. I don't speak any French but her English is near perfect. Real sexy accent.' Travis grinned. 'I love French girls. Don't meet many in Oz.'

'Sounds great,' said Spike. 'I love them, too. Why don't you bring her down to our boat for a drink after the show? Meet my partner, Ama. She runs the theatre in Arcadia. I'm heading down there to work with her – soon as I get my boat fixed.'

He told Travis of their near miss with the reef and the problems with the autopilot. Travis said he could come down and have a look at it, then directed him to the theatre and launderette and they agreed to meet later.

Ama arrived in time for a drink before the 'Taming of the Shrew' performance. She had dropped everything in response to Spike's call and driven over from Arcadia in her old Toyota. Justin and Emily had met with him after rehearsal and both seemed excited at the prospect of a joint production. They gave him complimentary tickets for the evening show.

At the tiny old Majestic Theatre, he and Ama finished their drinks and then sat in the small balcony. They watched the stalls fill with summer visitors dressed casually in shorts and tee shirts. There was a sprinkling of people more formally clothed like themselves.
'I think those must be locals,' said Ama. 'Dressed for the occasion.'
Spike looked around at the elaborate decoration and gilded ceiling. 'Is this like your theatre, Ama?'
'It's older and smaller. Our balcony is much bigger and there are box seats on the sides.'
'Late Victorian and well preserved,' Spike said. 'Even at this size, I doubt if they're often sold out.'
The first half of the play moved at a lively pace and the audience enjoyed Katharine, the shrew, stealing the show as Ama had predicted. She made a few notes before Spike remembered he was supposed to be doing the same thing. But by the intermission he had only jotted down three or four phrases to remind him of where he thought the audience might be puzzled. As they planned to meet Justin and Emily for a post show drink at the pub, they stayed in their seats and

compared notes. They had discussed how to assess when the audience might be struggling with the Elizabethan language, expressions and phraseology and to make notes during the show. Ama had the most.

When the second half began, Spike paid more attention at first and wrote down several points, but as the struggle between Justin and the red-haired Emily grew fiercer, he became caught up in the action and forgot his notes. As they left the theatre, she pulled him aside.

'I want to look around backstage, Spike.'

She gazed up to the fly-loft at the flown scenery and sighed. 'If only ours was functioning again. I love watching scenery flown in – it's magical.'

'What's wrong with yours then?'

'Condemned by the fire marshal. Too dangerous.'

'Couldn't you put in new ropes?'

She shook her head. 'It's not that simple. The wooden staircase is rotten with woodworm and the roof timbers won't support any heavy weights. Have you any idea how much a new roof costs?'

'A lot.'

'A fortune. It's out of the question.'

'What will you do? No sense looking at me. I'm hopeless with heights.'

She took his arm. 'My secret weapon. My new designer who performs miracles on a daily basis'

'What's her name again?'

'Claire – but I call her my goddess of clever ideas.'

'I remember now – she does it all with smoke and mirrors.'

'Still wish I had a fly-loft, though. Let's check out the Green room and find your new friends. I'm anxious to meet up.'

They found them in Emily's dressing room, removing their makeup and arguing fiercely.

'Are you rehearsing?' said Spike, 'or are we interrupting something.'

'No. This is a proper full-blown argument, not a rehearsal,' Emily said. 'Didn't you see the way he deliberately kept upstaging me, mugging to the audience?'

'It wasn't deliberate and I was only playing for laughs – it's supposed to be a comedy,' said Justin.

'A comedy, not a stupid knockabout farce,' she said, scrubbing her face makeup off and glaring at the mirror. 'And don't roll your eyes at them behind my back.'

Justin appealed to Ama. 'You saw for yourself, she's an inveterate scene-stealer and whenever I try to get a laugh, she accuses me of upstaging her.'

Ama laughed. 'Well I thought you were both wonderful.'

'Spike, don't just stand there grinning – tell him I was right,' said Emily, after they were all introduced.

'You're both right and you were both outrageous. Perfect. I loved the ending.'

Emily's frown changed to a smile. 'And you're both cowards. Afraid to take sides.' She embraced each in turn. 'You're supposed to say, loved her, hated him.'

'Absolutely agree,' said Ama. 'I hope you give him hell every night, Emily. He deserves it.'

'This could turn nasty, Spike. Shall we go and have a drink?' said Justin.

'Spike's coming with me,' said Emily. 'We actors have to stick together. You two directors can re-hash the play on the way to the Sail Loft.'

Although it was after ten o'clock, the air was still warm and the sky was light enough to see where they were walking.

Ama and Justin were already talking animatedly and Spike and Emily dawdled behind.

'Okay, Spike, now he's out of earshot you can tell me honestly – did you feel it worked or not?'

'As a hardened feminist, I think the play's flawed,' he said.

'Of course, and Shakespeare's a flawed playwright, no question,' said Emily.

'I happen to think he deliberately wrote it to be controversial,' Spike said. 'He sets us up to think one thing, then turns it upside down to be something else – and I thought you got the balance about right. In the end it's the two of you in a compact against the rest of us – outsmarting everyone and having a good laugh at us into the bargain.'

'I wanted to sidestep the battle of the sexes thing. Play it as two opinionated people resisting falling in love, and in denial almost to the end. Did any of that come across?'

'And a lot more besides,' said Spike. 'After all, it's Shakespeare.'

'Pity he's such a flawed playwright.' She took his arm. 'But enough about Shakespeare, let's talk about me. Did you like me?'

'Adored you, couldn't get enough. I want to come and see you every night,' he said.

'You're such a discerning critic, Spike. Why can't Justin see me like you?'

'Well if you will persist in hanging out with callow youths, what can you expect?'

'You're right, I need a mature older man.'

'Much older, like me.'

'Like you.'

'About forty years older, in fact.'

'Mmm... Perhaps I should wait until I'm more mature.'

'Perhaps. Besides, I'm already in love with Ama. She wouldn't approve.'

'Neither would Justin – he'd upstage me even more.'

'He's young, you can train him.'

'I suppose. Let's catch them up and have a drink.'

In the Sail Loft, it was standing room only but Travis and Anna-Lise waved them over to their table. Emily and Justin were almost immediately surrounded with friends and well-wishers. Ama and Spike sipped their drinks, smiling and nodding to everyone introduced to them, unable to sustain a conversation above the din.

'I know we were going to compare notes after the show,' said Ama, 'but I don't think I could concentrate with all this noise. Maybe we can do it over coffee in the morning.'

'I'm ready to call it a night, too,' said Spike.

They excused themselves and walked along the dock toward the Mongoose, which was swallowed up in the darkness. They tiptoed on board, past the unfinished deck saloon were Fergus was snoring and down the steps to the cabin, where Spike switched on the bare light bulb over the sink.

'Let's have candles instead, Spike. That light is too stark.' She found some candle ends on the counter and lit them with the gas igniter by the stove, carrying them over to the vee-berth. He waited until she had climbed onto the bunk, then turned out the bare bulb, took off his jacket and shoes and sat beside her to remove his pants. She handed him her dress to put on the chair and lay waiting for him.

'I feel suddenly shy taking all my clothes off, it's been so long.'

'Not that long.'

'I know but it seems like it.' She pulled him down beside her and they embraced in silence for several moments before kissing. 'It's just like I remembered.'

'Better.' He kissed her again, more thoroughly this time.

After a while she said, 'I guess we can finish undressing now. I've stopped feeling shy.' She rose on one elbow so he could undo her bra, then lay back and raised her hips for him to slide her knickers down her legs. She kicked them off and pulled his down to his knees. They lay naked in the candle light stroking each other, feeling the warmth of the summer night on their bare skin.

'This is enough for me but I suppose you want more,' she said running her hand down his thigh and onto his groin, coaxing him semi-erect.

'And I suppose you'd prefer to talk,' he said kissing his way down over her breasts to her stomach.

'That would be nice. But this is nice, too. Which will it be?' she asked, gripping him firmly.

'I'm in your hands, as they say,' said Spike.

'In that case, we'll talk later.' She swung her leg over his and pulled herself on top of him. They made love with long languid couplings, before collapsing together in a loose embrace.

A shiver from her made him draw the newly-laundered sheet up over them, as the perspiration cooled on their bodies. She sat up and reached across him to blow out the candle stubs, then lay back down in the hollow of his arm.

'"Put out the light and then put out the light." I always think of that line whenever I blow out a candle. It's so sad.'

'Are you feeling sad now?'

'Only a little – and not about you. Just residual stuff about my daughter. I'm sorry, Spike.'

'Don't be. We can't help how we feel.'

'Can't we? Sometimes, if I catch myself in time, I can stop certain feelings. But sometimes they sneak up and wash right over me.'

'Is that what happened just now? You didn't seem sad when we first arrived.'

'I wasn't. I was so excited about being alone with you again.'

'Me too. I didn't want to compare notes in the pub with the others. All I could think of was getting you back here to myself on the Mongoose,' Spike said.

'Yes, it's lovely being naked with you and holding you inside me again. What I've been dreaming about since you left.'

'And then something changed,' he said. 'You left me. Why, what did I say or do to put you off, Ama?'

'Nothing – nothing, you were wonderful, it was wonderful...'

'Then what?'

'Just old stuff. It was a feeling that snuck up on me.'

'You scared me. I thought you'd gone off me. We hardly know each other and here I am, pushing myself on you as if nothing had happened in the years since we separated. Do you think we're making a mistake, rushing back into it?'

'Now you're scaring me, Spike. Are you having second thoughts about us?'

'Only when I feel you moving away from me. Then I get worried. We barely know anything about each other's lives in all those years. Why's that, anyway?' he said.

'I was afraid I'd swamp you with all my old baggage. I'm not proud of my failed marriages. Some parts were sordid and degrading. It took me a long time and quite a few therapy sessions to get my self-respect back. My daughter is about all I've salvaged from my train wreck of a life.'

'No good friends?'

'Some good, very dear friends. Or I wouldn't be here to tell the tale.'

'Anyone in particular I should know about?'

'If you mean, men, only one at present. And not in the way you think. We're not having an affair or anything.'

'So, why's he special?'

'He's an old beau from way back. A lawyer who's helping me find Ocean and bring her home. I've only recently met him. He had a runaway daughter himself and he agreed to help me.'

'Should I be jealous of him, Ama?'

'Envious maybe. He has an elegant French-Canadian wife, who is a juvenile court judge, three adult children and three beautiful grandchildren.'

'Now I'm envious as well as jealous. Will I get to meet him to see if I'm still in with a chance?'

'Seeing as I'm lying here stark naked in your bed and he is a happily married man, I'd say you have nothing to worry about. It's me who should be worried.'

'What about?'

'Like you say. I know almost nothing of your past life, except when we were together and your behaviour then was not above reproach, as I recall.'

'I freely admit I was a callow youth in those days and not immune to the occasional bit on the side. But if we are going to get into mud-slinging, there was plenty to go around.'

She turned in his arms and looked into his face for a few moments, then smiled and lay back with one hand on his cheek. 'It's fun to joke about our youthful indiscretions. They were harmless enough, I suppose. I'm talking about more serious relationships, longer lasting ones with baggage attached. Don't you think we should discuss them at some point?'

'Make sure there aren't any unexploded mines which could blow up on us, you mean?' he said.

'At least if we knew where they were, we could avoid stepping on them, couldn't we? Although I'm not sure I like the idea of living in a minefield.'

'Well, speaking for myself, I don't know of anything that would cause serious damage. More like embarrassment or discomfort than pain. Do you think we should have full disclosure right away? Why not on a need to know basis?'

'Okay,' said Ama. 'Is there anyone in particular I should know about, Spike? Currently, I mean, not past history, over and done with.'

'Family, that's all. And my ex, who I keep hoping is over and done with, but she has a way of reappearing in my life at unexpected moments.'

'You mean she's not over and done with you yet? Do you think she might surface again if you and I get back together, Spike?'

'She's always been a sort of loose cannon ever since we split up. Hard to predict what she may do. However, she's in another country with an ocean between us.'

'So does ex mean divorced or only separated?'

'She doesn't want a divorce and won't agree to one. As I had no plans to re-marry, I haven't bothered pushing for one. Contested divorces are expensive. So, she remains Mrs. Drummond.'

'Sounds as though you prefer us to remain under the radar.'

'Not a bad idea for the time being, don't you think, Ama?'

'I'll take you on any terms, Spike, I'm so glad to have you back in my life.' She hugged him close and pressed herself against him.

For awhile, they lay silent, content to stroke and kiss each other, then curled together on the vee-berth, feeling the slight movement of the boat beneath them.

'When will you be able to bring the Mongoose down to Arcadia, Spike?'

'I'm not sure and neither is Fergus. The autopilot broke down and I don't know whether I can get it fixed here or not. Travis said he'd come and have a look at it.'

She burrowed closer to him. 'I don't want to go back home without you, Spike. It feels so good having your arms around me again.'

In the morning, sun pouring through the porthole above the bunk woke Spike up, bathed in sweat. He crawled out of Ama's sleeping embrace and had a quick shower in the tepid water from the storage tank. He put the coffee on while he prepared fresh fruit for the pancakes he was planning. Although he tried not to wake her, she was sitting propped up with pillows in the vee-berth when he brought the tray from the galley. He placed it across her knees and went back for the coffee. She patted the space beside her for him to sit.

'Mmm, perfect,' she said, kissing his cheek. 'Will it be like this when we live aboard properly?'

'The menu may change from time to time. Porridge one day, kippers another.'

She shuddered. 'Perhaps I'll have the continental option on those days, just coffee and croissants.'

'Wait until the snow and ice is a foot thick on deck, then you'll change your finicky foreign ways.'

'Maybe. Aren't you having any, Spike? They're delicious.' She fed him a fork-full from her plate.

'Not hungry yet. I'll just watch you eat while I have my coffee,' he said. 'I want to remember you like this, maple syrup dripping off your chin.' He reached over to lick it off, then kissed her sticky mouth.

'Let me finish my breakfast first, Spike.' She pushed him away and wiped her mouth and then his, with a napkin. 'Sit still and talk to me, till I'm done.'

'What shall we do this morning, Ama – go for a walk around the port?'

'I'd rather lie on the deck in the sun. I feel like I've been non-stop since I came back from the wake. Have we got any deckchairs on this ship?'

'Only boat cushions – I can spread them on the hatch, will that do?'

'Perfect. I'll lie on the cushions and you can entertain me.'

'With everyone watching us? I'd rather stay right here.'

'I was thinking more of you reading to me, while I sunbathe. Nothing too strenuous in my weakened state. I need to regain my strength. Is there any more coffee?'

'Yes. I'll have some too. I feel dehydrated after all that alcohol last night.'

'It was a lovely evening, Spike. Lovely dinner, lovely acting, lovely play.'

'Yes, we need a copy of the script to make sense of our notes. I can probably borrow one from Justin.'

'But not now, Spike, I want you to myself for today. Then I really must go back, or I'll get fired for abandoning everyone in mid-rehearsal.'

He took the tray back to the galley to clear up, while Ama was in the shower. He lay on the vee-berth, waiting for her to come out. She emerged with a towel round her and drying her damp hair. He removed the towel from her and slowly dried her off as she stood in front of him, then pulled her down on top of the tangled covers. For over half an hour they rolled about, first one then the other on top until finally they lay side by side fingers interlaced, replete.

'Ama, I know you have to go but I don't want you to. Couldn't you stay another night?'

'And then another and another,' she said. 'What's the use, we'd only keep thinking about having to part and spoiling our time together. I must get back, I promised.'

'You're a hard woman, Ama, I'd forgotten that part of you. I was always the weak one, making promises and breaking them.'

'Don't joke, Spike. You know it was exactly the opposite. I was the promise breaker. But I've changed. I try to keep my promises now. People depend on me. Don't make me let them down.'

He turned to face her and saw tears on her cheeks. 'I've made you cry. I'm sorry. I've become more selfish in my old age, always thinking of myself first.' He wiped the tears away with the corner of the sheet.

'It's not your fault,' she said, 'I keep thinking of those lost years when we might have been together, had children together, worked in the theatre together. Now I really am going to cry.'

'But we have children, Ama, you have a daughter, I have a son. We can't un-wish our children. If we hadn't separated, they wouldn't exist.'

'Oh, I know that, but sometimes I wonder what our children would have been like, don't you?'

'It's too late to wish for that, but we could pretend any grandchildren are ours, couldn't we?'

'I hope so, Spike. Somehow, I doubt if Ocean will ever have a child. But your son might grant our wish.'

'Well, Patrick has been with Caroline, his live-in girlfriend for three years and nothing's happened yet.'

'Perhaps we can go and visit them and urge them to get started,' Ama said.

'They live in a small flat in London behind King's Cross Station. They have a tiny garden that backs onto the Regent's Canal. They'd have to give it up if they had a baby.'

'Maybe we could buy a canal boat and moor it at the end of their garden. It would be like an extension of their flat and we'd stay in it when we came to visit,' said Ama. 'I loved the old canal boat we rented that summer.'

'Bit different from the Mongoose, floating through farmer's fields, stopping at canal-side pubs for lunch. Remember that time we took it to Stratford and moored up in the basin beside the theatre? What was the play we saw?'

'Measure for Measure but don't ask me who was in it.'

They talked for awhile about his arrival in Arcadia and whether they would live aboard the Mongoose, or stay in Ama's big rambling house-sit. They tentatively decided to begin at her place, while he worked on fitting out the boat.

'I suppose if we're going to eat with Justin and Emily, we'd better get some clothes on, Spike.'

'They'll be expecting us to turn up at the theatre to go over the notes with them from last night,' he said. 'But I don't want to do either. I prefer to stay here and massage your breasts all afternoon and then take you below and do all sorts of unspeakable things with you.'

She only smiled, pushed his hands away and went into the toilet cubicle to run some water in the hand basin. He lay on the vee-berth watching her through the open door as she soaped her torso. She finished washing and came back to stand in front of him. He sat up and put his arms round her naked waist and pressed his face to her breasts. 'I'll promise you anything, Ama, as long as I can hold you like this.'

'Okay, promise me you'll make the hard decisions about how irresponsible we are to everyone from now on.' She pushed him back down on the bed and lay on top of him, kissing his face. 'Do you think I wouldn't rather do this all day than have to go and eat lunch with the gorgeous green-eyed, flame-haired Emily?'

'Hmmm, when you put it like that, I see where my duty lies.'

He rolled her off him and kissed his way down to her feet, then stood up and put on his clean shorts and shirt. He picked up the damp towel and snapped it at her bottom.

'Up you wanton and make yourself decent. Up, up, I say.' He snapped the towel at her again. 'You want discipline, I'll show you discipline.' He continued snapping the towel in the air as Ama dodged off the vee-berth, clutching her clothes and ducked into the toilet cubicle, locking the door. He brushed his hair, found his notepad and rapped on the door. 'I'll be waiting for you on deck and if you're not topside in five minutes, I'll break the door down.'

'Please yourself, it's your door,' she called.

'Don't you sauce me, my girl, or I'll have you over my knee,' he called back, as he climbed up the companionway steps to wait for her.

She reappeared a few minutes later in her new summer dress and sandals. She hoisted her dress up to show him a pink welt on her thigh. 'I don't think much of your new self-discipline.'

He bent down and kissed it. 'Sorry, I got a bit carried away with my new role as captain. I have to maintain the great traditions of the navy. Rum, sodomy and the lash.'

'Next time, I'll just have the rum, please.' She took his hand and he helped her ashore.

They wandered up to the theatre but Justin and Emily were rehearsing some new business they wanted to try out. The four of them chatted briefly about the possibility of a joint production of Shakespeare in modern English and Spike and Ama shared their notes of where they felt the audience lost them because of the language.

'We won't disturb you any longer now,' said Spike. 'We can catch you up another time.'

'Yes, let's arrange to meet again in Arcadia when Spike gets there and we can have a proper talk about working together,' said Ama.

'I love the idea,' said Emily, hugging them goodbye.

'And I think we'd make a great team,' Justin said. 'Let's make it soon.'

They left the theatre and walked out to the point and sat staring out to sea, beside the red and white lighthouse.

'When do you think you'll arrive, Spike?'

'I don't know – in a few days probably. In the meantime, I'm going to dismantle the autopilot to find out what's wrong.'

'I wish I could help but I'm not much use, am I?'

'You will be, once you get familiar with the Mongoose. She's not high tech, Ama, you'll catch on in no time.'

They lay sprawled on the smooth cushiony lava rocks around the lighthouse a while longer, then strolled back to the Mongoose to gather Ama's belongings and put them in her dusty old red Toyota.

'Make me go, Spike, or I'll just stay here hanging around your neck forever.'

'Suits me,' he said, leaning against the car and holding her close to him.

'Exert some of your new self-discipline,' she said, 'I can feel mine evaporating.'

He opened the door for her but she made no move to get in, clinging to him.

'Don't start crying, Ama, or I'll never let you leave.'

'I can't help it, Spike. I don't want to go back alone. You'll have to be brutal to me – tell me I'm old, ugly and fat and you've had enough of me.'

He eased her into the driver's seat and buckled her seat belt. 'You're younger than me, more beautiful than I deserve, slimmer than I remembered and I can never get enough of you.' He closed the door and kissed her through the open window. 'Now go before I change my mind and lock you below deck.'

He stepped back away from the car and waved her off as she drove along the quay and turned the corner by the Sail Loft, to disappear from his view. He stood staring at the empty street before turning to walk back to his boat.

CHAPTER NINE

Ama drove back to Arcadia in a state of deepening sadness, tears leaking down her face. She felt too depressed to bother to wipe them away, occasionally licking the salt taste off her lips. The old red Toyota went slower and slower until she finally drifted to a stop on the shoulder of the road, put her head on the steering wheel and gave in to the sobs which convulsed her body. She got out of the car and walked first in one direction, then turned and stumbled along the gravel shoulder back towards Bridewell.

After she had been walking for some minutes, her crying stopped. She stood uncertainly at the side of the road, looking back at her little red car in the distance. She tried to analyse what had come over her to cause this outburst, as she walked back to the car but could come to no conclusion. Whatever had triggered it had released something inside her and she felt unaccountably better, almost light-headed by the time she sat again behind the wheel.

On the rest of the drive to Arcadia she was full of plans for the joint theatre venture with Spike and Justin and Emily. It was only when she was pulling into the driveway in front of her big rambling house-sit that she realised what had overwhelmed her. It was a feeling of despair about Ocean. She let herself in and dropped her bag in the hall. She went through to the large open-plan kitchen with its old harvest oak table, still cluttered with things just as she had left them, to go to see Spike in Bridewell.

Her laptop stood open on the table and she switched it on to see what messages had accumulated while she was away. She checked her email and almost marked one as junk before she recognised it. It was the law firm of her old friend and former lover, Jasper Falkenham. She opened it with mounting nervousness.

Sorry to have been so long getting back in touch with you, Ama. I finally have some news for you. Not all good, I'm afraid. As I suspected, your daughter's boyfriend Clay had gone to ground in Ontario and I managed to track him down to a trailer park in Stratford. But the police had got there before me and he was already in custody by the time I arrived. Fortunately, Ocean had been absent when the police took him away. She was staying in a farmhouse outside the city which belonged to his supplier. They were using it as a marijuana grow-op and she had been working there with them when I finally found her.

It took awhile to gain her boyfriend's confidence and persuade him to tell me where she was hiding. I offered to defend him in court in return for providing the information of her whereabouts. It turns out that he has a string of charges against him in several provinces, because they moved about staying one jump ahead of the drug police. To his credit, Clay hasn't implicated her, saying that she was only his girlfriend and knew nothing about his drug dealing. The police didn't believe him and want her for questioning but so far haven't found her.

I advised her to leave with me, because if she were found at the grow-op she would definitely wind up in jail. I persuaded her not to go on the run but to return to Montreal and stay with her father while awaiting a court appearance. With a little help from my wife Delphine, your ex-husband has reluctantly agreed to this arrangement, as she has him completely in her sway and they have become fast friends.

I must admit to finding Ronnie amusing and entertaining and not quite the black-hearted villain you led me to believe. He has even offered to find Ocean a minor role in his new TV mini-series, after I told him it would help me to get her leniency when her court case came up. And Delphine assured him the courts always rule in favour of any attempts at rehabilitation, rather than prison.

So that is where things stand at present, with one proviso. Ocean is adamant that she does not want to return to live with you, but only with her father. I have my own views on this, and will give you chapter and verse on the whole situation when we meet - soon – for our next boozy lunch in Halifax. Give me a call in my office and we'll arrange something. Your devoted solicitor, Jasper.

Grinning with relief, Ama re-read the email twice before ringing his office, but it was after hours in Montreal and she only got his answering service. She left him a fervent thank-you and said she would call again tomorrow. Pouring herself a large glass of red wine, she tried to do some work while she ate, but couldn't settle to anything. She needed to talk to someone. Spike? No, something warned her against it. She finished her meal and got back into her car to drive across town to see her old confidant.

It was still early evening as she parked in front of the big Georgian colonial house with its wrap-around veranda and fine view of the harbour. Mrs. Spengler and Kitty were sitting in rocking chairs knitting and chatting.

'You two look very industrious – knitting socks for our troops, or Gerald?' She climbed the front steps to hug each of them in turn.

Mrs. Spengler shook her head and held up a partially finished child's cardigan. 'Neither. These are for a new family at the refuge. You've been neglecting us, Ama. For that old flame, I expect.'

'I heard you'd disappeared suddenly,' said Kitty. 'I thought maybe you'd had news of your daughter.'

'You're both right. I've just been to spend a couple of days with Spike in Bridewell on his old boat. And when I got back here there was a message from an old friend who's been helping me locate Ocean.'

'Good news, I hope,' said Kitty. 'Sit down and tell us all about it. This tea's gone cold, maybe we should have something stronger, Sarah. Let's have a whisky sour to celebrate your news. Sarah makes a wicked cocktail. I can never get them to taste as good as hers.'

'Be right back,' said Sarah. 'You two go ahead, Kitty can fill me in later.' She padded off into the darkened house.

'It's not all good news, Kitty. Jasper, my lawyer friend, has tracked them down to Stratford, Ontario but he says the police found where they were and arrested her boyfriend, Clay. Ocean had gone to a farm to stay and he didn't tell them where she was. Jasper has spoken to her and advised her to leave immediately before the police find her there.'

'Leave the farm – why?'

'Because it's only a cover for a marijuana grow-op, he said, and if she's caught there she'd be arrested too.'

'Where did she go. Does he know?'

Ama nodded, 'You'll never guess. She's with Ronnie.'

'Ronnie – your ex?' said Kitty. 'But I thought you told me he wouldn't help...'

'That's just it, he wouldn't when I asked him but apparently Jasper's wife persuaded him to take Ocean in – Delphine's a juvenile court judge and thinks Ocean might get off with a suspended sentence in her father's custody, so Ronnie agreed to do it.'

'This Jasper must be a very good old friend, Ama, to get so involved.'

'You'd love him, Kitty. He's wonderful. Long ago we had an affair but he's married with three children and three grandchildren. He's doing all this as a favour. I told him I could only pay some of his expenses.'

'Perhaps he's hoping for some other kind of payment, Ama.'

'That's what I said and I told him I was in love with Spike and couldn't sleep with him or anything.'

'And he's doing this just as an old friend?'

'That's when he told me the story of his own daughter, who ran off and disappeared for over two years. He travelled half the globe trying to find her and his wife had a nervous breakdown,' said Ama.

She recounted the tale of Jasper's daughter Elvire and why he wanted to help her find Ocean.

'He does sound a wonderful man, Ama. I'm sorry I sounded so cynical. You don't often meet people like that. If he ever comes down here to see you, you must bring him round. I'd love to meet him and so would Sarah.'

Mrs. Spengler pushed open the screen door with her ample backside and set a tray of drinks down beside them. 'Who's this I'd love to meet, Kitty?'

'Another one of Ama's old beaus – a lawyer from Montreal.'

'By all means, bring him around, Ama. Kitty and me will entertain him while you're busy with your old sailor,' said Sarah.

'I could use a good lawyer,' said Kitty. 'My one here is getting too old, he says, and wants to retire.'

'Well, I'm supposed to call Jasper tomorrow to meet him for lunch – that's our deal – I take him out to lunch and we exchange information on Ocean. He mentioned that there's some fish restaurants in Arcadia he'd like to try.'

'He can come here for his lunch and we can proposition him, Ama,' said Sarah.

'If it's something unusual he just might take you up on it. I got the impression Jasper's not overly busy with clients but he likes to keep his hand in. If he does come down here all the way from Montreal for lunch, I'd like to show him the theatre and ask him for his ideas. He still loves theatre, that's how I met him.'

'If he's coming from Montreal, he'll need to stay over, Ama. We can offer to put him up here for the night,' said Kitty. 'He's bound to enjoy the view of the harbour from the front guest room.'

'I'm not sure I should trust you two with Jasper from what you've told me,' said Ama. 'Especially as his wife is being so kind about helping Ocean.'

'Ancient history,' said Sarah. 'We're boringly respectable nowadays, aren't we, Kitty?'

'Sad but true,' said Kitty, 'However we can still appreciate the company of a handsome man. I take it we can assume any ex-lover of yours is good-looking, Ama.'

'I'm afraid he's more than that, Kitty. He will charm the pants off you. He nearly did with me again. The only thing that stopped me was being in love with Spike. And his wife,

Delphine. And his three children. And his three grandchildren.'

Sarah handed them each a whisky sour. 'Here's to Jasper and his three grandchildren, lucky devil.'

'Invite him soon, Ama and we'll arrange a dinner party with some of your theatre friends. That will appeal to him more than an evening with two old widows,' said Kitty. 'You can take him to lunch at the Lobster Pot and discuss news of Ocean, then show him around the theatre and come back here for the party. How does that sound?'

'How can he refuse,' said Ama, 'he'll be putty in our hands.' They drank off their whisky sours and Mrs. Spengler poured them another from the cocktail shaker.

'We'll get him in a good mood with a few of these,' said Sarah, 'before we hit him with our propositions.'

'You haven't told us why you raced off to Bridewell to meet Spike,' said Kitty. 'Nothing wrong, I hope, between you two?'

'The only thing wrong is that he's stuck in Bridewell for the time being. His boat's automatic steering has broken down and he and his friend Fergus are trying to fix it.'

'How long before he arrives, Ama?' asked Kitty. 'You must be getting way behind schedule at the theatre.'

'I tried to wring a date from him but he couldn't say. Maybe another week – depends on his friend.'

'What with going to Halifax for the wake, then chasing off to Montreal after Ocean and then again to be with your sailor in Bridewell, they must wonder who's minding the store here, Ama,' said Sarah.

'I know, and that's not all. Spike wants me to take on a joint project with the Bridewell theatre group. As if I don't have enough on my plate.'

'What kind of project, Ama?' Kitty asked. 'Anything I can help you with?'

'It's all still at the discussion stage, Kitty. Basically, it's a new approach to doing Shakespeare by modernising the language, to make it understandable to contemporary audiences.'

'But isn't that why people go to see Shakespeare – to hear the language?' said Kitty.

'Up to a point, yes, I suppose. But if they can't understand it, then it's sort of like watching a play in a foreign language. You can't follow it.'

'Just like the opera – you haven't got a clue what they're saying,' said Sarah. 'Kitty likes to go but I gave up on it. Sit there for three hours and only hear two or three good tunes.'

Ama said, 'It all makes a change to live in that fantasy opera world for a few hours, before coming back down to earth in our old theatre, where we have to do everything on the cheap and expect the actors to work for nothing.'

'Not nothing, Ama. For love. Isn't that why we all do it?' said Kitty.

'At least you get paid a little, Ama, to make it all happen,' said Sarah. 'And I'm sure I'll enjoy whatever you do, more than the New York Metropolitan Opera with all its millions.'

Ama hugged her. 'Thanks for reminding me, Sarah. I'd better get moving. I have a ton of things to do at the theatre in the morning, if we're ever to keep to our scheduled opening date in September.'

'Do you think you'll be able to keep to it, Ama, if Spike won't be here for another week or more?' said Kitty.

'I'm determined we'll have some kind of opening, even if it's just a taster and a party. Right now, I'm heading for bed so I can make up for lost time in the morning. I always feel better after visiting both of you.'

'It's the whisky sours, not us,' said Sarah. 'Drive safely.'

Ama had set her alarm for 8am and was about to leave for the theatre when she remembered Jasper's email. She knew it was too early to call him. He told her he wouldn't be in his office before ten, so she sent him a quick email, knowing if she waited till after ten, she would be embroiled in other stuff and unable to call him till the evening.

Dear Jasper, What a relief to hear from you with your news of Ocean. I'm amazed at how soon you've found out so much, when I had spent fruitless months and got nowhere. I had no idea you intended to get so personally involved. I assumed you would just phone some of the people in your network you told me about, to see what you could learn.

Although I'm very happy you've done all this, I'm embarrassed to have embroiled you so deeply in my personal problems. Are you sure you want to defend Ocean's boyfriend in court? Stratford is a long way from Montreal. The fact that you and Delphine have persuaded Ronnie to take on Ocean's custody just bowls me over – I can't quite believe it yet.

I want to hear all about it but I simply can't take anymore time off from the theatre. I'm already hopelessly behind and Spike is delayed with his old boat in Bridewell. He can't join me for another week or so. You mentioned that you might like to come down to Arcadia so I can take you to lunch again and we can talk about Ocean's situation. I can do better than that. Two very dear women friends would like to host a party for you, with some of our theatre actors and designers at their lovely old colonial house, where they have offered to put you up for the night while you're here.

I have to confess that I painted such a glowing character portrait of you that they can't wait till you arrive. I, too would love it if you will say yes and I promise to take you to the

Lobster Pot, which is the best fish restaurant in Arcadia. Short of offering you my body, which is already spoken for, this is the best I can do by way of recompense for all you're doing for my daughter.
Please say yes.
Much love, Ama.

She clicked send, closed her laptop and headed for the theatre.

There were only two other vehicles in the Regency Theatre car park. This must mean that Frankie, her costume maker, was here already as well as Arthur, the stage carpenter. She went in through the unlocked stage door to look for them. Nobody was in the wardrobe department or onstage but she could hear loud voices arguing in the front-of-house foyer when she walked through the darkened stalls.

'You've got it inside out, Arthur, we'll have to take it all back down,' said Frankie, who stood at the bottom of the long electrician's step-ladder. He was bracing it for Arthur at the top, almost invisible under the voluminous folds of gauze draped over his shoulders.

'Are you crazy? It's taken me half an hour risking my neck to get it up here. No way I'm taking it all down again.'

'I'm back,' said Ama. 'Sorry I had to rush off and leave you to it but I'm here now, rested up and ready to work.'

'Ama, thank god you're back,' Arthur called down to her. 'Will you please tell this finicky fusspot that it doesn't matter which side is showing. It's just bloody gauze.'

'It matters to me, all the seams are showing, aren't they, Ama?' Frankie said.

'Nobody will even notice once it's back-lit. I can't tell the difference and I'm right in the middle of it,' said Arthur.

'Well we can, can't we, Ama, and I want it back down to turn it right side out,' said Frankie.

'No sense asking me, my eyes aren't adjusted from outdoors yet. It's brilliant sunshine this morning.'

'I had it all folded properly so it would fall the right way when you attached it, Arthur. I don't know how you messed it up.'

'To hell with it, do it yourself. I haven't got time to fiddle around with this. I only offered to do it as a favour because I know you hate climbing ladders. If I take it down, Frankie, I'm not putting it back up again,' said Arthur.

'Why don't we leave it for the time being and see how it looks fully unfolded,' Ama said. 'Come on down and we'll have a coffee and go over our work schedule, Arthur. Maybe we'll have time later to change it.'

'Claire's going to notice it straight off,' said Frankie. 'She'll insist we put it right.'

'Then she can climb up there and do it herself,' said Arthur. He dumped the bundles of gauze off his shoulders and they floated down, billowing out like a parachute over the foyer.

'It looks wonderful, Frankie, just like Claire said. Once we have it back-lit it will transform the whole front-of-house,' said Ama.

Arthur climbed down and the three of them gazed up at the shimmering cloud above them. Mollified by her remark, the grim set of Frankie's face relaxed as he smiled at his handiwork.

'That Claire is a wonder alright. I have to admit this wasn't such a crazy idea,' Arthur said.

'Let's bring our coffee out here and we can talk while we admire it,' said Ama.

They fetched coffee from the Green room and sat at the bar to drink it and consult the work sheets which were long and daunting.

'No way we're going to get through all this by ourselves, even with a wonder-worker like Claire,' said Ama. 'Spike won't be here for another week or so to help us.'

'We need to organise a work party,' said Arthur. 'With a bunch of volunteers, I could start to make inroads into this backlog. Lots of it is unskilled. Like hanging that canopy.' He winked at Ama.

'Couldn't do any worse than the skilled help,' Frankie said.

'But who could we ask? Gloria is always so busy with her bakery,' said Ama. 'Kitty and Mrs. Spengler have offered but they're getting a little old for heavy work.'

'Better not let Sarah hear you say that,' said Arthur, 'she reckons she can work as well as any man in this town. She always worked right alongside her husband before he drowned.'

'I'm gonna need plenty of extra hands, making all the hangings Claire has in mind to cover up the shabby auditorium,' said Frankie. 'Did she tell you she wants to make slipcovers for all the seats in both the stalls and the balcony? Can you imagine how long it would take me? I'd want a dozen volunteers just for that.'

'What time is Claire coming in today, did she say?' asked Ama.

'Around ten,' said Arthur. He pulled out his old pocket watch. 'It's quarter past already, she's late.'

'That playboy friend of hers must be pretty demanding,' said Frankie. 'She's always late.'

'Don't forget she's holding down a big museum contract. We're only a sideshow and lucky she can spare us the time,' said Ama. 'Let's be grateful we have her at all.'

'No wonder she's so skinny, everybody is wearing her out,' said Arthur.

'Claire's not worn out, she's anorexic,' said Frankie. 'Have you seen what she eats? God knows where all that energy comes from. I reckon she's on drugs of some kind.'

'Stop gossiping about her and leave her alone,' said Ama. 'As far as I'm concerned, she's a godsend and her personal life is none of our business. We need her help. Something's got to give and I don't know what.'

'That's what I been telling Frankie – we haven't got time to waste fiddling with gauze canopies.'

'And I've told him, that Claire said it was a priority. She says it's important as it sets the tone when people arrive,' said Frankie.

'Stop bickering, darlings. Mother Theresa is here to perform more miracles. But first I require a handmaiden, Ama.'

'Claire – thank god... we've ground to a halt,' said Ama, as Claire air-kissed her.

'Stop whatever you're doing and come with me, all of you.' She linked arms with Ama and led them back out the stage door to her big silver SUV van. Opening the rear access, she began pulling out a large rolled up poster. 'I've been to my favourite poster shop in Halifax and brought you these to cover up all the mirrors everywhere. Look at this.' She unrolled a colourful railway design of a steam train running out of a tunnel in the Rockies. 'Go ahead, open them up. See what you think.' She hauled out an armful and passed them round.

'I love this one,' said Frankie. 'It's the Banff Springs Hotel at Lake Louise.'

'There's a whole series of those we can spread around the front of house as people enter. From Atlantic to Pacific,' said Claire.

'Look at this sepia tint of street jazz musicians,' said Ama. 'Is there any more of these, Claire?'

'At least a dozen. I can't decide whether to group them or intersperse them around the theatre. What do you think?'

'I'd have to wait and see when we get them inside.'

'What have you brought for behind the bar, Claire?' asked Arthur. 'There's an acre of de-silvered mirrors to cover up.'

'Well, we are in Nova Scotia so I thought it ought to be a maritime theme. I found lots of Cunard steamship posters, with all these elegant art deco people posing on sweeping decks of ocean liners.'

Ama gathered up an armful of rolls. 'Let's bring them all inside and spread them out to see what you've got. We can hold them up for you to decide, Claire.'

They emptied the back of her car and carried them into the theatre foyer to unroll on the faded red carpeting, while Claire paced about looking at the empty mirrored spaces, deciding how to display them. For the next hour, she tried differing combinations around the foyer and up the curving staircase to the balcony. Ama and the two men held them up for her, turning and swapping them at her dictates while she photographed them on her cellphone and tried to make up her mind. At last, she paused.

'Alright, I think I have a tentative layout, so here's what we'll do. Ama and I will put them up with sticky-tack temporarily, so you and Frankie can get on with your own jobs,' said Claire. 'Frankie, I saw some bolts of cloth in your car for the seating in the stalls. Will you cut out and roughly pin one seat cover in each of the patterns we chose and then we can make a choice which to use. Arthur can start removing the centre seats from the first four rows so we can begin framing the thrust stage. This is just donkey work, Arthur, so get some volunteers in to help you, and you can supervise while you rough out the side ramps. Okay?'

'We were talking about a work party when you arrived, Claire,' said Frankie. 'I'm going to need lots of help to recover all these seats here and in the balcony, too.'

'Well, we all have networks so let's each put the word out. Nobody shows up here tomorrow without at least two volunteers in tow. Tell them we need each of them to find two more and we'll work out a rota, so they come when it suits them.'

'I've already lined up my first two,' said Ama. 'Kitty and Mrs. Spengler have volunteered and between them they know everybody in Arcadia, I think.'

'You mentioned using some old fishing nets for our canopies, Ama. We could use a few of those unemployed fishermen as well, to help Arthur with our new staging. Do you know any of them, yourself?' asked Claire.

'Not personally, but Sarah - Mrs. Spengler, is a fisherman's widow and she knows all the families.'

'Good. When you bring her in, she and Arthur can start recruiting. Meantime, let's see what we can do ourselves.'

Ama found a package of adhesive blue tack in the office and she and Claire used it to stick up the posters in a montage on the old bar mirrors until they were covered to Claire's satisfaction.

'I'm longing to hear about your latest liaison with your old flame, Ama. When am I going to meet him?'

'Not for awhile yet, I'm afraid. He's having problems with his old boat. And he has to wait for his friend to fix it and sail down here with him.'

'Did you do any sailing with him?'

'No, we didn't have any time, we were too busy. But we stayed on the boat while I was there. It was a lovely break from here. Things have been snowing me under and I needed to get away.'

'And is he still as keen on you as before, or has he cooled down after your first encounter?'

'You wouldn't believe us, Claire. We were at it like two ferrets in a sack, to quote Spike. I don't quite understand what's happening and neither does he, but whatever it is, we want it to continue.'

'Takes you by surprise, doesn't it? At our age, to still have those powerful feelings for someone. Even if it doesn't last,' said Claire. 'Enjoy it while you can.'

'Oh, oh... are you trying to tell me something. Are you having problems, Claire? I thought you told me Antony was devoted.'

'He's not the problem, Ama. I am. I've had some tests done recently and the results are not good.'

'What do you mean tests, what sort of tests?'

'Blood tests. You know how I haven't been able to put any weight on and my GP was getting worried. She ran some tests and she was right. Something is wrong. Seems like I might have pancreatic cancer and that's why I'm so thin.'

'Oh Claire, you're so full of energy. I can't believe you're ill. Are you sure?'

'That's what I said. I feel okay but I keep getting thinner.'

'I'm not surprised, you eat like a sparrow. What will they do? Will you have to be in hospital?'

'More tests for now, until they're sure. Then treatment, I guess. I didn't want to ask.'

'Does Antony know?'

'I haven't told him yet. He's so emotional I couldn't handle it – he'd upset us both.'

Ama climbed down from the stepladder to hug her. 'This is awful, Claire. What will you do?'

'Keep working, that's what my GP said. She says it's not the end of the world so I'm not to start imagining the worst, there's lots they can do these days.'

'Well, that sounds promising anyway.'

'Oh, she's very upbeat, my GP, talks a good line. But then she's not the one with the cancer, is she?'

'Are you sure you want to keep doing this, Claire – shouldn't you be resting?'

'Definitely not. Sitting around feeling sorry for myself would be fatal. I want to be occupied with something that takes my mind off my diagnosis.'

'But you've got your big museum project looming. Won't doing two projects be too much?

'Not if they stop me from brooding on myself. The busier the better. And if this isn't enough, I may look for something else as well.'

'Oh god, Claire, I feel terrible. Is there anything I can do? Will you come and stay with me for awhile till you get the results of these new tests?'

'I couldn't, Ama. Antony would get suspicious. I'm sorry, I shouldn't have told you, but I had to tell someone and Antony's hopeless. He'd probably try to send me to some Swiss clinic in the Alps or somewhere.'

'We'll tell him I asked you to stay, as I'm stressed out because my daughter is missing and the theatre is in a critical state. Both of which are true. And besides, it will switch the emphasis on to me, so he won't suspect anything.'

'I'm tempted, Ama. I'm all over the place since I heard the news. I'm frightened I might start to cry at any time and give the game away.'

'You can cry on my shoulder as much as you like. And any time in between, we can keep busy with all your plans for the theatre. Perhaps you'll let me help with your travelling museum project, too.'

'Maybe just a few days with you, till I come to terms with this new me.'

'Good. That's settled then, you come home with me tonight and I can make you some of my comfort food and fatten you up. You can keep me company till Spike arrives.'

'This is such a relief for me to have someone to talk to about this. I've been going round and round in my head and getting panic attacks...oh Christ, Ama, now I really am going to bawl.'

Ama steered her to a faded plush banquette and held her, while big gulping sobs shook her thin frame. Ama stroked her back and waited for the emotional turmoil to subside. She gave her a package of tissues from her pocket to mop up the aftermath.

'Sounded like you needed to get that out, Claire. Did it help?'

'Wonderful, I loved spilling it all out. I'm such a drama queen, Ama. I hope you know what you're letting yourself in for. I told you, I'm all over the place.'

'So am I these days. We can take turns. Let's go to the Green Room and have some coffee and you can repair the damage. We wouldn't want Arthur and Frankie to see you and have to explain everything.'

'God forbid. They'd want to sort me all out and tell me what to do. Men love solving our problems for us, don't they?'

They avoided the main auditorium and went backstage to the Green Room. Ama made fresh coffee while Claire washed her face and re-did her makeup. Ama found an open package of chocolate brownies in the fridge and they sat side by side on an old sofa, eating and drinking.

'Chocolate, the best medicine. The cure for everything, Claire.'

'That and a good weep. I feel better already. Thanks, Ama. It will be like having a sister, living with you for a few days. You can be the big sister I never had.'

'Neither did I. We can regress to being teenagers. Watch old Cary Grant videos.'

'Paint each other's toenails.'

'Eat pastries in bed,' said Ama.

'Do each other's hair,' Claire said. 'Try on our clothes.'

'None of yours would fit me and you'd drown in mine, Claire. Except for our shoes – we have the same size. I tried your kinky boots on, remember?'

'I suppose we'd better get back to work, Ama, or Arthur will come looking for us.'

'Okay, but only if you feel up to it.'

'I'm raring to go, thanks to you, sis.' She stood up and hugged Ama and they went upstairs and onstage to find Arthur.

'Where've you been?' he said. 'I wanted to ask you about these seats and you weren't in the foyer.'

'Claire needed a coffee break – we were in the Green Room. What's the problem?'

'I saw what you did with the bar mirrors. Looks great. Big improvement already. Claire, can you spare me some time to figure out exactly where the ramps will go? I phoned a couple of my retired pals to help me remove seats and they're coming after lunch. I don't want them taking out the wrong seats.'

'I can't do any more posters without Claire. You two go ahead and I'll make some phone calls while I wait,' said Ama.

She went through the stalls to sit in the foyer and study the montage Claire had created behind the bar. The gauzy canopy stirred above her head from a draft in the balcony. Although this had already made a difference to the shabby front of house, she realised it would take a lot more work on Claire's part to achieve the transformation she had promised. Ama wondered how much longer her friend could continue if the diagnosis was correct and she did have pancreatic cancer. Surely once she had to begin treatment, it would knock her frail body about so badly she would be unable to work. Ama knew only too well from other friends and family members who endured cancer treatment, the debilitating effects of chemotherapy and radiation.

With a guilty start, she realised she had been thinking of the effects on her plans for the theatre, rather than on the devastation it would bring to Claire's life. She chastised herself for even contemplating these selfish thoughts and tried to put them out of her mind. She needed to talk to Kitty and tell her of the dilemma she foresaw. Or Spike. Perhaps it would be better to talk to him instead.

In the end she did neither, for when she opened her phone to call, she saw there was a message from Jasper. As she had predicted when she sent him the email, she had forgotten all about him once she became caught up in the distractions at the theatre. She hadn't expected to hear from him so soon.

The message only asked her to call him back. As she called his office number, she wondered if he had more news of Ocean. He picked up on the second ring.

'Jasper Falkenham here,' he said, in his aloof lawyer's tone.

'Hello Jasper, that was quick. I hope it means your answer is yes.'

'Ama. I didn't recognise your number. I've cleared my desk and my calendar for the next two days. If it suits you, I can arrive tomorrow in time for our lunch engagement.'

'That's great, Jasper, shall I meet you at the airport? When does your flight get into Halifax?'

'All taken care of by Madame Laurent, my legal secretary. She has arranged a car rental and a scenic route along the lighthouse coast to Arcadia. The flight arrives in plenty of time for me to avoid the motorway.'

'And Delphine can spare you for a night? She won't mind you consorting with an old actress from your past?'

'*Au contraire*, she positively urged me to go, now that she is championing Ocean's cause. Your wayward daughter is now firmly tucked under her wing, while she awaits your ex-husband's takeover of his parental duty. Ronnie is in thrall to her and she is his keenest admirer.'

'I long to meet her in person, Jasper. Do you think she could bear to meet me, or has Ronnie painted too black a portrait of me?'

'All in good time, Ama. For now, you are my sole responsibility and I have much to tell you.'

'I hope it's not more bad news, Jasper. I don't think I can handle another dose.'

'What happened, the theatre roof collapse? You told me the fly-loft was condemned.'

'Worse. You know my amazing designer who's been transforming the place for us? She's ill and may not be able to continue.'

'I'm sorry, Ama. Is Spike there yet to help out?'

'Not for another week at least. Boat problems.'

'Sounds like you could use my assistance in more ways than one. We can talk about it over lunch when we catch up. I'll see you at about one tomorrow at the Lobster Pot. I looked it up online. Very impressive reviews.'

'Thanks for agreeing to come, Jasper. I'll phone my friend Kitty to tell her you're on the way.'

She rang Kitty next to warn her of the short notice.

'Plenty of time for Sarah and me to get organised, dear. His room is all ready for him. Who would you like to ask to the party from the theatre?'

'My new stage designer, Claire, for a start. You should see what she's done to the foyer already, Kitty. And Gloria, the baker from the market. You've seen her act in our last show. When we did the revival of Noel Coward's *Brief Encounter*.'

'Yes, she played that insufferable busybody neighbour, didn't she? Marvellous.'

'Who were you thinking of inviting, Kitty? Any of your former paramours? Or Sarah's?'

'Sarah wants to ask one or two from the women's refuge, to see if they can persuade your friend to be a patron and tap into all that old money in Montreal. I want him to meet some of our theatre board and ginger them up with some new ideas.'

'They sound a bit stuffy, Kitty. I was hoping it would be a bit livelier for Jasper. He likes a good time, as I remember. It won't be a sit-down formal dinner, will it?'

'Don't fret, Ama. Sarah and I are well-known for our parties. He won't be bored. Sarah has lined up several of her musician friends to play. And we've already planned to make it buffet-style food.'

'Sorry, Kitty. I didn't mean to tell you how to hold your own party. It's only that I suspect with Jasper's wife being a judge, they have to go to a lot of formal white-tie affairs. I was hoping this could be more casual and fun.'

'I promise you I've been honing my party skills since before you were born, Ama. He'll have a good time and so will you. I won't let anyone button-hole him for long. We want him to enjoy himself so he'll come back again. I have a feeling we're going to need his expertise if your theatre is going to be a success.'

'Let me know what I can do to help prepare, Kitty.'

'You just take him to lunch and discuss Ocean's plight. Then give him the grand tour of the theatre to meet the crew and see what you're up against. After that you can show him the town. Then leave the rest to us.'

Ama hung up and went to see Frankie in the costume loft. She found him cutting out upholstery materials for the auditorium seating.

'Hi Ama, have you come to help me cover 150 stalls seats, or would you rather make another canopy out of burlap sacking instead?' He grinned at her and indicated an empty stool for her to sit.

'I'll have to pass on both for now, Frankie. I've got something else to tell you. A change of plans. Are you ready?'

He put down his shears and faced her. 'I'm all ears.'

'You know how Claire's ideas to drastically change the staging to a multi-level open space will alter what we'll be able to do. I've been thinking, instead of doing a modern dress version of Twelfth Night, we should do a commedia del arte version of 'Oh What a Lovely War,' to take advantage of our radical new staging. What do you think?'

'But you've already started rehearsing for Twelfth Night.'

'I know. We haven't started building any of the set, though. Or making any of the costumes, either.'

'Because Claire has us side-tracked into making canopies and new seat covers.'

'If we can manage to form a work party to do the seat covers and revamp the stage, it would free you up to focus on making new costumes for 'Oh What a Lovely War.' I think you like commedia style costumes, don't you Frankie?'

'I love them, Ama. Is it a large cast? I don't really know the play. And commedia outfits are very elaborate.'

'I'm afraid it is a big cast, so we'll do lots of doubling. And I know we have some old costumes already. I've seen them in here somewhere.'

He got up from his stool and began browsing through the racks. 'I haven't seen them for ages either but you're right, they're in here somewhere.'

The two of them searched up and down the aisles until Frankie emerged triumphant, holding up a Harlequin diamond patterned costume. 'Here we are. There should be more in around here, Ama.'

'Yes, I've found a Pierrot white outfit,' she said.

They found several others which had been made for a Christmas panto and carried them all back to Frankie's cutting table.

'When you're fed up with making canopies and seat covers, Frankie, you can start refurbishing these. I'll order copies of the script online so we know what we'll have to make for the show. I haven't even begun to think about casting yet, so you can spend time researching costumes and props. I want to tell Claire about this change of play to get her thoughts on staging it.'

Ama returned to the stage and found Claire in one of the box seats off the balcony. A ladder was leaning against it from the stage with Arthur perched on it, dangling a measuring tape to the floor.

'It's going to be a steep staircase to the downstage area,' he said, 'unless we angle it further upstage.'

'Perhaps we'll put in a half landing, Arthur, to break it up and give us an extra acting area as well,' Claire said. 'What do you think, Ama?'

'Great idea. Will you do the same on the other side?'

'That's what I thought at first. Now I'm thinking of something asymmetrical. Provide more interesting opportunities for staging. Arthur wants a mirror image of this side and I want to reverse the stairs to project out over the audience and angle back to the front of stage from another half landing. You can be the final arbiter, Ama. We can go either way.'

'Will it block the ramp entrance, Claire? I love the idea of actors running up the slopes with banners and signs and stuff.'

'Not if we cantilever it over the ramp and run it back above head height. Will we, Arthur?' said Claire.

'I'd have to put in at least one support for the half landing,' he said. 'Easier to make both sides symmetrical, Ama.'

'What I had in mind allows a continuous flow from stage to box to balcony on one side, and back to stage on the other side without repetition,' Claire said. 'The same with the ramps from the stalls, one longer and shallower, the other shorter and steeper. The asymmetry opens everything up and integrates the auditorium with the stage. Makes it all more visually interesting with more possibilities for different kinds of staging. Symmetry will look more like a set for an opera or Hollywood musical.'

'You've convinced me, Claire, but Arthur has to build it. Is it do-able, Arthur, or too difficult?'

'I can do it but it will take longer and we already have a lot on our plate with all the front of house revamps Claire has in mind.'

Claire swung her long pencil-thin legs over the balcony and began to climb down the ladder, backing him down to Ama on the stage. 'This is simply a problem of logistics, Arthur, and the solution is simple, too. Delegate. You supervise and demonstrate. Put volunteers to work and only do the tricky bits yourself. I've learned not to assume all volunteers are just free labour. They all have skill sets we can use. We just have to find them. Put out the call for whoever you need at the moment. This is a community project so let them take part. You might be surprised how many respond. An hour or two on the odd afternoon or evening isn't asking that much. Get them involved, find the movers and shakers out there and get them onside. End of pep talk. It's time to get back to work. Come on, Ama, those posters are waiting for us and Arthur's pals will be here soon to yank these seats out.'

Ama and Claire continued covering the mirrors in the entrance foyer and up the wide staircase walls to the balcony landing. Along the corridor to the washrooms, the walls were lined with blistering mirrors, with the silver backings peeling off. They left the ones over the hand-basins uncovered, as Claire said they would have to replace these with cheap mirror tiles, for people to see themselves. When they finally ran out of posters, they had managed to cover every old mirror except those in the box office.

'We'll make those ones big posters of the current and upcoming shows,' said Claire.

'What shall we do about all these threadbare entrance carpets?' said Ama. 'They make the place look so shabby.'

'We rip them all out and up the staircase too,' said Claire. 'I have a contact who's an exhibition display contractor in Halifax. Arnold let's me have slightly used exhibition carpet by the mile for almost free. All we need is a good carpet layer to fit them. We can use volunteers to collect the stuff and help him, but it has to be a professional to make it look good. Maybe Arthur knows someone local we can ask to take charge, in return for some free advertising.'

They decided the auditorium carpets could be revived with a rental carpet cleaning machine.

'Refitting all this carpet would be a mammoth task unless we took all the seats out first and we haven't the time. The new seat coverings will brighten things up enough, I hope,' Claire said. 'Let's go and see if Frankie has finished the samples yet.'

In the wardrobe department, Frankie was hunched over his heavy old industrial sewing machine, surrounded by lengths of the patterned cloth he had brought that morning.

'I like this one, Frankie,' said Ama, holding up a piece of bold Art Deco material.

'I'm just sewing up the last one if you wait ten minutes. We can try them out in the stalls,' he said, not stopping as he fed the cloth under the chattering needle.

'We'll take these finished ones through and start laying them out for you,' said Claire.

She and Ama carried the covers into the auditorium stalls and draped them loosely over the seats, separating them in different rows to gauge how they looked. A few minutes later, Frankie appeared holding the last one. Taking a mouthful of pins, all three of them covered a seat each, separated far enough apart to judge. They studied the end results from different angles, trying to decide.

'I like the plain dark green best,' said Claire, 'but the zigzag pattern will disguise the old carpet better.'

'My choice, too. I like the Art Deco pattern because it fits with the theatre period,' Ama said.

'This dull gold corduroy is my pick. It will look rich when the whole house is done out the same. The zigzag is too jazzy,' said Frankie.

'Let's see what Arthur says,' said Claire. She shouted his name until he appeared on the stage, with a heavy pipe wrench in his hand.

'The bolts on some of these seats are rusted solid,' he said, peering into the darkened stalls.

'Which seat cover style do you like best, Arthur?' asked Ama.

'I like the cheapest one,' he said.

'Don't be such a philistine and give us your opinion,' said Claire.

'Okay, I like the same one you do.'

'And which one do you think that is?' she persisted.

'The navy blue with the jagged red pattern, of course.'

'Correct,' said Ama. 'Almost a unanimous verdict if we don't count Frankie.'

'Don't mind me,' said Frankie. 'I'm only the drudge who makes them.'

'Now don't sulk, Frankie,' said Claire, 'you've been consulted. And if everyone hates them, think of how you can gloat about it later. Anyway, you're not making them, your volunteer work party will stitch them all together, like Santa's elves.'

'Don't remove the covers yet. We'll leave them overnight and look at them again in the morning,' said Ama. 'Now I have some good news for you. I've persuaded Claire to stay with me for a few days, so we can go over what to do next in the evenings and she doesn't have to drive in all that way. We can plan how to stage our first production which is not going to be Twelfth Night, even though I've started rehearsals. Instead, I want to take full advantage of Claire's makeover of the theatre and do a commedia del arte style production of Oh What A Lovely War. It's perfect for all these levels and acting areas. She's even promised me a trap door to do the trench scenes, isn't that right, Arthur – you will be able to make one?'

'Yep. I looked up some different plans on the internet that all looked too complicated, so I've come up with my own version. Claire's already approved it.'

'Frankie and I went on a hunt in the costume loft and located some old Pierrot outfits already that we can use.'

'I found a few more costumes that might work, Ama. Columbine and Pulcinella.'

'Will you want to use masks or makeup?' asked Claire. 'I love designing masks but we need a good prop maker. Do you have anyone, Ama?'

'No, I'm hoping the drama students in Dartmouth will help out. Spike and I met some of them at the wake I went to in Halifax.'

They were interrupted by the arrival of Arthur's two retired pals. They left them to remove the redundant rows of stalls seating, to make room for the new apron staging and auditorium ramps. Claire and Frankie went back to the wardrobe department to continue searching out possible commedia costumes from the loft stores.

Ama drove downtown to Gloria and Garth's bakery, to speak to her friend about the work party and tell her of the change of plays. She had already cast Gloria in Twelfth Night. The G&G cafe and bakery looked empty when she arrived. She went around the back and found Garth having a coffee break, at one of the outdoor tables overlooking the inner harbour.

'If you've come to steal my wife away from her duties, you're outta luck. She's on a delivery. Should be back soon.' He heaved his bulky frame out of his chair. 'Sit down, Ama, you can have a coffee with me while you wait.'

He disappeared into the shop and came back in a minute with a mug and a plate with a Chelsea bun on it. 'These are still warm from the oven. Nice and sticky.' He set the mug of coffee and plate in front of her and sat back down. 'Fill me in, Ama. Haven't seen you around for a bit. Gloria said you've been off gallivanting around the country, instead of working on your show. When's the grand opening?'

'More like a grand fiasco, Garth. We're hopelessly behind and Gloria's right – I have been neglecting my theatre duties for personal reasons, haring off to Halifax and Montreal and Bridewell.'

'What were you doing in Bridewell - checking out the competition? Gloria said they're doing a Shakespeare there as well.'

'That's right. Taming of the Shrew. We saw it, me and Spike, my new co-director. I stayed on his boat.'

'He's not much good to you in Bridewell. When's he due to get here?'

'Not till his boat's fixed. Another week or two, he thinks.'

'Anything I can help you with in the meantime? The cafe's pretty quiet these days, as you can see and I do most of my baking early morning.'

'Arthur could use some extra muscle with the new staging we're installing. Lots of heavy lifting and carpentry work, Garth. You any good with a hammer and saw?'

'I fitted out this place myself when we took it over. I did all the shopfitting, counters and such. Gloria did the painting and we both did the baking at the same time.'

'Between the two of you, you must know most of the people in Arcadia. We're trying to organise some work parties to get things done in time for our September deadline. Do you think you could press gang any of your customers who might have some free time over the next month? There's so much to do and I hate to postpone our official opening.'

'When would you like me to come, Ama? I can't do mornings or late nights. Have to get up at four.'

'Just turn up whenever you're free and tell anyone else the same. Male or female, we'll take all comers. And if they'd like to be in the play, I'm looking for a large cast for our first show.'

'Gloria's already started learning her lines for Twelfth Night. Gives her something to do when I go to bed early.'

'That's what I wanted to talk to her about. I'm changing the order and doing the Shakespeare as our second show, so the rehearsals for it are on hold till Spike gets here.'

Garth rose and cleared the table. 'I'm free this afternoon once Gloria gets back with the van. Do I need to take any tools?'

'Arthur has most things in the scenery dock. What he wants is extra pairs of strong hands. He's going to make good use of your carpentry skills, Garth.'

While she waited until Gloria arrived, Ama helped Garth wiping down tables and display counters, until the G&G bakery van pulled up in front of the shop.

'Thought I spotted your old red Toyota, Ama. Come to check up on whether I've learned my lines yet?' said Gloria, hoisting her empty wicker baker's baskets up onto the counter. 'Haven't done any rehearsing since you've been away.'

'My fault, Gloria, not yours. However, you've got a reprieve because I've changed our play order. Spike wants to do a Shakespeare play in modern English when he arrives. The Bridewell community theatre group want to make it a joint production with us, and we're trying to figure out the logistics of who does what.'

'You mean we all have to learn new lines for Twelfth Night? Won't that be confusing for the cast?'

'I was thinking it would be easier learning a different play,' said Ama. 'They want us to do The Tempest.'

Garth took the van keys from Gloria and headed out the front door. 'I'll leave you two to duke it out. I'm going to help Arthur rebuild the Regency, Gloria. Apparently Ama's new designer has gutted it.'

'That's what I came to talk to you about, Gloria. The change of plays, since Claire came up with ways to rejuvenate the interior. Have you been in it while I was away?'

'Yes, I met her last week when I went in to see Frankie about my costume for Twelfth Night. Arthur and Claire showed me how the stage would look when she's done. She's a whirlwind, doing six things at one time. No wonder she's thin as a straw.'

Ama told her about her new plans to do Oh What a Lovely War, to take advantage of the re-jigged staging, but made no mention of Claire's illness. She did tell her Claire would be staying with her so they could speed things along, to make up for lost time. Gloria asked her if she had any results from her trip to Montreal, to talk to her ex-husband about Ocean's disappearance. Ama told her of the sudden change in Ronnie's behaviour as a result of Jasper and Delphine's involvement.

'That does sound miraculous considering what you've told me of his total lack of support in the past, Ama. I guess Kitty was right after all, urging you to give Ronnie one more try.'

'I still don't quite believe it myself until I hear it from the horse's mouth. I'll find out all the fascinating details tomorrow when I meet Jasper for lunch,' said Ama. She explained the deal she had made with him and Gloria just smiled, saying nothing.

'Will I get a chance to meet this legal powerhouse who works for lunches?'

'Kitty and Mrs. Spengler are throwing a party for him tomorrow evening and you'll meet him there. Garth too, if he wants to join us.'

'He has to get up too early so he tends to avoid parties and late nights. He leads a monkish existence most of the time. Up at an ungodly hour in the morning and in bed by nine.

'Fishermen and bakers have hard, demanding jobs,' said Gloria. 'Once in a while they have to blow off steam. Most of the wives know what they're letting themselves in for. My life is easy by comparison.'

'I expect they tolerate it because they have kids to think of, but you and Garth don't have any, so what makes you stay, Gloria?'

'I think it's because we don't have any children that Garth goes on his benders. I get involved in the theatre instead. Whatever floats your boat, they say in Nova Scotia. It's a different way of life down here that people 'from away,' especially city people, don't understand. You have to live here for awhile before you appreciate it, Ama.'

'Spike has an old converted fishing boat that we hope to use as a live-aboard. But I wish he was here now and it's only been one day since I left him in Bridewell.'

'I don't know how you juggle all these men in your life, Ama. Two old boyfriends vying for your attention, and a glamorous ex-husband back on the scene. And a missing daughter. It's like a Broadway play.'

'It feels more like a French farce, the way it has me running in circles. The faster I run the further behind I get, Gloria.'

'I'm sorry, Ama. I didn't mean to make light of your situation. I know you're having a difficult time. All these new changes at the theatre must be putting a lot of pressure on you. Whatever I can do to help, you know I'm on your side.'

'Thanks, Gloria. I was telling Garth before you arrived, that Claire says we should organise work parties of volunteers. Tackle the backlog of stuff to do before the September opening. I know you and Garth know everybody in town, and I wanted to ask if you'd be the co-ordinator? Sort of my sidekick until Spike arrives.'

'If I can fit it in and around my delivery runs, I'll be your girl Friday, Ama. When shall I start?'

'Claire and I will work out some schedules tonight. You can collect them at Kitty's party when you meet my lawyer-saviour, Jasper.'

Gloria began to fill a paper bag with Chelsea buns and savoury Arcadia tarts. She handed it to Ama. 'If you and Claire are working late tonight, you'll need some fuel to keep you going.'

When Ama offered to pay, she refused, saying that Garth always made too much and they'd only go stale overnight.

That evening Ama brought Claire back to her old house-sit and proceeded to make a big summer salad, to go with the savoury tarts from Gloria. She let Claire choose some music and pour out the wine from the chilled box in the fridge. They carried the food and drinks through to the long veranda at the front of the old colonial house. Claire had chosen an Aretha Franklin blues, so they left the door open to hear it.

An old swing double seat hung from the porch ceiling and they sat side by side, sipping their white wine.

'It's lovely here, Ama, such a quiet street with those huge shade trees along it. How long can you stay?'

'Indefinitely, according to Kitty. The owner is a widowed friend of hers who prefers to live in Italy. She's chronically ill and likes the heat. I haven't even met her. She took me on Kitty's recommendation.'

'Maybe I should go abroad to recuperate as well. Except I don't know any wealthy widows with spare villas.'

'Speaking selfishly, I'm glad, Claire. I don't want to lose you.'

'You may not have a choice if this diagnosis proves correct.'

'Have you thought what you'll do if it proves serious?'

'It depends how serious and how long I've got. In the meantime, I expect I'll soldier on and keep busy like my doc wants me to,' said Claire. 'What else is there to do?'

They ate in silence for a few moments before Ama spoke. 'We could talk about it. Spike says I'm a good listener. And we've got a few days together to mull it all over if you don't want to confide in Antony yet.'

'If I did, he'd go screaming back to his wife at the thought of me dying. And that would be the last I'd see of him.'

'You didn't say he was married, Claire, or is she his ex?'

'No, they're only separated. Permanently, he insists. Doesn't stop him from having lunch with her in L.A., whenever we have a row. At least, that's all they have, according to him. I'm not so sure.'

'I'm sorry, Claire. All the more reason for you to talk things through with me while you're here.'

'It would be better than the non-stop paranoia that passes for thought inside my head these last few days. What if I fall apart on you, Ama, are you ready for that?'

'All I know is that having a confidante to go to, is what saved me from disappearing into a black hole when my daughter went wild, after she discovered she had ALS. I would make a bee-line for Kitty and spill it all in her lap. And within an hour or so, I would realise it wasn't the end of the world after all.'

'What did she do? Is she like the Samaritans or something?'

'Nothing earth-shaking. We'd sit on her porch like this and drink gunpowder tea and sift through the mess I'd dumped on her, until I began to feel back in control of my life. Till the next time. Then back I'd go.'

'She sounds wonderful. Like being a child and having your mother make everything better again. Unfortunately, my mother died when I was a teenager so I never had that option, did you?'

'Not anymore,' said Ama. 'My mum's in a nursing home back in England. Last time I went back she didn't recognize me. Lost in her own strange world, repeating the same meaningless phrase over and over.'

'What did she say?'

'Motherbother.'

'Motherbother?'

'Motherbother, motherbother, motherbother.'

'What do you think she meant, Ama?'

'No idea. I often wonder about it. Just some words that have lodged in her brain that go round and round in a memory loop. Sometimes I find myself repeating them when I'm feeling defeated. In my case it's probably 'dementia praecox.'

'What on earth's that?'

Ama laughed. 'It's a line from a Tennessee Williams play I saw once on TV. Can't remember the title. Maybe Cat on a Hot Tin Roof – anyway Liz Taylor was in it. Someone said she had dementia praecox and it stuck in my mind. Maybe I'll end up like my mum, repeating it over and over, dementia praecox, dementia praecox. It's sort of soothing, like one of those Buddhist chants I used to know.'

'What does it mean?'

'Precocious dementia. Medical jargon for early stages of losing your mind.'

'Maybe I should try chanting it myself, when I start feeling a little crazy,' said Claire. 'Or motherbother. I like that better, rolls off the tongue – motherbother motherbother motherbother.'

'If you were Catholic, you could try 'mea culpa, mea culpe, mea maxima culpa,' said Ama. 'I had a boyfriend in my teens who used to repeat that while we were making out, to assuage his guilt for sinning. Sex outside marriage is a mortal sin for Catholics. Didn't seem to stop him, anyway.'

'Maybe he saw the chant as a workaround, provided by the church.' Claire said. They both laughed.

'They also say confession is good for the soul, Claire, so now it's your turn.'

'Oh god, don't get me started, I'll be here all night. Besides, I feel hungry and this tastes like soul food. Let's eat instead.'

They fell to, cleaning their plates, then went through to the kitchen for seconds and more wine. Their bags, which had been dumped on the long harvest table, reminded them they had planned to go through the endless list of things that needed their attention at the theatre.

'Do you feel up to spending a bit of time on these work schedules, Claire,' said Ama, as she riffed through the papers in her rucksack, which served as her briefcase.

'Sure, I'm up for it. What shall we tackle first?'

Ama told her that Gloria's husband was an experienced carpenter and strong to boot. He was willing to work on the staging with Arthur.

'Let's not waste him on manual stuff, dismantling the seating. We'll use him for the staircases, but first we have to find someone with a truck, to fetch them from the warehouse in Halifax. Do we have anyone?'

'Arthur has a pickup truck but we can't spare him,' she said. 'Maybe Gloria can find someone. She's offered to be the work party co-ordinator until Spike arrives.'

'A pickup would have to make several trips to bring them down in sections. What we need is a bigger truck that can do it in one journey. Tell her we'll offer to pay for the gas. It's too late to phone my friend, Arnold, at the exhibition warehouse tonight. I'll call him first thing and tell him what we need.'

'Won't we have to pay him for them, Claire? Stairs are expensive, aren't they?'

'Arnold will be glad to clear some of them out. Last time I was in there he had them piled outside, as his warehouse was crammed to the doors. He can't say no to all that free stuff and the exhibition firms pay him to haul it away. Nobody wants it once the conferences, shows and exhibitions are over. It just clutters up their workshops.'

'Surely they could recycle lots of it for other jobs?'

'They could but they prefer to build from new. It's faster and easier,' said Claire. 'Arnold's warehouse is like Aladdin's cave. It's where I'll get our exhibition carpet from as well. You should see the place, Ama, you'd love it.'

'I know I would, but I daren't take another day off, I'm so behind. I've got a feeling Arnold is going to see a lot of me in the future.'

'Leave it to me for now. We'll ask Arthur to estimate on the rolls of carpet and measure up the lengths of staircases, now we've worked out where they'll go.'

On and on they went, poring over the notes Ama had accumulated, prioritising jobs and calculating how many volunteers for each work party.

'Gloria is going to have her hands full co-ordinating this lot,' said Claire, when they finally stopped for the night. 'I hope she's ready for it, Ama.'

'She's not only a brilliant character actor, she's a great organiser. The perfect girl Friday, she calls herself. I feel a lot better since she agreed to step in and help.'

Upstairs, Ama showed Claire one of the several spare bedrooms and loaned her a nightie, as she had brought nothing with her. Claire stood in the doorway to the master bedroom with its antique curved sleigh bed, while Ama found the nightgown for her.

'Would you mind if we shared, Ama? I don't like sleeping on my own. Just for tonight. I'm feeling a bit fragile.'

'I don't like it either. I'm a terrible sleeper except when I'm with Spike. Then I sleep like a baby.'

'I'm a bag of bones these days. I don't know how Antony bears it. I'll try not to dig you in the ribs with my sharp elbows,' said Claire. She climbed into the king-size bed. 'I promise to keep to my side, Ama, but if I start hugging you, just push me away.'

'I'll pretend you're Ocean, my daughter. Whenever she felt depressed, which was frequently, she'd creep into bed with me.'

'I feel so exhausted by bedtime these days, I fall asleep instantly. Much to Antony's displeasure. He'd become used to me being all over him, and can't figure out what's come over me this last while.'

'We're like a pair of old spinster sisters dreaming about our missing men,' said Ama, turning out the bed lamp.

In the morning she woke to find Claire curled against her back, one arm flung over her, sleeping deeply. She carefully extricated herself and padded downstairs in her scruffy old slippers to make coffee. While it brewed, she pored over the work schedules drawn up the night before. Halfway through them, she remembered Jasper. The kitchen wall clock showed 9:15. He would probably already be in mid-flight from Montreal. She made some toast with honey and put a couple of bananas on the tray with the coffee mugs, then took it upstairs. Claire was still sleeping, curled in the fetal position. Ama set the tray down on the bedside table and opened the curtains. Her old work clothes lay on the chair by her side of the bed, as she had intended to put them on. Instead she flipped through her wardrobe, picked out a couple of light summer dresses and held them up to her, in front of the long wardrobe door mirror.

'The blue one, definitely,' said Claire.

'You woke up. I thought you were out for the count. I made you some coffee.'

'I smelled it, that's what woke me up.' She propped herself up in bed and reached across to pick up a mug. 'Mmm, cinnamon toast. Sometimes Antony spoils me like this if he's feeling randy. He thinks cinnamon toast is an aphrodisiac.'

'I must remember that when Spike arrives. You don't think this lemon one is more suitable for a business lunch? I don't want Jasper to think I'm coming on to him. He never needed much encouragement in the past.'

'I like the scalloped hem of the blue one and the plunging neckline. I could never get away with that but you've got plenty to fill it out,' Claire said. 'Put it on and let me see.'

'I need a shower first if I'm going out to lunch.' Ama sat on the edge of the bed and peeled a banana. 'I was kind of keeping the blue one for Spike. I bought it in Bridewell, on impulse, with a friend. You don't think it's too girly for my matronly figure? Mutton dressed as lamb, my mum would say.'

'Can't tell till you put it on,' Claire said. 'If I'm invited to this party tonight to meet Jasper, I'll have to go home to get something else to wear. And I'll need some more clothes if I'm staying for a few days. I can't fit into any of yours with my skeleton frame.'

Ama finished her breakfast and had a quick shower. She dressed in the bathroom in the blue number with the scalloped hem and modelled it in her bare feet for Claire, who sat in bed with her knees drawn up, going through her capacious bag looking for something.

'Sumptuous, Ama. But you're right – too provocative for your lawyer friend. Better save it for Spike, although I doubt if you'll have it on for long. If he's as keen as you say he is, he'll have you stripped off and popped into bed in no time.'

'Suits me,' said Ama. 'The sooner the better.' She slipped off the blue scalloped number and put on the pale lemon dress instead. 'There, this shouldn't distract Jasper from his legal duties.'

'Very ladies who lunch,' said Claire, 'very chaste and demure.'

'Hardly chaste. Jasper knows me of old with my string of ex-husbands. But it will keep his mind on business. I'll tell him there are other treats in store for him tonight, when he meets you and the glorious Gloria.'

'It will have to be my fine mind that attracts him, with you and Gloria there.'

'We'll see. Jasper has very eclectic tastes, he told me.'

'Where's he taking you to lunch, anyway?'

'He's not. I'm taking him, remember? That's our deal. I hope it's not too expensive. I've never been to the Lobster Pot before, have you?'

'A few times. I know the head waiter there. Have you booked?'

Ama shook her head. 'It's lunch time so I thought we'd just show up.'

'If you want a window table with a stunning view of the harbour, you should book. Would you like me to call Laurence for you? After all, Jasper is coming all the way from Montreal, so you ought to make an effort, Ama. Show him you appreciate his help.'

'I do, I do. I can't thank him enough.'

Claire phoned the restaurant and arranged the table for her, and Ama went downstairs to make some calls from her study overlooking the garden. She left Claire still ensconced in the big bed, already on the phone, launched on her heavy workload. She drove her little Toyota across town to Kitty's to liaise with her about Jasper and the party. Sarah and Kitty assured her they were on track with everything and didn't require any help from her, beyond squiring Jasper around as planned.

From Kitty's she drove to the G&G café to deliver the schedules to Gloria for the work parties. Garth was busy making dough, with his brawny arms and thick fingers forming incongruous delicate shapes with the pastry. He told her that he and Arthur's crew of volunteers had made serious inroads into removing the unwanted seats, in preparation for building the ramps. He said Arthur had already asked him if he would tackle the stairs, while he worked on the apron staging. They couldn't install the ramps until the new stage was constructed. What they mainly needed was more helpers.

At ten to one, she parked her car opposite the Lobster Pot and sat waiting for Jasper to show up. She watched the clusters of Asian tourists who dawdled along the narrow waterfront street, for any sign of him. The restaurant was on the second floor of a former dockside warehouse projecting over the water. It had a pedestrian wharf access as well as the main entrance where she had parked. She was about to go and check it out, when a large black sedan drove slowly past.

'Jasper!' she called out of her window, waving her arm at him. He turned his head, saw her, and braked to a stop. She motioned him into an empty space in front of her and waited for him to park and get out.

'Ama – that was easy. I thought I might have trouble finding you in these narrow lanes.' He gave her a bear hug then winced and rubbed his back. 'Long drive, but beautiful along the old lighthouse coast.'

'I'm so glad to see you again, Jasper. I'm longing to catch up. Shall we walk along the dock for you to stretch your legs before you sit down again?'

'What an amazing old town, Ama. Like driving back through time 300 years. It must be fun living down here.'

'Do you think Delphine would like it, Jasper? Maybe you could bring her next time.'

'She's a big city girl. Likes her amenities too much, whereas I'm a country boy at heart. I could fit right into small town life.'

Ama laughed and squeezed his arm. 'Montreal is the smallest town you've ever lived in, I'll bet.'

'You're right. But it's because of my chosen career. You have to go where the clients are.'

'People need lawyers in small towns, too,' she said. 'In fact, Kitty will be sounding you out about taking her on, so beware.'

'It would give me an excuse to come down and see you more often, Ama. I might take her up on the offer.'

They wandered back to the Lobster Pot and climbed the stairs to the entrance, which was decked out with fishing paraphernalia. Ama spoke to Laurence, the silver-haired headwaiter who came forward to meet them. He nodded when she mentioned Claire's name and led them to a table with an open sliding glass window, above the glittering water of the harbour. He pulled out Ama's chair for her and smiled.

'Claire said I was to defer to you, as the gentleman is your guest. Perhaps you'd like to decide what to eat before you choose the wine.' He handed them menus and indicated the chalkboard with the day's specials as he moved back to the bar.

Jasper raised an eyebrow. 'Why the special treatment, Ama, do you come here often?'

'Never been before. It was recommended by Kitty as the best place in town for seafood. What would you like, Jasper?'

He glanced at the specials. 'Well, it is called the Lobster Pot and the whole lobsters seem very reasonable. What do you say, shall we share one?'

'You must be ravenous after your flight and long drive. I think you'd better have a whole one and maybe I can ask for a small one,' she said. She signalled to Laurence they were ready and he came back to stand beside her.

'You have decided already?'

'My friend has travelled all the way from Montreal this morning and I've decided he needs a whole large lobster to himself. I've only come from across town so I would like a small one, if that's possible?'

'Perfectly possible. And how would you like it prepared?'

'I've only ever had it in a salad or chowder. I've no idea how to eat a whole one.'

Laurence looked around the half empty dining room and made a decision. 'Would you like to watch how they prepare them in the kitchen? It's not busy so the chef can demonstrate. But first, would you care to choose your wine and you can bring your glass with you?'

'You choose, Jasper, you're the expert.'

'No, this is your treat. I'm in your hands.'

'Oh god, I only recognise one or two. Would the Gewurztraminer go with lobster? I've drunk that before.'

'Definitely,' said Laurence. 'Nice and light for lunchtime, too.' He went over to the bar and then disappeared into the kitchen.

'You are getting the royal treatment, Ama. They never ask me to watch the chef. Your friend Claire must be very influential.'

'You'll meet her yourself tonight. I happen to think she's a magician but you can decide for yourself.'

Laurence returned with the wine, opened it and poured Ama a mouthful to taste first, then filled her glass when she nodded and poured a glass for Jasper. 'Now if you'd like to follow me to the kitchen.'

They carried their glasses with them through the bar area and into the kitchen, where the chef stood waiting for them with two red lobsters, one large, one small, in front of him on the counter top. Laurence introduced him and left. Alonzo nodded to them.

'You wish to see how to prepare a whole lobster, Laurence says. It is very simple. First we remove the large claws by breaking them off.' He laid them on the wooden chopping block and picked up a heavy meat cleaver. 'Then we crack the shell with the flat side of the blade,' he said, whacking each claw in turn with the cleaver. 'Next we snap off all the small legs like this.' He demonstrated, deftly stripping the thin legs from the body of the large lobster and set them aside with the claws. 'Now we turn it face down and split it in half – from stem to gudgeon, as the fishermen say.'

He placed the cleaver between the eyes and pressed down with the flat of his hand on the top of the blade. It crunched through the shell from head to tail and opened the insides like mirror images. 'Finally, we remove this long black vein which is the intestine and stomach, being very careful not to break it and taint the meat with a bitter taste.' Alonzo scooped it out with his fingers to lay aside, then laid the split lobster on a prepared bed of lettuce on a plate and set the claws and legs to either side along with several wedges of lemon. 'And it's ready to serve. As I said, quite a simple operation, but it helps if you have one of these.' He smiled and held up the heavy cleaver. 'Not necessary, of course. The fishermen often use a hatchet at sea to chop them open.'

They watched as he repeated the operation on the smaller lobster. 'And now you know how to do it at home, and not have to bother coming to the Lobster Pot. Laurence loses a customer, you buy direct off the boat, cutting out the middle man and soon I am out of a job and back working on a fishing boat.' Alonzo grinned at them and led them back out of the kitchen.

'We promise not to tell a soul,' said Ama. 'Your job is safe with us.'

They thanked him for the demonstration and returned to their table to await their meal.

'I suppose you've done that yourself many times, Jasper.'

'Not at all. Delphine is the expert on shellfish. I stick to the barbecue or the restaurant.'

'It may come in useful when Spike and I live aboard on his boat and we catch our own. Are you allowed to do that, Jasper or do you need a licence?'

'Not my area of expertise, but I've often seen sailboats with a lobster pot on deck so I assume it's possible,' he said. 'You're not really thinking of living aboard an old fishing boat, are you, Ama?'

'That's Spike's dream and I've agreed to try it, if he agrees to help me with the theatre. And I'm in desperate need of him if we're going to open on time.'

A young woman arrived with their plates of lobster and a pot of aioli. She set it down and returned with a basket of warm bread rolls, then proceeded to pin large white napkins round their necks.

'Attack,' said Jasper, picking up a claw and pulling out the meat with his fork to dip into a dollop of the garlicky mayonnaise.

Ama followed suit, unsure about what to eat and waiting until Jasper ate some of the body meat before she sampled it. Soon she was squeezing lemon wedges and spooning aioli on everything and wiping her hands on her bib. Jasper showed her how to use the crackers to crush the thin leg shell and pull out the meat with a pick. He leaned across the table to feed it to her and juice dribbled down her chin.

'God, it's like a scene from 'Tom Jones,' Ama said, mopping her chin with the huge napkin.

Jasper poured them more wine and sat back to watch her eat. 'This was worth coming all the way from Montreal, Ama. You sure know how to show a guy a good time. I'm already thinking about my next visit. I don't think I'll tell you all my news. Save some for the next trip.'

'When are you going to give me all the details, Jasper? I've been trying not to ask.'

'Let's not spoil our lunch, shall we? I'll tell you everything afterwards.'

'Now you're making me nervous - is it bad news?'

'It's mixed, Ama. Enjoy your meal first. I'll give you the whole story later.'

'I'm sorry, Jasper. I didn't mean to rush you, we've got all afternoon. I've waited all this long, I can wait a bit longer.'

'Tell me more about your theatre project. Will I get to see it?'

'You can't escape it. I want to show you the whole enormous pit I've dug for myself and listen to your hollow laughter at my folly, for taking it on in the first place.'

'Sounds like fun. I'll bet you're loving it.'

'Strange to say, I am, most of the time. When I'm not panicking at what I was thinking of, at my advanced age.'

'It will keep you young, Ama, doing something important and satisfying, instead of sinking into old age like me.'

'I don't know how important it is, except to me, but it is very satisfying. You're the one who's doing important work, upholding the law, defending people in trouble.'

'If you only knew how trivial my life has become, Ama. Handling divorces of selfish people with too much money and nothing to do, except keep changing partners. Not much upholding of the law involved. Unlike my wife. Delphine loves being a judge in Juvenile court.'

'The more I hear of Delphine, the more I want to meet her. You're a lucky man to have found such a life partner, prepared to tolerate all your philandering, Jasper. I suppose she can't resist you with your silver-tongued sweet talk.'

'She resists me very easily, I'm afraid. It's like trying to make love to a porcupine. She bristles when I attempt any advances. I've learned to keep my distance. As I told you before, we've come to an arrangement. We share a house, not a bed. Why I keep working I suppose, nothing at home for me anymore.'

'There must be other compensations. Your social life together, part of the glitterati of old Montreal. Being lionised as a powerful trial lawyer.'

'Pretty mangy old lion these days.'

'Not to me you're not, Jasper. I have nothing but admiration for the way you've been helping Ocean. And Delphine, too. Please thank her for me.'

'I suppose I can't stall any longer, Ama, now that we've eaten all the lobsters and drunk all the wine. If you want to settle the bill, we perhaps ought to go somewhere we can speak privately.'

She caught Laurence's eye and made writing motions on her palm. He nodded and came over to them with the bill.

'I hope you enjoyed your lobster enough to come here again and try some of our other specialties?'

'It was both delicious and educational, Laurence. I shall start saving right away for the next time,' said Ama.

They shook hands and left the restaurant to walk along the docks towards the empty fishery warehouses, past the huge old tall ship, thronged with tourists snapping selfies in front of it. They found an empty bench and sat watching the quarrelling seagulls.

'I wanted to speak to you in person, Ama, because it's hard for me to explain what I feel is happening with Ocean. She's a very disturbed young woman and I can't quite get through to her about the risks she's taking. Mixing with the drug dealing gang her boyfriend Clay is involved in. I've talked to him at length since he's been arrested and he's fully aware how dangerous it is, but he told me he doesn't care. He says he has late stage AIDS and will probably die soon. Selling drugs is the only way he can get money to live until then.'

'Oh God, Jasper, are you trying to tell me Ocean is infected too?'

'She told Delphine she wasn't, but she didn't want to find out for sure. It's almost as if she's been in some sort of solidarity pact with him. Is there something you haven't told me I should know about her, Ama?'

'She doesn't confide in me anymore, Jasper. I'm completely in the dark about her present condition. I can only guess she may have had some further confirmation of her ALS diagnosis and that's why she's acting so erratically. Do you think that might be why she's linked up with Clay – because they both think they're dying?'

'It's one explanation, I suppose. It would account for them behaving like some present-day Bonnie and Clyde couple. I haven't said too much to Ronnie yet – didn't want to scare him off. It's possible she may confide in her father. You said they've been close in the past.'

'Do you think I should talk to him, Jasper – see if he can find out anything? Only....'

'Only what, Ama? I can't help her if you keep information from me.'

'It's just that if he thinks she's HIV positive, he won't want her anywhere near his new family. I'm sure his young wife will freak out if she catches wind of it.'

'Delphine and I've talked through the different scenarios and can't see any happy long-term outcome, Ama. If Ocean and Clay are hell-bent on this mutual self-destruction, it's hard to predict what they'll do next.'

'But you said Ocean had agreed to stay with Ronnie and that he was giving her a job on his new TV mini-series.'

'That's what Delphine has managed to have them both promise to do. Meantime, I'll try to get Clay a reduced sentence doing community service.'

'It's more than I'd hoped you could do, Jasper. I was sure Ocean would end up in prison.'

'None of this has happened yet, Ama, so let's not get ahead of ourselves. If what we've been saying about some kind of suicide pact between them is true, I can foresee them both jumping ship.'

'Why? Did she say anything to Delphine?'

'Not in so many words. She told her she wouldn't abandon Clay. He needs her. And when I spoke with him in jail, he said he wouldn't implicate her in the charges against him. So, putting two and two together, both Delphine and I think Ocean will wait for him to be released and then skip town again.'

'And you're going to all this trouble, knowing what the probable outcome will be, Jasper?'

'We don't have much choice, unless you want them both to end up with prison sentences.'

'God, Jasper, I'm so sorry to have embroiled you and Delphine in this affair. I should have known better than to ask you in the first place.'

'No free lunches, Ama. It's the price I'm prepared to pay to be back in your life again.' He grinned at her. 'And as for Delphine, she's delighted to have Ronnie gracing her dinner table and making her the envy of all her women friends.'

'What do you think I should do, Jasper? Do you see any way out of this mess I've got us all into, with Ocean?'

'For the present, there's nothing you can do. Just wait and see. We've all done what we can. The next move is up to them. The best thing is to get on with your life and we'll keep a watching brief on our star-cross'd lovers. Do you believe in Fate, Ama?'

'Fate? I don't think I believe in anything anymore – except old friends. Like you.'

'To fill up my slow days in the office, I've started re-reading the classics. Filling in the gaps in my narrow legal education. I've worked my way through the Greeks from Homer and Hesiod, including all the big-name dramatists and now I'm onto the philosophers. And to a man, they're all big believers in Fate. Everything is in the lap of the gods with them. I guess that's where we are now, Ama.'

'Nothing to be done. Sounds like Beckett – Waiting for Godot.'

'Not at all. We do everything we can and then let it all play out. You can't second guess the gods, according to the Greeks, or it will all end in tears.'

'In that case, I will follow your sage advice and get on with my life. Which means my theatre project. Are you ready for your tour of inspection, Jasper?'

'Lead on,' he said, steering her towards his large black rental car.

She directed him to The Regency Theatre and he parked the car behind it in the half-full lot. Ama led him round the front and in through the partially refurbished entrance foyer to admire the effect of Claire's work. He stood staring up at the filmy canopy, now fully opened above the huge chandelier and pinned over the bar and curving elm staircase.

'Impressive, Ama. Quite a transformation from what it must have been before you started, I imagine.'

'All Claire's ideas. We merely do as she tells us.' She took his arm up the wide stairs to see the poster displays covering the blistered old mirrors and then to lean over the balcony railing to view the foyer and bar and gauze canopy from above.

'Shame all those big brass sconces everywhere have turned black,' said Jasper, rubbing his thumb over the nearest one. 'Do you think it's possible to restore them?'

'With enough volunteers and a giant can of Brasso, Claire says they'll gleam again. They're solid brass.'

'Is it a problem finding volunteers, Ama?'

'It is for me, but Claire has a way of press-ganging everyone she meets into helping.'

'Will I get to meet her? She sounds like a miracle worker.'

'She is and you will, so be warned. Grown men eat out of her hand.'

'I can hardly wait to fall under her spell.'

'She might still be onstage, let's have a look.' She opened the heavy hardwood doors to the balcony seating and ushered him through.

'What's happening, Ama? It looks like they're gutting the place.' Jasper went down the carpeted stairs to lean over the balcony railing.

A group of men were dismantling seats from one section while another gang of volunteers, mostly women, bent over another section, fitting the new art deco zigzag pattern covers, under Frankie's supervision. Ama pointed to Arthur, down in the newly opened empty space, talking to Garth who was laying out sheets of plywood for a ramp. There was no sign of Claire.

'That's Arthur, the stage carpenter who's making it all happen. I'll let him explain to you what's going on. Come on.'

She led the way back down through the foyer and into the auditorium and introduced him to Arthur and Garth. Frankie had disappeared back to the costume loft.

'Give him the VIP treatment, Arthur and we may persuade him to let us put his name on the program as a patron. I'll go and find Claire and Frankie.'

She left them and threaded her way through the auditorium to backstage. There was no one in the Green Room so she tried the costume loft. Frankie stood talking to three older women seated at his worktable, each with a sewing machine in front of them.

'These are my three elves sewing fine seams, Ama. They even come equipped with their own machines. Lucy, Clara and Joyce. I have an assembly line here that would rival Henry Ford for efficiency. How many have we covered already, Lucy?'

'Over thirty,' said Lucy, 'but we're running out of supplies. We need to stop and cut out some more patterns.'

'I'll pull two people off the fitting team and show them how to cut. You keep stitching, Lucy.'

'Have you seen Claire, Frankie? I can't find her anywhere.'

'She left half an hour ago to meet Gloria – something about organising a truck to collect stairs in Halifax. She said she was going home afterwards and would see us tonight at the party.'

'I want you to come and meet my lawyer friend, Jasper. I've been giving him a Cook's tour of Arcadia and the theatre, hoping to interest him in our project. He's with Arthur at the moment.' She drew him aside. 'Where did all these people come from, Frankie? The place is swarming with volunteers.'

'We all did what Claire told us to – contact our networks and this is the result. Who did you bring besides your lawyer, Ama?'

'Gloria and Garth. And tonight, I hope to tap into Kitty and Mrs. Spengler's networks, so have your list ready of who and what you need. Now come and meet Jasper.'

For a moment she couldn't spot Jasper in the group of workers, until his head appeared above a sheet of plywood he was holding in place for Garth. He had taken off his jacket to help.

'Good god, Arthur. Is this your idea of VIP treatment? After all my wining and dining to persuade Jasper to visit our project, you have him sweating like a stage-hand. Next thing you'll have him sweeping the stage.'

'All Garth's fault. He was showing him how the ramp will fit under the staircase.'

'I told them I was renovating our old week-end cottage in Hudson Heights but was scared to tackle the loft staircase,' said Jasper. 'Garth was giving me some tips.'

'Frankie, this is Jasper Falkenham, a very big fish from the St Lawrence I hope to persuade to come and swim in our local waters. You may call him sir.'

Frankie bobbed a curtsy. 'Pleased, I'm sure. Allow me.' He picked up Jasper's jacket from the seat and brushed imaginary dust off it before helping him on with it. 'I expect you'd like to come and meet my harem, the flower of Arcadia?'

'Now that is exactly the right way to appeal to Jasper,' said Ama.

'Don't you want to see how we're going to cantilever the staircase?' asked Garth.

'Be right back,' said Jasper, following Frankie backstage.

'What do you think, Arthur, does he seem interested in our project?' asked Ama.

'If he's not convinced, wait till Claire gets her claws into him this evening,' he said.

'I told him if he came by tomorrow, I'd lend him some work clothes and he could help with framing the staircase landing,' said Garth.

'I'm astonished by how much this group has accomplished already, Arthur. I can almost begin to picture what it will look like when you're finished. I'd better get cracking on the play or we won't have it ready to put on for the opening.'

'There's still miles to go yet, Ama. Me and Garth figure your deadline is too unrealistic and we may have to delay the opening, if we do everything Claire wants.'

'All this new staging is pretty ambitious,' said Garth. 'We may have to cut corners to be ready on time.'

'What kind of corners, Garth? You won't do anything unsafe and have the fire officer condemn the place?'

'No. More like only putting in one ramp and one staircase to the balcony, is what we had in mind.'

'Oh no! Claire will be so disappointed,' said Ama.

'It's just an idea. Kind of a fallback plan if we need one,' Arthur said. 'You may have to make a choice, Ama. Either delay the opening or settle for one ramp and staircase. It will still look terrific. Don't look so glum.'

'When will I have to decide? Not right away, I hope?'

'It will depend how long it takes us to build the first ramp and set of stairs,' he said. 'Then we'll know whether we have time to do the second ones.'

'Don't tell Claire yet, Arthur. Let's wait and see how you get on, first. Is there anything I can do to speed things up?'

'Not unless you can find two or three more Garths to make up another team. This bunch here are willing but they don't have the carpentry skills we need.'

'Okay. For now, don't mention this to anyone – we don't want the word to get out that the opening is going to be delayed – bad for morale.'

Ama made her way backstage to find Jasper. Frankie was showing him the few samples of commedia costumes he had found.

'Jasper's been telling me his wife is on the board of the Montreal opera house and she might be able to help with these costumes.'

'We can't afford to rent them, Frankie – they'd cost a fortune.'

'I already told him but he thinks they might loan them to us. From an old Magic Flute production.'

'I can't promise, of course,' said Jasper, 'but Delphine might be able to call in some favours. She's raised a lot of money for them over the years.'

'And just how would you persuade her to do this, Jasper? She's never even heard of us.'

'I told you – we have an arrangement. We scratch each other's back from time to time.'

'From what you've told me, Delphine's been doing most of the scratching lately.'

'You have no idea how many hundreds of opera tickets I've unloaded on my clients for her in the past. It's a question of picking the moment. Leave it with me.'

'Alright. Meantime, Frankie and I will be preparing a list of what we need, ready to pounce when you give us the nod.'

She looked round at the workroom with all the women cutting and sewing covers. 'Now if you can tear yourself away from Frankie's harem, I'll take you to meet your landladies for the evening.'

'Goodbye, ladies. *A demain*,' he said, waving to the smiling women.

'*Au revoir,* Jasper,' they called back.

Ama took his arm and led him to the stage door. 'You didn't waste any time, Jasper. I suppose you know all their names, too.'

Ample Make This Bed

'Gather ye roses while ye may,' he said. 'I've garnered three invitations to lunch already, Ama. I may have to extend my stay in Arcadia.'

'Remember this is not Montreal, Jasper. I have to live here. I don't want you causing any scandals.'

'Fear not, I'm nothing if not discreet. Besides, they were all merry widows.'

'Speaking of merry widows, you are about to meet two of our finest, Kitty and Sarah. Mrs. Spengler to you, as she is a local, born and bred. I am allowed to call her Sarah, now that we are friends.'

'And Kitty?'

'Kitty is 'from away,' as they say down here. New York to be exact. Married into one of the oldest families in Arcadia and is one of the most influential movers and shakers in the county. And my dearest friend here.'

Jasper drove his big rental car up the steep streets to Kitty's house and parked in front of the old colonial mansion house. He stood admiring its facade as Ama removed his case and suit zip bag from the back seat.

'Close your mouth and try not to look like a country bumpkin, Jasper. Remember they're expecting a sophisticated lawyer from Montreal. Don't let me down.' She climbed the front steps to the enclosed veranda while he followed her. 'Look behind you, now.'

He turned to take in the sweep of the harbour with the old town below them. 'You certainly know how to pick your friends, Ama.'

She pulled on the old doorbell and it rasped faintly inside. A moment later, Mrs. Spengler opened the door, pulling off her apron as she saw who it was.

'Ama – we've been expecting you. Come in. Here, let me take those things. Kitty! They're here.' She took Jasper's case and suit zip bag into the hall and laid them on a chair.

'Jasper, this is Mrs. Spengler. Sarah, Jasper Falkenham, my friend and pro bono lawyer.'

Sarah shook his hand and drew him into the drawing room off the hall. 'Have a seat, while I fetch Kitty. She's probably prinking in front of the mirror before she meets you.'

She left the room and Jasper gazed about it, looking at the old maritime paintings on the walls.

'This is finer than any hotel I might have expected to find. Are you sure I won't be putting them out?'

'Not at all, they're looking forward to having you. I told them what a prize you were.'

Kitty sailed into the room straight to Jasper and took his hand in both of hers. 'This is a rare treat for us. We seldom have such distinguished guests from Montreal. You've met my friend Sarah and I'm Kitty. May I call you Jasper? Ama has told us so much about how you and your wife have been helping her daughter, Ocean.'

'Ama and I are very old friends, Kitty. I'm only too pleased to be of some assistance to her and Ocean. I, too, had a wayward daughter, as she may have mentioned. I know how she feels.'

Kitty turned to Ama and smiled. 'He looks far too dashing to be a bona fide lawyer, Ama. We have such dry old sticks here in Arcadia, don't we, Sarah?'

'I can assure you he is the genuine article, Kitty. Don't be deceived by his appearance, or he may have you putting him in your will.'

'I expect you must be gasping for a drink after your long trip, Mr. Falkenham. I'm notorious for my cocktails. Would you like one?' asked Sarah.

'What a good idea, Sarah,' said Kitty, 'let's all have one of your whisky sours and then perhaps you could show Jasper his room, so he can freshen up before the party starts. The bathroom is right next door if you'd like to have a shower.'

'Better lock the door, Jasper, or you may have someone scrubbing your back,' said Ama.

'We won't be eating for a while so maybe you'd care for a snack to tide you over,' said Sarah. 'I can make you something while I do the drinks.'

'Ama stuffed me full of lobster and wine at lunch. If I have anything more, I'll fall asleep and disgrace her in front of your guests.'

'Plenty of time to have a nap as well,' said Kitty. 'Shall we sit out on the veranda with our drinks and then we'll let you escape upstairs.' She took Jasper's arm to lead him out of the room and Sarah went off to make the cocktails.

'I suppose Ama has shown you round our old Regency Theatre. What do you think of all the changes she and Claire are making?'

'Very inventive and radical. I know how these old public buildings can drink up money to restore to their original grandeur. This is more like a clever disguise, don't you think, Kitty?'

'I only have second hand reports from Ama. She won't let me visit yet – says it's too dangerous for decrepit old ladies.'

'I never said any such thing, Jasper. I just want to wait until there's something more to show than a building site. Right now, what we need are strong men with good carpentry skills. To help Arthur and Garth build ramps and staircases, in time for the grand opening in September.'

Sarah pushed open the door and set down a tray of cocktails and a plate of appetisers. 'These are for Mr. Falkenham to tide him over till the party. The fancy ones are Kitty's – but mine are more filling.' She handed round the whisky sours and sat down. 'It's a long time since I been in the old Regency but can't say I remember any such things as ramps and stairs on the stage.'

'That's because there aren't any yet,' said Ama. 'Arthur and Garth's team are just building them but we're running out of time. I was hoping you and Kitty might know some skilled carpenters you could inveigle into lending a helping hand.'

'Scarce as hen's teeth,' said Kitty. 'I've been trying to get someone to do repairs to the kitchen for months now.'

'Most of the skilled men I know are fishermen and boat builders,' said Sarah. 'There's a saying down here that boat builders can build houses but house builders can't build boats. So maybe I could talk to some of them. There's a lot of unemployed fishermen these days, pining for something to keep them occupied.'

'Too bad I'm so clumsy with my hands or I'd volunteer,' Jasper said. 'I've been pottering around our week-end cottage but my carpentry is very rough and ready.'

'I doubt if Delphine would lend you to us anyway, Jasper. You're more useful gracing her dinner party fund-raisers, I expect.'

'You'd be more than welcome to stay here, if you wanted a bit of a holiday from all the stresses of Montreal, wouldn't he Sarah?'

'Be nice to have a man around to cook proper meals for, instead of the sparrow portions I have to prepare for Kitty.'

'God knows we could use all your other skills, Jasper. But could you cope with being a big fish in a very small pond?' said Ama.

'You all make it sound quite compelling. And it would make a change doing something more meaningful than handling another society divorce.'

'Let him see his room with that perfect view of the harbour before he makes up his mind, Sarah,' said Kitty, topping up his whisky from the cocktail shaker. 'It would be like having Gerald back home again to make a fuss of.'

'I'll leave you to revive for the party, Jasper, and go home to get changed myself,' Ama said. She drained her glass and stood up. 'I'll collect my car on the way. The walk will sober me up after Sarah's powerful whisky sours.'

When Ama pulled up to her old house-sit she saw Claire's silver SUV parked in the drive and found her upstairs, perched on the old curved sleigh bed painting her toenails.

'Sit down and I'll do yours next,' she said.

'I must have a shower first, I smell like a ditch digger,' said Ama, heading into the bathroom.

She stood in the shower and let the warm water beat on her shoulders, feeling the tension of the theatre's problems draining from her body. After rinsing the shampoo off her hair, she turned the water to cool to close her pores, then pulled on her matted old terrycloth robe and went back to the bedroom to sit beside Claire.

'Ready? Same colour as mine, Sis?' asked Claire holding up the little bottle. 'Eau de Nile.' Ama nodded and stuck out one foot for Claire to start on.

'Matches my lemon dress only it's all grubby and sweaty from the theatre today,' she said, watching Claire expertly applying the pale green nail polish and pushing wads of cotton wool between her toes, to keep them separated.

'I've been going through your wardrobe and the news is not good, girl. You've been sadly neglecting yourself. However, I found a decent cream linen suit that might work for this evening,' said Claire, pointing to an outfit hanging on the old wardrobe door. 'Bit wrinkled and needs a good press. Just right for the artistic director image. And it won't show me up too much, I hope. But your lingerie drawer is shocking, Ama. Old industrial knickers is a more accurate description. If I wore things like that around Antony it would dampen his ardour permanently.'

'Well, it'll have to do for tonight. I don't know about you but I'm not planning to show my drawers to anyone this evening.'

'All I can say is turn the light off first before you let your sailor see them or he'll sail off into the sunset.'

She finished doing Ama's toenails and climbed off the bed. 'Tell me what you think of this little number Frankie discovered in the costume loft.' She took a shimmering little flapper outfit from the wardrobe and held it up for inspection. 'Kinda slinky, huh? Do you think I can get away with it for the party, or should I save it for opening night?' She slipped off her kimono, revealing flesh-pink silk French knickers and a push-up bra that made the most of her slender form. She slid the short flapper dress over her head and struck a twenties pose for Ama.

'Classy. You look as though you'd stepped straight out of a Noel Coward play. Of course, you'll make the rest of us look like lumpy frumps but the men will love it.'

'What about your big city lawyer – will he like it?'

'Jasper? Guaranteed. He'll probably try to swallow you whole. Dress and all.'

'Good. Just so I can keep his attention long enough to pitch some ideas to him about my travelling museum project.'

'Poor Jasper. Do you think I should warn him practically every woman in the room has designs on him? Me, you, Kitty with her charities and Sarah with her women's refuge. He was barely in their house before they were trying to lure him to move in.'

'I expect he doesn't mind being lionised by women, from what you've told me about his past. Now where's your steam iron and let's get you dressed to impress. From what Frankie tells me about Kitty's parties, Jasper won't be the only big fish there. Half the glitterati in the county cultural circles have been invited. We have work to do.'

'It's only a social evening for the local theatre workers to relax and enjoy themselves a little, Claire.'

'Ama, your naiveté is breathtaking sometimes. You said yourself practically everyone has an agenda to push tonight and this is our chance to push ours. Get your war-paint on and let's join the fray. But first, I need a little stiffener.' Claire opened her silvery clasp handbag and removed a small tube of pills. She popped one in her mouth and washed it down with a gulp of white wine from the bottle they'd been sipping while they dressed.

'What's that, Claire? Are you on some medication for your... condition?'

'Not yet. Antony gets these for me to keep my energy levels up. Want to try one?'

'What are they?'

'He won't tell me exactly. He says they're kind of like Ecstasy, only different.'

'Claire, are you sure you should be taking that kind of thing with your diagnosis? They might ...'

'Kill me, you mean? They might – but so might leukemia.' She put the little bottle back in her bag. '"Be bold and let who would, be wise.'" She opened the front door and they stepped into the silky warmth of the summer evening.

CHAPTER TEN

The walk to Kitty's old mansion was only a few short blocks so they left the cars at home. The street in either direction was filled with large expensive vehicles when they arrived. The sounds of live music came through the screen door of the veranda, as they climbed the steps. Two little girls in party frocks greeted them at the door and asked their names.

Claire told them and asked, 'What's yours?'

They giggled and one replied. 'I'm Shannon and this is Tracey. We're supposed to introduce you to Kitty first. It's your turn to stay at the door, Tracey.'

She led them into the drawing room on the left of the hall and over to where Kitty sat. She was on a chaise lounge between Jasper and a frail-looking elderly man, who was holding forth to a circle of guests gathered round them. Shannon squeezed through, holding Claire's hand and interrupted him. 'Kitty, this is Claire and this is Ama. You said we should tell you when they arrived.'

'Thank you, dear. Why don't you and Tracey have a break and get something to eat from Sarah. I'll look after them now.' She took Claire's hand in both of hers. 'Help me up so I can give you a proper hug, Claire. I'm showing off, wearing these high heels and I'm a bit unsteady. I nearly ended in Ralph's lap when I sat down.'

Claire took one arm and Jasper the other as Kitty stood unsteadily, smiling at Claire. 'From what Ama has been telling me of your exploits, I expected an Amazon, not a slip of a girl.' She embraced her and then held her away from her. 'You look delightful, doesn't she Jasper?'

'Stunning,' he said, taking her hand. 'I'm Jasper, Ama's lawyer friend from Montreal.'

'In that case, I want to give you a bear hug on her behalf. She has nothing but praise for how you're helping her, Jasper.' Claire put her arms out and he enveloped her with his, as she stood on tiptoe to kiss his cheek.

'And this is Ralph, my lawyer,' said Kitty as she helped the old man to his feet.

He took Claire's hand in turn. 'I'm sorry I haven't done anything to deserve a kiss like my colleague,' he said, 'but I shall live in hope that an opportunity will arise.'

Claire leaned forward and kissed him lightly on the cheek. 'Equality before the law. Now you're even.'

'I see that I've been supplanted in their attention,' said Kitty, 'so I'll leave you in their charge for now, Claire, and show Ama around.'

She took Ama's arm and led her through the room to meet some of the other guests, before heading for the big old-fashioned kitchen where the musicians were playing. Sarah was dispensing punch from a large pot-bellied glass urn and had a big apron over her flowered dress. She ladled a glassful for Ama. 'I've warned Kitty to pace herself, because this concoction is a bit stronger than I intended. She's alternating with fruit punch to keep her from falling off those high heels she insisted on wearing. An old woman like her.'

'She said I looked like a madame in a brothel, Ama. I took it as a compliment.' Kitty beckoned to a woman putting a plate of appetisers on the long oak table, already covered with food. She came over to them and Kitty introduced her. 'This is Karla. You've already met her daughter, Shannon, one of our official greeters.'

'We're some of Sarah and Kitty's waifs and strays from the women's refuge,' said Karla. 'If we seem out of place, it's because we're not used to this kind of treatment. They're pleased to call us their protégées when we're introduced.'

'And so they are,' said Kitty. 'And with their children, they make two old ladies very happy to be part of their lives.'

'Makes a change from being referred to as battered wives, Ama,' said Karla. 'Would you like to come for a visit and see how they've transformed the refuge? The kids love it there, don't they, Sarah?'

'Almost as much as I do,' said Sarah. 'Kitty thinks I should move in and be the resident grandmother.'

'I'm content with being honorary grandmother,' said Kitty. 'I love having the children visit but they do tire me out, they're so full of energy all the time.'

'I'd love to be an honorary member too, Karla. Maybe we could have the kids do something at the theatre, if they're interested,' said Ama. 'At the moment, it's too much of a building site to risk bringing them, but you'd be welcome if you fancied a break from the kids. There's masses to do before we open.'

'Introduce her to some of the other women here, Karla. They might enjoy a chance to do something different as well,' Sarah said.

Karla led Ama back through the old house to speak to several of the mothers with children present at the party. Ama had a chance to sound out some of the kids, and they all seemed keen to come and see what was happening at the old Regency. None of them had ever been inside it before.

In the kitchen the music had stopped. Ama went back to meet the musicians, conscious of Claire's remark about being there to work as well as enjoy herself. She asked Sarah to introduce her and the big woman took off her apron and gave Ama a tray of punch to give the players. She met each in turn and when the tray was empty, Sarah took it for a refill. She left Ama to talk to the musicians about the theatre project and whether they would consider playing in the opening production.

'We're mostly used to doing kitchen parties,' said a tall, skinny banjo player with a red goatee beard. 'Not many of us can read music, if that's what you need.'

The others laughed. The woman accordion player said, 'What Tim really means is none of us can, we just play by ear. We know a few basic chords and the rest we pick up with practice.'

'You sound pretty professional to my untrained ear,' said Ama. 'I don't think that would be much of a hindrance. Most of the songs in 'Oh What a Lovely War' are well-known ballads or old folk tunes.'

'Sounds like fun to me,' said the snare drummer. 'I'm game to give it a try. Maybe I could do some sound effects for you. I've got lots more drum kit at home I never get to use much.'

'Come by the theatre anytime you're free and see what we're doing. I need ideas for how to use music in the show. Would you mind wearing costumes for some of the scenes onstage?'

Bernice, the accordion player said, 'I suppose I could play a World War I camp follower with my old button accordion.'

'Type casting,' said Tim.

'And you could play a lamp-post,' she said.

'Tell us one of the songs, Ama,' said Bernice, 'maybe we already know it.'

'How about 'Mademoiselle from Armentiers, parley-voo,' asked Ama.

Tim began picking out the old tune on his banjo and the others joined in one by one, nodding and smiling. Ama started singing the words and soon others in the kitchen crowded round to join in the chorus. When they finished, Claire came over to whisper in her ear.

'I see you're doing your homework. Good girl.'

'What about you, having any luck?' asked Ama.

'Am I. I told Frankie this is going to be my good luck dress. I have wangled three business lunches already.'

'One of them with Jasper, I'll bet.'

Claire laughed. 'How did you guess. I suspect half the women here tonight will have received overtures from him, before the party's over.'

'I warned him to be discreet and not embarrass me with any scandals. Probably a waste of breath, though.'

'You ought to talk with Ralph, Kitty's old lawyer,' said Claire. 'He's a walking goldmine of contacts. I think his pillow talk would keep you awake all night, Ama, making notes.'

'I'm not that desperate yet.'

'Just a suggestion,' said Claire. She moved off again to work the room, drink in hand.

Ama spotted Gloria talking to Arthur in the hall and went to join them.

'You look very summery and cool, Gloria. Give us a twirl,' said Ama.

The big baker held out her pleated yellow skirt and turned around for them, ending with a deep bow that displayed her ample bosom. She had piled her blond hair up on top of her head with a curved amber clasp.

'Where's Garth? He'll be fending off the men before the night's out.'

'He's not worried. Says I look like a giant sunflower. Anyway, he's back at the theatre. He might come by later for a drink before he goes to bed.'

'I couldn't pry him loose,' said Arthur, 'he says he prefers working alone at night, he's used to it. I told him he can't burn the candle at both ends, with the theatre and baking bread but he said he's a workaholic.'

'I gave up trying to make him take it easy years ago,' said Gloria. 'He says he's as strong as one of those oxen he loves to watch. His idea of an outing is taking me to an ox-pull.'

'I've heard of them,' said Ama, 'they seem to be popular down here. What do they do? Is it a kind of tug of war or something?'

'No, they simply compete to see who can pull the heaviest load. After half an hour, I'm bored stiff. I refuse to go anymore.'

'It is a bit repetitive,' said Arthur, 'but they are magnificent animals with their long, curved horns and elaborate decorated harness and yokes. I know one of the farmers who owns several prize winners.'

'Claire said we should mingle and not talk shop amongst ourselves,' said Ama, 'but I don't know any of this crowd here, do you? I'm not very good at just walking up to strange people.'

'I know one or two by sight from theatre meetings,' said Arthur. 'Gloria knows practically everyone from her bakery rounds.'

'Frankie's the one to meet and greet with,' said Gloria. 'He's in his element at parties like this. See? He's over there holding court in the middle of that group around Kitty. But first I want to meet Jasper.'

She pulled Ama through the crowd to the kitchen where Jasper stood in a circle of children, each with a plate of Sarah's hors d'oeuvres, listening to him.

'What's going on, Jasper? Are you the gang leader here?' asked Ama.

'Kitty's worried everyone will get drunk if they don't eat some of this food, so I'm organising a competition with the kids. Whoever empties the most plates wins the prize and I'm keeping score. Okay, kids, spread out and don't cheat by eating them yourselves. I'll be watching you. I'll just top up your drinks while Kitty isn't looking,' said Jasper. 'Let me guess whether your friend is a thespian or a patron of the arts, Ama. My name's Jasper.' He held out his hand for Gloria to shake and she put her empty glass in it, then blushed when she realised her mistake and offered her other hand to him, flustered.

'Don't worry, Gloria. Jasper has this effect on all the women who meet him. I'm only immune to him because I keep reminding myself he's a grandfather with three grandchildren. This is Gloria, Jasper and she's a woman of many talents and not easily categorised.'

He refilled their glasses and raised his to them. 'Gloria, my guess is that you are first and foremost an actor and you deliberately tried to fool me, with that trick with the handshake. I didn't know what to say for a minute until I saw you smiling.'

'It's true I do some character acting for Ama but I don't usually play the clown,' said Gloria, regaining her aplomb. 'I'm used to meeting big men, though not quite so smooth. My husband is large and shaggy.'

'Ama, what have you been saying about me to create this false impression of an old roué?'

'Just friendly warnings, Jasper. Nothing Delphine wouldn't corroborate.'

'Ama is a very old friend, Gloria but she has this irritating habit of holding my wife up to me as some paragon of virtue, when she hasn't even met her. Whereas she continuously poor-mouths her ex-husband, while I find him quite charming.'

'I haven't met either your wife or Ama's ex so I shouldn't take sides,' said Gloria. 'However, I've seen Ama reduced to tears enough times to assume he's not quite as charming as you make him out to be.'

'And I'm willing to bet good money Delphine is not the harridan he likes to portray her as, either,' said Ama.

'I can see you're determined to gang up on me,' said Jasper, pulling a long face, 'and I was having such a good time up till now.'

'Don't be so touchy, Jasper. What is the point of being old friends, if we can't share a few home truths? You know I love you dearly, as I expect Delphine does too. And probably Gloria will as well, given the chance.'

'On that reassuring note, let's go and preach the gospel of the theatre to all these good people. I understand from Kitty that's the main reason for this gala affair.' He offered an arm to each and they processed around the house, talking to the great and the good of Arcadia.

Gloria tapped a man on the shoulder who was chatting with Frankie. 'Here's someone you should meet, Ama. A potential actor I've been trying to recruit. Maybe you'll have better luck than me. Howard masquerades as an accountant but I think he'd make a better actor, wouldn't he Frankie?'

'Definitely. I was just telling him the same thing,' said Frankie.

Ama and Howard shook hands. 'Frankie's been giving me the lowdown on your opening play, Ama. I saw it years ago in Halifax at the Neptune. Quite an ambitious piece to start off with, isn't it? I seem to remember a large cast.'

'We want to make a big splash to begin with, which is partly why I chose it. You're right though, we will need a large cast, so I hope you'll consider a part, Howard.'

'You don't even know me. I might be a terrible ham.'

'If Gloria and Frankie recommend you, that's good enough for me. Will you at least come along and see what we're doing with the old Regency, before you make up your mind?'

'I've already promised Frankie I'll lend him a hand with props. When I was at college, I made all the props for The Crucible.'

'That's all I need to hear. Come and meet Claire, our set designer. She'll put you straight to work. Have you seen her, Frankie?'

'Last time I saw her she had button-holed the board chairman in the front living room.'

'Can I make a confession to you, Howard? I haven't even started rehearsals for Lovely War because I'd already begun working on Twelfth Night, so I'm desperate to get it underway. You'd do me a great favour if you'd take on a role, as well as doing props.'

'Anything as long as it doesn't involve number crunching or fund-raising. I get asked to do that all the time by local groups.'

'I promise. We won't even mention the word accountant to Claire,' said Ama. 'Here she is.'

Claire turned to look at them and smiled. 'Douglas wants to know when he can come to see the transformations, Ama. Shall we invite him now or wait till the new staging is done?'

'Unless you want to risk being dragooned for project manager as well as chairman, Douglas, I advise you to wait,' said Ama. 'This is Howard, Claire, who's offered to do props so I thought you'd better meet right away. He comes highly recommended by both Frankie and Gloria.'

'You mean you've done props before, Howard?' He nodded and smiled at her. She took his arm to lead him away. 'Excuse us Douglas, we have to talk shop urgently.'

The chairman watched them go. 'She's an amazing person, Ama. I can't believe half the things she's been telling me. Where did you find her, and can we afford someone that high-powered on our limited budget?'

'She's only on loan, I'm afraid. Claire has a much larger commission and we're only a sideline. The bonus is, theatre is her first love and she has included us as part of her main project. She comes to us free. I'm glad you like her. Frankly, I'd be floundering without her at my elbow, so whatever you can do to smooth her path, will be well worth the effort.'

'I like her even more now, Ama. Just the cost of materials for the renovations is straining the budget. We've got nothing over for paying any more wages, in case you were thinking of asking for a raise.'

'Better wait until you see the finished production, Douglas. You might want to fire me instead.'

'Not a chance. With you and Claire at the helm we've seen more happen than we have in the last three years. Even if some of the board are grumbling about rumours that we can't afford it.'

'Oh god, I'll bet they don't like the idea of a female A.D., do they?'

'They're a fairly conventional bunch even though they don't think so, being arts supporters. My guess is they just want to have their say and feel they're being consulted. They don't consider theatre renovations to be part of your brief as artistic director. I figure if we explain the changes are integral to the productions, they'll be back onside, Ama.'

'Do you think you can convince them, Douglas?'

'With you and Claire there beside me, yes. So perhaps we better have a board meeting soon.'

'God, I'm up to my ears as it is and so is Claire. Do you really feel it's that important right now?'

'If you want them working for you and not against you, I do,' he said. 'Ask Kitty, she's on the board. See what she thinks. By the way, when is your assistant director going to show up? Kitty told me about him awhile ago but I don't see him here.'

'I know and I really need his help, but his boat has broken down in Bridewell, waiting for parts.'

'Well don't let that Majestic Theatre crowd hijack him on you, Ama.'

'That's a whole other story, Douglas. They want to do a joint Shakespeare production with us and he's super keen on the idea. I'll tell you more when he gets here. Anyway, I'll have a word with Kitty, and see what she thinks I should do about the board, Douglas. She's my touchstone, I don't do anything without her advice.'

'Me either. I'm the chairman but Kitty is the power behind the throne. She has a way of making you think everything is your own idea.'

Ama left him to look for her hostess and found her talking with the two lawyers, Ralph and Jasper.

'Hello dear, have you come to check up that I'm not boring Jasper like I promised you?' Kitty said. 'I know it looks like I'm monopolising him, but he and Ralph came to me, with some plan they've been hatching together. Hard to imagine two high-powered lawyers asking an old lady for advice. I think they may have drunk too much punch.'

'Drunk or sober, I've been seeking Kitty's advice for years on the pretext I'm advising her,' said Ralph.

'I've been watching Jasper out of the corner of my eye all evening, Kitty, to see he doesn't seriously damage our reputations,' Ama said. 'Apart from the fact that Ralph seems to be the only male here he's spoken to, he appears to have been a model of decorum.'

'I won't deny that I have enjoyed meeting the ladies of Arcadia with Ralph's assistance, as he happens to know them all,' said Jasper.

'Only in an avuncular way or in my professional capacity,' said Ralph. 'They only have eyes for Jasper and they weren't looking for legal advice.'

'You should have seen him with that tall silver-haired lady over there,' Jasper said. 'He didn't look too avuncular to me.'

'Ralph is one of the few eligible widowers left in Arcadia,' said Kitty. 'He relies on me to fend off their advances. He pretends we're courting when he's here on business.'

'I won't ask you what plan you're hatching, Jasper. I'm too tired to hear anymore tonight. It's been a wonderful party, Kitty, just like you said it would be. But now I only want my bed. Do you think you could drive Claire back to my place when she's ready, Jasper? I'll sneak out the front and walk home, I need the fresh air.'

'I'll come with you, Ama. I have something to tell you,' said Jasper.

They slipped out the front door and the warm July evening enveloped them, as they strolled back the tree-lined streets of the old colonial town towards Ama's house.

'I haven't enjoyed myself this much in years, Ama. People down here are so open and friendly compared to Montreal – all suspicious and reserved. Kitty pretends Ralph is a dry old stick but he's as shrewd as they come and they're close friends.'

'What was it you wanted to tell me, Jasper. Was it about the plan you and Ralph were hatching?'

'Partly. But my daughter Elvire called me earlier tonight. She's been having heart to hearts with Ocean and gaining her confidence. It turns out our suspicions that she and her boyfriend might do a runner were justified. She told Elvire that's what they plan to do at the first chance they get. She's afraid Clay will get a long prison sentence and she wants to be with him when he's dying.'

'Is he really that ill, Jasper? Or just pretending?'

'He told me it's late stage AIDS when I spoke to him in jail. I've been thinking I could get him released on probation, on humanitarian grounds rather than on bail. I wouldn't risk putting up bail if they plan to skip town.'

'Did she tell Elvire where they'll go?'

'Out of the country. Elvire wouldn't say where. She feels she's betraying a confidence and only told me because she thought I might post bail for Clay and then lose it. Funny thing is, I liked him. Reminds me of my own son Bo, with all his insecurities. I know you dislike Clay for leading Ocean astray, but they seem to want to care for each other.'

'God, you make me sound callous, Jasper. It's true I've hated him for getting her into this drugs mess, but maybe it's because I've never met him and you have. I guess I have to take your word for it that there's some good in him. But I'm with Elvire – don't you dare even think about posting bail for him. Let his father take the chance if he wants to.'

'I promise. I also told Elvire to tell her mother that I may stay on down here for a while on business.'

'In Halifax?'

'No, here in Arcadia. Ralph wants me to meet some local investors who might put up some funding for the theatre project. He thinks the combination of his firm, with my city connections could persuade them. The fact that we both have backgrounds in arts sponsorship, as well as legal experience should convince them.'

'That's wonderful, Jasper, but this is a long way from Montreal and your law practice. Won't you have divided loyalties with the opera's claim on you?'

'The opera is awash with retired lawyers, Ama. My involvement is only token, to please Delphine. I can afford to spend more time here, on the theatre project and on Claire's major arts enterprise. She's already recruited Ralph and he and I see eye to eye.'

Ama laughed. 'I knew Claire must be behind your sudden enthusiasm. She didn't waste any time getting you on board. I hope you realise she has a very demanding new partner, so there's not much chance for you on that front.'

'I'm doomed to be a Johnny-come-lately. I'll have to settle for business lunches with her. Starting tomorrow.'

'Don't forget to bring her back here tonight, Jasper. We've got decisions to make in the morning. The chairman of the board is worried I'm not going to be able to handle all this work, unless Spike gets here right away. I've decided to call him tonight, and plead with him to leave the boat for now and come and help me out. Goodnight Jasper. It's very reassuring to know you're planning to be around for awhile. Will you stay at Kitty's for now?'

'If I can persuade her and Sarah to let me, and I think I might be able to, as they both told me of how the women's refuge could use my help.'

'You were a big hit with those kids tonight, Jasper.'

'Goodnight, Ama.'

She gave him a hug and entered the house, leaving the door unlocked for Claire. In the kitchen, she slumped into a captain's chair at the old table and punched a number into her cell phone.

'Spike? It's me.'

CHAPTER ELEVEN

'Ama? What is it? Is something wrong? I was sound asleep...'

'Spike... sorry... Spike, I...' Ama tried to swallow the lump that rose in her throat. 'Spike....'

'Ama! For god's sake – Are you all right? Did something happen?'

'No. I'm fine, really...' And then she let go a long animal howl that took her over.

'Ama, stop crying and tell me what's going on...are you sick, or what?'

'Just give me a moment, Spike. I'll be okay now that I'm talking to you. Sorry, I didn't realise how late it is. I've been at a big party and I think I'm a bit drunk, that's all.'

'You don't sound drunk. You sound like somebody really upset you. Was it someone at the party? Shit! I wish I was there.'

'I wish you were too, Spike. That's why I called. I need you to be with me. Will you come?'

'You mean right now? In the middle of the night? I don't have a car but I guess I could find a taxi if it's an emergency. Is it? Tell me the truth, Ama, are you in trouble?'

'No, it's not like you think, Spike. I'm not in any kind of physical trouble.'

'Then what? Christ, I was in a deep sleep and suddenly you're wailing in my ear like a banshee'

'You sound cross with me for waking you up. I said I'm sorry.'

'I'm not cross, Ama, I'm frightened. I still don't understand why you're so upset.'

She took a long deep breath before she spoke in a rush. 'I guess a whole lot of things came to a head for me tonight and I couldn't handle it and all I could think of was if you were here, I would be okay...' she trailed off.

There was silence on the line for a moment before he answered. 'I'm glad you called me, Ama. It's not working out for me either, being here without you. I feel stuck with no way to get around, and the parts for the boat are on back order from the States. I don't know how much longer it will take, just hanging around. They've asked me at the theatre if I'd like to work on the show here with them.'

'No Spike, no! Please. I need you here with me. Can't you leave the Mongoose where it is until it's fixed? You could ask Travis and Fergus to keep an eye on it.'

'I'll tell you all about it when you come and pick me up, Ama.'

'You mean it, Spike? You'll really come?'

'I can't do anything about it in the middle of the night. First thing in the morning, I'll sort things out with the Mongoose while you're driving down to collect me. Is that soon enough?'

'I won't sleep a wink thinking about having you here.'

'Except I won't have anywhere to sleep without the Mongoose there.'

'You'll sleep in my big sleigh bed with me, where you belong, that's where.'

'Sounds much better than the vee-berth.'

'Oh my god -'

'Now what?'

'I just remembered. Claire's sleeping there with me already.'

'A threesome – sounds exciting.'

'No chance. I'll boot her into the spare room before you get here.'

'Shame – I've never had a threesome before.'

'And you won't now either. It's not going to happen on my watch.'

'Even if it was only something harmless – like nibbling her toes?'

'I've got plenty of toes you can nibble on without bringing Claire's into it.'

'You're right, it was only a fantasy anyway.'

'I promise to indulge all your fantasies when you get here, Spike.'

'Ditto. I love you, Ama. Did I already say that?'

'Not often enough. Say it again, please.'

'I love you, Amarylis.'

'I love you too, Spike.'

'I guess that's it then, till tomorrow, unless you can make love over the phone.'

'If I could, I would. Do I sound happy, Spike?'

'Delirious. Like me,' he said.

Despite what she said to Spike, Ama fell into a deep sleep and didn't hear Claire when she crawled in beside her later. She woke early, around seven and sneaked downstairs to use the small bathroom to avoid waking Claire, who lay curled in a tight ball. After a quick shower, she dressed, made some coffee and toast, scribbled a short note to Claire and was on the road to Bridewell by 8 a.m.

Traffic was light on the winding coast road to Bridewell and the town was only beginning to stir into lazy mid-summer life when she pulled up in her little red Toyota onto the dockside. The Mongoose lay gently rocking at her moorings as Ama climbed on board, slid the hatch cover silently open and taking off her sandals, descended the companionway in her bare feet. The cabin looked semi-derelict with dirty dishes and clothes lying where Spike had dropped them. He lay on one side in the rumpled vee-berth, facing away from her. She slipped in beside him, curled against him and closed her eyes. A long sigh escaped her as she felt the tension drain from her body.

They both slept on until the morning sun finally awoke them.

'Ama, you're here.'

'Mmmhm. I'm not leaving without you, my love.'

They dressed and Spike made Ama a second breakfast, while she cleaned up the messy cabin for Fergus. He woke Fergus who was still asleep up in the deck saloon, to explain what was happening with Ama and to leave him enough cash for living expenses until he returned. He went along the dock to Travis's ice cream stall, to ask him if he'd keep an eye on the Mongoose and Fergus until the spare parts for the autopilot arrived from Chicago.

When he returned, he found his old duffel bag for Ama to pack his clothes in, while he went on deck to store anything lying about loose. Ama said goodbye to Fergus and said she hoped he'd soon be down in Arcadia when the Mongoose was fixed. The old man waved goodbye from the deck and they were ready to go before noon.

As Spike drove her old car back along the coast road, Ama brought him up to speed on what had been happening at the theatre, as well as the developments with Ocean in her current predicament. By the time she had finished they had almost reached Arcadia. She directed him via the back harbour, so he could see the layout of the old colonial town from the crest of the hill at the outskirts.

They unloaded the little Toyota and took Spike's belongings into the front hall.

'This looks more like a small hotel than a house, Ama. It seems huge after the Mongoose. You must rattle around here on your own.'

'I do. Another reason why I wanted you here so badly. It's a lovely place but I can't really enjoy it on my own. These big houses were built for large families not single old ladies.' She hugged him. 'I feel more at home here already.'

'I've got a feeling you won't want to be spending much time on the Mongoose, when it finally gets here. I can see I'll be there on my own. I can't compete with this.'

'Nobody's asking you to. Remember I'm only house-sitting for a friend of Kitty's until she gets back.'

'Fergus told me the Mongoose is no place to spend the winter, with no insulation and only the tiny wood-stove for heat. Maybe she won't come home until spring and by then the Mongoose will look like the Queen Mary inside.'

'First you have to get it down here, Spike. In a way, I'm almost glad it's been delayed. I can have your undivided attention at the theatre.'

They unpacked the cool-box and found enough leftovers from the boat to make lunch. As they ate at the long harvest table, she told him her new plans for 'Oh What a Lovely War' and they thumbed through copies of the script, trying to remember the plot.

'Does it feel as if we're at the start of something or a continuation, Ama?'

'How do you mean – us or the theatre?'

'I'm not sure. Both, I guess. You don't think we're too old to be taking on major projects like this? I wish I felt as confident as you, Ama. Nowadays my confidence ebbs and flows almost daily.'

'Is it because I've press-ganged you into leaving the Mongoose before you're finished?'

'No, it's more the feeling that you're relying on me so much, and I may let you down. I'm not the man you used to know. In fact, I don't know who I am anymore. I've been lying on my back in the vee-berth lately, trying to figure out the answer.'

'Am I part of it, Spike?'

'Right now you may be all of it, Ama. Does it worry you that I'm relying on you more than you are on me?'

'I think as long as we both want to be together, we can work out a balance that fits our strengths and weaknesses. You just need to be clear that my confidence is mostly for show – it fluctuates wildly from one day to the next. Right now, I'm high as a kite with you here beside me. If you were to leave again, I'd probably fall apart.'

'When we were together all those years ago, I would never admit to any weaknesses in front of you, Ama. Far too proud. I'm humbler now. Ready to admit my ignorance and lack of confidence.'

She rose and crossed to straddle his lap, facing him and cradling his head in her arms. 'Something happened to you in all those years you haven't told me about, didn't it?'

'I don't think I'm ready to unearth it yet and trouble you, Ama. One day, perhaps.'

'I've changed too, Spike. I'm a different woman from the one you knew in many ways. How could it be anything else?

We've been apart over forty years. It will take time to find our way back to each other.'

'And if we do, then what – live happily ever after like they do in books? That's the part that I can't figure out. My life doesn't make sense anymore. Does yours?'

'Do you remember that philosophy course you were doing when we met? You were full of Sartre's ideas then, always preaching his watchwords.'

'Anguish, abandonment and despair,' said Spike, 'I loved all that existential angst. A very good line with girls, as I recall.'

'You certainly practised on me enough. I remember you wrote on the bathroom wall, "life is meaningless but we must act as if it had meaning".'

'Great for contemplating in the bath, watching the water going down the plughole.'

'Only problem was, our lives weren't meaningless then,' said Ama. 'We were full of all the stuff we would do in the theatre. Brimming with confidence.'

'Sartre was just poser stuff at the time. It's all coming home to roost now,' he said.

'What do you suggest, Spike. Shall we make a suicide pact now or go and see the theatre first?'

He hauled her to her feet and stood looking at her. 'Amaryllis Waterstone, I hereby award you the Jean Paul Sartre award for contributions to contemporary existential philosophy. Let's go.'

They locked the house and drove through the quiet afternoon streets to the theatre and parked beside Frankie's car. Claire's silver SUV was still not there. They entered through the front doors so Spike could get his first glimpse of the foyer and grand staircase. Frankie's gauze canopy was now right side out and pinned up above the old chandelier which had been lowered to the floor and stripped of all its tear-drop crystals. The shabby worn red carpets had also all been removed revealing fine oak flooring beneath. An elderly man was demonstrating his French-polishing technique to two middle-aged volunteers at the long mahogany front-of-house bar, with its array of period posters covering every mirrored surface behind them.

Ama led him up the curving elm staircase to the balcony area and down the aisle, to look below at the stage and auditorium. The stage was strewn with timber and sheets of plywood, with Arthur in the middle of a group of older men, re-laying the deck which now extended out into the stalls area.

'Is that what I think it is?' said Spike, pointing to a rectangular hole in the new section of stage.

'A trap-door, for the foxhole scenes in Lovely War,' she said. 'I've never had a trap-door before. You can use it as Caliban's hiding place in the Tempest, as well.'

'I like that ramp running out into the stalls,' he said, 'but you must have lost a lot of seating space, Ama.'

'Look around you,' she said, 'this place was built when everyone went to the theatre. We'll be lucky to half-fill it most of the time, so Claire said why not make use of the empty space for more acting areas.'

'Is that scaffolding going to be a raised platform or what?' asked Spike.

'It's the framework for a cantilevered staircase up to the box seats and over the stalls into the balcony. Gives us two more acting spaces in the box seats and on the staircase landing, halfway to the side of the stage.'

'Four levels, counting the trap-door and the bottom of the ramp. It'll be quite a challenge to use them all in the Tempest,' he said.

'Come down and meet Arthur, our head carpenter. He's got a growing crew of aspiring woodworkers but he's still short of skilled volunteers, so he has to do most of the tricky bits himself,' said Ama.

They went back downstairs to the foyer and a strong smell of vinegar. Two of the women Ama recognised from the refuge who had been at the party, sat over plastic buckets full of the soaking crystals, polishing them and re-hanging them onto the chandelier.

'Thought we'd take you up on your offer of having a look around,' said Karla, 'and Claire put us to work bringing some sparkle back to the chandelier. It was Charlene's idea to use vinegar as the commercial cleaning fluid's so expensive.'

'A tip from my Gran who lived through the depression,' said Charlene. 'Notice any difference?'

'It's going to be glittering when it goes back up,' said Ama. 'This is Spike, my partner and co-director. We're both looking for new people to work on our opening productions, so I hope we can persuade you to join us.'

'On stage or backstage or both,' said Spike. Let me know when you can come and talk about it with us.' He handed them a card from his wallet. 'I'll be around here if you need a hand hauling the chandelier back up, when you're done.'

They went into the stalls and clambered over the spare seats which had been stacked in the aisles. 'What's happening with all these, Ama?'

'We'll keep a few for props and the rest is going to Arnold's Cave in Halifax, in exchange for some used staircases. All arranged by Claire through her contacts.'

She stood at the foot of the long half-finished ramp leading up to the stage right area, where Arthur stood talking to Garth. 'Is it safe to walk up it yet, Arthur?'

'Sure, try it out, Ama.' He watched as she and Spike walked gingerly up the ramp, which gave slightly under their combined weight.

'A bit springy,' she said, as they reached the top and stepped onto the new staging. 'Arthur, Garth, this is my partner and new co-director, Spike.'

'At last,' said Arthur, shaking hands. 'We were all beginning to think you were a figment of her fevered imagination. It's a relief to know she's getting some help at last. Too bad you missed Kitty's party, Spike. You could have met everyone at once.'

'I'll have to hope she throws another one soon. Ama seems to have been able to enlist half the town in your project. She tells me you're the master builder but not the mastermind, Arthur.'

'That's right. Claire holds that title by unanimous vote. But she's not here at present. Disappeared at lunchtime with another one of her band of followers.

'Ama's been giving me the grand tour,' said Spike. 'I'm amazed at what you've all done with this old place. I wouldn't have known where to start.'

'Neither did we, until Claire came along with her bag of tricks,' Arthur said. 'She's from a different world and sees old places like this as just interesting venues, to transform into spaces to put on shows of all kinds.'

'The difference with Claire is, she's used to doing things on the cheap,' said Ama. 'And she knows exactly where she can lay her hands on free or recycled stuff. She has contacts all over Nova Scotia and beyond. Like right now she's at lunch with my old lawyer friend, Jasper, plugging into all his Montreal networks, I'll bet.'

Garth interrupted her. 'Did you tell her yet about the changes we have to make to meet the opening deadline, Ama?'

'I meant to tell her this morning, Garth, but then I left early to pick up Spike from his boat in Bridewell. Can we keep on with doing one ramp and one staircase like we talked about, and see how long it takes, before I have to tell her?'

'But we've already yanked out all the seats for both ramps,' said Arthur. 'If we put them back, she'll want to know why.'

'Don't put them back then. It won't take long to do it later,' Ama said. She explained to Spike how the original plan would take too long to complete before the opening.

'What's wrong with delaying the opening?' said Spike. 'It will give us a breathing space too, on the production side, trying to rehearse two plays at the same time.'

'I hate delaying it. We'll lose all the momentum we've built up. Look at all these volunteers who think they're working to a deadline,' said Ama. 'They might all drift away if they feel there's no urgency anymore.'

'It's community theatre,' Arthur said. 'We run on crises.'

'Let me talk to Claire first, before we say anything to anyone. You and Garth keep this under your hat, we don't want any rumours spreading,' she said. 'And don't let them take all the seats away yet, either.'

She and Spike went backstage and she showed him the revamped dressing rooms and the old rehearsal hall that abutted the theatre. Ama switched on the lights inside it, a row of flickering neon tubes, that dimly lit the large rectangular room.

'What a mess. I haven't been in here since the last production. It's only been used as a storage space for old sets and furniture.'

'More like a junk room,' said Spike, 'but at least it's big enough for rehearsals – or it will be once all this stuff is out of here. Do you still want to go ahead with Twelfth Night?'

'It's already cast and people are learning their lines. It's a bit awkward dropping it now. Don't you want to direct it, Spike?'

'I'd rather do The Tempest as the first launchpad for a modern English version. And now that I've seen what you're doing with the stage, it will let us do lots of unusual things with the different levels for the ship and the island. And Caliban's cave could be under the trap-door.'

'I suppose I could tell the cast we're putting Twelfth Night on hold till the New Year. Topically it makes more sense to do it then.'

'Probably you can re-cast them into Lovely War. It's a big cast and it means they'll still be in the opening production so they won't feel disappointed. Do you think you can sell it to them that way, Ama?'

'They've already committed to rehearsals now, so I can jump right in and add others as needed.'

'You'd better get on the phone and start calling people, while I start chucking out all this junk.'

For the rest of the afternoon, Ama and Gloria phoned the Twelfth Night actors, as well as asking more people to come to an audition session tomorrow evening in the rehearsal room. Spike went back into the foyer and commandeered the two women who were cleaning the chandelier to help him in the hall.

While they worked, Spike asked about their life in the women's refuge and what kind of future was in store for them. He was surprised to find that Charlene had gone to art college, before she married and had two kids with a drunken husband.

'I was stuck for years with him until Kitty and Sarah opened the shelter. Then I was in there like a shot before it was even ready. I'm used to doing this kind of clearing out and redecorating for the women's refuge – there's always new families waiting to come in, isn't there, Karla?'

'Charlene helped paper and paint my two rooms for me and the twins,' Karla said. 'We were Kitty and Sarah's first customers, weren't we?'

'I don't associate a women's refuge with a small town like this,' said Spike. 'It seems more like a big city thing.'

The two women laughed. 'You don't know the half of it, Spike. I could walk you down the main street and point out several women, who would love to be able to move into the shelter,' said Charlene.

'We're bursting at the seams year-round but specially at Christmas,' said Karla. 'It's a bit quieter in the summer, with kids staying at relatives in the school holidays.'

'Wouldn't you rather have your own apartment instead of all having to live together? I mean, once you got back on your feet, with a job and so on.'

'We feel safer in the shelter,' said Charlene. 'When you're back on your own, you have a drunken husband banging on your door in the middle of the night.'

'I tried it once,' Karla said. 'No thanks. By the time the police arrived they needed an ambulance to get me out of there. At least at the shelter, the cops patrol regularly and the men know it. Anyone who busts in there gets a long spell in jail and a stiff fine.'

'Until my kids finish school, I'm not moving anywhere,' Charlene said. 'You can count on me as a volunteer indefinitely.'

'Me too,' said Karla, 'providing it's not all cleaning. We already have plenty of that at the shelter. Kids living all together can make a lot of mess.'

'I promise this is only temporary,' said Spike. 'I'll find you something more creative once we've cleared out this space.'

Ama appeared in the doorway of the hall and stared at the junk heaped in the centre of the rehearsal room. 'God - what a mountain of stuff – you weren't planning to throw it all out, were you Spike?'

'Do you want to go through it to see if you can salvage any more?'

She shook her head as she circled about the junk heap, poking at bits of it. 'No thanks, I'll take your word on it. Let's get rid of this before Arthur or Frankie or Claire see it, and want to reclaim it all again. I'll give you a hand. I've left Gloria lining up more prospects for the auditions for Lovely War tomorrow night.'

'I've got two right here who want to tread the boards, Ama. Turns out Charlene went to art college and Karla wants to play Hedda Gabler.'

'I might if I knew who she was,' said Karla. 'For now, I'm happy to turn my hand to most things.'

'Except more cleaning,' said Spike. 'She's over-qualified in that area and wants to spread her wings.'

'How about you, Charlene?' asked Ama. 'Would you like to work with me on costume designs or would you consider acting?'

'Can I do both? Karla and I could practise our parts together at the shelter in the evenings.'

'We could certainly use both of you for as much time as you can spare us,' said Ama.

'First things first,' said Spike. 'Let's get this stuff outside. Karla and I will stack up the salvaged bits against the building. You and Charlene toss out the junk around the back.'

When they had finished, Ama rescued the painted canvas from some broken scenery flats, to use as tarpaulin covers for the stuff Spike had piled along the side wall. They all went inside the theatre to the Green Room for a tea break. Claire and Jasper were huddled over some drawings she had produced.

'Jasper? – I thought you'd be sleeping off your lobster lunch back at Kitty's,' said Ama.

'Not a chance. Claire insisted I see her plans for the staircases, before I leave tomorrow morning on a mission.'

'He's offered to rent a truck for the day to go to Halifax and collect the stairs from Arnold's Cave,' said Claire. 'I can't go with him so I wanted him to see what we needed. We can't spare Arthur or the work will come to a stop on stage. And Garth has to do double baking shifts when Gloria's here.'

'This is Claire, Spike, our miracle worker. And this is Jasper, my lawyer friend from Montreal. He foolishly offered to help out when under the influence of too much punch, at Kitty's party the other night.'

'We've been waiting impatiently for you to show up, Spike, so this girl can concentrate on her work and not be mooning around or disappearing off to your yacht,' said Claire.

'She's obviously been fibbing to you as well,' he said. 'My yacht is just an old fishing boat.'

'Worse than that,' said Ama. 'It's a broken-down old fishing boat. But his bad luck is our good luck, because I pried him off it early this morning, to come down here and stop me from sinking without trace.'

'Esther was telling me we should think about creating interest in the plays by doing short sketches in town on market days,' said Spike. 'It's what she does with the university students in Dartmouth to promote their modern versions of Shakespeare.'

'You mean like a parade float on the back of a truck?' said Charlene. 'I helped design the one we used to raise funds for the women's refuge, in the annual Fishermen's Parade. We did it like the old woman who lived in a shoe and made a giant shoe full of kids and moms.'

'We've still got it in the back yard of the shelter for the kids to play on,' said Karla. 'I think we should repaint it and use it again in this year's parade.'

'When is it?' asked Spike. 'We could put a float in too.'

'Labour Day weekend,' Karla said. 'Charlene could help make it for you. She's always designing things.'

'They're only drawings,' said Charlene. 'I don't actually make them, Karla.'

'Perhaps I can persuade Esther to come down for a weekend to tell us how they do it in Dartmouth,' said Spike.

'If you went with Jasper tomorrow to get the stairs, you could all meet for lunch before you return,' said Ama. 'She could show Jasper some of the good fish restaurants on the docks.'

'But first you collect my stairs before you have any boozy lunches,' said Claire. 'Let's go check with Arthur on the right dimensions.'

On stage, Garth was up a ladder to the box seat area and Arthur was nowhere in sight.

'He's under the stage,' Garth said, pointing to the open hole for the trap-door.

Claire poked her head down the opening and beckoned him out. He appeared a moment later and climbed up beside them on stage.

'Jasper and Spike are collecting the sets of stairs tomorrow, Arthur. We want to confirm the sizes before they go,' said Claire. 'As long as Garth has the big ladder out, we can re-measure both sides again.'

'I've already done this side so it won't be necessary,' said Garth.

'But the other side is different. We'll have to move the ladder.'

'What's the point? We're only doing this side.'

Claire looked from Garth to Arthur. 'Since when?'

Arthur turned to Ama. 'I thought you were going to tell her?'

'Tell me what, Ama? Are you changing my design without any discussion with me first?'

'I haven't had a chance to speak to you about it, Claire. I'm sorry. Arthur and Garth say it's too much work to have it ready for the deadline, so they suggested doing one ramp and one staircase for now.'

'We can always add the other side later on, Claire,' said Arthur.

'And meantime we open with a lop-sided set that will look like a building site. Is that what you really want, Ama?'

'No, of course not, Claire, but we have to be realistic. If we end up with a half-finished set because we've run out of time, wouldn't that be worse?'

'I thought you trusted me? I know what I'm doing. We'll be finished on time, Arthur's only playing safe to cover his ass.'

'That's not fair, Claire. Me and Garth have been working flat out and we reckon it can't be done on time. Full stop.'

'And I say it can,' she said. 'The answer is we need more people on the job, Ama, so let's find them.'

'There aren't any more with the right skills locally,' said Arthur. 'Any more unskilled people will just be falling over each other and slowing us down even more.'

'Another good reason for delaying the opening, Ama. We all gain more time and the stage gets done the way you all envisioned it,' said Spike.

'I still say we need more skilled help,' said Garth. 'Me and Arthur are spread too thin. If we start cutting too many corners, we could have an accident.'

'Or the fire marshal could shut us down for health and safety reasons,' said Arthur. 'He's already skittish as hell about all these volunteers working in this old wooden building. He told me it just takes one untrained person to cut through an electric cable by accident, and the whole place could go up in flames.'

'You can't blame him,' Garth said, 'most of this town is built of wood.'

'Alright,' said Ama. 'Let's all think it over tonight and make a decision one way or the other when Jasper and Spike get back from Halifax tomorrow.'

In bed that night as they lay locked together too tired to do anything more than stroke each other, Spike said to her, 'I was thinking of Fergus today, when Garth and Arthur said they needed more skilled workmen.'

'I thought you said he was a boat builder – isn't that a lot different?'

'The point is, he's a brilliant wood worker and that's what we need. I know he's just tinkering with all that junk from Simon's workshop we cleared out for Esther. Suppose I asked him to stay after he's sorted out the auto-pilot, and then sail the Mongoose down here with Travis? I know he's keen to see more of the south coast again.'

'They could live on the boat in the harbour, I suppose. Is that what you were thinking?'

'And Fergus could supply the skills Arthur needs so badly.'

'Could he build staircases, Spike?'

'In his sleep.'

'But why would he want to stay down here in Arcadia, though?'

'Because he's bored and he told me he likes to keep working, so he doesn't stiffen up. Speaking of which, I thought I detected a slight tremor myself.'

'You'll have to be very quiet then. Claire's right next door, remember.'

'She could always join in. I'm very broad-minded.'

'Too bad I'm not. It's either me or nothing.'

'Well when you put it like that, I suppose I ... ahh. False alarm.'

'If you have to fantasize about a *ménage à trois* to get you going, it doesn't bode very well for our future, Spike.'

'It's more that I was put off by your bluntness. You forget what a sensitive plant you're dealing with, Ama.'

'I'll have to remember that next time. And perhaps you might consider being a little more tactful, too.'

'Does that mean we're going to sleep then?' he asked.

She reached down to touch him. 'I believe it does. Good night.'

CHAPTER TWELVE

In Halifax, Jasper and Spike found Arnold's Cave in a run-down industrial park. Claire's contact, Arnold, helped them unload the redundant theatre seats Arthur's volunteers had stacked in the rental truck. He took them round the side of the warehouse, to the stacks of stairs of all shapes and sizes and left them to sort out what they needed.

They finished loading the stairs and crammed in a pile of hand railings on top, at Arnold's suggestion and left the warehouse.

On the way back to Arcadia, Spike stopped off in Bridewell, partly to show Jasper the Mongoose, as well as see the tiny Victorian Majestic Theatre. And also to speak to Travis, the young Aussie sailor. They found him at work in the gelato stall near the harbour. Spike asked him if he could take a week or so off, to help Fergus sail the Mongoose down to Arcadia for him.

'I can do better than that,' said Travis. 'This job is getting to me and I need some action. Too much sitting around. I'm pretty handy round a boat and I can help the old boy with any of the heavy work getting her ready. If he can't fix the auto-pilot we can do without it. No worries. We sailed across two oceans and barely used one.'

Ample Make This Bed

He closed the gelato bar and came with them down to see the Mongoose. Jasper was intrigued with the layout and what Fergus had achieved with the cabin interior and the saloon area on deck so far.

'Quite a difference from the plastic yachts we have in Hudson Heights. This must have been pretty spartan accommodation for the crew to live in,' he said.

'Fish storage was the first priority apparently,' said Spike. 'Crew comforts were minimal. They were expected to work and sleep, not lie around.'

'Seems normal to me,' Travis said. 'You should see the inside of ocean racing sailboats – just a bare space with the narrowest bunks and thinnest mattresses available. Weight was the criterion, not comfort. You get used to it.'

'At your age you can get used to anything,' said Fergus. 'At our age, our old bones needs a few more creature comforts.'

Jasper sat on the vee-berth bed. 'Nothing the matter with this, Spike. You should sleep like a baby here.'

'That's what Ama says. It rocks her to sleep in no time.'

'Still, I imagine a touch more luxury wouldn't go amiss if you want her to live aboard,' said Jasper.

'That's where Fergus comes in. I'm hoping to persuade him to stay and help me finish the conversion, with Ama's design ideas, so she'll feel it's her place too.'

They left Travis at the ice cream stall and walked along to the theatre stage door. No one was about, so they went backstage to the Green Room. Justin sat reading a copy of The Tempest.

'Doing some prep for our joint project, Justin? Sorry to interrupt, I was hoping to find Emily here, too,' Spike said.

'She's in her dressing room in a huff about something I said. She'll come back in as soon as she's thought of a devastating reply.'

'I only wanted you both to meet Jasper, Ama's lawyer friend from Montreal. He's keen to help promote our modern Shakespeare production.

'Ama and Spike have both told me enough to make me want to be a part of the show, only I'm unsure what you mean by a joint production,' said Jasper.

'It's early days yet,' Justin said. 'We've barely had preliminary discussions and haven't even seen the revised script. That's why I'm reading this traditional version, to have something to compare it with. Emily disagrees, of course, and insisted we do it after we've read the modern version first, to see if it works as a play in its own right. That's why she stomped off.'

'Perhaps Jasper could jolly her back into talking to us, Justin. Ama assures me his charm is legendary.'

'Only with old ladies,' said Jasper. 'The young ones just laugh at me.'

'No harm in trying, I suppose,' said Justin. 'Her dressing room is two doors along the hall.' He and Spike watched from the doorway as Jasper rapped on her door and she called out to enter. He disappeared inside and they stood waiting for developments.

'She's not shouting so the charm offensive must be working,' said Justin, after a few minutes had passed.

On cue, her door opened and Jasper ushered her out and back down the hall towards them. She wore faded shorts and some sort of filmy top with her red hair piled up to keep her neck cool. She padded beside Jasper in her bare feet.

'Spike!' she said, air kissing him. 'I came rushing out because this gentleman said somebody important wanted to see me.'

'He's got it all backward, Emily. Jasper is the important person I wanted you to meet,' said Spike.

'What did he say exactly to get you to stop sulking?' asked Justin.

'I was not sulking, I was emphasising a point. Jasper apologised for being like a stage door Johnny. He said you and Ama had told him he shouldn't miss an opportunity to see my Kate. And now he wasn't going to be able to stay for tonight's performance, because you have to be back for auditions. But at least he could say that he'd met me. Which I thought was rather gallante, considering I looked like the cleaning woman in my rehearsal rig.'

'I see what Ama means,' said Justin. 'Anyway, you're here now and we can listen to what he has to say about the joint Shakespeare project. I gather there's been some news we should hear.'

Jasper outlined Claire's cultural commission from the federal tourism body, and how the joint production could slot right into it. Spike told them about the pageant wagon scheme, to promote the show all round the province.

'My main concern was how you will do the play jointly. Justin tells me none of this has been worked out in detail yet. Could you tell me how you see it developing, Emily?' asked Jasper. 'If I'm going to sell the idea, I need to have a clear picture of the project in my own head.'

'All I know is I want to play Miranda and I think Justin would make a good Caliban. He's too young to do Prospero, but Spike seems perfect.'

'I think we're talking more than just casting,' said Justin. 'We have to figure out which scenes and where to rehearse them. It's going to involve a certain amount of backing and forthing to Arcadia.'

'First of all,' said Spike, 'I don't want to play Prospero or any of the lead roles anymore. I can't remember lines and it's too stressful for me and the rest of the cast. However, I'd like to direct it, as my tribute to my friend Simon who revised the script. With you two as leads. I'm sure Ama has ideas as to who could do Prospero.'

'We should all get together soon and thrash out who's doing which scenes and where, now that Spike has the revised scripts for us,' Emily said.

'I can see we've opened a potential Pandora's box here,' said Jasper. 'We don't have time to get into it now because Ama wants Spike back for auditions. When can you both come down to Arcadia and see the revamped venue? We can all get together then with Ama and Claire, to share out the tasks. If you'll let me sit in on the discussion, I can get a clearer notion of what I'm promoting.'

'I'll phone Ama in the morning to fix a date soon,' Emily said. 'This is beginning to sound exciting, if we can tour it all over Nova Scotia, Jasper.'

'The federal grant money's there,' he said. 'We just have to convince them to buy it. With Claire and Ralph behind me, I think we can do it. We need to move quickly, as we're not the only game in town. They'll be looking at other projects as well as ours.'

'But Ama said they've already approached Claire,' said Spike.

'Yes, she's got a good track record of doing projects and keeping below budget. We still have to show them this will give them the best return on their dollar,' Jasper said.

'If this modern English Shakespeare clicks with the audiences, we could do a different one each year,' said Justin.

'Revitalise the whole summer Shakespeare festival scene, with its dwindling band of loyal devotees getting older and older.'

'I reckon it's win/win,' said Spike. 'Either they'll love it or hate it, but everyone will want to see it to have their say.'

'Bums on seats,' said Emily. 'The holy grail of theatre managers.'

CHAPTER THIRTEEN

Jasper's wife, Delphine had phoned to tell him that Clay, Ocean's boyfriend had his court appearance put forward to beat the summer recess.

In the end, Jasper was unable to convince the judge that Clay would abide by the community service order, as Clay condemned himself by conceding he would be back doing drugs as soon as he was released, if he lived that long. Due to the repeated offences of drug dealing, the judge pronounced a minimum sentence of two years in custody and no parole before 18 months was served.

He phoned Ama from Montreal, to tell her the outcome of the trial.

'Are you still at the theatre or back home?' he asked.

'I came home early, Jasper. Claire's not feeling well. She's had some bad news.'

'Is it about the project, Ama? I had to leave so suddenly I haven't had a chance to follow up on any of the things we planned to do. I will when I get back, so tell her not to worry.'

'I'm afraid it's worse than that, Jasper. I promised Claire I wouldn't say anything to anyone before she does.'

'Could I speak to her, Ama – is she with you?'

'She's in hiding, Jasper. Doesn't want to speak to anyone right now, not even me. She holed up in her bedroom with the door closed, just like Ocean used to do'.

'Where's her partner – what's his name. Why isn't he there with her?'

'Antony. He doesn't know and she won't let me call him.'

'That's silly. Why not? He should be there.'

'Antony is useless, she says, he'll run back to his ex-wife the moment he hears.'

'Can't you give me any idea of what's wrong, Ama? Is she in trouble of some kind? Drugs? What?'

'It's nothing like that, Jasper. All I can say is it's her health. Maybe by tomorrow when she's had time to get over the shock, she might be willing to talk.'

'Alright, I'll call in the morning. Listen, Ama. I called to tell you that Clay is in prison. I tried to get him community service but it didn't work. I wanted to talk to you before I tell Ocean. I don't know which way she'll jump when she hears.'

'How long did he get? Maybe she'll wait for him, Jasper.'

'Two years and no parole for 18 months. I doubt she'll wait that long, do you?'

'No. She might disappear again for all I know. Have you spoken to Ronnie yet?'

'I thought it might come better from Delphine. I'm seeing her this evening. She thinks Elvire seems to have some influence over Ocean.'

'Can I call you in the morning after you've spoken with them? Maybe Claire will talk to you then.'

'Sorry to dump all this on you, Ama. I'll talk to you again tomorrow.'

'Thanks, Jasper. Maybe it's just as well Clay's in prison. Ocean may see things differently now.'

'That's what I'm afraid of,' he said.

As she invariably did when in a dilemma, she turned to her mentor and old friend, Kitty. The old lady sat sipping tea on her wrap-around veranda, when Ama pulled up at her wooden mansion in her old Toyota.

'Does your heart sink when you see me arrive, Kitty?' Ama asked as she embraced her. 'Always bringing my problems to dump in your lap.'

'At my age I don't see them as problems anymore, Ama. Just opportunities to experience life in a different way.'

'I wish I had your outlook on life, Kitty. Maybe I wouldn't get into such a muddle, although I doubt it.'

'Comes with old age, dear. Don't rush it, it will be here soon enough. Tea? This gunpowder blend is very calming, I find. Go and fetch another cup from the kitchen and I'll pour you some.'

When she returned, Kitty settled her on the porch swing, gave her the tea and waited for her to drink it.

'Now what's upsetting you, Ama? I assumed you hadn't been to see me because Spike has finally showed up. Surely you haven't fallen out already?'

'God no. Spike is a rock, Kitty. He and Jasper prop me up almost daily.'

'And now Jasper has been called back to Montreal suddenly. We barely had a chance to say goodbye but he's promised to return soon. Sarah and I moon over him like schoolgirls.'

'I spoke to him awhile ago and he promised me the same. He wanted to talk to Claire but she refused. She won't speak to anyone she's so distraught. That's why I'm here, Kitty, I need your help.'

'What's happened to her, Ama? Has she had a nervous breakdown? It wouldn't surprise me at the rate she goes. And there's nothing to her. I'll bet I weigh more than she does and Sarah says I'm only skin and bones.'

'That's the problem, Kitty, she's sworn me to secrecy. I can only tell you that it's bad news she's had about her health and she's convinced she's going to die. She's shut herself up in her room and won't come out.'

'Do you think she might talk to me, Ama? We only met briefly but we seemed to hit it off.'

'Would you, Kitty? You're the only person I think she'd open up to. I'm so worried about her. I can hear her weeping in her room but she won't talk to me at all.'

'Of course, dear. Let me put my coat and shoes on and we can go right now. I'll leave a note for Sarah – she's at the refuge and won't be home for awhile.'

Ama helped the old lady down the front steps to the car and drove the few blocks to her house-sit. Claire's bedroom was upstairs but Kitty went first to the kitchen to make some tea. When it was brewed, Ama carried the tray with two cups upstairs behind her. She set it down on a small hall table outside the bedroom door. She watched as Kitty listened at the door for a few moments, then tapped softly on the door and entered. The old lady gestured to Ama to go back downstairs and closed the door. Ama retreated to the foot of the stairs and sat down.

For what seemed an age the only sound coming from the room was a low murmur. She couldn't make it out at first and then identified as Claire, as it rose in volume before dissolving into heavy sobs, which went on and on. Eventually they subsided. The door opened and Kitty took the tray of tea into the room, leaving the door ajar.

Feeling too much as if she were eavesdropping, Ama rose and went back to the kitchen to pour herself some tea and wait. She thought of calling Spike at the theatre but something restrained her. She knew he would insist on coming home to be with her and trying to help. Kitty was her best hope and she trusted her old friend, even while she felt there was little to be done for Claire except give her comfort. She recalled how often she had relied on the old woman to help her to see her way out of what seemed intractable situations, mostly involving Ocean. The antique wall clock ticked its way round to the half hour chime, before she heard Kitty's voice calling her from the landing. Ama tiptoed up the stairs to her.

'She wants you to come and join us, Ama. We have some things to talk over together.'

In the bedroom, Claire sat cross-legged on the bed with a chair brought up to the side of it, where Kitty resumed her seat. She motioned Ama to sit on the edge of the bed. Claire's usually immaculate clothes were creased and her hair hung lank and uncombed around her sallow face. She gave Ama a weak smile and reached out her hand, saying nothing. They both turned to Kitty.

'Claire has told me her shocking news and we've been turning it over together to see what the way forward might be, Ama. For the present, we both agree that what the politicians call damage limitation, is the best option until she knows the full extent of her diagnosis. There might be more bad news to follow but we'll deal with that when it happens. There's more than enough for now.' She smiled at Claire and took her other hand. 'First though, the good news. Claire has agreed to move to my big old house and make it her base of operations, with Sarah and I to look after her. She may have to go into hospital later, but for now we can hold the fort and allow you to get on with plan B. You can't be in two places at once, Ama, so Claire would like you to be her stand-in at the theatre and she'll direct operations from my place. We'll put a bed in my enclosed veranda so she can enjoy the view and hold court in private with whoever she pleases. Her doctor, Laura, is the daughter of a good friend of mine and I've known her since she was a child. I'm sure she'll be happy to visit Claire at my house whenever she needs to. For everyone else, you can let it be known she's been overdoing things and has been ordered to have bed rest to regain her strength.'

'What about Antony, Claire – what will you tell him?'

'I don't know. Nothing yet. He's away in the States on one of his periodic business trips to L.A. I'll think of something before he comes back.'

'Wouldn't it be better if you just rested and forgot about the theatre? Let me do the worrying for awhile and you concentrate on recovering, Claire.'

'My doctor is very clear that there is not going to be any recovery, Ama. The most I can expect is a stalling tactic. She calls it remission and I'm not sure how it works or for how long. Meantime, if I don't keep busy, I'll lie here and brood.'

Over the next two days, Claire transferred to Kitty's enclosed veranda room and Spike and Ama set up her HQ there. A steady stream of people from the theatre began coming, to discuss the ongoing transformation of the old Regency playhouse. Sarah took on the challenge of enticing Claire to eat. Encouraged by Kitty, Charlene became Claire's design assistant. She shouldered much of the burden of fielding calls and regulating the flow of visitors, to prevent her from becoming overtired, which became an increasing problem.

Kitty monitored her patient under the guise of afternoon tea. Spike and Ama came by to chat and talk shop with her, after they finished at the theatre if it wasn't too late. Often Claire was asleep at her chart table. Arthur had rigged it for her to roll over her bed, so she could work propped up with pillows. At other times, she was flushed and animated when they arrived and wanted to keep them there, talking over a glass of white wine which she loved most of all. When Ama had asked Laura, her doctor, if this was wise, the medic shrugged and said why not, if it made her feel better.

Jasper had ordered video conference call equipment to be set up permanently in her room, so they could all sit round her bed and talk together with him in Montreal. Kitty's old lawyer friend, Ralph, had taken to stopping by after hours to discuss the progress of the cultural project by video. It had received approval before Claire's sudden change of circumstances. Jasper and Ralph had talked about curtailing the whole scheme, or putting it on hold but Claire was adamant it should continue.

Arthur and Garth had a change of heart when they heard the news. They told Ama it might be possible to go back to Claire's original plan of both staircases and both ramps. The official opening had been postponed to the end of September, instead of the beginning. They insisted on telling Claire in person.

'You were right after all, Claire,' said Garth. 'We've been talking it over, haven't we, Arthur?'

'That's right,' Arthur nodded. 'With the promise of Fergus's experience and assistance, we reckon it could now be done – with you overseeing it, of course.'

They were rewarded with smiles and hugs from Claire, who graciously apologised for pushing them too hard.

Ama had allowed herself to hope that she might be reunited with Ocean, when Jasper phoned to tell her of her daughter's reaction to the fate of Clay.

'What did she say, Jasper? Tell me.'

'Well, she told me she had half expected it, so it wasn't a surprise. In fact, she was already considering what she would do next, when her custody order was relaxed.'

'It sounds like she's accepting her situation, doesn't it?' Ama said.

'Ronnie has come up trumps, and found her a small part in his TV mini-series,' said Jasper. 'That's an encouraging start, Ama.'

Ama found she could now focus on rehearsals for Lovely War, which she was fitting in and around the work happening onstage. With the breathing space provided by the postponement of the official opening, the frantic pace of work relaxed and people returned to a more normal routine. It almost seemed to Ama, that progress on her rehearsals for Lovely War became less fraught. Now the actors had time to explore all the possibilities the three levels of the revamped stage provided. They pored over the rich body of material that existed from the original East London production. They discovered it had largely been a process of improvisations. This knowledge gave them the freedom to search for contemporary parallels to the horrors of the 1st World War. They didn't have to look far to find them once they started.

Where the 1960s Theatre Workshop production in London had made use of tabloid newspaper headlines, with a rear screen to project large static images of the war and mind-numbing statistics of the daily slaughter, Ama's troupe could use the modern media equivalents, with TV news clips and film archive excerpts.

'Ama, why don't we ask Esther's grad students to dig out recent material modern audiences can relate to?' asked Spike. 'With their research expertise, they'll draw their own parallels with the present-day wars, don't you think?'

She agreed and the students responded, by inundating them with equally horrific images and statistics on civilian casualties. Particularly children, the euphemistically termed 'collateral damage.'

To contrast with all this stygian gloom, the popular songs with their sometimes naive and sometimes ironic lyrics, would provide much needed comic relief for the audience. A chance to catch their breath and reflect on what they were seeing. Bolstering this, were Frankie's commedia del arte Pierrot costumes, to lend a distancing effect. A stark change from the continuous visual back projections, rolling out behind the actors.

Spike sat in the stalls offering his feedback to Ama. She paced back and forth from the stalls to the stage, energised by the opportunities offered from both the multi-level set and the enthusiastic cast. She stayed open to, and encouraged, their ideas and suggestions, while reserving for herself the final decisions.

'You're an actor's dream of a director, Ama,' Spike told her in bed one evening. 'I love the way you let them try their way of playing a scene and then your way after, to see which works better. Not many directors have the self-confidence to use that approach.'

'Do you really mean that, Spike, or are you just sweet-talking me?'

'A bit maybe, but it's true.'

'It takes longer, but often their way is the most effective. And I don't find dictatorial directors last long in community theatre. People don't want to work with them if they're not enjoying themselves.'

'Professional theatre is at a distinct disadvantage there,' said Spike. 'When you're being paid, you do what you're told, whether you agree or not. Often, it's cold comfort to know you were right, if the show suffers.'

'One of the reasons I didn't mind changing horses. But I miss the money sometimes,' she said.

Back at Claire's veranda HQ after rehearsals, they told her the successes and disappointments of the day and how much they loved her revamping ideas.

'I keep thinking of different ways I can make use of the ramps and stairs in the Tempest, Claire,' said Spike, 'especially for the storm scene at the opening. Do you think you could create the effect of an Elizabethan galleon with sails at two or three levels?'

'The problem will be striking them when the scene finishes,' said Ama. 'You don't want to have a fifteen-minute break to clear the stage.'

'I've been reading the script a few times looking for ideas while I'm lying here,' said Claire. 'As the storm scene ends with the shipwreck, wouldn't it be natural to have the masts and sails come crashing down on stage and the sailors trying to salvage them by dragging them off into the wings? Lots of lightening bolts and sound effects in the darkness to cover the action. We'd have to cheat on the sails,' she said. 'Canvas is heavy and expensive. I'd need something like silk, to be light and billowy enough and quick to remove.'

'Silk! It would cost a fortune,' said Ama.

Claire shook her head. 'Army surplus old parachutes. I think I know where to lay my hands on some. I might have to call on Ralph's old regimental contacts to get them.'

Walking home afterwards in the warm summer evening, arm in arm, Ama turned to Spike.

'You know, despite all the concerns with Ocean and Claire, I feel perfectly content. Isn't that perverse, Spike?'

'Not at all. With me here to solve your problems, it's roses, roses, all the way.'

'No, I mean it. I should be floundering and full of doubts and instead I'm feeling confident.' She leaned over to kiss his cheek. 'I'm happy to concede you're a lot to do with it, though.'

'It's catching,' he said, 'I feel the same way. I guess we're both on a roll with all this theatre stuff bolstering our morale. Does it make you feel nervous that it could just as easily be reversed?'

'Don't even think it, Spike, it's bad luck'.

'I know,' he said. 'Maybe it's the sentimental nostalgia of all those 1st World War songs we've been practising.'

'I prefer to think it's a good sign,' she said.

They linked arms again and marched down the darkened street singing together.

"What do we want with eggs and ham,
When we've got plum and apple jam,
Rinky dinky parley-voo."

CHAPTER FOURTEEN

In the days that followed, Spike and Ama re-discovered how well they worked together in their professional theatre capacity. They were helped immensely by Jasper's willingness to take on the role of producer, even though he often had to return to Montreal on legal business. At Kitty's insistence, he made her upstairs guest room his base. He could often be found conferring with Claire, in her new studio-cum-bedroom on the main floor of the rambling old house. Sarah plied them both with food and kept an eagle eye on Claire, to make sure Jasper didn't overtire her.

Fergus had returned to Halifax for his ancient pickup which he had loaded with his carpentry tools, plus an assortment of parts that might come in handy repairing the faulty autopilot on the Mongoose. He phoned Spike when he got back to Bridewell.

'That's great, Fergus. Travis said he'll help you out. He's an experienced sailor and good with his hands, he tells me. Should be a useful assistant for you while you dismantle the autopilot,' said Spike.

'Good. I'll need his help to do some sea trials with the Mongoose to find out what's makin' her play up,' Fergus said. 'May take us a while to track down the problem. I been thinkin' over how to finish what Simon and me had planned. It might be best to wait till we get the boat down to Arcadia before I tackle anything else. I figure you'll have your own ideas of what you want changed.'

'Yes, I'd like to talk it through with you, Fergus, and include Ama's ideas too, so let's wait till you get here.'

'Between Travis and me we should have her sorted out in a few days, Spike. I'll let you know when she's fixed.'

'Sorry I can't be there to help out, Fergus, but I'm fully committed down here with Ama's theatre opening. In fact, I'm glad you're waiting till you get here to start work on the Mongoose. We desperately need your expert advice on some tricky stage cantilevered stairs we're building. We've got plenty of willing volunteers but nobody with your experience. Do you think we can persuade you to supervise them, Fergus, so it doesn't all collapse on opening night?'

'Make a change from workin' on boats, I suppose, but probably not all that different, Spike. I've built and rebuilt a few companionways over the years. Be happy to put my oar in when we get the Mongoose down to Arcadia.'

'I was hoping that's what you'd say. I'll phone Travis to get in some supplies. He's a good cook, he tells me, so you'll be well looked after, Fergus. I'll be in touch in a couple of days.'

At the theatre he broke the good news to Arthur and Garth that expert help was on the way.

'If Fergus is as good as you say he is, Spike, we might just be able to build both staircases and ramps the way Claire wants them after all,' said Arthur.

'Have you told Ama yet?' asked Garth. 'She'll be relieved to hear he's coming.'

'Not yet. Where is she? Not rehearsing this time of day. She left the house before I got up.'

'Last time I saw her she was talking to three people at the same time,' said Garth. 'Gloria tells me she can't keep up with Ama since Claire's been ill, trying to juggle her work as well as rehearsals.'

'Maybe you should have a word with her, Spike,' said Arthur. 'That's all we need, to have Ama burn out on us as well as Claire.'

In the wardrobe, Frankie and Charlene were unpacking several large woven wicker costume hampers with official opera stencils on them.

'Have a look at this, Spike,' said Frankie, reading a document from the hamper. 'Courtesy of the Montreal opera company. It's in French, can you read it?' He handed it to Spike.

'It's signed Delphine Falkenham,' said Spike. 'Jasper's wife. She's on the opera board, he told me'

'Just look at this,' said Charlene, holding up a white satin commedia dell arte costume with bold glossy black buttons down the front. 'Wait till Ama sees these, Frankie.'

'Good old Jasper,' he said. 'It must have taken some smooth talking to persuade them to lend us these.'

'Where is Ama anyway?' said Spike. 'Have you seen her, Frankie?'

'She was in here earlier, before these arrived. Said she had to go to Kitty's to meet Claire's doctor.' He lifted out another multi-coloured velvet Harlequin outfit from the hamper. 'Why don't you take one of these over to show Claire, Spike? She'll love it.'

Ama's old Toyota was not in the theatre parking lot so he walked over to Kitty's, carrying the costume Frankie had wrapped in tissue and put in a bag for him to show Claire. At the old mansion, the little red car was parked between

Jasper's black Citroen and Claire's silver SUV. He tapped at the door and Sarah let him in.

'If you're looking for Ama, she's with Claire and the doctor in her room. Shall I see if it's okay for you to go in? Kitty's in the kitchen.'

'Will you give this to Claire, Sarah? I'll wait in the kitchen with Kitty.' He handed the parcel to Sarah and went down the hall to the big old kitchen. A worried look on Kitty's face made him fear bad news. She rose to give him a hug.

'What's up, Kitty? They told me at the theatre the doctor's here.'

'More tests results, I'm afraid.'

'She's not getting any better, is she, Kitty? Ama and I both notice how easily she tires these days.'

The old lady nodded. 'I wonder just how therapeutic all this endless activity is, Spike. Claire insists it's what she wants.' She shrugged and gave him a wan smile. 'It seems so unfair an old creature like me is hale and hearty, while a vital woman like her is fading away.'

Spike shook his head. 'And Ama's daughter, too. I suppose she's told you Ocean has some suicide pact with her AIDS boyfriend. Three terminal cases all at once for Ama to worry about.'

'She's another one who's driving herself too hard. Can't you make her ease up, Spike. Share the load more with you?'

'I'm trying, Kitty, but she's very stubborn. And she does love the work.'

Sarah entered the room, smiling at him. 'That was an inspired surprise, Spike. Claire wants you to go in and model it for them.'

The three women looked up, smiling at him as he walked into Claire's enclosed porch room.

'You're all looking chirpy. Is this the effect of my little surprise present?'

'Don't try to take the credit, Spike, this is all Jasper's doing,' said Claire, as he bent over the bed to give her a careful hug.

'Not quite all,' said Ama. 'Jasper's wife, Delphine, is who we should thank for arranging this loan. Are there many more like this, Spike?'

'Crates of them. Charlene and Frankie were just starting to unpack them, oohing and ahhing over each one.'

'Seems like you've stolen my thunder,' said the doctor. 'Shall I tell him or will you, Claire?'

'These latest tests have come back negative, Spike. Laura says it means I'm in remission. For awhile anyway,' said Claire. 'I feel like Lazarus. I want to rise from my bed and go over to the theatre with Ama to see all these fantastic costumes.'

The doctor smiled, shaking her head. 'I don't want to be a damp squib, Claire, but remission doesn't mean you're cured. More like a breathing space or a pause. They happen quite a lot. You can think of it as a reprieve.'

'How about if I model this Harlequin costume for you for starters?' said Spike. 'Ama can be my dresser.'

She took the costume and went out into the hall to put it on him.

'Did the doctor say how long this remission will last, Ama?'

'She said it could be weeks or even months. Depends a lot on whether she overdoes it or not.'

'That could be problematic, knowing Claire. You saw how she wanted to jump straight out of bed,' said Spike. 'Sarah may have to tie her down.'

He pranced back into the room, circling the bed with exaggerated gestures to Claire and the doctor, ending with a sweeping courtly bow to them all. The women all applauded, admiring the elegant costume.

'Wonderful,' said Claire. 'Isn't it a pity we've lost the significance of all these commedia costumes. Each one was a specific character. Do you remember who Harlequin represented, Spike?'

'I'm not sure. I don't think he was a clown, was he, Ama?'

'No, he was more a mischievous servant and the lover of Columbine the maid. I've been boning up again on the whole commedia dell' arte characters and history, for Lovely War, and it's full of fascinating stories. Traditionally, Harlequin usually carries two sticks tied together to make loud scary noises. It's where we get the term –'

'Slapstick,' said Laura.

'How did you know that?'

'When I was an intern, all the junior doctors used to put on comedy shows at Christmas for the kids in hospital. I played il Dottore, the comic doctor, performing all sorts of funny operations like pretending to cut off a leg or a foot. We got most of our ideas from reading about commedia sketches. The Tooth Puller was a favourite with the kids, pulling out three or four teeth and still not getting the right one.'

'Ama, do you think you'll be able to use many of these traditional characters in Oh What A Lovely War?' asked Claire.

'I'd love to. In the original production they mainly used the most recognizable, Pierrot and Pierrette, and Punch and Judy. That's nearly all we have left today in the theatre, except for circus clowns.'

'And pantomimes,' said Spike.

'Yes, of course, the pantos,' said Ama. 'Apparently, right up until the 20th century they used to be called Harlequinades, because he was the main character. But it's changed gradually over the years to include fairy tale characters and music hall routines. You should read up on it,' she said, 'it's wonderful stuff – goes right back to the Greeks and Romans – that's where the word comes from. Pantomime literally means act all the parts. Originally, one person acted out all the characters in the old myths and legends.'

'Is there anything that didn't begin with the Greeks, I wonder,' said Laura.

'What was news to me, was that women first appeared in commedia dell' arte plays, long before they ever showed up on the English stage,' said Ama.

'It's got me thinking how we could adapt our stage for commedia style acting,' said Claire. 'I know they were mainly travelling players touring around Europe, playing outside to the public. Maybe we could have them appear as a play within a play, Ama.'

'Like the Players in Hamlet,' said Spike. 'I once acted the First Player in my rep days. We had a wagon we pulled around the stage to act on.'

'Shakespeare loved using commedia style characters and plots,' said Ama. 'His plays are full of them. Look at Falstaff – I'll bet he originated as a commedia character.'

'You know how Esther suggested we use the old pageant wagon idea to promote the plays,' said Spike. 'Why not design something we can use both onstage and around the town, with lots of actors dressed in commedia style doing mime shows.'

'Who's going to volunteer to tell Arthur he has to build a pageant wagon on top of everything else,' said Claire. 'I'm already in his bad books for insisting on two ramps and two staircases.'

'Maybe he won't have to, Claire,' said Spike. 'Esther told me if you can find the funding, she can send her grad students down to make one, as part of their coursework.'

'Before you all get too carried away, I'd like to register one caveat,' said Laura. 'Just because Claire's tests show she's in remission, doesn't mean she can plunge straight back into her normal schedule. I've told her of the risk of a relapse, but I expect you all to make sure it doesn't happen. I have to go now so I'll leave you to it. All sounds very exciting, I wish I had the time to be part of it.'

'We could find you a cameo role as il Dottore,' said Spike, 'and you could reprise your student intern days.'

'Don't tempt me,' said Laura. She gathered up her black bag and coat, gave Claire a quick squeeze and left to speak to Sarah and Kitty about their charge.

'We'd better get back to the theatre. Leave Claire to rest and mull over how she can adapt the stage,' said Ama.

'I want to come with you,' said Claire, 'but Laura has put the fear in me of what will happen if I overdo it. I think I'll stay here and decide on my next move. Do you think you could send Charlene back, so I can bounce some ideas off her, Ama?'

'If I can tear her away from all those commedia costumes, I will. Meantime you could cheer Sarah and Kitty up with your good news.'

'I'd better get on to Esther and see how soon they can come down to build the pageant wagon,' said Spike, as they drove back to the theatre.

Ama nodded, 'And I was thinking we'd better warn Arthur to make a long ramp shallow enough to push the wagon up onto the stage. I love the idea of using it for entertaining the troops.'

'When I hitch-hiked to east Berlin as a student to see Brecht's theatre,' said Spike, 'his company was performing Mother Courage. They had a big wagon she dragged across the stage with her camp followers. I can still picture it – made a very powerful impression on me.'

'Perhaps I can ask Charlene to design one with Claire. We can use it in the Labour Day parade, as well as in the theatre, Spike. It might help keep Claire occupied while she's recuperating.'

'I'll ask Esther to liaise with her and send her some pictures of what her students used in the past,' he said.

At the theatre, Spike saw that Arthur and Frankie's teams of volunteer workers had begun to transform the shabby old theatre into what was beginning to look like an intriguing space. The thrust staging with ramps on either side extending into the audience was surrounded with the newly-covered zigzag art deco seating. The trap door now had a cover which dropped down out of sight so it could be controlled from below.

Ama had been rehearsing her Lovely War cast in the cleared out old rehearsal hall at the rear of the theatre. She was now able to move them onstage in the evenings, to become familiar with the revamped theatre.

Arthur and Garth were working on the support structure for one of the staircases.

'How soon will I be able to let the cast use all three levels, Arthur?' asked Ama.

'Well, when me and Garth finish the landing area between the stage and the box seats, we can rig you some temporary steps for rehearsal so you can have access in both directions.'

'Will it be safe for the actors to use though?' she said, studying the skeleton structure.

'Oh, it will be safe enough, it just won't look very beautiful. And it will only be for this side of the stage. You'll have to wait for Spike's ship-building expert, for the cantilevered staircase on the other side.'

'Yeah, when can we expect him to arrive?' asked Garth. 'Me and Arthur can manage this side, it's fairly straightforward but the other one defeats us.'

'Not for awhile,' said Spike, 'he's rebuilding my faulty autopilot in Bridewell and then he and Travis will sail it down here to live on, while he works on these stairs.'

'But the good news is, Claire's doctor has said she's recovered enough to come back to doing light duties, so she'll soon be down here egging you on, Arthur,' said Ama.

'It will be great to have her back, even if she does give me a hard time, Ama. Her enthusiasm is catching. I miss her.'

'We all do,' said Ama, 'but her doctor says we have to make sure she doesn't overdo it.'

'We'll make sure she takes plenty of breaks,' said Garth, 'even if we have to tie her down in the stalls.'

'I think she'll be happy just to be here in the thick of things,' said Spike. 'She knows she has to pace herself.'

'Claire only knows one speed,' said Ama. 'Flat out. It may not be that simple to slow her down. She's the queen bee and we'll soon all be buzzing round her like before. I'm worried.'

'What are you worrying about now, Ama?' said Frankie, calling up from the stalls where he was supervising the last of the seat coverings. He joined them on stage and Ama told him Claire's news.

'Why don't we set her up in the Green Room for her office? We can all take turns consulting with her and there's a big sofa for her to take naps on.' he said.

'The intercom's in there so she'll hear everything that's happening,' said Arthur, 'and I'll get Reggie to run a phone extension in for her.'

'She won't agree to stay put, that's the trouble,' said Ama. 'She'll insist on supervising everything herself.'

'Then we'll make sure she has a regular assistant,' said Spike. 'She likes working with Charlene. Let's ask her if she'll be her go-between, Ama.'

Charlene came onstage to tell Spike someone wanted to see him. 'He's waiting in the foyer.'

Spike followed her out and found a big farmer staring about him. The carpet-laying team was spreading rolls of royal blue exhibition carpet up the curving elm staircase under the supervision of one of Gloria's volunteers. The farmer pumped Spike's hand and said he was Lloyd Kramer, a friend of Arthur's.

'Arthur tells me you might be looking for a team of oxen to pull a fancy wagon around town to advertise your show. The farm keeps me fully occupied with very little free time. I'm on my way back home now and just dropped in to see you. You look kinda busy yourself with all these renovations. I hardly recognise it from when I came here as a schoolboy to see Julius Caesar. When do you plan to open?'

'Not for a while yet – we've had to put back the opening date till the end of September.

'My son Derek is learning to drive our show team of oxen. I told Arthur he'd like a chance to appear in public with them. I'm trying to encourage him to stay on the farm. But I don't like to push him too hard.'

'Fathers and sons – tricky combinations, Lloyd. My son left home because we couldn't get along. You're fortunate your boy wants to be with you.'

'That's what Beattie says. We only have one child. I'd hate to lose him. What happened to your lad, then?'

'He's back in London, in the antique business with his partner – no kids yet. I don't hear much from him.'

'I can't imagine how that would be – havin' my only son livin' in another country. Farmers don't stray far from home. Not like theatre people, I guess, used to travellin' all over.'

'I think I'm finally ready to settle in one place,' said Spike. 'I like it here. If things work out for Ama and me with the theatre, I hope to stay.'

'Be nice to get to know each other better, Spike. I hope you stay, too.'

The next afternoon, when they had Claire ensconced in the Green Room holding court, Ama and Spike found Derek Kramer, the big farmer's son waiting for them in the foyer.

'Dad told me you might have a job for me and our show team. He told me to drop by after school and have a word. I was never that interested in ox-pulls but I'd still like to show them at fairs and stuff. He said he's had enough of them, too. He's won practically every medal there is, so he's ready to retire and just farm. That suits me.'

'So, you and your dad will be showmen instead of sportsmen,' said Spike. 'Maybe you'd like to bring your team to the Fishermen's Day parade in town. We're planning to put a float in it to promote the re-opening of the theatre. It would be a chance to show off your prize oxen and we'd have you and your dad to lead the pageant wagon we're going to make.'

'I think I can persuade Dad and I'm sure mom wouldn't object either.'

'That's wonderful,' said Ama, 'we'll let you know when we need you, Derek.'

As they drove back home, they decided to call Esther to tell her they had a real yoke of oxen to pull her pageant wagon.

'That ought to spur her to get the students down here working on it,' said Spike.

Jasper's big black sedan was parked outside Ama's house-sit when they arrived home after rehearsal that evening. He was nowhere to be seen, so they went indoors. Twenty minutes later he knocked at the door.

'I went for a walk downtown while I waited for you,' he said. 'I didn't want to disturb you at the theatre. Lots of tourists wandering about but not much for them to do, except eat and look in closed shop windows. It will be good to be able to offer them some live entertainment when you open.'

'First we have to attract them there,' said Spike. 'We're working on a pageant wagon to drum up interest. We've even got some prize oxen to pull it around the town.'

'Was it something particular, Jasper, or a social visit?' asked Ama. 'We don't get to see much of you these days with Ralph and Claire monopolising you. Come in and have a drink and tell us all your latest news from Montreal.'

'I was hoping you wouldn't be too tired for a chat,' said Jasper. 'I brought a very nice bottle of single malt scotch from a grateful divorcee we can sample.' He put the bottle on the kitchen counter while Spike found some ice and glasses.

'Let's sit out on the veranda,' said Ama, leading the way. 'It's too nice to stay indoors. I've been in a darkened theatre all day.'

'We should be treating you, Jasper, after all those amazing costumes you commandeered,' said Spike.

'I haven't actually seen them,' said Jasper. 'I just gave Ama's list to Delphine and she did the rest.'

'I want you to make me a promise, Jasper, that you'll bring your wonderful wife down here for the opening, so I can personally thank her. And for all she's done for Ocean, as well.'

'That's what I wanted to see you about, Ama. I have some more news of her I needed to tell you privately. Have you spoken to Ronnie?'

'No, not a word. What is it, Jasper?'

'Ocean's disappeared. She hasn't been back home at Ronnie's for three days. I thought maybe she might have come down here to you. She's violating her parole Delphine and I arranged, by leaving her father's custody.'

'Oh god, I was afraid it was all going too smoothly,' said Ama. 'Where do you think she is? Does Ronnie have any idea? Did she leave him a note or anything?'

'Nothing. None of us have any idea. I was hoping she might have at least been in touch with you, Ama.'

'Well, Clay presumably hasn't broken out of prison, so we can rule him out,' said Spike.

'Ronnie feels he has to tell her parole officer soon but I asked him to wait until I'd spoken to you first. Have you any idea where she might have gone, Ama? A relative or a friend maybe?' said Jasper.

'Did Ronnie search her room? Is her passport missing? That's all I can think of. She might have gone back to that retreat place in France she stayed at before.'

'That's what he figured, too, but he found her passport in a drawer,' said Jasper. 'I wondered if she had gone to that grow-op farm where I tracked her down, remember? Those druggie friends of Clay's. I asked a local contact in Stratford if he'd check it out for me. I heard back from him before I left Montreal.'

'And she wasn't there?'

Jasper shook his head. 'I've run out of ideas, Ama. That's why I'm here, to see if you have any.'

'Oh god, Spike, here we go again. I haven't got a clue where she'd be. I've no idea who her friends are these days, if she even has any. I'm sorry, Jasper. All your good work, and Delphine's. I don't know what to say.'

'It's not entirely unexpected, Ama. We discussed this possibility before and now it's happened. Only not with Clay. She's on her own and she's broken her parole so she's made things more difficult for herself when she does surface again. The court won't be so lenient with her next time.'

'It looks like we'll just have to wait and see,' said Spike. 'She hasn't left the country so she's bound to show up somewhere soon.'

Jasper rose from his seat. 'I think Spike's right, Ama. I only wanted you to know the situation. Delphine and I have lots of contacts and we'll keep feelers out for her. Try not to worry.' He gave her a hug. 'I'll be at Kitty's for the next week or so. Now that we've had Claire's good news, Ralph and I will be renewing our project plans with her.'

After he left, Ama and Spike fell into bed, exhausted.

'I've had an idea, Spike,' she whispered to him, but he was already asleep.

The next morning, Ama was up early and left the house before Spike awoke. She wrote him a note stuck on the bathroom mirror.

'Please hold the fort, Spike. I'll be out of town for a couple of days. Call you tonight. I love you. Ama xxx'

She put her overnight bag in the old red Toyota and drove slowly out of Arcadia, heading west. On the motorway to Montreal and Toronto she tried to work out her idea from the night before. By the time she reached Montreal she had formulated her plan, and she stayed at the same little *pension* she'd found on her previous visit. The same corner take-out kebab house was open and she took the food back to her room to eat before calling Ronnie. His wife answered and said he had a night shoot and wouldn't be home till very late. Ama left her name and said she'd call back in the morning. Next, she rang Spike.

'Ama, where are you? What are you doing?'

'I'm sorry, Spike. I knew if I woke you up this morning, you'd try to talk me out of it.'

'Out of what? Where are you calling from? Everybody's asking where you went.'

'I'm in Montreal. On my way to London.'

'England? What on earth for?'

'London, Ontario. But first I wanted to talk to Ronnie, so I've stopped in Montreal for the night. He's on a night shoot, his wife says and he won't be home till morning.'

'Couldn't you have called him, Ama? Why drive all the way to Montreal?'

'It's probably no use but I wanted to hear what he knows of Ocean, before I go to London.'

'I don't understand, Ama. Why London?'

'That's where Clay is in jail, Spike. Jasper told me. I have to speak to him.'

'And you think Clay knows where Ocean is?'

'Yes, don't you?'

'I suppose it's possible,' he said. 'If she and Clay really have made this suicide pact.'

'Jasper's daughter, Elvire, thinks they have. And Jasper says she's become a sort of confidante of Ocean's.'

'Why don't you talk to her first, before driving all the way to London? It'll take you a whole day just to get there and he probably wouldn't want to speak to you anyway, Ama. He knows you hate his guts.'

'I just thought he might tell me if I spoke to him in person.'

'Why would he tell you anything if they are planning something together. He knows you'd try to prevent it happening, so he won't say a word.'

'How do you know what he'd say, Spike? It's worth a chance. I have to do something.'

'Why not talk to Elvire? She's in Montreal and so are you. She might know something, Ama. It's better than a wild goose chase half-way across the country. You don't just turn up at a prison and demand to see one of the inmates. They have regular visiting days. You have to make an appointment. You might have to wait a week to see him. Or he might say he doesn't want to see you.'

'You don't know this, Spike.'

'I've seen enough TV cop shows to know the procedure, Ama. At least, try to talk to Elvire before you leave Montreal. And call me back afterwards. Promise?'

'I'll think it over and decide in the morning, Spike. I'm too tired to think straight right now.'

'If I thought it would do any good, I'd come with you, Ama.'

'It's alright, Spike. I'd rather you stayed there and covered for me. I'll be back as soon as I find out anything.'

'Don't disappear on me, Ama. Keep in touch, okay?'

'I'll call you tomorrow, Spike.'

'And Ama – no more wild goose chases. Not without me. Promise?'

'I promise.'

In the morning she called Claire, to ask her if she had a Montreal phone number for Jasper. She knew if she spoke to him herself, he would want her to let him handle things. When she rang the number Claire gave her, it was Jasper's wife, Delphine, who answered. Ama explained why she was calling and thanked her for everything she had done for her daughter, then asked her if she could speak to Elvire. Delphine listened in silence until she had finished speaking.

'Per'aps we should meet for lunch to discuss this further. I will ask Elvire to join us.' She gave Ama the name of a small bistro downtown and agreed to meet there at 1pm.

The bistro was not far from Jasper's office and she found it without any trouble, arriving ten minutes early. She had a feeling Delphine would be punctual and didn't want to keep her waiting. Sure enough, promptly at one, two smartly dressed women entered the restaurant and looked about. Ama half-rose as the older woman approached. She gave Ama a firm handshake and introduced herself and her daughter, then glanced at her wristwatch.

'I'm sorry I have less than an hour before I'm due in court, although Elvire is free until the children are out of school.' Delphine signalled to a waiter who seemed to know her. 'Léon, I'll have my usual omelette and some *eau gazeuse, s'il vous plait*. Would you like a drink, Ama?'

'I would, yes. I feel the need of one.' She and Elvire ordered white wine spritzers. The two women smiled at Ama and waited.

'Thanks for agreeing to see me on such short notice,' she began. 'I feel I'm very beholden to you already and now I'm asking for even more help.'

Delphine waved this aside with a flick of her wrist. 'Your daughter's case is very troubling, Ama. From everything Jasper has told me, I can understand how distressed you must be. Elvire and I would like to help in any way we can.'

'I understand from your father that you've befriended Ocean and she confides in you, Elvire.'

The young matron nodded but said nothing.

'You may already know she disappeared three – no, four days ago without a word to anyone and I fear the worst, or I wouldn't have troubled you further,' said Ama.

Delphine spoke first. 'Her father, Ronnie, phoned me two days ago to tell me she had not turned up for work nor been home. He has not heard anything since and is quite worried about her parole conditions.'

'Is there anything you can tell me which might help me find her, Elvire?' asked Ama.

'Before she disappeared, I saw her briefly after work and she was very upset. We went for a drink to calm her down. She said how hopeless she was feeling, since Clay had been imprisoned without parole.'

'Is that the only thing that was upsetting her?' asked Ama.

'Apparently her health is deteriorating faster than she had anticipated. She said she doubted she would live long enough to see Clay get out of prison.'

'Oh god,' said Ama, 'did she say why she thought this? Ronnie hasn't told me she'd been having more tests. Did she tell either of you?'

'She just said the last results held out no hope at all. I asked her what she would do, now that Clay would be imprisoned for two years. She told me they had worked out a plan for such an eventuality. She said Clay's friends at the grow-op farm could give her some drugs she would use. Clay had hidden a razor blade so that he would slit his wrists when the time came.'

'Oh my god. Did she say when they planned to do this, Elvire?'

Elvire shook her head. 'All she would say was that they would have a last meeting and then do it that night at the same time. She made me promise not to tell my father or he would try to prevent them. I asked her to think it over first before meeting Clay. She said she had made her mind up and refused to tell me when they would act, because I could be implicated if I knew.' She looked at her mother. 'I have not even shared this with my mother, because as a judge she might be obliged to act on the information.'

'This is terrible, Delphine. I don't know what to say,' said Ama. 'It sounds hopeless.'

'Even if we knew and managed to prevent it happening this time, they would only do it again when they had a chance,' said Delphine.

'What are you saying. That I should simply let it happen?'

'I cannot tell you how to act, Ama. Only point to the inevitable. Ocean is doing this because it is her choice. She knows her disease will soon remove her ability to choose, so she wants to act now.'

'Clay told my father at his trial that he was in the late stage of AIDS,' said Elvire. 'I think he and Ocean have decided to do this as a last act together, that will be meaningful for them. I agree and I hope you will let them do this, as a show of their love for each other, Ama. I only told you all this to help you understand their position.'

'Do you agree, too, Delphine? As a mother, you would let this happen and do nothing?'

Delphine shook her head. 'No, I would do something, Ama. I would try to find her to say goodbye, before she acts. So she would know I loved and supported her in her decision.'

'She is my only child, Delphine...'

'She is also a woman, Ama, and she is in love and beloved. As a mother, will you deny her what is her dearest wish?'

Ama rose abruptly from the table clutching her handbag and stumbled to the washroom. Inside, she began to cry, muffling her mouth with her handkerchief. After a moment, the door to the washroom opened and Elvire entered. She put her arms around Ama, stroking her back but saying nothing. Ama wiped her face and tried to smile.

'For almost four years I have watched my daughter, my only child, slip further and further away, alienated from me by this hateful disease. Everything I tried to do only made matters worse between us. Your mother and father know something of what it's like to lose a child, Elvire. But they did get you back. That is how we differ. I'm not going to get Ocean back, no matter what I do.'

'Think about what my mother said, Ama. I'll try to help you find her to say goodbye, but my parents must not be aware of our intentions, or their careers could be jeopardised. Will you agree?'

Ama nodded and Elvire led her back to their table. Delphine rose to embrace her, then picked up her briefcase and the three women left the bistro. Delphine said goodbye and hailed a taxi. Ama and Elvire agreed the best thing was for Ama to return home and wait. Elvire said she had extracted a promise in return from Ocean. She would not act without first being in touch with the Right to Die group in Montreal. She suggested Ama could do the same with the local group in Halifax. They might be able to arrange a meeting for her, to say goodbye to her daughter. Elvire walked with Ama back to her *pension* before leaving to collect her children from school.

It was easy for Delphine to say Ama should honour Ocean's wishes, she had Elvire back, and grandchildren as well.

For the next few hours of darkness Ama argued with herself. She rehashed the lunchtime conversation over and over, during the long drive home. Home. What would that mean anymore with Ocean gone from her life? Not that her daughter had spent much time with her in the last few years. Nonetheless, she thought of themselves as a family, however small and fractured. Now she would truly be alone. Except Spike. Would she fasten on him like a limpet and drive him away with her neediness in the process?

The thought of Spike temporarily distracted Ama from dwelling on Ocean's plight. She concocted scenarios of life together on the old Mongoose, cocooned in the vee-berth, when they weren't jointly engaged in new productions in the Regency Theatre. She even allowed herself to dream of the possibility of Spike's son providing them with some grandchildren to share.

She became aware of the stars fading from the sky and by the time she crested the long undulating hill leading into Arcadia, she could make out the incoming tide in the harbour. The street lights were still on, as she drew up in front of the old house-sit. Upstairs, Spike would be sleeping. She eased off her shoes and crept up the stairs. Slipping out of her crumpled clothes, she slid in beside him and pressed herself against his bare back. The corners of her mouth turned up as she drifted into sleep.

It was Spike's turn to wake up first. Ama didn't move from her sound sleep as he crawled out of bed and went downstairs to make some coffee. He drank a cupful on his own, mulling over what to say to her, while he made a plate of toast to take up to her in bed. He cradled her in his arms, stroking her back but she slept on. He wanted to wake her to talk to him. She seemed in such a deep sleep, he decided against it and climbed out of bed again. Time enough later, he thought, to have it out with her about Ocean. He dressed in the bathroom, had a last look in on her and left for the theatre. Driving by Kitty's, he stopped the old Toyota to check if Claire wanted a lift in with him. He found her and Jasper sitting in the kitchen over a breakfast of pancakes and bacon.

'Sit down, Spike,' said Sarah. 'Plenty left as usual. Claire eats even less than Kitty, if that's possible.' She set him a plateful and poured out some coffee.

'I just dropped in on my way to the theatre to offer you a lift, Claire. I thought Jasper might need your car since he gave up his rental one. Just one rasher of bacon, please Sarah. It's against my religion but I can never resist a taste.'

'I'm glad you stopped by, Spike,' said Claire. 'Jasper and I have been discussing Ama's situation and we need to talk to you. Do you know when she'll be back?'

'She's already here, or at least a zombie resembling her appeared in my bed in the middle of the night. I didn't dare wake her this morning. She looked comatose from sleep deprivation.'

'That's what we've been talking about,' said Jasper. 'I had two phone calls last night, one from my wife and one from my daughter. They're both concerned about Ama. They think she's heading for a nervous breakdown, Spike. Did you know she intended driving all the way to London to try to speak to Clay in prison?'

Spike nodded. 'She told me over the phone and I tried to persuade her to speak to Elvire first. It sounds like she did.'

'Elvire said she promised to help locate Ocean, provided Ama wouldn't try to prevent her suicide pact with Clay. Ama agreed and said she'd go home and wait to hear from her. She must have driven through the night from Montreal, if she's home now.'

'I blame myself for what's happening with Ama,' said Claire. 'I've been leaning on her too much. Allowing her to do my job as well as her own and dumping all my personal problems on her, too. It's no wonder she's a basket case, Spike. That's why we want to talk to you.'

'Claire's right, Spike. We need to put our heads together, preferably while Ama's not around and work something out.'

'You're already doing more than your share, Jasper, and we don't want Claire having a relapse from overwork again. So that leaves me, I guess. Funny, I was just lying in bed this morning, rehearsing how I would have it out with her. But she seemed so exhausted I left her to sleep it off.'

'My wife, Delphine, thinks Ama has become obsessed with rescuing Ocean from herself. She tried to get her to see that her daughter is not a child. Ocean wants to be in charge of her own life and how to end it. Delphine wasn't sure how much of what she said sank in and asked me to reinforce it.'

'The point is,' said Claire, 'We have to make some changes and make them now. So far, everything I've suggested, Jasper has vetoed.'

'Because they all involved you in taking on too much. Next thing we'll have two basket cases on our hands,' he said.

'You're too important in your advisory and consulting role to start doing any hands-on stuff, Claire,' said Spike.

'What do you suggest we do?' she said. 'Jasper thinks you should take over the running of the theatre. Give Ama some breathing space to sort out her personal life.'

'I'm ready to be the go-to person for dealing with day to day stuff at the theatre, if Ama will agree. But it's her baby and I doubt she'll give it up.'

'Well, it's our job to make her see reason, so let's call her in and persuade her,' said Claire. 'If you both agree?'

Jasper and Spike nodded and they proceeded to draw up some guidelines as to who should do what. They all agreed to ask Gloria if she would take on more of the decision making. She had proven to be very effective in her girl Friday role for Ama. Claire also wanted to give Charlene more responsibility as her design assistant, and have Karla be Frankie's official number two.

'These are all things that should happen further down the road anyway,' she said. 'We're simply bringing them forward. It's not as if we won't all be here to provide backup.'

'I think that's the line we should take with Ama when we meet up,' said Jasper. 'Present her with a *fait accompli* and hope she'll see reason.'

'That will be my role,' said Spike. 'I'll practice being tyrannical. Lock her in the house if need be.'

'Okay team, let's go to work,' said Claire putting on her coat. 'Come on, Spike, we'll go in your car, Jasper needs mine for official business with Ralph.'

'Ralph is a powerhouse,' said Jasper. 'I can barely keep up with him. He's taken Claire's big cultural project and put wheels under it. I just rubber stamp his decisions and oil the wheels.'

'And I need to get Esther's grad students down here to start work on the pageant wagon,' said Spike.

'Why not delegate that to Karla?' asked Claire. 'You're going to be busy with the productions and rehearsals and she's been keen on rebuilding the refuge float for the parade. Let her combine the two. She and Charlene can oversee them.'

'I'd like to propose we make Jasper our official producer. I think we can convince Ama to ease up, if she knows Jasper is at the helm,' Spike said.

'Actually, it would make it easier for me, too,' he said. 'If I have an official reason to base myself down here for the interim, it will make Delphine happier. Knowing I'm not just drifting around.'

'If she only knew we're exploiting you ruthlessly, she might not be so happy,' said Claire.

At the theatre, they told everyone of the new arrangements they wanted to put in place, in order to ease the strain on Ama. It was common knowledge that she had been having on-going problems with her sick daughter, and they accepted this was just another episode. No one complained of their increased role in running the theatre.

'Sarah will be glad to have an excuse to spend even more time at the refuge,' said Karla. 'Filling in for me and Charlene.'

The lion's share of the extra workload fell on Gloria. She was already doing much of Ama's paperwork and running errands. Now that she was deputising for her, she would need some backup herself.

'I'll have to base myself here now that I'm acting producer,' said Jasper. 'Why don't you and I share Ama's office, Gloria? There's bound to be a lot of overlap so it makes sense we work together.'

There was no room in the tiny office for a second desk so Arthur found a small table in the prop store for Jasper to use.

When everyone was clear on their new roles, Spike drove home at lunchtime to break the news to Ama. She was still sound asleep, the coffee and toast untouched and cold. He took the dishes back downstairs and made some fresh coffee. He was about to pour her a fresh cup when his cell phone rang.

'Hello Spike, it's Fergus. Glad I caught you. Wanted to tell you we finally sorted the autopilot out. It was Travis spotted the problem. One of them chains was too slack on the autopilot, so it was gradually losin' ground and runnin' off course. Each time me and Travis took the Mongoose out to test it, she'd start fine, then slowly go off-track. We took a link out of the chain and presto, back on course.'

'That's great news, Fergus. Now we just need to get it down here. My problem is, I'm flat out at the theatre because we're up against a deadline. I don't know when I could get away for a couple of days.'

'We been talkin' it over whiles we been doin' the sea trials and Travis is keen for us to bring her down ourselves. I been watchin' him and he's a good sailor, Spike. Only trouble is my old pickup – it's got all my tools and bits 'n bobs I need, if I'm gonna be buildin' staircases.'

'Do you think Justin would drive your pickup down and Travis could drop him back to Bridewell in Ama's car?'

'I'll ask him. I know he's dead curious to see what you're all up to with the theatre, Spike. If the weather stays good, we can head off tomorrow – should be there before dark.'

'I've lined up a free space on Fisherman's wharf where you can tie up. Tell Travis to call me on his cellphone when you're in the outer harbour and I'll be waiting to help you dock, Fergus.'

He rang off and poured out Ama's fresh coffee to take up to her. Putting the cup on the side table, he sat on the edge of the bed and took her hand from under the covers, stroking it until she opened her eyes.

'I thought I heard voices downstairs but I was too tired to get up,' she said, reaching out both arms to pull him down to her.

They embraced in silence until he felt tears against his face. He sat back to look at her, shaking his head.

'Why do you do this all alone, Ama? We're supposed to be sharing our lives, not living separately.'

'I'm frightened to alienate you with all my messy past, Spike. And anyway, it's hopeless. I've got to let her go, everyone says so.'

He handed her the hot mug. 'Here, drink your coffee and tell me what you've been up to without me. Move over a bit.' He shifted her over enough to sit on top of the bed with his arm about her while she drank.

'I don't know where to start, Spike. It's all such a muddle in my mind. I spent the whole trip back from Montreal with it going round and round in my head.'

'Tell me about your meeting with Elvire. What's she like?'

'She's a bit like Jasper. Very clever and thoughtful. She persuaded me not to go to London to try to see Clay. I think she feels I would only fight with him and he wouldn't tell me anything. She's trusted by Ocean and maybe she can win Clay's trust, too.'

'He might tell her where she is, you mean?'

'She was very reassuring. She asked me to leave it with her and she promised to keep in touch, as soon as she heard anything definite.'

'About what? Where Ocean is hiding?'

'And when they plan to commit suicide together.'

'Together? How can they with Clay in jail?' asked Spike. 'They'll have to wait at least two years till he's free.'

Ama shook her head. 'They have no intention to wait. They've made a pact, Elvire says, and they plan to carry it out soon. Ocean feels she's near the end of her ability to act and Clay knows he has terminal AIDS. Doing drugs was all he had left. Now he just wants to die and so does she.'

Ama began to cry uncontrollably. Spike took her mug of coffee from her. He held her close until she stopped shaking and mopped her eyes with his handkerchief. When she had control of herself again, she described to him how they would carry out their plan, according to what Ocean had told Elvire.

'Delphine, Jasper's wife was with her. We met in a restaurant. I've been wanting to meet her since Jasper told me all she's done for Ocean. And now her help with the opera costumes for Lovely War.'

'Did she agree with Elvire?' asked Spike.

'Yes, but she doesn't know the details of their suicide plan. Elvire couldn't tell her or Jasper. Only me, because of their legal positions.'

'What did she say. Is she angry because Ocean broke her parole agreement?'

'No, but she convinced me I had to let her go. She said Ocean is her own woman now and this is her choice. I shouldn't try to prevent it.'

'And will you?' asked Spike, 'let her go I mean?'

'I don't know if I can. She's my only child, Spike. Without her, I have only my mother who's in a care home back in England and doesn't even know who I am anymore.'

'What about me, don't I count?'

'More than ever, Spike. But you may not like the idea of me clutching on to you. You told me you don't like needy people, they make you want to run a mile.'

'I'll make an exception for you, Ama,' he said, hugging her closer. 'Anyway, you're not exactly a clinging vine, always disappearing on me. I'm the one doing most of the hanging on.'

She struggled to a sitting position. 'And I have to disappear again. I've got a hundred things to do at the theatre, as well as for Claire.'

He drew her back onto the pillows. 'Not anymore. Not for awhile.'

'What do you mean, Spike? Has something happened to Claire?'

'Claire's fine. It's you they're all worried about. Me, too. You've been pushing yourself too hard, Ama. Everyone says so. They've had a meeting and decided to provide you with a support team. To give you a break, so you can focus on your own problems with Ocean.'

'I already have a support team, Spike. You and Gloria.'

'We've been coasting on your coat tails. For the next while they've asked me to relieve you in running the theatre, with Gloria, and Jasper in his role of producer. Claire will have Charlene more or less full-time, so she doesn't overdo it as well.'

'But what am I supposed to do? I just told you what Elvire and Delphine said. I should leave Ocean to make her own decisions and they would be in touch when they know anything. I can't simply hang around the house, waiting to hear. It could be ages.'

'For a start, you could switch your attentions to me. I'm feeling sorely neglected. And I shall be coming home exhausted from taking on your role,' he said.

'Don't make me feel even more guilty, Spike. I know I've been distracted. I promise to do better in future.'

'You could start right now,' he said, 'assuaging your guilt.'

'First you have to reassure me that it's alright with everyone, for me to take a back seat for awhile – just till I find out what's happening with Ocean. I can't concentrate on the theatre projects until I know where she is and I can speak to her.'

'That's why we all feel you need some time out. Take as much as you feel you want, to sort things out. Just keep me in the loop and don't disappear on me again, please. In the meantime, I'm happy to mind the store.'

'I have to confess it's a big relief to hear you say this, Spike. I felt it was all getting too complicated for me to deal with. And Ocean as well. But I really don't want to sit around and dwell on how she is. I think what I'd like, is to be able to leave the theatre project to you and just come along to rehearsals for Lovely War in the evenings. Would that be alright with you, Spike?'

'Perfect. We can make it our joint production. And in the daytime, you can go down and see how to make our future home more livable.'

'The Mongoose? You mean it's ready to move down here?'

'Yep. That was Fergus you heard on the phone earlier. He wants to leave tomorrow.'

The following day, Spike and Ama went down to the docks to wait for the arrival of the Mongoose. Travis had phoned them on his cell to say they expected to arrive late afternoon about five. Spike made sure the space he'd rented on the wharf was unoccupied and ready. By 6pm there was still no sign and Spike paced the dock, while Ama went off to do some shopping to feed them. They had agreed that Travis and Fergus would live on the boat while they were in Arcadia and use shore power and dock facilities, to finish the work on the Mongoose.

At a quarter past six, the Mongoose appeared in the harbour entrance and by six thirty she had moored alongside.

'Ran into a bit of a blow awhile back,' said Travis. 'Slowed us down a bit bucking the headwind.'

'Didn't help that the tide was runnin' against us, either,' said Fergus.

Ama appeared in the companionway, her arms loaded with paper bags. 'Welcome to Arcadia everyone. Take some of these groceries, Spike, or I'll fall down the stairs.' She followed him down into the cabin to hug each of them in turn. 'I've got a cold bottle of bubbly here to toast your arrival and look what else I found on the way.' She removed a cardboard package with half a dozen wine glasses from one of the bags. 'It's time we stopped celebrating by drinking out of tea mugs and toothbrush glasses. Will you do the honours, Travis while I rinse these out?'

'Sure thing. Among my many skills of seamanship, I learned to pop champagne corks sailing at a forty-five-degree angle without spilling a drop.' He poured out the fizzy liquid and handed them round. 'To the Mongoose and all who sail in her.'

'But not at a forty-five-degree angle, I hope,' said Ama. 'I planned to cook you all a welcome dinner but it smells as if Travis has beat me to it. Just have to save this till tomorrow, then, I guess. I brought a whole fresh salmon. Hope it will fit in your little fridge.'

'Why don't we all eat topside,' said Travis 'and take advantage of the balmy weather. Plenty of Spike's beer when the champagne runs out'

'Sounds like you've earned it,' said Spike. 'You two relax on deck and Ama and I will wait on you. Tomorrow we'll take you up to see the theatre but tonight just take it easy.'

'Can't put me to work on them staircases till my pickup arrives with all my toolkit anyways,' said Fergus.

'I've been thinking of the storm scene in the opening of The Tempest,' said Spike when they were all seated on deck, eating and drinking. 'It would be a powerful effect if we could have one of the sailors aloft, high up the mast with the sails billowing all around him. Do you have much of a head for heights, Travis?'

'Doesn't bother me at all. Once we had a halyard jam at the top of the mast in a Force 7 gale and I climbed up to free it so we could reduce sail. Quite an adventure,' said Travis.

'Sounds terrifying,' said Ama. 'I'm sure I would have been rigid with fear.'

'Do you think you could help me stage it, Travis, if we rigged you up with a safety harness?'

'I'll give it a go. Worth it, just to brag to my girlfriend, Anna-Lise, I'm in a Shakespeare play.'

'It's not for awhile – after we do Oh What a Lovely War,' Spike said. 'We'll have plenty of time to practise. Maybe we can even persuade Fergus to rig the block and tackle with the new ropes and pulleys from the Mongoose.'

'Fergus would make a perfect ship's boatswain for the storm scene, too,' said Ama.

'Long as I stay on deck and it's Travis goes aloft, I'm game,' he said.

'You can both suss it out in the morning,' said Spike.

Next morning, Fergus started into the building of the cantilevered staircases, with Travis handling the high-level work, while Fergus directed it from the stage level.

CHAPTER FIFTEEN

In the midst of this, Esther's group of grad students turned up to begin construction of the pageant wagon. A heated discussion ensued as to what sort of performances they should put on with it.

'I think we should do sketches based on Lovely War,' said Ama. 'Like a preview or teaser.'

'We could alternate with scenes from The Tempest, to promote our next production,' Spike said.

'And it's important we have some musicians to be part of the show to attract a crowd. Some of us students can play early music instruments,' said Ivy, Sy's girlfriend, who had come with them.

While work began on the wagon in the rehearsal room, Claire and Jasper were asked what they thought would be the best use of it for promotion.

'We've got all these beautiful commedia costumes,' said Claire, 'why not do some mime shows using the stock commedia characters to get the audiences used to seeing them before they come to the theatre?'

'I'll ask Charlene to design some leaflets the actors can hand out while they perform,' said Jasper.

With the enlarged production team meshing well together and Jasper overseeing everything, the end of September deadline began to seem within their grasp. Ama relaxed into directing evening rehearsals of Lovely War and left all the rest to Spike and Jasper. Gloria devised a rota of volunteers to spread the work, so that people came and went from early morning to after midnight.

Each day when Spike arrived, significant changes appeared. He and Travis slowly began to figure out the best way to make the opening storm scene of The Tempest most effective. Thanks to Sarah's fishermen contacts, they were given an old wooden mast to rig the parachute material to. Fergus helped them with a block and tackle arrangement that allowed them to raise it upright and then drop it in slow motion across the stage. Their experiments could only happen after all the volunteers had gone home for the night, so they had the stage to themselves.

'I reckon if Fergus can rig me a bosun's chair beside the mast, I can jump clear when it's lowered near the deck,' said Travis. 'With all the sails flapping about me it will look like I was on top of the mast.'

'You'll need a set of block and tackle separate from the mast and someone to lower you at the same time,' said Fergus.

'The fly-loft has been condemned as unsafe by the fire marshal,' Spike said. 'We'll need to hang the tackle from one of the metal bars of the lighting grid. I guess they're strong enough.'

'Only one way to find out. Let's give her a try,' said Travis. 'Get your tackle together, Fergus, while me and Spike set up the long extension ladder.' He hauled the heavy set of ropes and blocks high up the ladder to attach it to the metal lighting bar.

'You be careful up there,' said Fergus, helping to steady the swaying ladder.

'No worries, boys. I'm used to this. One hand for the ship and one for the work I was taught, when we were racing. Okay, here comes the rope, watch your heads.' He dropped the heavy coil down to the stage and waited for them to take the strain on it before looping it under his armpits and stepping off the ladder. 'Okay, pay it out nice and slow. That's it, lower away.'

His body turned in a slow circle as they lowered him towards the stage. Fifteen feet from the floor he lurched downwards as one end of the metal bar broke free and angled down, letting the pulley block slide off the end of it. 'Watch out!' shouted Travis as he plummeted down on top of Spike and they crashed to the floor in a tangle of rope.

Fergus pulled Travis free of the pile of rope and helped him to his feet. Travis gave a yelp when he put his weight on his left foot and crumpled to the floor. 'My ankle – I think I've sprained it. Help Spike, Fergus, I think I kicked his head.'

The old man turned to pull the ropes off Spike who lay stunned and inert. He tried to lift him up to a sitting position but Spike shouted and lay back, eyes wide with pain. He lay panting and staring up at Fergus.

'My back – I've done something to it.'

Travis looked across at him from his sitting position, then turned to Fergus. 'Better find a phone and call an ambulance. We shouldn't move him.'

The old man nodded, then headed backstage.

Less than an hour later, both men were in the emergency ward of the small local hospital, waiting to hear the results of the x-rays. Travis had an ankle fracture and Spike had a crushed vertebra. When Fergus arrived in his old pickup to hear how they were, he was told they would be kept in overnight and to come back in the morning.

Instead of phoning Ama, Spike called Jasper as it was after midnight.

'Sorry to wake you, but we've had an accident at the theatre. Travis and I are in the local hospital. Looks like we're both going to be out of action for awhile, Jasper, so I'm afraid you're going to be dropped in at the deep end. I don't want to wake Ama at this hour – there's nothing she can do except get upset. Would you call her first thing in the morning? Tell her it's not too serious, she can phone the hospital for news.' He gave Jasper a brief rundown on what had happened.

'I'll phone the hospital myself before I call her, Spike, and call you in the morning.'

.

By the time Ama arrived at the hospital, Spike had been transferred to a ward where he lay flat on his back unable to move and heavily sedated with a morphine drip which he could use to control the pain when it got too great. Travis sat propped up in the bed next to him with his leg raised up on pillows with the foot encased in plaster. He grinned at Ama and gave her a potted version of what had happened.

'Good thing I didn't land on Fergus, Ama. Might have finished him off. As it is, I managed to do some serious damage to Spike's back. I don't think he'll be going back to the theatre for awhile from what I hear from the doc.'

Spike only gave her a weak smile as she sat beside his bed, clutching his hand. 'How serious, Spike? Have you broken any bones?'

He shook his head. 'I injured my spine during a sword fight, doing Henry the Fifth years ago and it left me with a weak back. This accident damaged it even more, the doctor says. It's going to take me quite awhile to recuperate.'

'But you'll be alright, won't you? You'll be able to walk, Spike?'

'Not for awhile, I'm afraid. Seems I have osteoporosis, so it's going to be a slow recovery.'

'Osteoporosis – I thought only women got that?'

'So did I. But apparently men get it too, only not as much as women.'

'Oh my god, Spike, this is awful.' She began to cry and he patted her hand, unable to do more.

'I'm sorry, my love, I've dropped you in an awful mess with the theatre.'

'The theatre? It's you I'm worried about, not the bloody theatre.'

'I'll be alright eventually, it's not life threatening, Ama.'

She tried to give him a hug but he winced with pain and she pulled away in fright. 'Sorry, sorry. God, I'm not thinking straight, I'm so scared, Spike.'

'Nothing to be scared about. I'm going to be fine, you'll see.'

'Sure thing,' said Travis. 'Once we get him in a wheelchair, he'll be scooting up and down those new ramps of yours and around the stage like Jack Brabham.'

'Jack Brabham?' said Ama.

'Only the greatest racing driver ever to come out of Oz. Won the Grand Prix three times.'

'Not a very good example, Travis,' said Spike. 'Didn't he crash a couple of times as well?'

'Yeah, whatever. Anyways, soon as they get me one of them surgical boots, I'll be hoppin' out of here and back to the theatre. Me and Fergus will get that lighting bar anchored good and solid, so there'll be no more freak accidents. I still reckon it will look terrific once you add in bolts of lightning and crashing wave sounds, Spike.'

'I want you to stay firmly on the ground till that ankle's healed,' said Ama. 'We don't want anymore accidents, freak or otherwise, Travis.'

Ama was shooed out by a nurse before the consultant did his rounds. She made her way to Kitty's, to see if she could catch Jasper and Claire before they left for the theatre. She was too late, Sarah told her, leading her into the old kitchen to join Kitty for a coffee and a slice of her plum tart. Ama told them both the bad news about Spike, as Jasper hadn't mentioned it to them yet.

'Leaving it to you, I expect,' said Kitty. 'Men are such cowards when it comes to telling bad news.'

'Right now, I'm so upset about Spike injuring his back, I can't even begin to decide what to do next, Kitty. It seems like the whole project is collapsing around me, including the theatre. First Claire's illness, then Ocean's suicide pact, me nearly having a nervous breakdown and now this accident, with Travis and Spike both in hospital. I'm almost afraid to leave the house for fear of more bad news.' She began to fumble for tissues in her pocket as tears ran down her cheeks.

'You are doing absolutely the right thing,' said Kitty. 'Let it all come pouring out. We'll work out what to do afterwards. We're right here with you, Ama. Aren't we, Sarah?'

The big woman stood over her as she sat crying, pressing Ama against her and stroking her back while Kitty held her hand. The three of them remained linked together until her tears subsided. Ama scrubbed at her face with a tea towel Sarah handed her. She sniffled and blew her nose in a handful of wet tissues.

'I feel like one of the three witches in Macbeth,' she tried to smile at them.

'"Double, double, toil and trouble," Kitty said, smiling back at her.

'Trouble comes in threes, they say,' Sarah said, moving to the big Aga to put the kettle on. 'I reckon you've had your dose for awhile, Ama.'

'Sarah's right. Let's have another cup of tea and see what our next move is, shall we?' said Kitty. 'Some of that gunpowder, and better make it double strength, Sarah. Why don't we have it on the veranda? I always think clearer while I'm looking at that view.'

The three women sat together, drinking the strong brew and mulling over Ama's options.

'The way I see it, Spike is out of the picture indefinitely but Jasper is our ace in the hole,' said Kitty. 'Let's get him over and hear what he has to say. He's a very resourceful man and he thrives on problems, wouldn't you agree, Ama?'

'Perhaps it might be best if I met him at the theatre, Kitty.'

'Sarah shook her head. 'Claire's there with him and she'd be bound to dive in straight away. She's too delicate to be takin' on anything more. I wish she was back home here where I can keep a closer eye on her.'

'I agree. Once we're clear on our plan, then will be soon enough to let her in on it,' said Kitty. 'I'll call him right now.'

They were still sitting on the veranda when Jasper pulled up in Claire's big silver SUV. He climbed the front steps to join them, easing his large frame into a woven wicker chair.

'This looks like a council of war,' he said looking at Ama's grim face, still white and tear-stained. 'I think I know why I'm here.'

'We felt we're in dire need of a smart big city lawyer's advice, to help get us out of a very large hole, Jasper,' said Ama, 'so naturally we thought of you.'

'First rule at law school,' he said, 'when you're in a hole, stop digging.'

'And do what?'

'Call for help. They fill in the hole and soon you're back on level ground.'

'Looks like we got that bit right anyway,' said Sarah, standing. 'Help's arrived – better get him some fuel to keep his strength up.' She gathered up the tea tray and headed into the kitchen.

'I don't know what to do next, Jasper, I'm stuck.'

'I've had all night to think about it. Couldn't sleep much after Spike called,' he said. 'We've had a run of bad luck, but I'm not ready to give in just yet. Fortunately, we have a good strong team of people, since we regrouped after Claire's illness and your overwork problems. It's tough having Spike laid up but we can still use his expertise, even if he'll be joining Claire in the sick bay. I can take over his role co-ordinating the theatre redevelopment, but I can't fill his shoes on The Tempest production. I made a couple of phone calls this morning and have some promising news. I spoke to Justin and Emily at Bridewell and told them what had happened. They're keen to take on the modern Shakespeare production with Spike's help. Seems like they were feeling a bit sidelined, with everything happening over here and this is their chance to make it a real co-production.'

'That's wonderful news, Jasper. What a relief,' said Ama.

'That just leaves you. As you and Spike will be spending lots of time together anyway while he convalesces, I thought you could work together on Lovely War and not have to think about the Tempest production. It will be in Justin's competent hands with Emily to co-ordinate it all.'

'You make it sound as if Spike's accident was a stroke of good luck, Jasper,' Ama said.

'I don't think he'd see it that way. But it does mean you will still have the time to focus on Ocean for the immediate future and not be worrying about the theatre.'

'It does seem a workable solution, Jasper,' said Kitty. 'But couldn't I be of some help as well? Sarah is busy at the refuge most days, now that Karla and Charlene are spending so much time at the theatre.'

'What do you suggest, Kitty?' he said. 'You're already hosting Claire and me as semi-permanent house guests.'

'I meant something more than just being a theatrical landlady. I'd like to take a more active role to help Ama, besides being a shoulder to cry on.'

'Would you consider attending rehearsals with me, Kitty, until Spike is well enough to come back?' asked Ama. 'It would mean giving up some evenings and weekends but you'd still have the days free.'

'What would I be doing, Ama? I haven't been to a rehearsal for years.'

'Observing. Being my assistant to bounce ideas off and give me feedback. Tell me what works and what doesn't, that sort of thing. Moral support.'

'Moral support I can do, Ama. Not sure about the rest but it sounds exciting. As long as you don't take anything I say too seriously. I'm at least two generations out of date.'

'All the better,' said Jasper. 'Provide an objective point of view, Kitty.'

'In that case, when do I start?' she said.

'Monday, Wednesday and Friday evenings. Saturday and Sunday afternoons.'

'Now that's all in-train, Ama, I think it's time you and I talk to Claire and the rest of the team,' said Jasper. 'Shall I give you a lift to the theatre?'

At the theatre parking lot, the grad students were unloading their belongings from a university minibus and carrying them into the rehearsal room, which would be their base for the next month.

'How's Spike, Ama?' asked Ivy, who was acting as team leader. 'Will I be able to see him today? I spoke to Jasper early this morning, before we left Dartmouth and he told me what had happened.'

'He's okay, but he's going to be flat on his back for awhile. Maybe we can get your students settled in here and then let Arthur show them around the theatre. To meet everybody before they get started.

'Esther put me in charge as the senior grad student,' said Ivy. 'We've talked over the pageant wagon project together and I'm keen to get them started.'

'Let's go over to the hospital. You can see if Spike feels up to talking to you about the Shakespeare co-production.'

At the local hospital, Spike was asleep or drowsing when they arrived. Ama spoke to the nurse who said he was still in a lot of pain, so they kept topping him up with pain killers which made him very sleepy. It took Ama several minutes of stroking his hand and face and whispering to him, before he at last opened his eyes to look at her. He made a move to touch her face but stopped, wincing with pain.

'Ama – you disappeared again. Please stay with me.'

'I will, I promise. Ivy's here to see you, Spike. Do you feel like talking?'

'Feeling a bit woozy with the morphine. They keep me doped up with it for the pain in my back. The slightest move makes me yelp.'

'Perhaps I should come back tomorrow, Spike, we can talk then,' said Ivy.

'No problem, as long as you do the talking. I'm not too coherent.'

'We just wanted to tell you what's happening,' said Ama. 'We had a meeting after your accident and made a few changes, to cover for you while you're out of action. That's why Ivy's here.'

'I thought you came for the pageant wagon project, Ivy. Aren't you doing it now?'

'Don't worry, it's all going ahead,' she said. 'We've got lots of help on it, Spike. Everyone wants to get involved. They love the idea.'

'Jasper was in touch with Emily and Justin at the theatre in Bridewell, to tell them what happened,' said Ama, 'and they've offered to take over the Tempest production until you're back on your feet again.'

'That won't be for awhile, according to the surgeon,' Spike said. 'He was around this morning to give me the bad news. They want to fuse the lower vertebrae together or something, but not until the swelling goes down.'

'At least you won't have to worry about our modern Shakespeare production going ahead,' said Ama. 'Jasper reckons with Emily and Justin onboard and me co-directing, he'll be fine taking over the rest of the theatre renovations you were overseeing, Spike. Which means you can be my *éminence grise* on Lovely War instead. And Kitty wants to be my assistant at rehearsals.'

'Sounds like I'm redundant. I guess I can go back to my boat and help Fergus,' said Spike.

'I don't think the doctor will like the idea of you clambering around on a fishing boat just yet,' said Ivy. 'Maybe later, but we have first dibs on you when you come out of here. There'll be plenty for you to do, even from a wheelchair.'

'Travis says he'll be pushing you up and down the ramps in no time,' said Ama.

'I think I'll just lie here and stay stoned on morphine – it's wonderful. Not surprised Clay and Ocean are hooked on it. Have you heard anymore from Jasper and Elvire about them, Ama?'

She shook her head. 'Nothing yet. Your little escapade has pushed them right out of my mind.'

'Well, that's something anyway,' he said. 'Sorry, I think I'm fading,' said Spike. 'Must be the morphine...' His eyes fluttered shut.

'I've got some phone calls to make before he wakes up again, Ivy.' She handed her the keys to the old Toyota. 'You can drive back to the theatre to unpack.'

Ivy left the hospital, and Ama went into the small cafeteria to buy a coffee and use her cell phone. It took her awhile to track down the number she needed but eventually she got through to a Halifax address. A woman answered.

'Hello, Evelyn Wallace speaking.'

'Is this the 'Right to Die' office?' Ama asked her.

'Yes, may I help you?'

'I'm calling about my daughter. I was hoping you'd be able to help me find her. She's dying of MLS – Lou Gehrig's disease, and is planning to end her life.'

'I'm sorry but she will have to be in touch with us in person. What is her name?'

'Ocean Waterstone.'

'Does she live in the Halifax area?'

'That's what I need your help with. I don't know where she is, but I understand she's been in touch with your Montreal branch.'

Ama briefly explained to the woman why she had contacted her.

'And she won't talk to me anymore, because she's convinced I'll try to stop her suicide pact with her boyfriend, who has terminal AIDS. My friends have persuaded me I should let her go, but I must at least say goodbye. I was hoping you might act as an intermediary for us. Convince her I only want to see her one last time. Tell her that's all I ask.'

'And you say she has been in touch with our Montreal branch, Mrs. Waterstone?'

'That's what my friend in Montreal tells me. She was the one who suggested I speak to you. Do you think you could arrange for me to meet her somewhere?'

'You understand our loyalty must be to her, of course. But I can call Montreal and see if they can do anything for you.

'And you will let me know, either way?'

'I promise.'

Ama finished her coffee and then emailed Elvire before she went back up to Spike's room.

He was sleeping when she entered, so she sat down and took her copy of Lovely War from her handbag and flipped through to the scenes they were currently rehearsing. Now that she had been able to focus solely on the play and not worry about the theatre, she felt the rehearsals were going well. She would miss not having Spike beside her, to bounce ideas off and give her instant feedback. She had Kitty and afterwards, she could visit Spike to tell him everything they were doing. If not a perfect solution it was at least a workable one.

With Fergus advising Arthur and Garth, the twin cantilevered staircases were almost finished. Soon she'd be able to move the actors on to the stage in the evenings. Then they could work on all three levels and tie the scenes together with the musical numbers. It would also be time to bring in the musicians she had recruited. She realised the tech rehearsal would be very complicated and decided to break it up into two or three sections, when the time came. For now, she could focus on the actors' performances. Get them used to working in the stylised commedia manner, with broad brush comic strokes to undercut the harsh wartime statistics, projected on the screens behind them.

'You look very busy.'

She looked up to see that Spike was watching her.

'How long have you been awake?'

'A few minutes. I didn't like to disturb you. But then my selfish actor's need for attention took over.'

'That's what I'm here for,' she said, putting down her script and moving to the chair beside his bed. 'Can I do anything for you?'

He moved his head to one side very carefully. 'No, unfortunately. What I had in mind is too painful to contemplate right now. I'll settle for some chaste kisses.'

She bent over the bed being careful not to move him and caressed his face, kissing him very lightly on the forehead, cheeks and mouth. 'Does that hurt, Spike?'

'A little, but it's worth it. Do it again, please.'

She repeated the performance, then sat back down and took his hand. 'Better not overdo it, I might get carried away and set back your recovery.'

They sat smiling at each other, saying nothing. She stroked his hand and felt tears building up. She blinked hard, trying to squeeze them back but a few escaped down her cheeks.

'Hey, it's okay, Ama. I'm not dying or anything, just immobile.'

'I know, Spike. I guess it's only relief that you're going to recover. I've realised that I don't want to continue at the theatre, unless we can do it together. While you were sleeping, I spoke to a woman at the 'right to die' group, about meeting Ocean for one last time.'

'What did she say?'

'She couldn't promise anything except to say she'd get back to me, about whether Ocean agrees to see me or not.'

'I'm sure she'll see you, Ama, if you've said you're on her side and won't try to stop her.'

'Will she, Spike? I don't think she trusts me anymore, according to Elvire.'

'Let's wait and see, shall we? I think she'll want to be reconciled with you before she dies, wouldn't you?'

'If it was me and not her dying? Of course. But you don't know Ocean.'

'I know she's your only child, Ama. If they can find her, I think she'll agree.'

Ama wiped her eyes on the bedcover. 'I want to believe you, Spike.'

'And you promise not to run off and leave me, Ama? Until I can go with you?'

She smiled. 'If they'd let me, I'd move right in here with you, Spike.'

'I've been thinking about us, too, Ama. Wondering how we should proceed when I get out of here.'

'And what do you think we should do?'

'I'm not sure you'll want to hear what I say, but will you give it some thought, for my sake?'

'You're making me worried, Spike, what is it?'

'When we've got these first two productions up and running, Ama, let's step back from this full-time involvement in the theatre.'

'And do what instead?'

'Offer to do one production a year. Let the younger members take over the running of it.'

'What would we do the rest of the time?'

'Finish our bargain. Work on the Mongoose, live aboard, travel. Visit my son in London. Tell him to get into production.'

'Did we agree to all that, Spike?'

'Not exactly. Some of it is the morphine talking, perhaps.'

'All the same, it sounds a nice vision. Even if it is drug-induced.'

'Like Coleridge's,' said Spike. '"In Zanadu did Kubla Khan,

A stately pleasure-dome decree..."'

CHAPTER SIXTEEN

As he drove Claire back to Kitty's house, Jasper made up his mind to tell her of his plan. Although they had all been careful not to let her assume anymore of Ama's duties, he found it was almost impossible to stop her, when he wasn't around. The two of them had become very close during the course of her illness and he knew her remission wouldn't last indefinitely. Her doctor had told him in strict confidence, that Claire probably had only a matter of months. He drove her silver SUV down the narrow streets of the old town to a lookout point over the inner harbour and parked.

'Claire, I want to ask you something personal. All the time you've been ill, you've had no contact from Antony. Do you know why?'

'It's an old story, Jasper. He's gone back to his wife in Los Angeles. He said he was going on business but when he met up with her again, they decided to get back together.'

'I'm sorry, Claire.'

'Don't be. It's happened before. Like I said, it's an old story. I knew it was never going to work for us and this time when he left, I decided to end it.'

'It makes what I want to say easier then, because I have a suggestion I want you to consider. It's no secret that my wife and I live separate lives, and that she's quite relieved that I've moved down here to work, indefinitely. It suits us both. These past few weeks living and working with you have turned my life around, Claire. We make a good team and I'd like us to make a secret pact to strengthen it, if you agree.'

'A secret pact. I wonder what that could be, Jasper?'

'I think you know what I mean, Claire.'

'I think so, but I'd like to hear you say it.'

'I want us to live together, Claire, to be able to hold you close and be with you, not just while we're working. We don't have to shout it from the rooftops, simply present it as a *fait accompli*. I'm sure I can persuade Kitty to rent us the two guest rooms upstairs, now that you're in recovery mode. She and Sarah are fond of us both and they like having us around. We can join forces in the Green room at the theatre and come and go together. As far as everyone is concerned, we're partners, with your big culture project looming we need to work as a team full-time.'

'Ama was right, Jasper, you are silver-tongued. You make it all seem so easy,' said Claire. 'But you're forgetting something. I'm damaged goods. I couldn't be what you want. I'm not strong enough anymore for a full-on relationship, much as I would love one, especially with you.'

'Do you mean that, Claire? You'd like to be with me, too?'

'Do you think I haven't fantasised about it since we first met, Jasper? Only I'd disappoint you, in my condition.'

'Not possible. I'd have you on any terms, Claire, you know that.'

'Well, we could try an experiment, I suppose,' she said, leaning over to kiss him. 'As long as you understand I'm not the woman I used to be.'

'Nor I the man,' he said as he held her to him. 'Enough is as good as a feast, they say.'

'Mmhmm, we'll see,' she said. 'Meantime, *carpe diem*, as they also say. Shall we go back and let you use your silver tongue to ask Kitty if we can share your room for tonight?'

Ivy and her group of grad students had been working on two possible sketches for the pageant wagon. One was a pastiche of music hall comedy songs from Lovely War. The other was a mime show of the Tooth Puller from the medieval commedia repertoire, which Claire's doctor had told them she used to perform in medical school. They tried them out on the cast and backstage crew, to get their reactions and ideas.

'Be great if they had some music to go with it,' said Arthur.

'I've already asked Sarah's kitchen party musicians to play for us,' said Ama.

'Are you going to dress the musicians up in commedia costumes, too, Ivy? We've got extras left, from all the ones Jasper's wife sent us from the Montreal opera,' said Frankie.

'Some of our students have learned to play early music instruments so we plan to use them as well,' Ivy said.

'Where's the wagon? Is it ready yet?' asked Fergus. 'I'm finished on them staircases if you need any help. My uncle was a wheelwright and I used to work with him as a lad.'

'I've been making a few enquiries myself,' said Arthur. 'I spoke to Lloyd Kramer, Ama. He said he had an old hay wagon with wooden wheels we could have but it's not in very good shape. Been sitting out behind his barn for years and will need some repairs, but it's free if we want it. I drove out to have a look at it the other day and it's got a broken wheel, so we'd have to haul it in on a trailer. I'm too busy to try to fix it but if Fergus thinks he can...'

'You get her here an' I'll fix her,' said Fergus.

Jasper arranged a truck rental with a tailgate hoist and he and Garth, with some students went out to collect it.

'What you planning on usin' it for?' asked Lloyd Kramer when he showed it to them. 'Arthur just said you needed it for a play of some sort.'

'It's going to be like a parade float,' said Jasper. 'Spike said you'd agreed to bring one of your ox teams to pull it.'

'That's right, I did tell him I would. But I wouldn't want one of my show teams pullin' that old wreck.'

'Wait till you see what we do with it, Lloyd. You won't recognise it,' said Garth. 'We've got a professional team of restorers to transform it into a medieval pageant wagon. You'll be proud to have your team pull it in the Fishermen's Parade.'

'Mmhmm. Maybe I'll reserve judgment on that till I see it,' said Lloyd. 'Meantime, I'll be glad to give you a hand fixin' her up. It's a shame to see it rottin' away in the field. My dad used it regularly when I was a boy.' He helped them load it on to the truck. 'Where's Spike?' he asked. 'How come he didn't come along if he's so interested?'

'In hospital,' said Garth. 'Had an accident in the theatre and injured his back pretty bad.'

'Sorry to hear that,' said Lloyd. 'Maybe Derek and me should go visit him.'

When Ama went to see Spike on her daily visit a few days later, he already had two visitors. One of them had flaming red hair. They rose to greet her.

'Justin, what a surprise. And Emily. How lovely to see you both again.'

'Visiting the halt and the maimed, Ama. And you too, of course,' said Justin, giving her a hug.

Ample Make This Bed

'Let me give her an extra hug,' said Emily, 'seeing as Spike is untouchable.'

'You may kiss him very carefully,' said Ama, 'but no hugging allowed.'

'How marvellous to have such total control over him, Ama. How long will it last?' Emily asked.

'Quite awhile, if my surgeon is to be believed,' said Spike.

'That's why Jasper pressed you into service,' Ama said. 'It's wonderful of you to volunteer.'

'The show must go on and all that,' said Justin, 'and besides it's our project, too.'

'Yes, it was very thoughtless of Spike to get us all fired up on this modern Shakespeare production, giving us starring roles,' said Emily, 'and now he drops us in the deep end. Still, we are troupers, aren't we, darlings.'

'You are, you are,' said Ama, 'and we are suitably grateful for coming to our rescue.'

'Yes, well enough of this sycophancy,' said Justin, 'how shall we start?'

'Just plunge in,' said Ama. 'Spike is laid up, so he's relying on you for casting and bringing in your people to get it back on track. It's going to be a mammoth job and we're both out of the picture. Me with Lovely War and Spike flat on his back. Are you sure you're up for it?'

'We thrive on crises, Ama. It's our stock in trade,' said Justin.

'Trust us, darlings. We'll be marvellous. Lead on. Jasper first, I think,' said Emily. She stood and crossed to kiss Spike on the forehead, her flame-red hair falling around his face.

'Well, I can't shake his hand and I'm not kissing him, so I'll kiss Ama instead,' said Justin.

They all left together for the theatre and Ama introduced Emily and Justin to everyone backstage. Their main concern was choosing a suitable older actor strong enough to play the lead role of Prospero. Ama offered to put them up on nights when they were too late to return home to Bridewell. Spike languished prostrate in hospital, awaiting his operation. Jasper had asked one of his grateful divorce clients, a back specialist, if he would agree to operate. He agreed and a date was set.

The Lovely War cast was now rehearsing onstage, familiarising themselves with acting on three levels instead of just one, plus the trap-door which now served duty as a foxhole in the trenches. Ama had them marching up and down the ramps, and pouring down the cantilevered staircases. Gradually, they overcame their timidity with the unaccustomed heights and acting areas and kept suggesting new possibilities to Ama as they rehearsed. She was in full flow one evening, when Kitty passed her a message. It was from Elvire asking her to call her back. As soon as the rehearsal was finished, she went to her empty office to return the phone call.

'I 'ave some news for you, Ama,' said Elvire. 'We 'ave located Ocean at the farm near Stratford. She 'as been staying there all this time.'

'How did you find her, Elvire? You're not in Stratford, are you?'

'Oh no, I am in Montreal. I 'ave a nephew who is studying English at Western University in London, and he agreed to go to the prison to speak to Ocean's boyfriend, Clay. I asked him to explain to Clay your request for a final meeting and Clay told us where she was.'

'How did you get him to agree, Elvire?'

'My nephew Maurice said Clay is in a very bad way. Clay said it was the right thing for Ocean to see her mother one last time, now that you 'ave promised not to try to stop their suicide pact. He already 'ad a visit from his father, from the Stratford theatre where he works and told him of their plan. His father agreed with him, and so Clay gave Maurice his phone number.'

'Have you got the number now, Elvire? Maybe I could talk to him.'

'I 'ave already done so, Ama. Clay told his father where Ocean was, and he offered to go and speak to her about a meeting with you. He would also like to meet you, too, and said he could act as a go-between if Ocean agrees to it.'

'This is wonderful news, Elvire. Thank you so much for all you've done.'

'I 'ave become quite close to your daughter, Ama, and she trusts me completely. I told her I would not do anything to betray that trust, so I must ask you something before we go any further.'

'I know what you're going to say,' said Ama, 'and I promise you I won't interfere in any way to stop them. I only want to see her one last time, I give you my word, Elvire.'

'It will take a few days to make all the arrangements with Clay's father. I'll phone you as soon as we can fix a date, Ama.'

'Is there anything, I can do to help? Should I phone Clay's father, too?'

'It will be best to leave it to me until you meet him, Ama. After that, the two of you can handle the rest of the final details. You realise there will 'ave to be all the funeral arrangements for both of them.'

'Oh god, I hadn't even thought of that, Elvire.'

'I'm sorry for you, Ama. None of this is going to be easy. Do you 'ave someone to help you with all this?'

'I'm not sure. My partner, Spike, is in hospital awaiting an operation on his back. I don't think he will be out for some time.'

'Is my father there, Ama? Perhaps you could ask him to help.'

'Jasper is very busy with so many different roles as acting producer and he's done too much already, Elvire, I wouldn't like to ask him.'

'Papa, too, 'as become quite fond of your daughter, Ama. I will speak to him myself and tell him what the situation is. I will call you soon.'

CHAPTER SEVENTEEN

Esther and her students had designed the pageant wagon to be viewed from either side, so that it was open in the centre. Folding wings could be lowered down, to make a platform stage when it was stopped to perform. A painted curtain provided a hiding place, for the actors to make exits and entrances as needed. With the new wheel fitted by Fergus, they began to paint and decorate the whole wagon with traditional medieval designs and bright primary colours.

Karla and Charlene helped with the decorating, in return for assistance from the students to get the refuge centre float ready for the Fishermen's Day parade. The old giant shoe house had become shabby and worn from being used as a playground climbing frame in the women's refuge garden. The students decided to refurbish it and add a roof and front porch and a slide from one of the windows.

Sarah had persuaded one of the fish packing companies in Arcadia to lend a truck with a flatbed trailer to pull it in the parade. All the refuge kids helped make decorations for the trailer, with paintings and streamers and a long banner to promote support of the refuge centre.

When Karla and Charlene's two young girls saw the comedy sketches that the grad students were rehearsing, they wanted to do something too, besides just waving from the float. The two girls rehearsed the little ones endlessly at the refuge centre, in preparation for the big day. They persuaded Sarah to be the old woman who lived in the shoe and made her join their rehearsals. Sarah readily agreed as a good way to keep an eye on the children, while they were on the float.

Spike had some news of his own a few days later, when Ama came to visit him in hospital as he waited for his operation.

'Guess who paid me a visit yesterday? – Lloyd Kramer and his son Derek. Apparently, Arthur told them about my accident. He's going to concentrate on breeding oxen for show. Seems he and his son have been helping to build the pageant wagon with Esther's students. Derek told me how they repaired the broken wheel at the shipyard with Fergus. Lloyd promised me they will definitely bring one of his show teams, to pull the pageant wagon in the Fishermen's Day Parade.'

'Jasper'll be delighted and so will I. That should certainly draw the crowds,' Ama said.

'That's the good news. The bad news is I won't be able to see them – or the pageant wagon plays. My operation isn't until the day after the parade.'

'I'm sorry, Spike. Maybe Jasper can arrange to film the whole thing for you. And we could use clips for promoting the plays as well.'

'You don't look sorry, you look delighted. I always seem to play second fiddle to the theatre.'

'Don't sulk. I'll make it up to you, I promise.'

'When, though.'

'I can't do anything while you're laid up, so don't go getting any ideas.'

'I've been lying here thinking – maybe we could use one of those sling contraptions they use for broken legs. You could get in it and lower yourself down on top of me with ropes and pulleys. And I could lie perfectly still, what do you think?'

'I think the nurses would be thrilled to help you carry out your sexual fantasies. All part of their job description, I'm sure.'

He grinned. 'I've had other ideas if you don't think that one will work, Ama.'

'The best idea is for you to focus on The Tempest and how to stage it. I could ask Emily to come and discuss it with you.' It was her turn to grin.

'Now that's an even better idea. I'll bet she'd approve of my sling contraption scheme.'

'On second thoughts, perhaps I won't suggest it. You can just lie here pretending you're the Marquis de Sade and entertain the nurses with your fantasies. I had some news of my own to tell you but perhaps it might have an adverse effect on you. I'll save it for later.'

'Tell me now, Ama, I can handle it. This morphine drip makes me feel like Superman.'

'It's about Claire. And Jasper.'

'What scheme are they up to now? She's not overdoing it again, is she?'

'I'm not sure. It seems she and Jasper have come to an understanding.'

'Go on, I'm listening.'

'This is all hush, hush and you're not to let it go outside this room. They've moved in together at Kitty's. No one knows except the four of us. Sarah's in on it too, of course.'

'But Antony? And Jasper's wife. Do they know?'

'Claire says it's because she finally heard from Antony in Los Angeles. He's gone back to his wife over there. And Jasper and Delphine live together but separately, he says.'

'The lucky devil. I always thought it was you he fancied.'

'I made it plain from the start, I was otherwise engaged. We're just good friends.'

'Now I guess we'll never get to try out our proposed threesome with Claire, Ama.'

'You can add it to your collection of fantasies here in the hospital. It will keep you occupied.'

With Kitty to help her in rehearsals and Jasper dealing with any renovation problems, the Lovely War production was beginning to coalesce into a viable show. Not having to concern herself with anything else except Spike, meant that Ama could focus her whole attention on the play. She sat in the stalls with Kitty, watching the first full run-through of the show. They used recordings of the musical numbers, as the musicians wouldn't be available until closer to the final rehearsals. But they did have some of the sound effects and some general background lighting. Each rehearsal they added more of the real props and bits of costumes as they became available from Frankie and their new props man.

'This seems more and more like a show and less like a train wreck every day, Ama,' said Arthur.

'We'll take that as a compliment, shall we, Kitty?'

'It's nothing short of a miracle the way everything is coming together,' said Kitty. 'Arthur, you've done wonders with all your team.'

'Still a long way to go,' said Arthur, 'but I'm convinced now you can pull it off, Ama.'

'Kitty's right,' she said, 'it is miraculous. I only wish Spike could be here to see it happen. He was even more dubious than you when we started. Thought it was way too ambitious.'

'So did everyone at the beginning,' said Kitty. 'Except Claire. She never faltered for a moment, finding answers to everything. Small wonder she had a breakdown. But now look at her, coming back stronger every day.'

'Jasper has his hands full stopping her from over-doing it,' said Ama. 'I hope you and Sarah keep a sharp watch on her at home, Kitty.'

'Too bad I'm not in the show,' said Arthur. 'All that running up and down those staircases and ramps like the rest of the cast would keep me in trim, Ama.'

'You don't think I'm overdoing the action, do you? I just can't resist making maximum use of all these levels and I keep dreaming up more ways to try them out. Spike was a spear-carrier at the RSC in Stratford once, years ago during a season of the Roman plays. He remembers a slow-motion charge of Caesar's army, coming straight towards the audience out of the fog of battle, running on the spot, miming shouts and cries that went on for five minutes. The Guardian theatre critic said it looked like the Royal Ballet in a rugby match. Not quite what the directors were hoping for, Spike said. That's what I'd like to try doing, something like that.'

'You've got the perfect space to do it in,' Arthur said. 'Why not start with an empty stage and then have everyone come pouring in from all directions and all levels, musicians included.'

'Sounds better than the Grand March from Aida,' said Kitty. 'Maybe you could use Verdi's music.'

'I was thinking of something circus-like with a ringmaster and music from Entrance of the Gladiators,' said Ama.

'Why not the yoke of oxen pulling the pageant wagon across the stage?' Arthur said.

The run-through had finished and the cast were gathered onstage, waiting for notes from Ama. She stood at the bottom of the ramp and spoke to them.

'We've just been tossing ideas around for a big impressive opening number, to get the audience on the edge of their seats. I'd like to hear what you think would work best. Kitty thought something operatic like the Grand March from Aida. I suggested a ring-master cracking his whip to circus music and everyone tumbling onstage. Arthur wants to bring the ox-team on pulling the pageant wagon. Now let's hear from you.'

Everyone started talking at once... '... bring the musicians on in full commedia costume... clowns popping up out of the trap-door on the floor, chasing each other with slapsticks.'. the ideas and suggestions kept coming.

Finally, Ama held up her hands for quiet. 'Just one thing. I get to have the final say, so convince me. Right now, I'm off to the hospital to see Spike and hear what he thinks we should do.'

After visiting hours, Ama drove back home to the empty house-sit. She lay in the old carved sleigh bed wondering how long it would be until Spike could be in it with her. Despite his bravado, she worried he was sinking into depression, lying on his back without moving day after day. Although he seldom spoke of it, they both knew the success rate for spinal operations was not high, with often only marginal improvements. What would happen to all their brave new plans for sailing, travelling and producing plays if he made only a partial recovery.

The bedside phone rang in the midst of her reverie.

'Hello, Ama? It's Elvire. I 'ope this is not too late.'

'Elvire. No, I've only come home from the hospital now. Did you ring earlier?'

'Twice. I 'ave heard from Mr. Fordwich, Clay's father. He's been to the farm and spoken to Ocean in person.'

'Is she alright, Elvire? What did he say?'

'She didn't want to talk to him at first. She thought he 'ad come to try to get between her and Clay and prevent their suicide pact. He told me Ocean was very agitated and he 'ad a hard time convincing her he was on their side.'

'How did he convince her, Elvire? Maybe I should say the same thing too.'

'Per'aps. Or per'aps not, Ama. It might make her suspicious you were both planning something. I think you must use your own words.'

'But will she even talk to me?'

'Mr. Fordwich says she will. He told her how he and Clay 'ad talked everything over, and how much better they both felt afterwards. He said they were both crying and smiling at the same time.'

'Was Mrs. Fordwich there, too, Elvire?'

'No, she died three years ago. Clay was their only child. Mr. Fordwich sounded very sad on the phone, Ama. He broke down and cried while he was telling me about their meeting. Clay 'as promised to let him know the night he and Ocean will end their lives.'

'I would like to meet him. Do you have his phone number?'

'He thinks you should phone Ocean as soon as possible; in case she changes her mind. She's waiting to hear from you. Do you 'ave a pencil there, I will give you both their numbers.' She dictated the phone numbers to her twice. 'Please call me after you speak to her, Ama. Ask her if she wishes me to call her again. This is a sad time for me, too.'

For some time after Elvire had hung up, Ama sat staring at the scrawled numbers, wondering if it was too late to call her daughter. Ocean had always been a night owl, sometimes staying up all night, prowling round the house when she lived at home. Perhaps the morning would be better. Or was she just being a coward now, frightened to make the call after waiting for so long.

She went downstairs and made a cup of tea, then sat in her armchair in the little vestibule she used as an office. She drank her tea and took the crumpled piece of paper with the phone numbers, from the pocket of her faded old dressing gown. Claire had tried to persuade her to throw the gown away in favour of something more glamorous. She smoothed out the paper and picked up her cellphone to dial Ocean's number. It rang several times before she answered.

'Ocean? It's me. Mom.'

'Hello Mother. I've been expecting your call.'

'Have you, darling? I've been out at the theatre for rehearsal, then I went to the hospital to see Spike and when I got home Elvire phoned – she said she'd been calling several times and I've only just finished speaking to her...' Ama heard herself babbling on but was too nervous to stop. '... I was going to wait until morning to call you and then I remembered what a nighthawk you were –'

'I'm glad you phoned, Mother. I needed to talk to you.'

'And I couldn't wait to talk to you again, when Elvire gave me your number.'

'Yes. It was Elvire persuaded me to get in touch with you. She's been a good friend to me since we met and I trust her completely. I hope she hasn't been wrong this time, suggesting we meet.'

'If you mean you're worried I might interfere in some way, Ocean, I gave Elvire my solemn promise not to. I only want us to see each other again before...before –'

'Before what? Say it, Mother. I want to hear you say it.'

'Before you end your life, darling.'

'Before I commit suicide with Clay. That's what I want to hear you say. No euphemisms, no religious claptrap, Mother.'

'Why are you acting so hard, Ocean – aren't you frightened? I am. But I know it's what you want.'

'Yes, it is. It's what we both want, Clay and I. And we need to be hard to get through this together. I don't want to risk you messing things up for us, Mother.'

'I promise, I promise. And if it feels right for you, you must do it. I'll support you any way I can.'

'Us, Mother, us. Clay and I love each other, regardless of what you think. We want to be with each other till the end, and this is what we've decided to do when the time comes.'

'I understand, Ocean and I accept your decision. Only please don't exclude me. I want to support you – both of you if this is what you really want.'

'What are you saying, Mother – exclude you? You're not planning to do anything, are you?'

'No, no, of course not. I promised you. I only meant, wouldn't you let me be with you at the end? To hold you while it happens, so you wouldn't be all alone. I hate to think of you doing this all by yourself.'

'I won't be by myself. I'll be with Clay, in the only way we can.'

'I know that, darling. I just meant to support you. Please, Ocean, let me do that.'

'Oh, Mother, I'm sorry. I don't want to be hard. It's the only way I know to get through this when I can't be together with Clay. We have a little ritual ceremony we'll each perform at the same time, even though we can't hold each other.'

'I wouldn't disturb that, I promise, Ocean.'

'Alright, Mother, I promise, too. I'll let you know when we fix the exact date.'

'Thank you, darling, I'm so happy you agreed.'

'I'm happy too. It's almost like it will be a wedding in some strange way. Goodbye, Mother.'

'Goodbye, Ocean.'

CHAPTER EIGHTEEN

The Saturday morning of the Fishermen's Day parade, the parking lot of the old Regency Theatre was pulsating with over-excited children racing around the floats. The plan was to have both the women's refuge float and the pageant wagon, join the main body of the parade at the edge of town, where it was assembling for a noon start. The grad students had hauled the replica model of the medieval pageant wagon outside, for the oxen to be hitched to it when they arrived.

Lloyd Kramer's heavy-duty pickup truck had pulled into the parking lot. Kids seethed around the trailer as he and his son Derek, lowered the tailgate ramp and led out the massive team of oxen. The placid animals stood unmoving, as the big farmer tied them together with the painted wooden yoke, lashing it tight to their polished horns with long leather thongs. Derek adjusted the gleaming brass decorations on the collars round their thick necks, and brushed their shining deep red hides with a curry comb.

Lloyd led them over to the front end of the pageant wagon and he and Derek harnessed them to it with the special chrome-plated show chains he had brought with him.

'Better let them have a practice turn around the parking lot to get used to the feel of it,' he said.

'Good idea,' said Ivy. 'I'll get the players on board and they can see what it's like when it's moving. They've only rehearsed with it standing still.'

Ama and Ivy rounded them up and the performers took their places on the wagon. Lloyd stood at the head of his team with his long leather goad raised above their heads. On his signal, the oxen lowered their heads as they took up the strain and the pageant wagon lurched forward, with the students clutching for support at the unfamiliar movement. Children danced about on both sides and one or two of the musicians joined in behind. Lloyd led the yoke of oxen around the perimeter of the parking lot, to get them used to turning corners and stopping and starting on his command. Satisfied, he led them over to his pickup and tied them to the trailer, while Derek fed them some hay from inside.

While they waited for the rest of the parade to swing by the theatre, the students took the opportunity to have a final run-through of their performances. The kids climbed down from the shoe float and gathered round, as the performers and musicians on the pageant wagon began their comedy sketches. The kids shouted and joined in the action as the actors in their commedia characters got into their stride. They milked the young audience for laughs, as the long-nosed Tooth-Puller yanked out whole sets of false teeth with his huge pliers. He offered to pull the kids' loose teeth for them. They screamed and scattered, when he climbed down off the wagon to pursue them.

Jasper, who had been sent to reconnoitre the progress of the parade, pulled into the theatre parking lot. He told everyone it would be arriving in ten minutes and where their positions would be in the procession. The parade marshal wanted to put the pageant wagon near the head, behind the high school marching band, so the slow oxen would set the pace for the whole parade. The women's refuge float would follow the town band, somewhere in the middle.

A few minutes later the music from the marching band could be heard approaching. The parade hove into view, led by a group of high-kicking school cheer leaders in front of their marching band. The marshal halted the parade as they passed, to create a space for Lloyd to lead his oxen and the pageant wagon in behind the band. When the town band appeared, the marshal halted the parade again and motioned the driver of the children's float to pull into position behind the musicians.

With Lloyd's oxen now determining the speed of the parade, many of the gathering crowd of tourists and onlookers moved along with the floats, lured by the actions of the performers and singing children. Jasper had positioned Ama, Arthur and Frankie around the pageant wagon. Each had bundles of leaflets promoting the re-opening of the Regency Theatre, to hand out to the crowd. Frankie's wardrobe volunteers had made wide diagonal sashes for them to wear, advertising 'Oh What A |Lovely War'.

The Fishermen's Day Parade was a long-standing tradition in the town. The Arcadia Tourist office promoted it widely, as a highlight of the end of summer season. The tourists poured into town.

Claire, Gloria and Jasper had previously covered the entire route of the parade. They put theatre posters on every shop window and lamppost along the way, to catch the attention of a captive audience waiting for the parade.

Jasper dodged about with his video camera, filming the action of the passing floats as they went by, following the one-way system. The route took them through the main street of the ancient town, past the old shipyards. It passed the multi-coloured fishermen's warehouses and down along the docks, to end in the open space on the wharf, in front of the museum. The floats formed a large circle around a cluster of green and yellow marquees, provided by the local fish-packing businesses. The stalls sold seafood and drinks to the crowds, as they strolled round the circle of floats watching the performers and snapping pictures of the oxen and pageant wagon.

Jasper stood beside Claire, beaming at the crowds with satisfaction. 'If this doesn't guarantee Ama a full house for the theatre re-opening, I shall be very surprised, Claire.'

'Especially as Lloyd and his son have promised to bring the oxen again for opening night,' she said. 'I've produced my share of big shows but this one tops them all. You've done an amazing job, Jasper.'

'We did it together, Claire. You're the brains and I helped make it happen. Call it teamwork.'

'I call it a labour of love – by everyone. What a rotten shame Spike can't be here to see it all, Jasper.'

'What do you think this is all for?' he said, holding up his video camera. 'I'll be giving him a private viewing of the whole parade, in his hospital room tonight. Ama asked me to do it for him.'

At the hospital that evening, Ama, Claire and Jasper sat around Spike's bed, to view the video footage Jasper had filmed of the parade. Spike was in a good mood and teased Claire about some of the shaky shots she had taken.

'There's plenty of usable stuff that Jasper took,' she said. 'We can blow-up some of the stills for the foyer displays and edit a loop of the video of the pageant wagon material to run in the bar area.'

'I promised Sarah and Kitty to make them a copy of the whole parade for the kids as well,' said Jasper

'Well, I've got some good news for you all,' said Spike. 'My operation has been brought forward, as they think I'm ready for it now. I'm on the operating list for tomorrow, so wish me luck.'

'That's great, Spike. You're in good hands. Napier is one of the best surgeons in Montreal,' said Jasper. 'Come on, Claire, we'd better let him rest for the big day.'

Jasper and Claire left and Ama stayed on to the end of visiting hours to sit with him.

'Are you as nervous as I am, Spike?'

'About the show?'

'About you. It seems like forever we've been waiting, and now that it's finally going to happen, I'm frightened.'

'You heard Jasper. This guy is a top surgeon, Ama. I'm ready for this. Lying here day after day, wondering if I'll ever walk again. At least tomorrow by this time I'll know for sure.'

'And you're not nervous or frightened it might go wrong? Oh god, I'm going to cry – I'm sorry, Spike.'

'It's my fault, Ama. All this self-pity about becoming a basket case. I'm sorry I upset you.'

'I just want to hug you and hold you close,' she said, 'and all I can do is hold your hand.'

'After tomorrow things will be different, one way or the other.'

'Don't talk like that, my love, you're frightening me again.'

'I only meant that... listen, Ama. I want to tell you something. I've been thinking about it for a long time. I was going to wait until after the operation but it's better I say it now. If anything should go wrong tomorrow and I can't walk again, I don't want you to stay with me. It wouldn't be fair. You didn't sign up to be my care-giver. We're not married, so none of that 'in sickness and in health' stuff, okay?'

'Now you really are frightening me, Spike. Please don't talk like that.'

'I have to, Ama. I might be too afraid to say it later.'

'If you're not sure, maybe we should get a second opinion. Not rush into it...'

'What good would that do? Sooner or later I have to face this and take the chance. But you don't, Ama, that's all I'm saying. My choice is not binding on you.'

'Has it never occurred to you, lying here all this time, that if it weren't for me, you wouldn't be in this predicament, Spike. I didn't notice you running away from my problems with Ocean and the theatre. I'm not going anywhere, especially not now. We may not be married but we're together, full stop.'

He smiled at her. 'Okay. Fair warning, you may not get the chance again.'

'And neither will you, so don't even think about it in future.' She leaned over the bed and kissed him lightly but for a long time, before she left.

CHAPTER NINETEEN

With the re-opening of the theatre only a week away, Ama had no time to dwell on Spike or Ocean's fate. She was glad of the chance to immerse herself in the final preparations for Oh What A Lovely War. The Fishermen's Day parade had produced a burst of renewed interest and volunteers flowed into the old Edwardian theatre, offering help of every sort. Claire absorbed each one in some aspect of the work still needing to be done. She plied Arthur and Frankie with helpers and chastised both, if she caught them doing anything other than supervising. Arthur chafed under this unaccustomed role.

'It's faster if I do it myself, Ama, instead of riding herd over this lot.'

'Maybe the first time, Arthur, but Claire's right. Unless you delegate these last time-consuming little jobs, we'll never finish on time. You're too valuable to be fussing over things even I could do. Let them get on with it and just keep an eye on them. They may not do it as well as you might but they'll learn. Maybe they'll stick around for our next show, if you make them feel needed. Look at Charlene and Karla.'

'Yeah, you're right about them anyway. You'd think they'd been around for ages instead of just a few weeks.'

When Ama drove her back to Kitty's, Claire took an armload of work with her.

'You must be so relieved that Spike's operation is over,' said Claire. 'I was worried there might be complications from what Jasper told me. Dr. Napier told him it was a tricky job.'

'I spoke to him right afterwards,' said Ama. 'He feels it went off successfully but we won't know for sure until it starts to heal. He had to go back to Montreal, but he assured me his colleagues in Halifax would keep him up to speed on Spike's progress.'

'That all sounds promising, Ama. Too bad Jasper can't find me a magician like that.'

'What do you mean, Claire, are you alright? You haven't had any more test results, have you?'

'I don't get results anymore, Ama, just reports. None of them good.'

'But I thought your doctor said you were in remission. And you and Jasper seem to be so happy these days.'

'I am. We are. That's the problem. It won't last. I can feel myself getting worse again. I don't need Laura to tell me. She just confirms what I already know.'

'Does Jasper know, Claire? Have you told him?'

'No. I tried to tell him but he's convinced I'm getting better, or at least stable. For a while he almost had me believing him. I told him it's the 'Jasper effect.' I haven't been this happy in years, Ama. That's what's so sad.' She began to cry, tears streaking her makeup.

'What about Kitty, have you talked to her?'

'What's the point? There's nothing she can do and I don't want to upset her. She and Sarah think Jasper and I are the perfect couple.'

'And Laura says there's no hope, Claire? Nothing more she can do?'

'She just says no one can tell how long remission will last, so make the most of it. But it's not as easy as it sounds. I look at Jasper sometimes, so full of plans for us and I know they won't happen. I try to pretend, only lately it's becoming more difficult to hide it from him.'

'You think he must know, too, Claire?'

She nodded and dabbed at her eyes, trying to smile. 'Dying isn't for sissies, Ama. I'm not much good at it. It's a lonely business most of the time. Thank God you let me fall apart with you sometimes. I know it's not fair, when you have so much to distress you with Ocean and now Spike...'

'Maybe you should let Jasper share this with you, instead of both pretending and being brave. You don't have to do this alone. Jasper will love you even more for letting him in. He's a good, kind man. Don't hold him off, Claire. It works for Spike and me, anyway.'

'I'll try, Ama. I promise.'

When Ama arrived at the hospital the next day to see Spike, Jasper was already there. They had been talking about his release.

'How soon will that be? Do you know yet, Spike?' asked Jasper. 'I understand one of Napier's colleagues is taking over your case, now that he's been called back to Montreal.'

'That's right. Dr. Leevis is an old boy, just does consulting now. Dr. Napier told me I'm in good hands with him. He was in to see me this morning.'

'What did he say, Spike?' said Ama. 'Will they let you out soon?'

'Dr. Leevis said if he had his way, he'd keep me in under observation for three weeks, like they used to do. But nowadays they send you home as soon as the anaesthetic wears off, according to him.'

'My god, I'd be terrified to move you, Spike,' said Ama. 'He can't be serious.'

'He was exaggerating, of course but it will be a few days not a few weeks,' Spike said. 'Don't worry, they send you home in an ambulance and I'll be all strapped up so I can't move.'

'Now that Claire is back on her feet you could have her hospital bed,' said Jasper. 'It's still in Kitty's veranda. Travis and I can move it over in Fergus's old pickup. Sarah has offered to cook for you and all Ama has to do is keep you entertained.'

Three days later, Dr. Leevis reluctantly agreed to the arrangements, and Spike was duly installed in Claire's ex-hospital bed, in Ama's downstairs front room. The elderly consultant promised to make periodic house-calls. Arthur dug out a folding cot from the props department so Ama could sleep beside Spike, which she insisted on.

As they lay side by side that night linking hands, Spike told Ama some surprising news.

'While I was waiting in hospital for my operation, I had plenty of time to think over what I should do after I got out. I remembered you saying once, that we should go back to England to visit my son and his girlfriend. One night when I couldn't sleep, I persuaded a nursing assistant to write a letter to him for me. I told Patrick about my accident and asked him to get in touch. I didn't have an email address or a phone number, so she had to send it by post. Two days ago, I heard back from him.'

Ama squeezed his hand. 'That's wonderful news, Spike. After all this time, out of the blue.'

'He wants to come over, but he can't leave his girlfriend.'
'Why not, is she ill?'

'Not exactly – she's pregnant.'

'What?'

'Apparently she's had two miscarriages previously. Her doctor warned her not to fly or it might happen again.'

'Oh god, this is amazing news, Spike. Why didn't you tell me before?'

'I've been waiting for the right moment so we could share it together, Ama. Do you want to hear what else he said?'

'They're getting married.'

'No. More surprising than that. Her doctor doesn't want her to fly because she's expecting twins.'

'Good God – twins...'

'Yes. They've been having fertility treatment, because she was finding it hard to conceive and that was a possible risk – multiple births.'

'I don't know what to say, Spike. How soon is she expecting?'

'Around Christmas, providing there's no complications.'

'What a Christmas present for us. You did tell Patrick about us? I'll be able to share them with you?'

'Of course. He wants us to come over for the birth. He said he was planning to write earlier but wanted to be absolutely sure first, before he told me. Then when he got my letter, he decided to risk it.'

'It's like a dream. The children we never had together.'

'We can spoil them rotten, Ama. It's allowed with grandchildren. Twins – one for each of us. I hope they're girls.'

'Perhaps there'll be a boy and a girl. Is that possible with twins or do they have to be the same?'

'I'm not sure, maybe that's what they call fraternal twins' he said.

'No, I think that just means they're not identical.'

'Who cares as long as they're healthy, Ama. Two grandchildren. Hard to believe at our age.'

Ama sat up on her cot. 'I'm too excited to sleep, Spike. Let's have a drink to celebrate.'

She rose and padded into the darkened kitchen to search the fridge. A bottle of sparkling wine she had put in for Spike's home-coming, lay on the bottom shelf unopened. She took it back into the living room with two wine glasses.

'Look what I found.' She switched on the bedside lamp by the hospital bed, and handed him a glass. She peeled off the foil, untied the wire cage and popped the cork, trying not to let it foam over too much. They clinked glasses.

'To our grandchildren,' Spike said.

'To our good fortune,' said Ama. She drank and then kissed him, licking the foam off his lip. 'Like our first night on the Mongoose, remember? Drinking warm champagne. It's nice to be able to kiss you again, without being afraid of hurting your back.'

'Seems a long time ago, Ama. I'd love to be lying in the vee berth with you again.'

'You will, all in good time.'

'And with two squirming grandkids climbing all over us.'

The remaining days, before the opening night of 'Oh What A Lovely War' were so crammed with final rehearsals and finishing off the renovations, that Spike was almost abandoned in the house by himself. Claire and Jasper threw themselves into last minute details but the to-do list only seemed to grow longer each day.

Ama focused her attention on resolving the tech rehearsal snags, trying to co-ordinate all the sound, lighting, and special effects. She had two late-night sessions with the local musicians, practising the links with the back projections and the actors, until they at last felt ready for opening night.

Under Claire's supervision, Charlene's design group painted all the sets and props in garish mock music hall motifs, to match the pageant wagon. Ama wanted to have Lloyd's team of oxen pull the wagon through the loading doors of the scenery dock and onto the stage during the opening number. She persuaded Garth, Arthur and Fergus to build a rough ramp to lead the oxen up into the theatre, next to the stage door loading bay.

Frankie and Claire nearly came to blows over the beautiful commedia silk costumes, on loan from the opera in Montreal.

'The students can't wear these outside on the pageant wagon all around the town,' said Frankie. 'They'll get torn and dirty. Let them wear some of the old Halloween party outfits.'

Claire insisted. 'The whole point of them, is to get the audiences familiar with the commedia-style acting Ama's using in the show.'

Finally, they appealed to Jasper for a decision, as it was his wife who had arranged the loan of the costumes from the opera.

'I think we should risk it, Frankie. Claire's right, the crowds will love them and want to see more. I'm prepared to take the blame from my wife if anything happens,' he said.

'I'll give Ivy's students a special pep talk to be careful, and not get carried away with the clowning around,' Ama said.

In the end, Claire had her way as she had known she would, the minute she appealed to Jasper. He was incapable of refusing her anything these days. He watched her with increasing concern, as she glowed almost incandescent, with the excitement and delight of seeing the results of her vision. At one time or another, she had been alone in believing the transformation of the old theatre would ever come about. Everyone was in total awe of her abilities, now that they saw what she had achieved.

It was up to Ama now to bring it to life. And she leapt in, being everywhere at once, inspired by Claire's vision, and determined she would make it all happen. She urged her cast to a high pitch of attention to detail, as they ploughed through the last tech rehearsal and prepared for the final dress rehearsal before the opening night.

Spike ordered a wheelchair to practise manoeuvres. Each day after Ama left for the theatre, he eased himself into the wheelchair and wheeled around the empty house. By the opening night, he felt he was ready to appear in public, with some assistance from Travis and Garth to get him into the theatre. He was determined he would be there for Ama's big night.

As promised, Lloyd Kramer and his son Derek showed up with their team of oxen by six p.m. The graduate students arranged to help position the pageant wagon at the bottom of the ramp by the stage door. Lloyd would lead the oxen up it and right onto the stage, when they returned from their parade through the town. The big farmer yoked the oxen to the decorated wagon and gave them a practice turn up and down the ramp, before setting off with the musicians and cast of students. Everyone wore the colourful opera's costumes of the commedia characters and Jasper filmed them along the route. The pubs and seafood restaurants were full with the end of summer tourists. At each stop the cast lowered the wings which formed the platform stage, to present one of their well-rehearsed comic sketches, and invited everyone to come see the show.

By the time they reached the pubs down by the docks, they had a swelling crowd of kids and strolling visitors. The locals as well, accompanied the pageant wagon with its band of performers and musicians. Jasper had calculated an hour and a half to do the circuit back to the theatre. This would leave over half an hour for the audience to enjoy the delights of Claire's magically transformed foyer bar, with its billowing canopy and huge, slowly turning glitter ball. Coloured lights danced round the whole of the entrance area, reflecting off the mirrored globe from the central chandelier, now restored to its former glory.

The audience coming through the entrance doors crowded round the gleaming mahogany bar to place their orders for intermission drinks.

Ama glanced at her watch for the tenth time, as the eight o'clock performance time came and went with no sign of the crowd abating. She caught Jasper's eye across the foyer and tapped her wrist at him. He shook his head at her and pointed to the line-up of people, still queuing for tickets at the box office. She edged her way over to him and Kitty, who were talking to Ralph by the foot of the curving staircase.

'We're all set backstage, Jasper. What shall we do? It's past eight already.'

'Give them another ten minutes, Ama. I'll speak to the box office to hurry them along,' he said.

'Enjoy your fifteen minutes of fame,' Ralph said, raising his cup of punch to her.

'Don't rush them, dear,' said Kitty. 'Everyone's having a wonderful time marvelling at Claire's handiwork. Where is she, anyway, I want to congratulate her.'

'She's with Emily and Justin somewhere,' said Ama. 'They're already talking about our next show.'

Jasper came back and caught her elbow. 'I've warned them at the box office that we go on in ten minutes. Late-comers will be seated at the first break. They can wait at the bar. I'll make an announcement here and you can make one from onstage to the auditorium.' He shooed her off backstage and mounted the first few steps of the staircase.

'Welcome, everyone. Will you please begin taking your seats? The performance will start in ten minutes. Thank you. Late-comers will be shown in at the first opportunity.'

Ama spotted Emily's flame-red hair in the archway to the stalls and waved to her.

'What is it, Ama, something wrong? It's ten past eight already.'

'People are still pouring in to the box office for last minute tickets. Jasper's giving them ten more minutes and then we start. He wants me to make an announcement from the stage. Will you do it, Emily and I'll go backstage to warn everyone we're on standby.'

'Of course she will, Ama,' said Justin. 'Emily has a wonderful stentorian voice when she's onstage.'

'I prefer to think of it as bell-like,' said Emily. 'Here, hold my drink, Justin.' She made her way down to the long ramp and mounted it on to the stage, while Ama and Claire hurried backstage to warn Lloyd and the cast.

The oxen stood patiently waiting outside at the foot of the ramp, while Lloyd and his son made last minute adjustments to the shining harness. The musicians hung about behind the pageant wagon, smoking and waiting for the pre-arranged signal. Jasper had kept one of the trumpet players with him to play a fanfare when everyone was seated and the houselights were out.

Ama made sure the cast with the pageant wagon were on standby, then peered through the hanging blacks masking the wings, to see if all the extras were in position. She waited while the lights dimmed.

The trumpet blared a ragged fanfare and the stage burst into sound and light. The oxen appeared through billowing gun smoke and distant cannon fire, pulling the pageant wagon surrounded by capering actors and musicians. Lloyd led them in a slow loop around the stage perimeter, as extras poured down the staircases from both sides. They ran up the long and short ramps waving banners and four of the refuge children dressed as war orphans, popped out of the trap door in the stage floor and ran after the wagon.

Lloyd led the oxen downstage centre and stopped. The sides of the pageant wagon unfolded and the commedia characters performed a mimed sketch. A firing squad shot their bloated officer, instead of the blindfold deserter and the whole cast sang the theme tune of "Oh, Oh, Oh What a Lovely War."

The song came to the final chorus as Lloyd and his yoke of oxen pulled the wagon back offstage and down the ramp. The crowd of extras followed, amidst delighted applause from the audience.

Ama stopped holding her breath as the play began. She slipped out to watch it with Spike from the back of the auditorium. He had positioned his wheelchair underneath the lighting booth and Ama perched on a folding stool beside him, to hold his hand.

'You did it, my love, you did it,' he whispered.

'We did it,' she said, kissing him.

'And I've got the war wound to prove it.'

They watched the audience from their observation post. People sat engrossed with all of the spectacle unfolding from different levels, and pointing out the action to their companions. They laughed and clapped in all the right places, as the timing rehearsed so painstakingly, paid off. Spike grinned at her and squeezed her hand as tears of relief slid down her cheeks.

The first half rolled on, with only slight hitches in the complicated technical cues and the odd fluffed line. The clever plotting, with the farcical live action and stylised commedia performances, played out against the mixed media backdrop projected behind the actors. It reinforced the appalling statistics of war and parodied all the jingoistic posturing of its proponents.

The intermission arrived to enthusiastic applause and the audience streamed back out to the foyer, chattering in excited groups in the crush for the bar. Jasper dished out glasses of champagne from his private horde at one end of the bar, to Ralph and Kitty and Claire. He held out two flutes to Ama for her and Spike, who remained at his post for her return. She hugged Claire, who wore a sleek black designer number and an amber pendant Jasper had given her.

They all stood congratulating each other, until Claire was commandeered by a group of admirers in dress suits, who were obviously from the government arts council. She glowed in their midst like an animated puppet, while Ama watched her perform. She hadn't seen her so agitated and distracted before and turned to see if Jasper had noticed. He gave Ama a quizzical look and slowly shook his head. She wove her way through the drinkers and handed Spike his glass of champagne. They toasted each other and sat watching the stage crew clearing the stage for the second half performance.

'It's going to be hard topping this show, Ama. I don't envy Justin and Emily their task but they seem undaunted.'

'They have youth on their side,' she said, 'unlike us. I think I may quit while I'm ahead. This may well be my swansong. I don't think I could survive another production like this.'

'Perhaps we can retire gracefully to the sidelines and just perform occasional cameo roles in future,' he said. 'Besides, we have other fish to fry.'

'Are you by any chance referring to small fry, Spike?'

'I am, indeed, my love. Would you care to hear about it after the show?'

'Yes, please. And I also have a suggestion to make later, concerning Emily and Justin.'

Charlene came hurrying up to them. 'Ama, we've been searching for you front of house and backstage – there's been an urgent phone call for you from your daughter.'

'Oh my god, what is it?'

'She's been trying to reach you all evening but your phone isn't answering, so she finally got the theatre stage door number.'

'Is she still on the line, Charlene? I turned my phone off before the show so I wouldn't be disturbed. It's in my bag in the office.'

'She left a number for you to call back, Ama. I was too busy to find you until the intermission.'

Ama followed Charlene backstage to get her cellphone and call the number for Ocean. Her pulse raced as she dialled the number, dreading what it was.

'Mother? Where have you been? I've rung and rung.'

'I know, darling, I'm sorry. My phone was turned off. Has something happened? Are you alright?'

'I've had my last visit with Clay this afternoon, Mother and we've agreed on tomorrow morning. I told him I promised you I'd call first to let you know, if you still want to come.'

'Of course I do, you know I do. Where are you, Ocean? How will I find you?'

'I'm still in London, in a motel by the prison. It's where relatives stay when they come to visit. Riverside Lodge. Room Eleven. It's as near as I can be to Clay for our last night. We've set the hour. Dawn tomorrow morning and we'll both die together at the same time.'

'Oh darling, are you really going to do this?'

'Yes, Mother, we are. And you made a promise, remember?'

'I know I did, Ocean. I'm coming right away. Wait for me, please. I'm in Nova Scotia. I'll be there as soon as I can.'

'You have to come tonight, Mother. Dawn is at six. We've agreed. It's too late to change now.'

'I promise I'll be there, darling.'

'And Mother? I promised Elvire to let Dad know. I've left a message for him but he's filming a night shoot in Montreal. If I don't speak to him will you say goodbye for me?'

'I promise, Ocean. I must go and catch a flight. Please wait, darling.'

'I'm waiting. I'll be here until dawn. Goodbye, Mother.' She hung up.

For a minute, Ama stood rooted to the desk, her mind churning. She rummaged in her bag for the keys to the old red Toyota. No time to pack a bag. She studied her wristwatch, staring at the second hand sweeping round the dial. Less than nine hours till dawn. How could she possibly make it? Spike

– she must speak to him first and then go. She grabbed her coat and bag and fled back to the auditorium where people had begun to return to their seats.

'Ama – what's happened? Is Ocean okay? She hasn't...' he stopped, waiting for her to speak. He knew of Ocean and Clay's suicide pact. Ama had told him the night Ocean first called her about it.

'No, she hasn't done it yet. Not till dawn tomorrow. Six a.m. They've agreed the time to do it together. Spike how can I possibly get there in less than nine hours? I'm going right now to Halifax but I'm afraid I'll be too late.'

'We're in a different time zone, Ama – you've got an extra hour. Ten hours – you'll do it, but you must leave now. Get Travis to drive you to the airport. Ask Claire if she'll lend you her SUV. She's with Jasper. I just spoke to them. Travis is backstage helping Arthur. God, I want to come with you, Ama. This damn wheelchair...Go, find Claire. I'll call Travis on his cellphone to meet you in the bar. Go, go...'

'I'll phone you when I arrive, Spike.' She gave him a hurried kiss and pushed through the returning audience to the bar. Jasper and Claire stood chatting to well-wishers. She clutched Claire's elbow and pulled her aside to tell her what had happened.

'Take my car and give me your keys. Travis will have you at the airport in under an hour on the motorway, if he puts his foot down,' said Claire. 'Here's my keys. I'll tell Jasper and the others after the show. Give Ocean my love, Ama. Go, there's Travis now.' She hugged Ama and pushed her towards him, as he stood looking for her by the box office.

She handed him Claire's keys and they hurried outside to find the big silver SUV in the theatre parking lot. Spike had briefed Travis on the phone and he concentrated on following Ama's directions out to the motorway. It was not until the

SUV was purring through the darkness at 30mph over the posted speed limit that he asked her about her daughter.

It was a relief for her to pour out her fears for Ocean to someone and Travis listened without interrupting, until she finally stopped to mop her wet face and blow her nose.

'This must be bloody hard for you, Ama, to just stand by and not do anything. But it sounds from what you say, they've been planning this for a long time and it's not some knee-jerk reaction. I don't know what I'd do in your situation, though.'

'I don't know what I'm going to do either, Travis. I've made Ocean a promise to be with her when she dies. All I can think about at the moment, is to get there before it's too late. Can we go any faster? There's no traffic this time of night.'

For answer, Travis put his foot down hard and the big silver car leapt forward on the darkened motorway. In under an hour he pulled up in front of the departures area of the Halifax airport to drop Ama off.

'You won't get a direct flight from here, Ama. Your best bet is to go to Montreal or Toronto first where you'll have more options. Good luck. Wish I could be more help.' He hugged her and she ran into the near-empty departure lounge.

Travis was right. There were only a few flights out. The soonest one was in half an hour to Toronto. She got her ticket and then bought a sandwich and coffee, while she waited for her flight to be called.

The plane was over half empty when she boarded. The young flight attendant let her sit in one of the empty rows, where she could put the armrests up and stretch out across three seats. She sat for some time staring out into the darkness and tried to empty her mind, the way she was taught in her meditation group. Concentrating on recalling the old familiar Buddhist chants helped to stop her brain racing in repetitive circles. She took the proffered blanket from the attendant, lay on her side full-length on the seats and closed her eyes. Although she couldn't sleep, the steady throb of the jet engines blocked any thoughts from her mind. She dozed in a state of limbo for the rest of the flight. They arrived in Toronto just before two a.m.

Scanning the electronic departures board, Ama found a local flight to Windsor-Detroit making two stops on the way at Hamilton and London. It would arrive in London at 4:20 a.m. and was already boarding. She scrambled to buy her ticket from the automated machines, ran to the boarding gate and joined the last few stragglers passing through the security scanners.

On board, a large party of elderly tourists blocked the aisles, storing all their duty-free liquor and souvenirs from a Caribbean cruise. They all seemed to know each other from their holiday and called back and forth during the short hop to Hamilton, where many of them got off.

As the plane took off again for London, Ama had only one person beside her. The woman looked at her several times to catch her eye, wanting to talk.

'Have you been on holiday, too, dear?' she said. When Ama shook her head, the woman took it as an invitation to tell her of her own Caribbean adventures. 'I've had such a wonderful time, I hate to be returning to dreary old London. My husband hated cruises. I had to wait until he passed on before I could go on one. I'm so angry with myself for not just going anyway. It turns out lots of women my age take cruises on their own or with a group. I'm determined to make up for lost time.'

'I'm going to London, too,' said Ama. 'I'm supposed to be meeting my daughter. She's staying at a motel called the

Riverside Lodge. Do you happen to know if it's near the airport?'

'Why, yes dear, although I don't think you'll enjoy staying there. It's practically opposite the prison. I think it's mostly used by people visiting the inmates, although I've never been there. It has a bit of a rough reputation. I can't imagine why your daughter's staying...' her voice trailed off. 'Oh, I'm so sorry, I didn't mean to... oh dear.'

'It's alright,' Ama said. 'That's why she's there. Her boyfriend is inside and she's been visiting him.'

'We fly right over the prison, you can't miss it. It's all floodlit, like a football stadium. If you take a taxi you should be there in a few minutes. Ask him to drop you right at the motel reception. I wouldn't advise you to walk around there at night.' The older woman studied her. 'I hope it's not a serious offence, dear. Will he be out soon?'

'No, he won't, I'm afraid.'

'But your daughter will wait for him?'

Ama nodded her head and started to cry, fumbling for a handkerchief.

'Oh, my dear, I'm so sorry, I didn't mean to interfere. Here,' she handed Ama a tissue from her handbag. 'Please forgive me. When you live alone you long for someone to talk to.'

Ama wiped her eyes and tried to smile. 'It's not your fault. I'm in a state of shock, I think. I can't stop crying all the time.'

'Would you like me to come with you? We could share a cab. I know the town inside out. I've lived here all my life.'

'Yes, I would,' said Ama. 'I'm very late meeting her and I'm pressed for time. It's kind of you to offer.'

'Nonsense, dear. I've only an empty house to return to. I'd feel better making up for my thoughtlessness in upsetting you.'

The plane began making its descent into London. The woman pointed out the window at the bleak floodlit prison below. Ama tried to picture Clay sitting alone in his cell, preparing to take his own life. A terrible sadness welled up inside her and she sobbed aloud, as she stared out the window. How cruel that her daughter could not be with him, she thought, to share their last hours together. She tried to suppress a wail that arose in her throat.

'Oh dear god, I've done it again,' said the woman, leaning across to stroke Ama's arm. 'How could I be so insensitive. Please let me help you. What is your name, dear?'

'Ama.

'And your daughter's?'

'Ocean.'

'Ocean. What a peaceful soothing name. Mine's Evelyn.'

'I suppose I can tell you the truth, Evelyn. The reason I'm such a wreck is that Ocean and her boyfriend Clay have planned to commit suicide this morning and I'm afraid I may be too late.'

'To try to stop them? But how? You said he's in prison.'

In the time remaining for the plane to land, Ama poured out the little she knew of their joint suicide pact.

'I promised I wouldn't try to stop her. I only wanted to be with her at the last, so she wouldn't be all alone at the end.' She looked at her watch. 'I only have an hour and a half until 6 a.m. or I'll miss her. She won't wait longer she said. They've chosen the same time to die.'

'And you've chosen to be with her. That's very brave of you, Ama, to take this risk by yourself. Would you let me come with you? – just for when it's over, I mean. We could go back to my house for awhile. For you to recover a bit.'

'I don't want to involve you in this, Evelyn. But if you'd come to the motel with me, I'd appreciate that. Perhaps we could meet afterwards. I'm not sure what I'll do next. I haven't really thought that far ahead. I'll have to call a doctor when it's over, I suppose.'

'Try not to think about that now, dear. I'll wait outside in the motel lounge for you and we can work out what to do.'

'There's a risk you might be regarded as an accessory or something, so you mustn't come in with me, Evelyn. Someone at the motel might report you.'

Only a handful of people left the airplane. They collected Evelyn's bag from the carousel and went to the taxi stand outside arrivals. Evelyn checked with the cab driver first, that he knew exactly where the Riverside Lodge was, before they got in. He nodded assurance and they left for the motel. It was ten to five by Ama's watch.

'You should have nearly an hour with Ocean,' said Evelyn. 'I'll drop you at reception, then go home to get my own car and come back for you after six.'

The taxi pulled up to the motel entrance at ten past five and Ama entered the empty lobby. There was no one at the desk but she could hear a vacuum cleaner humming in the distance. She followed the room arrows to number eleven on the ground floor and tapped at the door.

'Ocean? It's me, Mother.'

In a moment the door was unlocked and a dishevelled Ocean with tear-streaked face stood there in bare feet. Her face crumpled as she looked at Ama and stepped forward to embrace her. Ama pulled her over to the messy bed and sat beside her, stroking her hair and making soothing noises.

'I made it, darling. I'm here now. I won't leave you.'

'I thought you weren't going to come, Mother.'

'I was so scared I'd be too late. I had to change planes and they kept stopping. I'm sorry I made you worry.'

'It's okay, Mother, you're here now anyway. We still have some time together to talk.' She hugged Ama and they clung to each other for several moments.

'Have you been here all night on your own, Ocean?' said Ama, wiping her daughter's face with her handkerchief.

Ocean nodded. 'I came here right after I phoned and left the message for you.'

'All that time I've been travelling across the country you've been sitting here alone, waiting for me.'

'I wanted to be alone so I could be with Clay, just like we planned. I'm ready to meet him, Mother. See?' She pointed to two small vials and a glass sitting on the bedside table.

'It makes me so sad, darling, to think you can't be together with him now.'

'But I have been. All night. Reliving all the things we've done, places we've been and friends we've had. I've been so happy these last few hours.'

'Your eyes are all red, Ocean. You've been crying. Are you frightened?'

'Some of the memories were sad ones, Mother. They made me cry. But I still wanted to remember them, too.'

'I know I promised I wouldn't try to stop you or interfere in any way, darling, and I won't. I only want to be with you. I think I understand why you're doing this, and only you know when it's the right time.'

'Clay and I know we've almost reached the end. If we left it any longer, we'd both be too sick to do anything about it. You do realise that, Mother?'

'I believe you, Ocean. It's hard to accept that you'll be gone from my life, that's all. It doesn't feel natural that children should die before their parents. Can you understand that?'

'I wish it could have worked out that way, but I've accepted I have to go first. I didn't choose my life. It chose me. This is who I am and I'm ready to go. I'm not going alone; Clay will be with me.'

'I'm glad you believe you won't be alone, darling. It's something for me to hold onto as well.'

'We're not religious, Clay and me. It's the journey we'll be together for. Who knows what the destination will be, we don't. We often talked about death and dying. We knew we wanted to die together and thought we could be in control of that part. But death is different. All you can do is accept it. What we didn't expect, was not to be together at the end. This is the best we could manage.'

'You make me ashamed of my petty worries and problems, Ocean. I feel as though you were the parent and I am the child.'

'I'm still your child, Mother. I still need your love, even now.'

'And I need yours, too. Is there anything I can say or do for you, Ocean?'

'Just hold me while I go, so I'll feel loved by you.'

'I will. I'll always love you as much as the day you were born.'

'Would you help me get ready, Mother? I've brought a clean nightdress to wear. I want to feel like a bride for Clay. I told him I would be.'

'Of course I will. May I brush your hair for you? Let's wash your face first and then you can put on your bridegown.'

Ama opened her daughter's small suitcase and took out the nightdress. She helped her out of her crumpled clothes and folded them into the case, along with her shoes. Ocean sat passively on the bed and let her mother wash her face with a warm cloth from the motel bathroom. Her hairbrush lay on the night table beside the waiting medicine. Ama spent a long time brushing Ocean's shoulder-length hair, after she slipped the nightdress on her. From the toilet bag in the bathroom which Ama brought over to her, Ocean removed a small velvet box. She opened it to show her mother.

'It's a ring Clay gave me before he went to prison. It's from a thrift shop, it's not stolen. I promised to put it on when I take the medicine. He's getting ready now, too. We have it all worked out to the last minute, so we can picture each other. We only have a little more time,' she said, looking at her watch. 'In my suitcase is an envelope for you to open, with all the instructions the 'Right to Die' people gave me. There's a phone number to call and someone will come and help you. They said it's important that you leave the room before I take the medicine, so you can't be accused of assisting me. Go to the reception and wait for five minutes and then come back in and hold my hand, Mother. Can you do that?'

'I promise,' said Ama, tucking her daughter into bed and smoothing the covers.

'I want to be alone with Clay at the end. Will you just sit with me and not say anything when you come back in? And hold my hand.'

They sat smiling at each other for a few more moments, until Ocean held open her arms to embrace Ama. They kissed each other and Ocean motioned for her to leave.

'Come back in at five past six, Mother?'

'I will, darling.'

She left the room and walked down the hall to reception. The night clerk sat behind the desk, thumbing a text message and took no notice of Ama. She decided to go outside to see if Evelyn had returned, but there was no sign of her. At five past six she went back inside to the reception desk.

'I'm in room eleven with my daughter, Ocean. She's waiting for me.' The girl only nodded and Ama read the name Denise on her uniform, before walking back down the hall to re-enter the room in silence.

Ocean lay propped up on the pillows with her eyes closed. Her hands were at her sides and the plain gold band was on her ring finger. Ama sat on her left side and took her hand. Ocean opened her eyes and smiled at her mother, then closed them again and held her hand tight. Her hair was spread round her shoulders and Ama wanted to stroke it but forebore, remembering her daughter's request. She sat watching her child's face as the smile faded and she looked asleep, but she still clutched her mother's hand. It was only after several more minutes that the grip loosened, and Ama placed Ocean's two hands together on her lap. She leaned forward to feel for her breath, then held her wrist to see if there was any pulse. Only then did she allow herself to stroke her daughter's hair and put her arms around her limp body to hold her close.

She didn't know how long she remained like this, stroking Ocean's hair and wiping her own tears off her daughter's face. At last, she stood at the foot of the bed staring down at her dead child. When she had looked her fill, Ama left the room to go outside to find Evelyn. A dark green sedan sat near the entrance with Evelyn behind the wheel. Ama opened the car door and got in beside her.

Evelyn waited for her to speak but Ama only sat staring at the envelope clenched in her fist.

'Is it over, Ama?' asked Evelyn.

Ama nodded, holding up the envelope. 'These are my instructions from the 'Right to Die' people.'

'All in good time, dear. You're not in a rush any longer. Did you have enough time with Ocean?'

'She was amazing, right to the end. So calm and peaceful.'

'Like her name. Would you like to go and have a coffee and tell me about it before we start, Ama?'

'No, Evelyn. I think I want to do this last bit for her, the way she planned it.' She opened the envelope but her eyes blurred with tears and she handed it to Evelyn to read.

'It says first you must call this number and they will call a doctor to come to write the death certificate. Someone will come from the group to be with you, in case the doctor decides the police need to be informed. The person will bring a list of local funeral homes for you to choose one. This is for you, Ama.' Evelyn handed her a sealed letter. 'It's her will.'

Ama opened the letter and read: 'This is my only request, that I will be buried beside Clay as we both wanted. His father has a family plot where Clay's mother is buried, and he has agreed to us being together there. Clay's will says the same thing. To my mother and father, I leave my love and gratitude for all they have done for me. Ocean.' Ama folded the letter and let out a long sigh. She began to weep.

Evelyn pulled Ama over on to her shoulder and held her there till the weeping slowed and came to a stop. She handed her several tissues to wipe her tears and dry her face. 'Shall we make this phone call now, Ama?'

Ama took out her cellphone and put in the numbers, as Evelyn read them to her. A woman answered and asked who she was calling about. She knew already where they were, and said someone would come to be there when the doctor arrived. Ama was told to wait in reception for them. She hung up and sat listening to Evelyn say that she hoped Ama would stay with her, until everything was settled and the funeral was over. They waited in her car for twenty minutes and then sat in the lobby until a woman came in, looked around and approached them.

'Are you Ocean's mother, Ama Waterstone? I'm Anthea Jensen from 'Right to Die.' The doctor should be here in a few minutes and we can all go in together.'

While they waited, the woman talked through the procedure and asked Ama if she had followed Ocean's instructions, about leaving the room while she took the medicine. When Ama nodded, she then explained that the doctor might have to notify the police, because it was a young person who had died. She explained that it was not a crime to commit suicide, but assisted suicide was still illegal, although the law was being challenged and a supreme court ruling was awaited.

Another woman arrived and introduced herself as Doctor Blakely. She said she was sympathetic to the 'Right to Die' movement and had offered to act for them, in any suicides in the London area where she practised. Anthea Jensen led the way to room eleven and they all entered and closed the door. After the doctor had made her examination and pronounced Ocean dead by drug overdose, she pulled the sheet up over Ocean's face.

When she had finished writing out the death certificate, Doctor Blakely rang a number at the police station. She spoke with a senior officer, for authorisation to release the body to the funeral director Ama had chosen. After some questions, permission was given and they said an officer would contact

Ama for further questioning. Ama was assured the interview would be routine and that a lawyer from the 'Right to Die' organisation would be present. Dr. Blakely shook hands and left a copy of the death certificate for the undertakers.

Anthea Jensen had phoned the funeral home. Their ambulance arrived to remove Ocean's body by the service entrance to Riverside Lodge, at the request of the manager. Ama paid the motel bill and took her daughter's suitcase with her. Evelyn drove her back across London to her home near the university, where she used to teach. She took Ama upstairs to a spare bedroom and told her to rest for as long as she wanted. Ama kicked off her shoes, curled up in the foetal position and sank into a deep slumber.

CHAPTER TWENTY

Spike too, was in a deep sleep after the opening night celebrations. Travis had driven him home and helped him into bed. He lay on his back in the borrowed hospital bed but couldn't sleep. He had left the first night party early after having a glass of champagne with all the cast and crew. Everyone was overjoyed with the success of the show and even Ama's absence couldn't dampen their celebrating. They knew only what Travis had told them, that Ama had been called away on an emergency about her sick daughter. Spike didn't want to put a damper on their high spirits and despite Claire's pleading, he slipped away with Travis in Ama's old Toyota. Before he left, he pulled Jasper aside.

'Is Claire alright, Jasper? I've never seen her so flushed and agitated. I think she's been overdoing it. Maybe now the show is up and running you can persuade her to take some time off.'

'Everyone's been saying the same thing, but you know Claire,' Jasper said. 'Short of tying her down I don't know what to do. She's having her moment of triumph now, but when the party's over I'm banning her from the theatre, if I have to sit on her.'

The two of them watched Claire flitting from group to group with a champagne bottle in her hand, topping up everyone's drink as well as her own.

'Let me know as soon as you hear from Ama, Spike. I hope she'll make it in time.'

'I'll call you the moment I hear, Jasper. Keep an eye on Claire.'

'That's all I can do right now. She won't leave till after the dancing. The musicians have promised her they'll play for an hour or so. Goodnight.'

In the darkened old house, Spike picked over the possible effects of this sudden change of circumstances. He knew Ama had been expecting a call at any time. When they hadn't heard for awhile, he hoped that Ocean had second thoughts about the suicide pact. But with Ama at last confronted with her daughter's death, he knew things would change. This would destroy any desire she had to continue at the pace they had been going, since they met at Simon's wake.

Spike felt he had been sucked along in the undertow of excitement over the re-opening of the theatre and the success of Ama's show. Now, when it was his turn to stage the new modern English production of The Tempest, he had backed off. His accident to his spine had given him the excuse to turn the whole show over to Justin and Emily. Although they were sorry he wouldn't be involved, he could tell they were delighted. The opportunity to put on such a ground-breaking performance, as well as the prospect of touring productions all over Nova Scotia, was too good to pass up.

Ama had already mooted the suggestion that Emily and Justin take over her role as joint artistic directors. Jasper and Claire would provide them with the experience and financial backing, from Claire's government funded cultural project. Now it seemed, with Ocean gone, he and Ama must make some decisions about their joint future. He drifted off to sleep and didn't waken until his cellphone rang the next morning.

'Spike, it's me. I'm sorry I didn't call before but...'
'Ama. What time is it? Where are you?'
'It's nine o'clock here. I'm in a friend's house. Evelyn. Someone I met on the plane. She's been with me the whole time.'
'Ocean – is she...?'
'She's gone, Spike. But I made it in time to be with her at the end.'
'Are you alright, sweetheart? God, I wish I were with you. I've been worrying about you all night. I even dreamed I was there.'
'I wish you were, too, my love. I'm okay now, just feeling sort of numb. She was wonderful. So courageous right to the very end.'
'You must be feeling horrible, Ama. And now, with all the funeral and everything. Will you bring her back here?'
'No, she wanted to be buried with Clay. They had it all planned.'
She explained to him how the 'Right to Die' group had taken over, and even provided a lawyer for her police interview.
'Police – how did they know?'
'The doctor had to phone them so Ocean's body could be released to the undertakers. The police said they will need to talk to me today. But the lawyer will be there with me, so it should be routine, I think.'
'When will the funeral be, Ama? When can you come back?'
'Not for a couple of days. I need to talk to Clay's father about the joint burial. We don't know when the prison authorities will release his son's body for the funeral. I have to go, or I'll be late for the meeting with the lawyer. I'll call you tonight, I promise.'

'I'll be waiting, Ama.'

Later in the afternoon, Travis drove Spike to the theatre. He wheeled himself up the ramp for the oxen, onto the stage. Arthur and Garth were fiddling with the hatch on the trap door.

'Have you seen Jasper, Arthur?'

'Nope. No sign of him or Claire. I hope he's making her stay home and rest.'

'She looked shattered by the time they left last night,' said Garth. 'Gloria said she was going to look in on her, during her delivery round this morning.'

'Emily and Justin are in the Green Room,' Arthur said. 'Any news from Ama?'

'Only a message to say she'd phone me tonight,' said Spike, not wanting to go into detail.

He would have to make an announcement to everyone, he realised, but would wait till after the show tonight, to tell them of Ocean's death. There was no easy way to put it without causing shock and upset. At least after the show, the cast had the whole night and tomorrow to absorb the news. He wheeled down the long ramp into the auditorium and made his way backstage to the Green Room. Emily sat curled on a sofa reading a script.

'Spike. What's happened, have you heard from Ama?' she said, bending over to hug him.

'Her daughter's dead, Emily. Took her own life this morning. Ama's dealing with the aftermath now, so she won't be back for two or three days.'

'My god, what a shock for her. Did she know her daughter was planning suicide, Spike?'

He nodded. 'She's known about it for awhile. Ocean was terminally ill. Don't say anything to anyone yet, Emily. I'll make an announcement to the cast after the show tonight. You can tell Justin.'

'What a pity you can't be with her, Spike. Poor Ama, this must be so distressing. And for you, feeling unable to help her. If there's any way we can do something here till she gets back, just ask, won't you?'

'Would you and Justin mind filling in for Ama? You know, give notes to the cast, let them know they haven't been abandoned. I'm worried the news will throw them for awhile and they'll need a steadying hand.'

'Of course. We saw the show last night so we can speak to them after you've told them about Ama's daughter. It's not as if they don't know us, as we've been around rehearsing for The Tempest. You concentrate on supporting Ama, Spike. Justin and I will deal with the show.'

'Emily, can I ask you something else while Justin's not here? With this business with Ocean and my back problems, Ama and I are considering stepping aside from the full-time running of the theatre. How would you feel about taking over from us? I wanted to ask you both separately. Then you can talk it over together. Do you like the idea?'

'This is a much bigger setup than the old Majestic in Bridewell. It would be a real challenge. I can't speak for Justin but I'd love to have the chance, Spike.'

'You wouldn't have to give up the Majestic, Emily. Bridewell's close enough to run them both with the two of you sharing.'

'What will you and Ama do?'

'My son wants us both to come over to England. His partner is expecting. Twins. Around Christmas.'

'Twins, that's wonderful. So, you'll still be here for the modern Shakespeare premiere next month.'

'We haven't said a word to anyone yet, Emily. Only to you and Justin. And of course, it's Ama's decision, she's the A.D., not me. I just wanted to sound you out first. I'll buttonhole Justin later, so don't say anything till it's official. I need to make sure you both feel the same way before I try to convince Ama to hand over the reins.'

'I'm sure he'll jump at the chance, Spike. He loves working here. I won't mention it till you've seen him.'

'I hope you're right, Emily. It will be a great relief to know it's in good hands.'

'If you wait here, I'll go and find him right away. He's supposed to be meeting Jasper and Claire to talk about The Tempest promotion. I think they're in the rehearsal hall.'

Spike wheeled over to the new coffee machine donated by the local coffee company and made himself a cup of espresso. He balanced it on the arm of the wheelchair to cool while he waited. He wondered if Ama would be cross with him for sounding out Emily and Justin without her. He would make sure the final decision was hers when she came back. It was hard to tell what her state of mind would be, by the time she returned from burying her daughter. The whole thing seemed to have been dragging on from the day he first met her at the wake.

He had barely finished his coffee when the Green Room door opened. Instead of Justin it was Jasper who entered. His normally impeccable appearance was rumpled and he was unshaven.

'Jasper. You look a little rough. Too much champagne last night?'

'I haven't been to bed. It's Claire. She's had a relapse. Her doctor's with her now.' He slumped onto one of the sofas and Spike wheeled back to the machine to get him a black coffee.

'What happened, Jasper – is she alright? We've all been worried about her lately.'

'She's in a bad way, Spike. I had to drag her away from the after-show party. She was all feverish and incoherent. Turns out she's been dosing herself with drugs that Antony, her old boyfriend, got for her. She's been stock-piling them for when she felt she was getting worse. It all came to a head late this morning. I couldn't make her go to bed, she was too high on alcohol and amphetamines, so I called Laura, her doctor. I wanted her to go to the hospital but Laura says there's no point. She's better at home.'

'What's the doctor planning to do?'

'Nothing. There's nothing she can do. Just monitor her and keep her sedated. Laura says I shouldn't be with her, Spike. I upset her too much and it makes her condition worsen. Jesus Christ...what a mess, and it's my fault for letting it get out of hand. Laura's blaming me for not calling her in sooner and she's right. I could see it coming, the way Claire's been acting lately. Laura says she may not recover this time. The remission period is over and she's going downhill. Goddam my dumb selfish ass....'

'I'm sorry, Jasper. Poor Claire, she's been hiding this from all of us. Did you know about the drugs?'

'She told me, but she said she needed them to make her feel better and I wanted to believe her. She seemed her old self until recently. I can't believe this is all happening so fast, Spike.'

'Look, come and stay with me for a couple of nights, give Claire a chance to unwind. Sarah will look after her like a baby. Let the doctor decide when you can visit without upsetting her. Ama's going to be away, coping with Ocean's funeral. She died this morning, Ama phoned me afterwards.'

'She made it on time. Claire will be pleased to hear that,' said Jasper. 'How long will she be away?'

'Not sure. She had an interview with the police this afternoon and she promised to call me tonight.'

'The police. How did they find out?'

'Ama says the doctor called them, because of the death of a young person and they want to question her.'

'She should have a lawyer with her, Spike.'

'It's all arranged. Ocean had planned it with the 'Right to Die' group. They got the doctor and the lawyer for her. They told her it should all be routine.'

'Let's hope so, unless they think Ama was assisting Ocean to commit suicide. The police are very touchy about these cases now, because the whole thing has become a national issue. I'd better speak to her and hear what they said.'

'Ama promised to call me tonight to tell me what's happened. I'll ask her to call you as well, Jasper.'

'Okay. I'll go back to Kitty's and explain I'm staying with you for a couple of days while Ama's away, if you're sure you don't mind, Spike?'

'No problem. You can speak to Ama when she calls, after I've had a word with her. What are you going to tell Claire, Jasper?'

'I'm not sure. I think I'll say that Laura has said no visitors for awhile, including me.'

Spike spent the rest of the afternoon writing up his notes for the cast from the opening show. He left them, with a note for Emily to pass them on. In order to avoid any questions from the actors, he decided not to come back until after the show, to make his announcement about Ocean. Garth was leaving to go to his café and gave Spike a lift home.

When the play was nearly over, Travis drove Spike back to the theatre to talk to the cast. He waited till the audience had left, then asked everyone to join him in the rehearsal room for an announcement.

Emily and Justin sat with him while he told them of Ocean's suicide and why she had chosen to do it. He said he and Ama were excusing themselves for the next few days, for the funeral arrangements.

Travis dropped Spike off at home to wait for Ama's phone call. Spike told him to keep the old Toyota at the boat, for running errands and driving him back and forth. Jasper's black suitcase sat in the front hall but he wasn't there. He'd left a note on the kitchen table for Spike, saying that Ama had phoned earlier and would call back after the show. The police had some new evidence of her involvement and were threatening to make trouble. He had gone to meet Ralph to discuss the best move and would speak to Spike later.

He made a stiff drink and wheeled himself into the living room to wait for Ama to ring. Spike sipped his drink, waiting for the phone call and wondered what evidence the police had found. He had thought at the time, Ama was taking a chance staying with her daughter until she died, but he understood how important it was for both of them and said nothing. Maybe he should have, if the police knew she had been with Ocean at the end. He polished off his whisky and went to the kitchen to make another drink. He was re-reading the note from Jasper when the phone finally rang.

'Ama? I've been waiting for you to call.'

'There's been some bad news, Spike. Ronnie called the police and told them I was planning to help Ocean commit suicide.'

'What? Jesus Christ. What did they say to you, Ama?'

'They questioned me for over an hour when I went for the interview. Thank God the Right to Die lawyer was with me.'

'Did you know Ronnie was against Ocean's suicide?'

'He was told by Jasper's daughter, Elvire. Ocean had asked her to speak to her father but not to tell him any details. When he did call the police, it was all over.'

'So now what's going to happen? Are they going to charge you as an accomplice, Ama?'

'The police detective said they could, but the lawyer said they have no proof to charge me.'

'But you were there when the doctor arrived, you said.'

'I know but I wasn't there when Ocean took the drugs and she had left a suicide note to say I had nothing to do with it. She and Clay had arranged it all. The lawyer thinks the police won't press charges. But they told me not to leave London until they had finished their investigation, or they would charge me.'

'What a mess, Ama. How long will you have to stay there?'

'The lawyer thinks if I wait until after the funeral, they'll probably let me go. She says the police don't like to take these cases to court these days. Judges won't prosecute, with the new assisted suicide laws being debated in parliament.'

'Let's hope she's right, sweetheart. Are you alright with all this worry on top of Ocean's death? I wish I could be with you there.'

'My new friend, Evelyn, is looking after me. She says I can stay with her till after the burial and she's helping me with all the arrangements for the joint funeral.'

'You're not dealing with Clay's burial too, are you?'

'No. I met his father today and he's handling most of the details with Evelyn. Thank god, because I'm all over the place, Spike. Can't think straight about anything yet.'

'This is rotten, Ama. The one time you really need me and I'm stuck here in Nova Scotia in a wheelchair.'

'I'll be alright, my love. I'll call you every day till it's over and I can come home.'

'Jasper wants to speak to you, too, Ama, but he's not here at the moment. He'll call you later. He just wants to be sure you're alright and to make sure you have a good lawyer.'

'I want to talk to him as well. He always reassures me, Spike. My reconciliation with Ocean would never have happened without his help.'

'He's a great guy. We owe him a lot, Ama.'

Later, after Jasper had spoken to Ama, he and Spike sat drinking in the big front room of Ama's house-sit, trying to decide their next move.

'From what she tells me, there's a good chance the police will try to make a case against her, as the Right to Die group has been involved. I need to talk to their lawyer in the morning to see how she thinks it will go. I told Ama I will fly over tomorrow to act for her and not to worry.'

'I'm really grateful to you for this, Jasper. Ama has been so worked up over Ocean's suicide, that having you there will put her mind at rest. She has total confidence in you, you know. She's convinced you can do anything, since you sorted things out between her and Ocean.'

'It's a stroke of bad luck Ronnie called the police instead of me. Ama said Elvire told him to speak to me before he did anything, but he couldn't get me because I've had my phone turned off. I didn't want to be distracted when Claire was so sick. Now I've been banned from visiting her because I upset her too much. I feel to blame for this mess Ama's in.'

'That's crazy. You didn't know Ronnie would do this.'

'No, but if I'd been thinking clearly, I might have anticipated it, Spike. I've been so distracted worrying about Claire and now I can't even see her.'

'Perhaps, I could go and visit her. We've become good friends, almost since I arrived. If I can't go to see Ama and you can't go to see Claire, we can change places. And report back to each other. I'd feel a lot better if I heard from you directly, Jasper.'

'Me too, Spike. I know Claire is very fond of you. I'm sure you wouldn't upset her. But how would you get into Kitty's house with all those steps up to her veranda?'

'Travis could help me and Arthur or Garth would lend a hand. I'll call them in the morning.'

Early next morning Jasper called the Right to Die lawyer in London, to make an appointment before driving to Halifax airport. Spike left a message for Travis, after he called Kitty to arrange a visit to see Claire. Kitty suggested he come for lunch, to put Claire at her ease that it was only a social call and nothing to worry about.

At noon Travis and Arthur collected Spike in Ama's red Toyota and took him and his wheelchair to Kitty's. They deposited him on the front veranda and told him to call the theatre when he was ready to be picked up. Sarah answered the door and wheeled him into the spacious kitchen to see Kitty first.

'I hope you're hungry, Spike,' she said, kissing him on the cheek. 'Sarah has become used to cooking hearty meals for Jasper. Now with him staying with you, Claire and I won't even make a dent in her offerings.'

'How is she, Kitty? I don't know what to expect,' said Spike.

'Fragile is the word I'd use, wouldn't you, Sarah?'

'Listless,' said Sarah. 'She just lies there starin' at nothing, much of the time. We hope you can cheer her up a bit. I wish Ama were here. Those two are like sisters.'

'Yes, when will she be coming home, Spike?' asked Kitty. 'I was so saddened for her when I heard the news about Ocean. Is she alright?'

He told them briefly about the joint funeral and burial but didn't mention the police investigation.

'She should be home in a few days when it's all over,' he said.

'Claire will want to know, too,' said Kitty, 'but please be careful not to distress her, won't you?'

Sarah led the way into the enclosed front veranda, where Claire lay propped up on a sofa with a low coffee table in front of her, set up for lunch for two.

'Aren't you joining us, Kitty?' asked Spike.

'We know you two have lots to talk about, so we'll come in later for tea.'

Spike wheeled up to the side of the sofa to take Claire's hand and she leaned forward to kiss his cheek.

'Aren't we a pair of old crocks, Spike?' said Claire, as she lay back on the sofa, giving him a wan smile.

'I think we both made the mistake of thinking we were a lot younger than we are, Claire. Me, anyway. Ama never says anything to me, but I know she thinks I'm a damn fool. First with my boat that's too big for me and now with my broken back.'

'Jasper would wrap me in a cocoon if I'd let him. I daren't show the slightest sign of weakness in front of him or he'd rush me into hospital.'

'It's your own fault, Claire. You've got him completely besotted with you. He never stops talking about what a wonder you are. It must be very wearing having such an effect on someone.' He grinned at her and squeezed her hand. 'But I expect you're used to it. I might have fallen under your spell, too, if Ama hadn't kept you strictly at arm's length.'

'You and Jasper are a pair of charmers, Spike. No wonder Ama and I are both so smitten. It's lovely to have you here. The difference is, I can say things to you I can't to Jasper. I'm afraid he'll go to pieces on me, if I told him the truth.'

'Tell me instead, Claire. Ama says I'm tough as old boots and never get emotionally involved. But when I see how she's become almost a basket case over Ocean, I can get very weepy at times.'

'Laura, my doctor, has tried to prepare Jasper for the worst but he won't believe her. It's as though he's convinced he can will me to be better. He studies me all the time, looking for the least little thing he can fasten on to prove he's right. I don't have the heart to tell him the truth, Spike.'

'How bad is it, Claire? Share it with me. I won't tell him or Ama, if you don't want them to know.'

'Laura says my relapse this time means I'm not in remission anymore. Weeks, not months now.'

Tears started to spring into Spike's eyes and he grasped her hand. 'Christ, Claire. I had no idea it was so soon. Who knows besides us?'

'Only Kitty and Sarah. And you. Now do you see how impossible it is for me to have Jasper here?'

He nodded. 'He'll be devastated, Claire. So will Ama. I'm in shock myself, now you've told me. What shall we do?'

'Keep it to ourselves for now. That's what I've been doing.'

'At least we can talk it over together from now on. Maybe we'll come up with some ingenious way to break it to them.'

'It's a relief to say it out loud to you, Spike. I feel as if I've been holding my breath since I collapsed.'

'Let's have some lunch, Claire. I always think better on a full stomach. Be a pity to waste this food Sarah's laid on for us.'

'For you, not me. I have no appetite anymore.'

'Got to keep your strength up to come up with a plan. Try a bit of this.' He helped her to some food.

CHAPTER TWENTY-ONE

Jasper's flight into the small London airport was early. By lunchtime his meeting with the Right to Die lawyer had finished. He called Ama's cell number and said he'd meet her for lunch in his rental car. He drove to a small restaurant by the river that Ama's new friend, Evelyn, had recommended. They sat out on the terrace while waiting for their meal. Jasper wanted her to begin, so he made small talk about Spike and Claire.

'I feel so bad about having to leave right in the middle of opening night without a word to anyone, Jasper. I hope they understood I had no choice.'

'Naturally the cast and crew were all shaken at the news of Ocean,' he said. 'Spike waited until after the performance to tell them, and then explained Justin and Emily would be in charge until you came back.'

'And what about Claire, Jasper? What does Laura say, is it as bad as I feared?'

'Worse. She told me I had to expect it was all downhill from now on. I asked her not to let on to Claire but she said it was too late. She'd already told her the worst, because Claire had made her promise to tell her the truth.'

'Oh god, Jasper. Our quicksilver Claire. I'm so sorry.' She leaned over from her seat to put her arms around him and they sat, heads touching for a few minutes, not saying anything. At last, Jasper wiped his eyes with a napkin and passed it to Ama who dabbed at her face.

'What are we going to do? You should be with her, not down here in London with me, Jasper. I can't leave until the police have finished their investigation, they said.'

'And I can't be with her right now anyway. Laura says I upset Claire too much and she needs to rest and be quiet for now. At least I can do something here and be occupied while I wait.'

'What did the Right to Die lawyer tell you, Jasper?'

'She said if Ronnie hadn't called the police, it would have been a routine case of suicide. Now they feel forced to launch a full inquiry. Because it was a joint pact, they must have had assistance to organise it. That's the crux of our case, to prove they didn't. Clay and Ocean planned it all themselves.'

'And carried it out together, Jasper. I did nothing but hold her hand at the very end. She was so strong. I was the weak passive observer. All I could think of, was how sad and cruel they had to be separated at the end. But they made it happen together, in time, at least. She was quite content and peaceful. It made me feel very close to her. I still do, I'm not agitated or distressed. It's only this police business that's upsetting. Do you think they'll charge me with assisted suicide, Jasper?'

'Not if I can convince them it was all the way you described it, Ama. The whole public debate in the country is in favour of the new legislation, to make it legal. Even if it goes to court, I feel confident any judge will dismiss the case. That's what I'll be impressing on the investigating police officer.'

'I feel better already, just having you here beside me, Jasper.'

'Good. Let's eat then. All this talk has made me ravenous. I only had a coffee and a Danish on the plane from Halifax this morning.'

Over lunch, Jasper fully debriefed Ama on everything that had transpired, from the time she left on her midnight journey to when he arrived today. When he felt satisfied he knew all that he needed to approach the police, his mind turned to his main preoccupation, Claire.

'Now it's your turn to advise me, Ama. What am I going to do about Claire? We were doing so well together, I couldn't believe my luck. And now everything is falling apart. She doesn't even want to see me. You've got to help me, Ama. I'm lost. I know you probably think with my track record as an old philanderer, that this is yet another infatuation. I wouldn't blame you. I know how it must look.'

He looked so forlorn and worried that Ama reached across the table to squeeze his hand.

'I believe you, Jasper. I've seen how fond you and Claire are of each other these past few weeks. This sudden change in her is a big shock to me, too.'

'I truly thought she might come to care for me, Ama. Not in the besotted way I am with her, but more than just fond. I don't understand what's happening. It must be something I've done, is all I can think.'

'Surely, it's the relapse from remission that's caused her to act like this, Jasper. I'm trying to imagine what she must be feeling. What it must be like, to be told you have only a short time left to live, with no hope of reprieve. Perhaps she only wants to be alone, to think it all through.'

'I guess I can understand that, if that's what it really is. I wouldn't feel quite so rejected. More shut out.'

'But if that's her decision, you have to respect it, don't you think? However painful it is for you. I know that's what I had to do with Ocean, when she decided to end her life. Ultimately I had to accept her decision.'

'Do you think it's the same, though. She'll never want to see me again? I don't think I could live with that.'

'You may have to, Jasper, if that's her final decision. It may not be. You can't know what's going through her mind right now.'

'This is cold comfort, Ama. I need something to cling to. Some shred of hope. Would you talk to her when you come back? Plead my case for me? She'll listen to you. Kitty says you're like sisters.'

'Of course I will, you know how much I owe you. I'll talk to her like a dutch uncle if it will help. But it may not. Claire can be very stubborn.'

'Thanks, Ama. That's all I ask.' He gave her a fierce hug and stood up. 'I feel ready to take on that police detective now. The sooner I can clear up this business here, the sooner I can get you back to see Claire.'

He drove Ama to the funeral home to meet up with Clay's father, who was waiting for the prison to deliver his son's body. He drove on to the police station to plead Ama's case, with a smile on his face.

When he returned to Evelyn's house he was smiling even more broadly. After she and Ama gave him tea and cake, Jasper helped clear up and told them of his meeting with the police detective.

'When I launched into a long defence of why the possible charges should be dropped, he stopped me in full flow. It seems his hand was forced by Ronnie's phone call, saying you were actively helping Ocean take her life. He had reviewed all the evidence provided by the Right to Die lawyer and Ama's interview. Plus, the statements from both doctors who had written the death certificates for Clay and Ocean.

After consulting with the public prosecutor, the police have decided to take no further action. It seems they didn't need any big city lawyer from Montreal to tell them their job. And which way the political wind was blowing.'

'Oh my god, what a relief,' said Ama, hugging him. She turned to Evelyn. 'Didn't I tell you he was a miracle worker.'

'I believe this calls for something a little stronger than wine. I have a bottle of cognac waiting for a suitable moment to be opened. I think this is it.' She fetched the bottle and poured each of them a hefty shot.

'To Jasper, old friends are best friends,' said Ama.

'To a happy ending, for everyone,' Evelyn said.

'To Clay and Ocean, to their Great Escape,' said Jasper. 'And now, I think I needn't impose on Evelyn's hospitality any longer, and head for Halifax.'

Ama walked to the rental car with him. 'Evelyn has offered to let me stay for a few more days until the burial is over. I need some time alone to mourn for Ocean, Jasper. Will you explain to everyone I'll be back as soon as I'm able? I promise to speak to Claire for you. Tell Spike I'll call him tonight. And thank you for being such a good friend, Jasper. To me and my daughter.' She embraced him, kissed his cheek and watched him drive away.

The burial was scheduled for two days later, after all the formalities with the prison and the cemetery had been arranged. There was space in Clay's family plot for him and Ocean to be buried side by side. They had even chosen to make it a green burial, with wool shrouds and woven wicker coffins. Only a handful of people attended. Ama, her new friend Evelyn, Clay's father, Rod, and a friend of his from the Stratford Festival Theatre.

No minister was there, and Rod read a passage from the Buddhist Dhammapada, Clay had given him. Ocean had selected her favourite poem from Emily Dickinson. Ama threw a handful of earth into the grave, then read the poem with a shaky voice to begin with, but strengthened as she continued:

"'Ample make this bed –
Make this bed with awe –
In it wait till judgment break
Excellent and fair.

Be its mattress straight –
Be its pillow round –
Let no sunrise yellow noise
Interrupt this ground.'"

Clay's father, Rod, cleared his throat with an effort. "'Those whom God hath joined together, let no man put asunder.'"

Evelyn placed a little spray of rosemary and violets at the head of the open grave.

The next day Ama wanted to take some flowers to place on the grave. Evelyn dropped her at the cemetery gates and Ama said she would prefer to walk back. The fresh earth lay neatly mounded and Evelyn's tiny spray of rosemary and violets had been placed on top of the grave. Ama placed her flowers on the bare earth and sank down onto the grass to wait. She studied the soil which was beginning to dry in the warm sunshine, brushing bits out of the grass like crumbs back onto the grave. Her mind began to dwell on Ocean's body lying down below her in the dark, while she remained above in the light and at last it came. Grief swept over her like a wave and she gave herself up to it, mourning her lost child.

She lay for a long time, pressing her cheek on the warm earth and staring at the autumn dahlias she had placed on her daughter's grave. No thought of Clay had been in her mind until now. She felt grateful to him at last, for accompanying Ocean under the ground. As she got up, her one leg nearly collapsed with numbness from sitting so long in one position. She realised there was nothing to mark Ocean's grave. Only the small numbered stake at the foot as if something had been planted. In all of the preparations, she and Rod had forgotten to arrange a headstone. A small inset marble slab beside the fresh grave had Clay's mother's name, with a blank space for her husband's. She would ask Rod to help her choose an inscription and then call her, so she could return to see it put in place. Maybe it would allow her to let Ocean go.

Ama didn't want to fly home. She needed more time to mourn and told Evelyn she would take the train to Halifax instead. Evelyn had made Ama promise to stay with her, when the headstone was ready. Spike would be expecting her now the burial had taken place, so she waited until she was on the train before calling him on her cellphone.

'I'm sorry about taking the long way home, Spike. I got cold feet at the thought of diving straight back into the theatre melee again. Can you understand? I'm still sort of numb.'

'I'm sorry too, sweetheart,' Spike said, 'but I guess I can wait another day and a half. When do you arrive in Halifax? I'll ask Travis if he'll drive me to the train station.'

'I'm not sure. I'll call when I get nearer, tomorrow. It will give me time to piece my life back together. I love long train journeys, staring out the window at the passing world, wondering where I fit into it all.'

'Wherever it is I hope I fit into it too, Ama. I get worried when you disappear on me, that you're having second thoughts about us.'

'And third and fourth ones as well, my love. My mind goes round and round and always circles back to you. It's where we go from here that I can't fathom. Maybe by the time I reach Halifax, I'll see clearer.'

'It's the end of the line, Ama, you can't go any further. Except by sea.'

'Maybe that's our next move, then,' she said.

'You mean to England. To Patrick and Caroline?'

'And the twins. Your grandchildren. New life, Spike. I want that. I'm weighed down with death.'

'On the Mongoose, my love. Over the wine-dark sea,' he said.

'Spike? Say something to me. Please. I need comforting. Something from Prospero. Your favourite audition piece. I loved to hear you practise it.'

'Shall I recite it for you now, Ama?'

'I would like that more than anything.'

'Good. Then I'll begin...

"Our revels now are ended. These our actors,
As I foretold you, were all spirits and
Are melted into air, into thin air:
And, like the baseless fabric of this vision,
The cloud-capp'd towers, the gorgeous palaces,
The solemn temples, the great globe itself,
Yea, all which it inherit, shall dissolve
And, like this insubstantial pageant faded,
Leave not a rack behind. We are such stuff
As dreams are made on, and our little life
Is rounded with a sleep."

Goodnight Ama, safe journey home.'
'Goodnight, my love.'

CHAPTER TWENTY-TWO

Despite his protests that he couldn't learn lines anymore, Emily and Justin combined forces to persuade Spike that he was the best choice for Prospero.

Emily said, 'Now that you're in a wheelchair, it makes all the difference, don't you see, Spike? Wheeling about the stage, making dramatic entrances suddenly from the wings.'

'Zooming up the ramps and storming onto centre stage,' said Justin.

'Waving Prospero's book of magic spells,' Emily said, 'which also happens to have your copy of the script inside it, right there on your lap the whole time.'

'No more lines to worry about, Spike. They're all right in front of you, when you want them,' Justin said.

'The audience will be mesmerised, wondering what you'll do next. Don't you think it's a brilliant idea? It was Justin's suggestion,' said Emily.

'I saw this amazing performance of King Lear last year at Stratford, with Lear in a wheelchair. The final scene with Cordelia sprawled across his lap was stunning.'

Emily said, 'Justin will direct, as he now knows the modern version inside out. I play Miranda, Justin is Caliban, and you star as Prospero.'

'What about Ama?'

'She co-directs with me and Claire does the design,' Justin said. 'Gives Emily and me the time to familiarise ourselves with taking over the theatre. When you and Ama bow out for awhile to go to England.'

'With Jasper at our elbows as producer, steering us over the hurdles, it's a winning team,' said Emily.

'And we'll still be able to run the theatre in Bridewell, with his help. But you're the key, Spike. With you as Prospero, it all comes together.'

'Without you, it all falls apart,' said Justin.

'The problem is not me, I'm afraid. It's Claire. I don't think she's well enough to do the show. I've had a long talk with her and it's all bad news for her, for Jasper and for us. I'll agree to do Prospero but first we all need to talk to Claire, Jasper and Ama. I appreciate your vote of confidence in me, as you haven't seen me act. I admit you make it sound appealing.'

'We've watched you in rehearsals, Spike. We have no qualms, do we, Justin?'

'Like Emily says, you're the key, Spike.'

'This is all between us for now,' said Spike. 'Claire doesn't want anyone else to know how bad her health is. Ama will be back tomorrow. Meantime, talk to Jasper, make sure he's in agreement, okay? I know the first thing Ama will want to do, is see Claire by herself. She's had a double blow with her daughter and now the shock of Claire's latest news. You may need to rethink the whole production.'

Once again, Spike enlisted Travis to take him to collect Ama from her long train journey in Halifax.

They had Ama's old house-sit to themselves. Jasper had left a note to say he was staying over at Ralph's to work on the Arts Council project, an obvious ploy to let them have some time alone. Travis helped Spike up the temporary ramp he and Garth had made to the side porch, and left for the Mongoose.

Spike put the kettle on to make Ama some tea. He decided not to bombard her with questions. He waited for her to begin what he felt must be a painful conversation. Ama took her bag upstairs to unpack and change. When she came back down, he was waiting for her at the foot of the stairs. He patted his lap for her to sit on, then wheeled her into the kitchen.

'Now what shall we do while we wait for the tea to steep, my love?' he said.

For answer, she put her arms round his neck and gave him a long gentle kiss. He held her away from him and smiled.

'It's alright, I won't break. You can kiss me properly.'

And she did. Over and over for several minutes. It ended with Spike holding her away again as he felt her tears on his face.

'We have a lot of catching up to do, Ama. Let's have that tea, shall we?'

Ama got up off his lap and poured out the tea for them.

'I thought all that time on the train was exactly what I needed. I could spend some of it mourning the loss of Ocean and a lot of it thinking about you and me and our future plans. And that's sort of what I did.'

'Sounds like a good plan to me.'

'That's what I thought. Only it didn't work out quite the way I hoped.'

'Don't scare me, Ama. You're not going to tell me bad news about us, are you?'

'Nothing like that, Spike. What I meant was I didn't get anywhere. Unless you feel going in circles is progress. Yes, I did mourn for Ocean, but I realised it's going to be a much longer process than I thought. It's not a one-off thing you do, then fold it up and put it away out of sight. I think it's going to be messy and prolonged and catch me off guard. At least that's how it's been so far.'

'That sounds like progress, in a way, isn't it? A kind of natural progression.'

'Maybe. What I also realised is that I have to do it alone. No one else can do it for me. Not even you, Spike. And I worry about you seeing me withdraw into myself. Somewhere I can't be reached, from time to time. Unexpectedly. That you'll come home and I'll have been curled up in the foetal position all day. I worry it will drive a wedge between us, that I'll be powerless to do anything about when it takes me over.'

'As long as I know you'll come out the other side, I'll wait for you, Ama. I may not be able to do your mourning for you, but I can share it, if you tell me what's happening.'

'They say people don't die of love, except in stories. But I believe they do from grief. You can wither up and die inside from loss of a loved one, especially if it's a child. That's what I fear might happen to me, to us.'

'Well, I won't let it happen, Ama, you'll see. I'll be right here beside you the same way you've been for me, through all my time lying on my back unable to move. Willing me to recover. I have a good model to follow, my love. And we do have our ace in the hole, remember. Two aces, in fact.'

'The twins. Just thinking about them makes me smile.'

'Do you think Patrick and Caroline will let us look after them sometimes?'

'If we're around. Not if we only turn up on occasion. They won't trust us. I wouldn't, we don't have good track records,' Ama said.

'Then we'll have to mend our ways. Be model grandparents. We're both actors, after all.'

He told her about his approach to Justin and Emily, to sound them out on their proposed takeover of the theatre and how they jumped at the idea. He also said they had surprised him, by asking him to take the lead in the Tempest, to do Prospero in a wheelchair and he had tentatively agreed.

'But you swore you were finished learning lines, Spike. Why the sudden change of heart?'

'I know, that's what I told them and that's when they said the wheelchair gave them the idea. I could keep the script on my lap the whole time to glance at, and nobody would notice. Because it's inside my magician's book of spells.'

'It's a big commitment, are you sure you want to do it? I thought we agreed before I went away, that we were stepping back, if Emily and Justin would take over from us.'

'We can't go to England until the Mongoose is ready. Fergus and Travis are still working on the conversion. And the hurricane season isn't over till mid-November. By then, I should be out of the wheelchair and Justin and Emily will be settled in to replace us.'

'You've got it all figured out, haven't you? What will I be doing in the meantime?'

'The hardest part of all. I was saving this till last,' he said. 'Dealing with Claire and Jasper. Since she collapsed after opening night, she won't let Jasper near her. He's been staying with me and he's an emotional wreck. Can't figure out what he did wrong. I've had some long talks with Claire at Kitty's. She knows she has only weeks left, according to Laura and the consultant oncologist. There's nothing more they can do, except keep her doped up to preserve her remaining strength. Claire's told me she's determined to finish her project and see The Tempest completed. It's partly why I agreed to do Prospero. She'll never make it without Jasper. That's why you have to reconcile them Ama. I can't convince her.'

'I'll go in the morning. I've already promised Jasper I'd speak to her. He sounded desperate when he came to see me after Ocean died. I owe him so much, Spike. I hope I can make Claire take him back.' She steered him back into the living room. 'Right now, I'm feeling drained. I just want to sleep, my love, with you.'

They undressed and she helped him into the high hospital bed, then squeezed in beside him. He showed her how to pull up the side so she wouldn't fall out. He lay on his back with one arm around her, and began telling her what he and Fergus and Travis had been doing to the Mongoose. He only stopped talking when he heard her deep, steady breathing and felt her body relax beside him.

In the morning he tried to get up without disturbing her but couldn't manage it. He lay stroking her arm which she'd flung across him, content to wait until she woke up. He knew she was going to have a difficult time with Claire, and let her sleep on. The ringing of her cell phone finally woke her. It was Jasper, checking to see she had arrived home safely.

'I know why you're calling, Jasper and I promise I'll see Claire this morning...yes, I'll call you back after...alright... we can meet for lunch in town... at Garth's café...no, I'll walk there...I won't forget to call, Jasper. Goodbye.' She closed her phone and lay back beside Spike. 'My god, he is in a state, isn't he?' She turned to face him. 'If I made some coffee could we have it here in bed, before I face Claire?'

'Bring the wheelchair to my side of the bed and I'll go and make it.'

'It's quicker if I do it. How do I get out of this contraption?'

He reached across to lower the side and she climbed out of the high bed.

'Don't go anywhere till I get back. I need more snuggling to fortify me,' she said.

'It's amazing the power Claire has over us all, isn't it, for someone as slight and fragile as she is,' Spike said.

'I love her dearly. But she is daunting,' said Ama, 'even for big old Jasper.'

'Size has nothing to do with it. Her energy is what mesmerizes us all,' he said.

She padded out to the kitchen to make the coffee. 'Do you want anything to eat?' she called.

'Just you.'

'Coming up.' She reappeared a few minutes later, pulling the hospital wheeled trolley over the bed with the tray of coffee, and climbed back in beside him.

'The hospital nurses never offered service like this or I might have asked to stay longer.'

'I should hope not. Anyway, don't start getting any ideas or you might end up back in there.'

'I admit I have had a few ideas I want to show you. Where there's a will, there's a way,' he said.

And they found it. As they lay back drinking lukewarm coffee afterwards, Spike said, 'You're quite the acrobat, Ama.'

'Mmmhm, I admit I've been around the block a few times. You forget I had three husbands. We all know what practice makes.'

'I never thought I'd be grateful to your exes, till now.'

'Good to know they were of some use,' she said. 'As were yours, of course. I would be an ingrate not to acknowledge the role of the fiery Fiona in your education.'

Spike laughed. 'My highland fling.'

'She of the orange-haired legs and nether parts, who stole you away from me. I was no match for her.'

'Neither was I. She married a crofter from Inverness.'

'Probably a big orange hairy one, like her,' Ama said, climbing out of bed. 'It's time I went to see Claire. I'll leave you to dream of your lost wild highland lass.'

The warm autumn sunshine gave her an excuse to dawdle on her way to Kitty's, planning what she should say to Claire. She tried to imagine what it must be like for her, to be under a death sentence, hanging over her like some sword of Damocles.

CHAPTER TWENTY-THREE

'Ama, thank God you're back,' said Sarah, enfolding her in a big hug. 'Kitty and me are so worried about Claire. We need you to bring her round. She won't listen to us when we try to get her to let Jasper come back here to be with her.' She led Ama into the kitchen where Kitty sat in her rocker by the table, stringing runner beans from a pile in front of her.

'At last, Ama. You don't know how it lifts my heart to see you home.' She embraced Ama, patting her back in a long gentle hug. 'Claire will be so happy to have you here. But you must be prepared for a shock. She is very weak and fragile. We're hoping that somehow you'll be the one person who can bring her and Jasper back together.'

'Would you like some tea before you face her, Ama?' asked Sarah.

'No, I think I want to speak to her right away,' she said.

'Have you thought of how you might convince her?' said Kitty. 'None of us have had any luck.'

'I've thought of her a lot on the train back from London and I think I may have an idea.'

'Sarah and I have been willing you to be strong through all your ordeal with Ocean, dear. I'm so saddened by her death and how you must be feeling.'

'It all seems so wrong for children to die before you, Kitty. I think it will take me a long time to get used to it.'

'Perhaps you never do, you just learn to bear it, Ama,' said Sarah. 'Kitty and me took comfort that you're a survivor and you have Spike to be with you.'

'If you can only persuade Claire that she doesn't have to face this alone. She has Jasper,' said Kitty.

'I'll do my best, Kitty. I think I'd better see her now.'

She gave them both a hug and went back down the front hall to Claire's haven in the enclosed porch. Claire lay back on her pillow, eyes closed and a sheaf of papers clasped in her hand. Ama eased them from her grip and sat stroking her hand until Claire opened her eyes. For a moment or two she seemed not to recognise Ama.

'Hello, Claire. It's me, Ama. Remember? Your big sister.' She smiled at her and waited.

'Hello, Sis. I thought you'd forgotten me. When did you come back?'

'Last night. On the train. I've been thinking about you all the way from London. I'm sorry I've been so long. Ocean's funeral kept me away.'

'I wish I could have been there with you. I thought of you all alone in a strange place. And your daughter dying.' She held out her arms and the two of them clung together for several moments. 'I suppose you know the worst about me by now, Ama. I wish I had better news to comfort you for Ocean's death, but it seems it's not to be.'

'Just seeing you again makes me feel better, Claire. I'm not leaving you again, I promise.'

'I feel so useless lying here not able to do anything, when there's so much left to do on The Tempest production.'

'The best thing you can do is rest and recover so you can come back and finish what you started, Claire. I'm afraid we're floundering without you. Especially now that Jasper is planning to leave.'

'What? Jasper – why?'

'I'm not sure. I've tried talking to him. But he only says he hasn't got the heart for it anymore and will probably go back to Montreal.'

'Oh god, this is all my fault, Ama. I told him I couldn't see him any longer. I made the excuse that the doctors said he was upsetting me.'

'Why, what did he do?'

'He kept saying I was getting better every day when I knew I was getting worse. It was too hard keeping up the pretense with him. I got so I dreaded him being with me, making plans for us when I'm better. I asked Laura to tell him it was best not to see me, as he was making my condition worse.'

'And was he, Claire? Making you worse?'

'He won't accept that I'm dying, Ama. He's in denial. I got upset struggling with him to face reality. I can't cope with him anymore. It's too difficult having him in my life. He saps my little remaining energy.' She slumped down amongst the pillows, turning her head away, her fingers twitching.

'Are you saying you don't love him any longer, Claire. Is that why you're breaking it off with him?'

'Jasper is in love with who I was, not who I am now. He keeps trying to resurrect the past and live in some false reality. I know I don't have much time left, Ama. Laura is crystal clear about that. You accept that and I can be truthful with you. Jasper can't accept it.'

'Can't, or won't?'

'He won't. I want to be with people who are honest with me and tell me the truth. It's all I have to hang onto now. People like you and Kitty and Sarah.'

'I know you feel Jasper is in denial and there's no use talking to him. What if I can convince him to see the truth – that you're dying, Claire. Would that make any difference to you?'

'You're wasting your breath, Ama. You don't know Jasper like I do.'

'That's just it. I do know him. Next to you, he's the truest friend I have ever had. He's fiercely loyal – god knows why, I'm such a mess. Will you let me talk to him? Please?' She clasped one of Claire's hands, stroking and smoothing the agitated fingers plucking the bedsheet.

'It won't do any good. He won't listen.'

'Let me try, Claire.'

'No. You know what he's like. God knows I've heard you describe him often enough. Silver-tongued, you always say. He'll make me agree to take him back, and I haven't the strength to go through it all again.'

Ama continued to soothe her trembling hand, saying nothing until she felt Claire's fluttering fingers stilled. Looking down at the translucent skin, she thought how different it was to the firm young flesh of Ocean's hand she had clung to so recently. Tears splashed onto Claire's hand as she pressed her face to it. Ama felt herself being drawn up into a fierce embrace and they clung together, weeping silently.

'Don't say I didn't try to warn you, Ama. I told you I might fall apart on you at any time, remember?'

'So you did. I guess this is as good a time as any. For both of us.'

'Do you know what I wish right now? I wish Jasper was here, Ama.'

'That's an easy wish to grant. Say the word and he'll be here, I promise.'

'Are you sure you can make him understand what I need, though?'

'I will, Sis. On your terms. When can I tell him?'

'Better tell him now, before I have second thoughts.'

'He's waiting for my phone call, Claire. I promised I'd ask you. Or do you want to ring him?'

'No, you do it. And please make him understand, Ama. That's my only condition.'

'I'll be your witness. We'll make him put it in writing.' She stood up and gave Claire a hug. 'I think I'll tell him in person.'

'And Ama? It's alright to tell Spike what a pathetic person I am – but no-one else. Okay?'

'Deal. The solidarity sisters, that's us.' Ama squeezed her hand and left.

CHAPTER TWENTY-FOUR

In the days and weeks that followed Claire and Jasper's reconciliation, a flurry of activity kept the theatre humming day and night. The original intention was to hold performances three nights a week on Thursdays, Fridays and Saturdays. The rest of the week would be kept free for rehearsals and set building for the next production. But this had to be extended to include Wednesday matinees, as the word of mouth spread through Nova Scotia of the huge success of 'Oh What A Lovely War'. Coach parties from clubs, women's institutes and high school groups, soon booked the old Regency matinees solid till the end of the run.

Jasper and Ralph capitalised on this demand, by offering a touring production. They extended the run to half a dozen other towns throughout the province, as part of the regional cultural project. Claire and Charlene hastily re-designed a scaled down set that could fit into the smaller venues, with portable ramps and simple towers, to replace the more elaborate Regency Theatre set.

Claire badgered Ralph into finding additional funding to repair the fly-loft, so that the fire and safety officer would allow her to use it for the storm scene in The Tempest. Undaunted by his accident with Spike, Travis was soon practising his spectacular descents from the falling mast. Claire had tracked down old parachute silk via Ralph's regimental contacts. Travis disappeared into billowing clouds of it, as he toppled from the fly-loft.

Ama and Ivy spent hours devising new sketches for the grad students to try out for the pageant wagon, to start promoting the Tempest production.
And always, attentive and capable, Jasper was at Claire's side to carry out her plans and implement her schemes. Whatever doubts and worries he had about Claire's weakening condition, he kept to himself, as he had promised he would. Instead, Ama became his confidante and the two of them monitored her feverish activity, reporting to Laura. They let her, as Claire's doctor, admonish her to slow down.

Arthur and Frankie had been quietly advised of Claire's determination to continue, until both the old theatre was refurbished and The Tempest production was launched. They tried not to show their concern in front of her. No mention was made to any of the volunteers or cast and crew. But somehow, the unspoken acknowledgement that this was Claire's swansong, spread throughout the whole company. Everyone became complicit in helping to bring her vision to fruition. There was always a cluster of people consulting her. She sat in the stalls, with Jasper on one side and Charlene on the other, fielding requests and passing on instructions. The pace became frantic.
'She can't go on like this much longer, Spike,' said Ama. 'She'll burn up in a puff of smoke if we don't slow her down.'
'It's how she wants it to be,' he said. 'Even Laura agrees it's too late to do anything for her, so let her be happy.'
'Jasper is the one I feel sorry for, trying to hide his worries from her,' she said.

'That was what he agreed to, if he wanted to be back in her life, Ama. Unconditional support. No more cotton wool, just be there for her.'

'And he is, but it's taking it's toll on him, too,' Ama said. 'Watching her grow weaker every day.'

'It's affecting everyone, including me,' he said. 'The cast is becoming edgy, seeing her burning up out there in the stalls during rehearsals.'

'It's no use, Spike. I've tried talking to her but she just brushes it aside. I only hope she doesn't succumb before we open.'

But inevitably she did. In the middle of the final technical rehearsal. A heated argument arose with Tommy, the special effects technician, over the thunder and lightning in the storm scene. Claire wanted more and more mist from the smoke guns to mask Travis's fall to the decks. At the third attempt, she insisted Jasper help her up on the stage. Incandescent with fury, she flared up at Tommy. Everyone fell silent. Cast and crew stared in disbelief. They'd never seen Claire lose her temper before. Always the level-headed one.

She stopped in mid-rant, aware of the awkward silence and looked about her. She turned back to the technician.

'Tommy. I'm so sorry. I didn't mean to shout at you....' She clutched his arm. 'I think I need to sit down.' She sank down onto the stage amid the tangle of parachute silk, slumped over on her side. Jasper bent down to lift her up and she lay limply in his arms. He carried her off into the wings toward the Green Room.

Spike wheeled after them in his wheelchair, his long Merlin's robe dragging behind him. Ama rushed up the ramp from the stalls to follow him. Justin stepped forward to address the cast and declare a short break, then turned to go after Emily, who had run off with the others.

In the Green Room, Jasper was on the phone to Laura, who told him to call an ambulance and she would meet them at the hospital. Claire lay on the battered sofa, with Ama holding her hand, telling her Laura was on her way. Claire said nothing, her eyes closed. Jasper shooed everyone out and shut the door. Justin and Emily conferred briefly in the hall, then returned to the stage to announce that Claire was being taken to the hospital. The best thing they could do, Justin said, was to complete the technical dress rehearsal, as she would want them to.

They began again where they had left off, with a shaken Tommy performing flawless special effects, for Travis's fourth daredevil fall from the newly-repaired fly-loft. He wore a safety harness Fergus had made for him from a bosun's chair rig. Justin led the subdued cast and crew from cue to cue through the rest of the tech rehearsal, that went off without a hitch. When it was over, Emily made an emotional speech to the cast, about how important it was to make Claire proud of them and everyone trooped offstage.

At the hospital, Laura and the oncologist arrived to make a diagnosis. They weren't long in agreeing Claire was probably in her last days, if not hours. They sedated her with morphine and hooked her up to a life support system, before they allowed Jasper to go in and sit with her. She was only semi-conscious, her eyelids flickering occasionally, when Ama and Spike went in to see her. Jasper said he would stay the night with her. They left after a brief visit, to drive back to the empty old house.

Ample Make This Bed

Spike wheeled into the kitchen and found a bottle of brandy and some glasses. He had removed Prospero's star-spattered magician's cloak at the theatre, but he still had on the rest of his costume and full makeup. He poured them out the brandy, while Ama removed his face makeup with some cold cream from the bathroom. They touched glasses and drank.

'I know it sounds awful, Spike, but I'm relieved it's finally happened. I couldn't have kept up that fevered pitch much longer.'

'Everyone was willing her to last. They're probably all secretly relieved, too,' he said.

'It won't be easy for Justin, either,' said Spike, 'trying to keep everyone focused on the final dress rehearsal.'

'You're the old pro, Spike, you'll have to set the tone for them.'

'In a way, it will help me keep my mind off Claire.'

'Come to bed now and let's talk about us,' said Ama, helping him from the wheelchair onto the hospital bed. She climbed in beside him and pulled up the side of the bed the way he had showed her. 'It's like hauling up the gangplank on the Mongoose, except this isn't the vee-berth.'

'Soon will be, I hope,' he said. 'Once The Tempest is over, we'll be on our way.'

'From the new world to the old. Isn't that the wrong way? Shouldn't it be the other way around?'

'Not according to T.S. Eliot. "In our end is our beginning...."'

'Let's hope he's right,' she said. 'A new beginning. But please God, a slower pace. This is way too frantic for trainee grandparents.' She burrowed down under his arm as he lay on his back.

'The nice thing about being grandparents, is you don't have to get up in the middle of the night when the baby starts to cry,' he said.

'With two of them we might have to take our turn. I wouldn't mind, though. I quite fancy the idea – What are you grinning about?'

'Do you think Caroline will breast-feed both at the same time?' said Spike. 'I was just picturing Patrick carting the twins in and hooking one up on each side. I expect they'll be having some practice sessions. I wouldn't mind helping with that.'

'The only practice you'll be allowed will be with a bottle,' said Ama, 'so don't get too excited about taking over your son's role.'

The next morning Ama phoned the hospital to see if there had been any change. The nurse on duty said Claire was drifting in and out of consciousness and Jasper was beside her all night. She decided to go and relieve him and left Spike to rehearse his lines for the final dress rehearsal that evening. When she arrived, a haggard-looking Jasper rose from the armchair he had pulled up beside the bed.

'How is she, Jasper? Has she spoken to you at all?'

He shook his head. 'I do all the talking, Ama. One of the nurses said people can hear you, even in a coma.'

'Why don't you go back to the house and catch some sleep, Jasper. I'll sit and read to her. I've brought a book with me. I promise I'll call you if there's any change. We can take it in shifts. You need to rest so you can be alert for Claire if she comes around.'

'I suppose you're right, Ama. I have dozed off a couple of times sitting here all night.'

Ample Make This Bed

'Why not walk back? It's not that far. Get some air. Spike is working on his lines for tonight. He'll be glad of a break. And you can have a shower and change your clothes. But get some sleep first.' She held up her cellphone. 'You can call me when you wake up.'

He left reluctantly and Ama settled into her chair to hold Claire's hand while she read to her. Occasionally a friendly nursing assistant brought her cups of tea. Nurses and interns looked in to check Claire's charts. Gloria dropped by after her bakery round. They sat on either side of the bed, holding Claire's hands and reminiscing about her. They caught themselves laughing aloud a couple of times at some of Claire's more outrageous behaviour, before they stopped with stricken looks at her delicate frame.

Jasper returned after only a few hours. Too agitated to sleep much, he told Ama, and anxious to take up his vigil, in case he might miss a moment of wakefulness from Claire. Sarah and Kitty turned up with a basket of home-cooked food for Jasper and any other visitors. The two old women took turns sitting with Claire while they served up hot food to him, insisting he must eat.

Ama drove Spike to the dress rehearsal, promising to return for him afterwards and went back to relieve Jasper for the evening shift. She stayed until the rehearsal was over and left him to go and collect Spike from the theatre. Jasper insisted he wanted to stay with Claire through the night. Laura had been in and told him sometimes if the coma was not too deep, people would surface briefly. He clung to this hope and refused to go far from her bedside all night. To no avail. The following day brought no change. Claire became progressively weaker, with both Laura and the oncologist saying it was only a matter of hours remaining.

Ama shuttled between the house, the hospital and the theatre. She reassured the cast and crew that Claire would be wishing them well for the opening night, even if she was unable to attend. An enormous bouquet of roses appeared in the Green Room, before the half-hour call for the first performance. The card, addressed to everyone had Claire's name on it. Jasper had ordered it on one of his short breaks from her bedside and signed it on her behalf. No one commented that it was not Claire's handwriting.

Ama had dropped Spike off at the stage door, where Travis met them and helped him from the old Toyota. There was a flurry of laughter from the front of the old Regency Theatre as the pageant wagon pulled up, with musicians and grad students capering about and performing for the arriving audience. Many of them were already inside. They streamed outside from the refurbished foyer bar with drinks in hand, to see the impromptu show and take pictures of Lloyd Kramer's son, Derek, standing proudly in front of the gleaming yoke of oxen.

After hurrying backstage to wish Spike and the cast good luck, Ama threaded her way through the crush in the foyer, to meet and greet the incoming crowd. She positioned herself between Ralph and Kitty, to make sure she said all the right things to all the right people introduced to her. Frankie had changed the foyer canopy on Claire's instruction. It was now a maze of fishing nets of different shades of startling luminescence, with the giant mirrored glitter ball sprinkling flickering light above everyone's head.

A modern English version of Shakespeare's Tempest was not everyone's choice, but Jasper as producer, had presented it as an experiment. By encouraging everyone to write their comments, he had disarmed the most vocal of the opposition, who prepared to wait and see. Ama had further put people at ease by saying she, too, was nervous about its reception and hoped they would keep an open mind.

The audience filed in, a hush fell as the house settled and the houselights dimmed to black.

Out of the darkness came a clap of thunder and a startling bolt of lightning. Confused voices became shouts and cries, as the storm seemed to roll round the theatre. Lightning flashes flickered over the huge swaying mast and billowing white sails. The storm raged and increased in intensity for several minutes, culminating in a great shout from high in the fly-loft. As the lightning lit the mast, it crashed to the stage in slow motion with Travis clinging to the ropes. He was shrouded in the mist from Tommy's smoke guns and enveloping clouds of parachute silk, as he sprang free. The sea roared in deafening waves, relayed about the auditorium through a series of speakers, positioned high in the balconies and fly-loft. The Tempest had begun.

Ama realised she had been holding her breath and released it with relief. A spontaneous burst of applause from the watching audience, greeted the re-appearance of a soaking wet Travis, hauled to his feet by the floundering seamen. Judging from the looks on many of the ruddy faces Ama could see around her, Claire had touched a common chord of experience in this maritime community. The audience was with them and remained with them, as the actors told their tale in language they could all understand at last. Shakespeare's renown as a playwright was brought home to them.

The experiment seemed a success in the first act. Ama listened to the crowd as they talked to each other on the way to the bar at intermission. She slipped backstage to spread the good news to Spike and the others, who were all speaking at high volume with relief and excitement. She found him in his dressing room repairing his makeup, his script still clutched in one hand. She hugged him from behind his wheelchair and spoke to him over his shoulder in the mirror. He grinned at her through the layers of slap he was applying.

'Thank god for this,' he said, holding up the magician's book of spells which hid his script. 'My brain went totally numb on at least three occasions.'

'You were wonderful, it was wonderful, nobody noticed it at all. I didn't realise how much of it you already knew by heart, Spike.'

'All the same, I'm hanging onto this till the final curtain. There's some big speeches to get through.'

'I kept thinking what a shame Claire couldn't be here to share your triumph. I've been with her on and off most of the day, spelling Jasper off. He won't leave her side for more than an hour.'

'I was so mesmerised by the storm scene I almost forgot my first lines. She must have put such a fear in poor Tommy, he went right over the top on the special effects.'

'It electrified everyone in the cast. They were all in top form. Travis was amazing. He terrified me the way he toppled off the mast from the fly-loft,' Ama said.

'What amazed me even more was how the audience is following the plot. No coughing or rustling programs, they understand what's going on. They're getting it, Ama. Every line. Esther and Simon have done a great job on the translation.'

'I must get around the dressing rooms to speak to everyone, Spike. I'll be back as soon as the curtain drops.'

She hurried round to encourage them all, then slipped out to take her seat for the second half. She was stopped in the foyer by Gloria.

'Jasper phoned. He's been trying to reach you. It's Claire. He thinks she's dying, Ama.'

She stood hesitating in the foyer, as people pushed past her to take their seats. She turned and headed out the front entrance to the parking lot. It took her several minutes to extricate her little Toyota from the crowded space and drive onto the road, filled with the audience's vehicles. She raced through the half-empty narrow streets of the old town, to the small modern hospital and dumped her car in the first space she saw. Once inside, she hurried down the corridor to Claire's room. The door was open and three medical staff were by the bed. Jasper pulled her aside.

'She started to come out of it, Ama. She even spoke to me.'

'Did she recognise you, Jasper?'

'Yes, I think so. It was hard to make out what she was saying, she was so groggy with the morphine. I called the nurse and she paged the resident doctor. That's her over there.'

'That's wonderful, Jasper. Do they think she's coming out of the coma?'

'The doctor's not sure. She's called the consultant on duty. He hasn't arrived yet. I tried to call Laura but only got her voicemail. Then I called you, Ama.'

'Laura's at the opening, Jasper. I saw her at the foyer bar earlier. She probably turned her phone off for the play.'

They waited for the consultant to show up and the resident doctor left to see another patient. One of the two nurses was called to emergency. The other one made notes on Claire's charts and adjusted the drips in her arms, checking the dosages. Finally, the consultant, an older man, showed up and asked if they would wait for him in the reception area. Jasper couldn't sit still and paced up and down outside the front doors. Ama got two cups of coffee from the machine and joined him outside in the cool autumn night. A salt breeze blew off the harbour as they both stood drinking the hot liquid and staring at the sky.

When the consultant eventually came out his face was unsmiling. 'We've managed to stabilise her but she's not responding to the medication. She appears to be sinking back into the coma and becoming weaker. It's only a matter of time now. I'm sorry there's nothing more we can do except monitor her. You might want to get some rest yourselves and come back later. The nurses will let you know as soon as they notice any change.'

He shook hands with both of them and left to go back inside.

'I don't want to leave her, Ama. There's no need for you to stay. I can call you again if anything changes. You may as well go back and see the end of the play.'

'I'll stay a bit longer, Jasper, just in case.'

Back in the room, Claire lay in the same position as they'd left her in. The nurse had brushed her hair back off her face and she seemed asleep, breathing shallowly. They took up their posts on either side of the bed and held her hands with the translucent skin showing all the veins. Ama turned the hand she was holding palm upward and felt the flickering pulse. She looked across at Jasper who sat staring at Claire's face. She sat several minutes longer, then turned to him again.

'I'm going to say goodbye to her now, Jasper. I want to be able to remember her asleep like this and I know you want to be alone with her for the end.'

Ample Make This Bed

She stood up and leaned over to kiss her forehead. 'Goodbye Claire, my magical friend. I love you.' Ama placed Claire's hand in Jasper's, then went around to kiss the top of his head, as he sat stooped forward with Claire's two limp hands held in his open palms.

'Please call me when it's over, Jasper. No matter what the time?'

'I will, Ama. And say thank you to everyone. From Claire and me.'

The night wind off the harbour had freshened and Ama drew the light silk patterned shawl Claire had given her, around her shoulders. She drove slowly back to the theatre, in time to hear Spike give Prospero's elegiac speech. He spoke it in his strong trained voice, not glancing at his lines.

'"*Now my charms are all o'erthrown...*"'

The powerful cadences rang out in the hushed and darkened auditorium and Ama let the famous lines wash over her. The lights faded slowly to black and the audience sat as though reluctant to break the spell. Some one began to applaud, perhaps it was her, and the audience joined in quietly at first then building to a heavy solid applause. Quite different, she thought to the outburst of almost hysterical clapping that Lovely War had received, but warm and generous too. She clapped happily along with them. Happy for Spike, happy for Claire, happy for Jasper.

People were in no hurry to leave, chatting animatedly amongst themselves as they evaluated this Shakespeare, who could still speak to them in words they all now could understand. Ama smiled at them, as she worked her way backstage to find Spike. Justin stepped out of a dressing room and saw her.

'Ama. Claire... is she – alright?' He had removed his Caliban wig but his makeup still formed a line round his face. He drew her aside. 'She's dying, isn't she? Jasper told me this afternoon she was fading. Only hours, he said. He asked me to make her goodbyes to the cast and be sure they helped celebrate her triumphs as she would have wanted. He has arranged champagne for everyone at the foyer bar for the first-night party. I'm just spreading the word for people to gather after the house has cleared. Emily's doing the same.' He put his arms around her. 'I'm sorry for you, Ama. I know how close you were.'

She nodded, unable to speak and pushed on to Spike's dressing room. His back was to her and he saw her in the big makeup mirror, wheeling round to hold his arms out to her. Emily stood smiling beside him, waiting her turn to hug Ama. He pulled Ama down on his lap and kissed her, holding her to him.

'You should hear them in the auditorium, Spike. They loved you. They loved the play. It worked. You said it would and it did. If only Claire could have seen you all.'

'Justin told me what Jasper said, Ama. I wish she could have been here, too. Is he with her now?' asked Emily.

Ama hugged her and tried to smile. 'Yes. I was with them until half an hour ago, then I said goodbye to leave them together for the end.'

'Soon?' asked Spike.

'Anytime now. A few hours at most,' said Ama, tears spilling down her cheeks. 'Oh god, I want to howl.'

'Howl away, Ama, you deserve to,' said Emily. 'I'll close the door and leave you two alone.'

She left and Spike held Ama in his arms until her sobbing became a low moan. He stroked her back and waited for the tears to subside. He could think of nothing but empty platitudes to console her. She took his proffered handkerchief to wipe her eyes and survey the swollen face. He drew a straight chair up to the big mirror. 'Why don't you sit here and put on some makeup while I take mine off, okay?'

They smiled at each other in the mirror as their faces took on their normal guise. She helped Spike out of his costume and hung up his Merlin robe on the back of the door. He pointed out his street clothes to her and allowed her to dress him. She handed him a long-handled shoe horn to ease his shoes on. She bent down to lace them up for him and he held out his hand to help her to her feet.

'Shall we join the celebrations? I understand Justin is going to make a speech and there may be some surprise guests to meet.'

He wheeled down the empty hall with Ama's hand on his shoulder. The foyer bar crowd of cast and crew had overflowed into the auditorium and onto the stage. Emily spotted Ama and cleared a path through the cast for Spike's wheelchair. Justin handed them each a champagne flute and poured their glasses full.

'A toast to our budding matinee idol, Porter Drummond, making a long-overdue re-appearance on the stage tonight. Known to his intimates as Spike and to you all now as Prospero. Cheers.'

Emily raised her hand next and refilled Ama's glass. 'I have the honour to salute the woman without whom we should all be sitting at home tonight, watching dreary re-runs on TV. Our visionary artistic director, producer extraordinaire and general theatrical dogsbody, Amaryllis Waterstone. To Ama. God's gift to community theatre. Cheers.'

Justin raised his hand for silence. 'In case any of you are wondering who our generous champagne benefactor is, I should like to thank our absent producer, Jasper, who has asked me to say a few words to you. It is no news to you that our most treasured colleague, Claire, has fallen irrecoverably ill. Jasper, her devoted companion throughout her illness, is with her now in our local hospital. It is my sad task to tell you she has only a few hours to live, as Ama will attest, having been with her this evening during the show. Jasper says Claire would have loved to be here with you, to celebrate our theatrical triumph and is with you now in spirit.

'He further asks that you will take this opportunity to toast her unshakeable faith in this project. Share your memories of her with each other tonight, with a rousing joyous send-off to her. To Claire. Our inspiration. She would have wanted you to sing and dance as well as drink and dine. Our musicians will play for us, once they are sufficiently lubricated. Our patron saints, Kitty, Sarah and Gloria have prepared enough food to see us through until morning. May every second toast be to Claire and Jasper. Let us raise high the roofbeams so they can both hear us. Thank you all.'

'A fine speech, Justin. I'll drink to that,' called Spike. 'To Claire and Jasper, everyone.'

The champagne corks popped and the cast and crew needed no further permission to celebrate their success. They took their drinks onto the stage and cleared the set for the musicians, who began in the bar. They played throughout the auditorium, up and down the ramps and cantilevered stairs with the cast, crew and volunteers dancing and drinking along with them. Even Fergus produced his vintage squeezebox and perched on the landing of one of the staircases he had helped to build. He waved to Spike below and raised his glass in salute.

Ama was dragged off by Ivy to find Esther, who had come down from Halifax to celebrate this production of

Ample Make This Bed

Simon's Tempest translation. Never one to hold her drink very well, Esther clung to Sy's arm. He had driven down with Esther. Ivy, who stood behind her, rolled her eyes and grinned.

Spike manoeuvred his way through to Ama. 'Emily just told me a contingent from Bridewell have driven over to see the play and should be here somewhere. Travis's girlfriend Anna-Lise is with them.'

Frankie and Arthur brought plates of Sarah's hot appetisers over to Spike and Ama. Frankie handed his plate to Ama.

'Is there any chance at all Jasper might turn up later?'

'None at all. He's determined to stay with her to the end.'

'God, this will be a sadder place without Claire here,' said Frankie. 'I used to love watching her bully Arthur into doing stuff he hated.'

'I only pretended, to get a rise out of her,' said Arthur. 'I loved working with her. She had more energy than the four of us put together.'

Justin and Emily came over to join them. 'I'm tired of dancing with Justin,' she said, 'so I've come over to ask Spike to dance.'

'If I'd figured out how to do that, I'd have been up there twirling Ama about, Emily.'

'What's stopping you then? I've already seen her on your lap in the dressing room, so why not on the stage? Justin will give you a push up the ramp and away you go. I want a turn when Ama's done.'

Ama followed them and plunked herself on his lap. The musicians changed to a slower tempo and Spike wheeled her around the stage with Ama bending over backwards each time they twirled about.

'This is lovely, Spike, why didn't we think of this before?'

'Do you think we can manage this on the Mongoose, Ama?'

'We could try it tonight if you like. I don't want to go back to the house, I want to be in the vee-berth again.'

'Why not?' he said. 'I'm ready to go anytime.'

'You can't go till you've given Emily a turn. I'll make our apologies and then we can sneak away.' She hopped off his lap and beckoned to Emily who ran up the ramp to them. 'Be careful of him Emily. He tends to get carried away with redheads.' She waited till Emily was sitting on his lap, winked at him and headed off through the dancers to the foyer bar, to begin making their excuses.

Spike twirled Emily around the stage as she stuck out her leg and swivelled them about in different directions in time with the music.

'This is dreamy,' she said, leaning back over the side of the wheelchair and waving one elegant leg in the air. 'You must lend Justin your chair so we can experiment a little. He's so conventional, Spike, I could scream. I do, sometimes but he simply ignores me.'

'I've told you before, Emily,' said Spike, lazily spinning the chair about, 'if you will choose these callow youths, what else can you expect. An older man now...'

'An older man in a wheelchair, maybe?'

'Perhaps not that old, no,' he said.

She grinned at him. 'What was that Ama said about you and some redhead?'

'She likes to exaggerate, Emily. It's one of her irritating habits.'

'Justin says all my habits are irritating, Spike.'

Ample Make This Bed

'Hmmm. Perhaps we should just stay friends then'
He pulled the wheelchair up in front of Justin who sat watching them. 'This is your stop, Emily. You should keep an eye on this girl, Justin. Her behaviour is borderline egregious. A less principled man might take advantage. I must go, Ama's waiting for me. Goodnight, you two.'
Emily kissed his cheek and climbed off his lap. Spike rolled off down the long ramp puffing on an imaginary cigarette and doing his Franklin D. Roosevelt routine.

He found Ama making her last goodbyes and they wheeled out the stage door to her old Toyota. She helped him get seated and shoved the chair into the back seat. They drove down the empty main street to the harbour and parked beside the Mongoose's makeshift gangway. Once on deck he sent Ama down to turn on some lights, to help him get below. He wheeled over to the vee-berth and flopped into it, suddenly feeling tired and deflated. The rush of nervous energy from the events of the day had left them both exhausted. They lay side by side fully clothed, only kicking off their shoes.
Ama turned to prop herself up on one arm to kiss him for awhile, then fell back down. Spike put his arm around her shoulders and drew her to him.
'The only way to get comfortable together is with you on top of me,' he said 'Let's get out of all these clothes.' He started unbuttoning his shirt but she moved his hand away and proceeded to undress him. He unzipped her dress and slipped it off over her head. He fumbled with her bra with one hand until she finished undoing it her self and let him slide it off her shoulders.
'How do you plan to remove my knickers?' she said.
'Clumsily I expect. Will you do it?' She pushed them down and eased herself on top of him with a slight shiver.

'We're going to need a quilt, Spike. It's getting cooler these nights.' She pulled one up over them from the foot of the vee-berth. 'Will it be cold out on the sea when we go?'

'Damn cold, it'll be November.'

She shivered again. 'I'm not very good in the cold. I tend to stiffen up.'

'Me too. In fact, I can feel myself stiffening up already.'

'We've left the light on, too.'

'I don't mind. I like looking at you. Especially when you're not wearing any clothes.'

'You won't see much of me in November. I love to bundle up from head to toe.'

'I tend to hibernate when it's cold,' he said.

'Spike. Sweetheart. Do we really have to go across the Atlantic in November? During the hurricane season? With you in a wheelchair?'

'When you put it like that, it does sound a mite eccentric, my love.'

'And so?'

'And so... perhaps we should consider other alternatives.'

'Like an aeroplane, for instance?'

'Out of the question. I can't sit up for six hours in one of those cramped little seats.'

'We could go business class. They have those reclining seats, you can lie flat on your back just like this.'

'What happens when I need to pee? I can't go six hours without a pee. I can't even go three hours.'

'We could get one of those bottles like they used in the hospital,' she said.

'The stewardess would never empty it for me.'

'I could empty it when they're not looking.'

'You would do that for me?'

'Of course I would.'

'It sounds very intimate. I'm not sure I could pee with you watching.'

'I won't watch. I'll just empty it afterwards.'

'Ama. My love. You really want to see these twins, don't you?'

'Very much.'

'What will we do with the Mongoose, if we're going to fly?'

'It will still be here when we get back. Fergus and Travis can live on it till then. They can finish it all off inside while we're away,' she said.

'What if we decide not to come back? Stay over in London to look after our twin grandchildren.'

'It's a nice thought. Do we have to decide now? I'm very tired.'

'I am, too. I just like talking to you like this. All naked and close. Unwinding. I got wound up very tight today. I'm not sure how often I want to do this anymore,' Spike said.

'Let's not talk now, sweetheart. We have all the rest of our life to talk. Let's go to sleep.'

'I love you, Ama. Maybe I've always loved you. All those years we were apart.'

'I love you too, Spike. Can we go to sleep now?'

'The light's still on.'

'I've got used to it... darling?'

'Mmm?'

'They're not called stewardesses anymore. They're flight attendants now.'

'Mmhmm. Good night.'

'Good night.'

The waves lapped against the hull of the Mongoose and they lay in a deep sleep. Until four a.m. A phone rang and wakened Ama. She blinked in the light from the bare bulb over the galley. The phone was her mobile, ringing on the bunk shelf. She rolled out of Spike's arms and sat up to answer it. It was Jasper.

'It's Claire,' he said. 'She's gone.'

For a few moments Ama sat still, listening to the waves lapping. Then she stood up and put out the light. She crossed back to the vee-berth and lay down beside Spike. A shiver ran through her and she pressed herself against him, before falling back to sleep.

THE END

AMPLE MAKE THIS BED is the latest novel after the **THIRD AGE TRILOGY.**

The first book of the trilogy is **IN HOT PURSUIT**, set in Vancouver and London. It charts the beginnings of Barney Roper's search for some meaning to this third age of his life, post-60. As empty nesters, he and his wife Alice, decide to go their separate ways and explore what life still has to offer. He goes back to discover his roots in Canada. She goes back to university to pursue an old dream. They both realise it is not going to be as easy as they thought to create a new life, as family ties pursue them.

Whatever else they expected their third age to be, it is a demanding challenge and they both rise to meet it head-on. With at times amusing but always unpredictable results, they enter the undiscovered country of the 'sixty-somethings.'

THE BLUE-EYED BOY, the second book of the 3rd Age Trilogy, follows Barney Roper and his wife, Alice as each plunges deeper into their new separate lives. He travels to China, Nepal and Tibet in search of answers to his dilemma of 'how shall a man live?' at this stage of life, pursuing the elusive wisdom of the East. Alice and her new-found partner, Heck, try to escape the constraints of academia, as they move from Oxford to London and Rome, with disastrous results. But Barney and Alice seem unable to extricate themselves from their past lives, that have them clutching each other for support. Living fully in the 3rd age makes heavy demands on them in unexpected ways.

A SINGLE STEP is the final book of the trilogy. Barney's search for a meaningful existence takes him from volunteering in an English county hospice, where he becomes deeply involved with the dying inmates, to the aftermath of the civil wars in West Africa, to search for his missing daughter working with child refugees. Alice finds her life in turmoil, as her health breaks down along with her new relationship. Both Barney and Alice struggle with what it means to be an older person in today's fragmented society, where the old rules and *mores* fail them, as they pursue a new understanding of their lives in the 3rd age.

If you would like to explore more of the **3RD AGE TRILOGY** as either paperbacks or e-books you can find out more at my website: ***3rdageworld.com*** as well as ***amazon.com***, ***booklocker.com,*** or any good bookstore.

Your comments and reviews will be welcomed on my website and blog.

3rd Age World Publishing, Victoria, B.C., Canada
2019
****

CPSIA information can be obtained
at www.ICGtesting.com
Printed in the USA
LVHW040915031219
639142LV00003B/7/P